The Daredevil Snared

In that moment, he understood and fully accepted that fate had brought him there—to her, to this.

To this moment of awakening.

To this second in which he finally comprehended what it was to desire, to want, to need one specific woman.

To the recognition that his destiny lay inextricably entwined with hers.

And that there was *no limit* to what he would do, what he would give, to protect her. So that ultimately they could and would reach for and seize that destiny together.

STEPHANIE LAURENS

The Daredevil Snared

MIRA®

MIRA®

Recycling programs
for this product may
not exist in your area.

ISBN-13: 978-0-7783-1964-1

The Daredevil Snared

www.MIRABooks.com

Printed in U.S.A.

First printing: July 2016
10 9 8 7 6 5 4 3 2 1

The Daredevil Snared

CAST OF CHARACTERS

Principal Characters:

Frobisher, Caleb — Hero, youngest Frobisher brother and captain of *The Prince*

Fortescue, Katherine (Kate) — Heroine, missing governess from the Sherbrook household in Freetown

In London:

Family:

Frobisher, Declan — Caleb's older brother

Frobisher, Lady Edwina — Caleb's sister-in-law, Declan's wife

Frobisher, Robert — Caleb's older brother

Hopkins, Aileen — Robert's intended, Lt. William Hopkins's sister

Staff in Declan & Edwina's town house:

Humphrey — Butler

Government:

Wolverstone, Duke of, Royce, aka Dalziel — Ex-commander of British secret operatives outside England

In Aberdeen:

Frobisher, Fergus — Caleb's father

Frobisher, Elaine — Caleb's mother

Frobisher, Royd (Murgatroyd) — Caleb's oldest brother

In Southampton:

Higginson — Head clerk, Frobisher Shipping Company Office

In Freetown:

Holbrook, Governor — Governor-in-Chief of British West Africa

Eldridge, Major — Commander, Fort Thornton

Decker, Vice-Admiral — Commander, West Africa Squadron

Winton, Major	Commissar of Fort Thornton
Babington, Charles	Partner, Macauley & Babington Trading Company
Macauley, Mr.	Senior partner, Macauley & Babington Trading Company
Undoto, Obo	Local priest
Muldoon	The Naval Attaché
Winton	Nephew of Major Winton, Assistant Commissar at the fort

At Kale's Homestead:

Kale	Slavers' leader
Rogers	Kale's lieutenant in the settlement
Fifteen other slavers, including "the pied piper"	

In the Mining Compound:

Mercenaries:

Dubois	Leader of the mercenaries, presumed French
Arsene	Dubois's lieutenant, second-in-command, presumed French
Cripps	Dubois's second lieutenant, English
Plus twenty-eight other mercenaries	Of various ages and extractions

Captives:

Dixon, Captain John	Army engineer
Hopkins, Lieutenant William	Navy, West Africa Squadron
Fanshawe, Lieutenant	Navy, West Africa Squadron
Hillsythe	Ex-Wolverstone agent, governor's aide
Frazier, Harriet	Gently bred young woman, Dixon's sweetheart
Wilson, Mary	Shop owner-assistant, Babington's sweetheart
Mackenzie, Ellen	Young woman recently arrived in the settlement
Halliday, Gemma	Young woman from the slums

Mellows, Annie	Young woman from the slums
Mathers, Jed	Carpenter
Plus eighteen other men	All British of various backgrounds and trades
Diccon	Young boy, seven years old
Amy	Young girl, six years old
Gerry	Boy, ten years old
Plus sixteen other children	All British, ranging from six to ten years old
Plus five other children	All British, ranging from eleven to fourteen years old

On board The Prince*:*

Fitzpatrick, Lieutenant Frederick	First Mate
Wallace, Mr.	Master
Carter	Bosun, goes into the jungle but returns to the ship
Quilley	Quartermaster, goes into the jungle and remains with Caleb
Hornby, Mr.	Steward, goes into the jungle but returns to the ship
Johnson	Midshipman, goes into the jungle but returns to the ship
Foster, Martin, Ellis, Quick, Mallard, Collins, Biggs, Norton and Olsen	Midshipmen and experienced seamen who go into the jungle and remain with Caleb

On board The Raven*:*

Lascelle, Phillipe	Captain, privateer, longtime friend of Caleb's
Reynaud	Bosun, goes into the jungle but returns to the ship
Ducasse	Quartermaster, goes into the jungle and remains with Phillipe
Fullard, Collmer, Gerard, Vineron	Midshipmen and experienced seamen who go into the jungle and remain with Phillipe
Plus four other seamen	All of French extraction, who go into the jungle but return to the ship

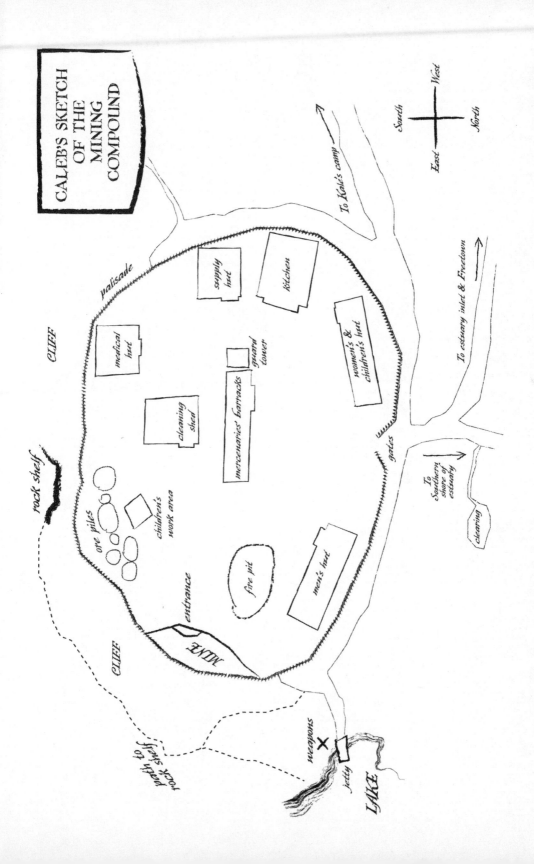

One

July 14, 1824
Jungle east of Freetown, West Africa

Caleb Frobisher moved steadily forward through the jungle shadows. His company of twenty-four men followed in single file. No one spoke; the silence was eerie, stretching nerves taut. Beneath the thick canopy, the humidity was so high that forging ahead felt like walking underwater, as if the heavy atmosphere literally weighed on their limbs.

"Hell's bells," Phillipe Lascelle, at Caleb's heels, breathed. "Surely it can't be much farther."

"It's only midmorning," Caleb murmured back. "You can't be wilting already."

Phillipe snorted.

Caleb continued along the path that was little more than an animal track; they had to constantly duck and weave under and around palm fronds and low branches festooned with clinging vines.

Somewhere ahead lay the slavers' camp they'd come to find—or so Caleb fervently hoped. Despite his determination to unwaveringly abide by the rule book throughout this mission, thus proving to all and sundry, and his family especially, that he could be trusted with such serious endeavors, sometimes instinct—albeit masquerading as reckless impulse—proved too strong to resist. His brother Robert's hand-drawn map described the location of the slavers' camp—Kale's Homestead—when approached from the west. However, Caleb had studied the camp's position and decided to come in from the north. From all he'd gleaned from Robert's notes, the slavers would be alert to any incursion from the west; they would almost certainly have lookouts posted, making west not the wisest direction from which to approach if one's intention was to seize the camp.

Which was, rather plainly, their purpose; why else would twenty-five strong men all armed to the gills be trooping through such a godforsaken place?

Three nights before, Caleb, in his ship, *The Prince*, closely followed by his old comrade-in-adventure, Phillipe, in his ship, *The Raven*, had slipped into the estuary on the night tide. They'd kept to the north shore, well away from the shipping lanes leading into Freetown harbor, and sailed deeper down the estuary and into Tagrin Bay, reducing the risk of detection by any naval vessels going into and out of the harbor; according to Robert's information, the West Africa Squadron should now be in port, and Caleb would prefer to avoid having to explain himself to Vice-Admiral Decker.

They'd anchored off the southern shore of the bay at a spot Caleb judged was due north of Kale's Homestead. According to Robert's map, miles of jungle lay between the slavers' camp and the ships' positions; Caleb hadn't known how passable that jungle would be, but his confidence had been bolstered by the intelligence they'd gained from natives living in a village nearby. Phillipe had a way with languages—another excellent reason for inviting him along—and he'd quickly established a rapport with the village elders. The villagers had known of the slavers' camp, but, unsurprisingly, avoided it with a near-religious fervor. Sadly, they'd known nothing about any mine or similar enterprise anywhere in the vicinity, but they'd been happy to point out a narrow track that, so they'd insisted, led more or less directly to the slavers' camp.

Unfortunately, the villagers hadn't known the name of the slavers' leader. Caleb clung to the hope that he and his men weren't going to find themselves at some other slavers' camp entirely—and trudged on. They'd set out on the previous morning, leaving skeleton crews on their ships and taking the strongest and most experienced of their men. Seizing a slavers' camp would be no easy task, especially if there were any captives currently in the slavers' clutches.

Turning that prospect over in his mind—wondering what he might do if it proved to be so—Caleb led the way on.

He almost didn't trust his eyes when, through the dense curtain of trees, palms, and vines, he glimpsed a pale glow—indicating a clearing where daylight flooded in, banishing the jungle's pervasive gloom.

Then their narrow track ended, opening onto a wider, better-maintained path, one clearly frequently used.

Caleb stopped and held up a hand; the men following halted and froze. He sent his senses questing. A rumble of male voices was faint but discernible.

Phillipe leaned close and whispered, "We're twenty to twenty-five yards from the perimeter."

Caleb nodded. "This wider path must be the one between the camp and the mine."

Rapidly, he canvassed his options. Although Phillipe was the more experienced commander, he waited, silently deferring to Caleb—this was Caleb's show. Another reason Caleb liked working with the man. Eventually, he murmured, "Pass the word—we'll creep nearer, keeping to the jungle, and see what we can see. No reason to let them know we're here."

Phillipe turned to pass the order back down the line. Of their party of twenty-five, thirteen were from Caleb's crew and ten from *The Raven*'s. Because of Caleb and Phillipe's previous joint ventures, their men had worked together before; Caleb didn't need to fear that they wouldn't operate as a cohesive unit in what was to come.

After one last searching look around, he ventured onto the wider path, placing his feet with care. He followed the well-trodden trail, but halted just before a curve that, by his reckoning, would expose him to those in the clearing. Instead, he slipped silently sideways to his right, into the cover of the jungle. Quietly, he skirted the edge of the clearing, continuing to move slowly and with care, shifting from north to west. Eventually, he reached the western aspect; on spotting a clump of large-leafed palms closer to the clearing's perimeter, he crouched and crept into the concealment the palms offered. A swift glance behind showed Phillipe following him, while the rest of their men hunkered down, strung out in the shadows, their gazes trained on the activity in the camp.

Caleb returned his attention to the clearing and settled to study Kale's Homestead. He recognized the layout from Robert's notes—the horseshoe-shaped central space with a large barrack-like hut across the head and four smaller huts, two on each side. Caleb and his men were at the open end of the horseshoe, virtually directly opposite the main barracks. According to Robert's diagram, that meant the path from Freetown should be somewhere to their right; Caleb searched and spotted the opening. The path he and his men had briefly followed entered the clearing to the left of the main barracks, while another path—one Robert had deemed unused—straggled away into the jungle from the right of that building.

Having established that reality matched the picture of the camp he'd carried in his mind, Caleb focused on the people moving in and out of the huts and sitting about the central fire pit.

Phillipe settled alongside him, and they tuned their ears to the low-voiced, desultory chatter.

After a while, Phillipe leaned closer and whispered, "That large one—he acts like the leader, but from Robert's description, he can't be Kale."

Caleb focused on the slaver in question—a heavyset man, tall, and with a swaggering gait. "I think," Caleb murmured back, "that he must be the man who leads Kale's men in the settlement." After a moment, he mused, "Interesting that he's here."

"*Useful* that he's here," Phillipe corrected. "If we eradicate all here, chances are Kale's operation won't simply rise again under some other leader."

Caleb nodded. "True." He scanned the area and the huts. "It doesn't look like they have any captives—the doors of the smaller huts are open, and I haven't seen any hint there's anyone inside."

"I haven't, either."

Caleb grimaced. "Kale's not out there. Is he here, but in the barracks, and if so, how many men are in there with him?"

Phillipe's shoulders lifted in a Gallic shrug.

Just then, one of the men hovering about the large pot slung over the fire pit raised his head, looked toward the barracks, and yelled, "Stew's ready!"

Seconds later, the barracks' door opened. Caleb grinned as a slaver of medium height and wiry build, with a disfiguring scar marring his features—from Robert's description, the man had to be Kale—emerged, followed by three more men.

"How helpful," Phillipe murmured.

Another man emerged from the path to Freetown. Caleb nudged Phillipe and nodded at the newcomer. "They did have a lookout on that path."

Phillipe studied the man as he joined his fellows. "It doesn't look as if they're seriously concerned over unexpected company—odds are there was only the one lookout."

"That's the way I read it, too."

"All told, that makes thirteen."

His eyes on the scene unfolding about the fire pit, Caleb merely nodded. Phillipe settled again, and they watched as Kale, handed a tin plate piled with stew by one of his henchmen, sat on a log and started eating. His men followed suit, sitting on the logs arranged in a rough circle around the fire.

They'd barely taken their first mouthfuls when the muted tramp of feet had everyone—Kale and his men, as well as Caleb, Phillipe, and their company—looking toward the path from the north. The path Caleb believed led to the mine—the same path they'd briefly been on fifteen or so minutes before.

Four men—slavers by their dress and Kale's men by their composure—appeared. They hailed Kale and exchanged greetings with others in the group.

"So you got our recent guests settled, then?" Kale's words came in a distinctive, gravelly rasp, further confirming his identity.

The man who'd led the group grinned. "Aye—and Dubois sent his thanks. That said, he made a very large point about needing more men. Emphasizing *men*. He says he wants at least fifteen more."

Kale swore colorfully. "I'd be thrilled to give him more if only those blighters in the settlement would just let us do what we do best." He grunted, then shook his head and returned his attention to his plate. "Sadly, they're the ones who pay the piper, and they pay his highness Dubois, too, so he'll just have to make do with those we can give him." Kale waved the newcomers to the pot. "Sit and eat. You've earned it."

The four did, gratefully settling with the rest.

Conversation was nonexistent while the men ate. Caleb would have felt hungrier had he not insisted that his party consume a decent breakfast before they broke their temporary camp that morning. He'd never favored fighting on an empty stomach, and he'd felt quietly confident that they would find Kale's camp that day.

"That's seventeen now," Phillipe murmured. "Not quite so easy." He sounded, if anything, pleased.

Caleb softly grunted. He verified Phillipe's headcount and, again, thanked the impulse that had prompted him to invite Phillipe and his crew to join his mission. A day out of Southampton, one of *The Prince*'s main water kegs had sprung a leak. Determined to adhere to the maxim of "take no unnecessary risks," Caleb had made the small detour to the Canary Islands. Before he'd even moored in Las Palmas harbor, he'd spotted the distinctive black hull of *The Raven*. While the keg was repaired and refilled and his men arranged for extra supplies, Caleb had spent an evening catching up with his old friend. And on discovering that *The Raven*, along with its experienced crew and captain, was presently unengaged, Caleb had invited Phillipe to join him on his mission. He'd made it clear there would be no payment or likely spoils, but like Caleb, Phillipe was addicted to adventure. Bored, he'd jumped at the chance of action.

Phillipe was a lone privateer, and while he'd originally sailed for the French under Bonaparte, exactly who he sailed for these days was unclear. However, the war with France was long over, and on the waves, any lingering political loyalties counted for less than longtime friendship bolstered by similar devil-may-care traits.

To Caleb's mind, twenty-five men against seventeen was precisely the sort of numbers he needed in this place, at this time, to eradicate Kale and his operation. The slavers would fight to the death and would do anything and everything to survive. Caleb didn't want to lose any of his men, or any of Phillipe's, either. Twenty-five to seventeen...that should do it.

By the time he'd sailed into Las Palmas, he'd already discarded the notion of leaving Kale undisturbed and, instead, picking up the trail north from the "Homestead" and making directly for the mine. That was his mission, after all—to locate the mine, learn what he could of it, and then get that intelligence back to London. However, heading north to the mine with Kale and his men effectively at his back didn't appeal in the least. More, returning to London without eliminating Kale and his crew would simply leave that task to whoever returned to complete the mission. No commander worth his salt would attempt to attack and capture the mine with Kale still in his camp, a potential source of reinforcements for whatever forces were already at the mine.

But Kale had to be removed in a way that would not immediately alert the villains behind the scheme—the "blighters" Kale had referred to—or Dubois and any others in charge at the mine. That was Caleb's first hurdle—the first challenge on this quest.

"If we'd arrived earlier," Phillipe murmured, "while they're all gathered as they are, distracted with eating, would have been a good time to attack."

Caleb shrugged. In days gone by, he might have leapt precipitously at the chance and rushed in, but for today and the foreseeable future, he was determined to adhere to the script of a reliable and responsible commander. He could almost hear the voices of his three older brothers, all of whom would lecture him to take his time and plan, and find and secure every advantage he could for his men in the upcoming skirmish, which was guaranteed to end as a bloody massacre.

He, Phillipe, and every man in their company knew and accepted that they would need to kill every slaver in Kale's camp. That Kale and his men were engaged in trading in others' lives—men, women, and children, too—had made the decision, the resolution, that much easier to make. The men gathered around the fire pit ranked among the lowest of the low.

Kale spooned up the last of his stew, chewed, swallowed, then looked across the fire pit at the large man Phillipe had earlier noted. "Rogers—you and your crew can rest up, then head back to the settlement midafternoon. If you don't find a message from Muldoon waiting—no suggestion of who to grab next—use your own judgment. See if there are any more sailor-boys we can snatch. Dubois, at least, will be grateful."

Rogers grinned and saluted. "We'll see what we can find."

Phillipe shifted to whisper in Caleb's ear. "We need to attack before Rogers leaves."

Caleb studied the group, then replied in the barest murmur,

"They've just eaten their main meal for the day, and it was stew. Heavy." He glanced at Phillipe. "In this heat, an hour from now, they're all going to be half asleep."

Phillipe blinked his dark-blue eyes once, then he grinned wolfishly and looked back at the camp.

Several minutes later, after having seen Kale retreat with three of his men into the main barracks while the rest of the slavers spread out in groups, quietly chatting, Caleb tapped Phillipe on the shoulder, then carefully crept back to where their men waited.

Phillipe followed. At Caleb's signal, the group moved farther back, away from the camp and deeper into the concealing shadows.

They chanced upon a natural clearing big enough to hold them all. Most of the men had been hauling seabags and packs containing their tents and supplies; Caleb waited while they shed them, then at his intimation, they all hunkered down in a rough circle. He looked around, noting the expectant faces and also the confidence—in him and his leadership—conveyed by their steady gazes; all had fought under his orders before, and his own men had been with him for years. "Here's how we're going to approach this."

Not recklessly but responsibly—with all due care for the safety of his men and prospective success.

Clearly and concisely, he laid out the elements of his plan— in essence a version of divide and conquer. He invited input on several aspects, and Phillipe and a number of others made inventive suggestions that he readily incorporated into the whole. In less than half an hour, they'd hammered out a solid plan, one to which everyone was ready to lend their enthusiastic support.

"Right, then." He looked around the circle, meeting each man's eyes. Then he nodded decisively. "Let's get to it. Move into position and wait for my signal."

The men melted away in twos and threes, some going west, others east, ultimately to encircle the camp.

When all others had left them, Phillipe dipped his head in wry acknowledgment. "That was well done."

Caleb knew Phillipe wasn't referring to how he'd made the plan but to the way he'd doubled up the less experienced, less strong fighters among their men. Five of his men and five of Phillipe's, as well as himself and Phillipe, were well able to take care of themselves in any company—even against slavers of the ilk of Kale and his crew, all of whom would, without a doubt, prove to be vicious fighters. Vicious and desperate, for they would quickly realize that they were outnumbered. Caleb shrugged. "I just want us all to walk out of this and, given this climate, with as few cuts as possible."

They'd brought various salves and ointments in their supplies, but in tropical climes, infection was always a danger.

"We'd better get into position." In such close quarters, pistols would be useless—as likely to hit a friend as an enemy. The fight would be all bladework. Both Caleb and Phillipe reached for their sword hilts and loosened the blades in the scabbards, then they checked the various knives strapped about their persons.

Satisfied they were as prepared as possible, Caleb indicated the spot from which they'd earlier studied the camp. He and Phillipe had, of course, taken the most dangerous positions. They would lead the charge—as they usually did—by storming into the camp from the open end of the horseshoe-shaped space, making as much immediate impact as they could.

Two other men would attack from positions to their right and left. Others would come in from the paths flanking the main barracks and also from between the smaller huts.

Meanwhile, their bosuns, Caleb's Carter and Phillipe's Reynaud—both hefty men too slow on their feet to be good in a sword fight on open ground, yet as strong as any wrestlers—

would prevent Kale and the three closeted with him in the main hut from immediately joining in the fight.

"So helpful of Kale to take three of them with him," Phillipe murmured as they scuttled into position behind the large-leafed palms.

"All he needs to do is stay there for just a few minutes longer..." Caleb peered across the camp, then grinned. "Carter's in position."

"Reynaud, as well." Phillipe met Caleb's eyes. "Whenever you're ready."

Caleb felt his grin take on a familiar unholy edge. *"Now."*

They sprang to their feet and rushed into the camp. They fell on the nearest pair of men lolling on the logs and dispatched both before they'd even struggled to their feet. No quarter, no fighting fair—not with cutthroats like this.

By then the other slavers had leapt to their feet, but before they could move to engage Caleb and Phillipe, they were distracted by, and then forced to turn and defend against, the rest of Caleb and Phillipe's company.

Straightening, Caleb glanced over the heads and confirmed all was on track.

Long before the first shout had sounded—before Kale was alerted to the disruption—Carter and Reynaud had clambered onto the barracks' porch and spilled their burdens of cleaned logs made from branches three and four inches thick before the door. Then they'd leapt back and put their spines to the barracks' front wall. Two others had joined them, waiting to pounce when Kale and company emerged at a run—and pitched every which way on the rolling logs.

Caleb swore as a loose slaver made a run for him, cutlass swinging; he had to look away and miss the action on the porch.

Clang!

Caleb's sword met the slaver's cutlass. He threw the man back, then advanced, sword whirling.

The slaver was shorter than Caleb's six-plus feet and scrawny to boot. Caleb's longer reach and greater strength soon put paid to the villain. He fell, eyes rolling up. Caleb yanked his sword free of the man's chest and turned.

Chaos filled the camp. The fighting was ferocious, every bit as desperate as Caleb had foreseen. There were more men down, but as far as Caleb could tell, all were slavers. The fighting in front of the barracks was intense, but his and Phillipe's men now held the porch itself, an advantage in the circumstances.

But he couldn't see Kale.

Another slaver rushed him, and he had to turn and deal with the man. That took longer than he would have liked—the man had had some training somewhere and was taller and stronger than most of his fellows. He actually managed to nick Caleb's forearm, which reminded Caleb that he wasn't fighting any gentleman; he lashed out with his boot, catching the slaver unawares and driving his heel into the man's midsection. The slaver doubled up, and then he was dead.

A sudden flaring of instinct had Caleb swinging around, counting heads—almost desperately searching for something going wrong.

His gaze fell on Phillipe, who was engaged in a furious battle with the man known as Rogers.

Phillipe was tall, but had a fencer's build—all supple wiriness. He was lethally fast with any blade. He was currently fighting with the traditional sword most captains favored; the blade flashed and gleamed as he countered Rogers's every strike.

But Rogers was stronger, heavier, and had a longer reach—and was wielding a much heavier, wickedly curved blade. From the feverish anticipation in Rogers's face, he believed he had Phillipe beaten. Phillipe was, indeed, hard pressed but still countering fluidly, his elegant features distorted in a snarl.

Caleb knew better than to distract his friend.

Then Phillipe gave Rogers an opening.

With a triumphant roar, Rogers swung and struck—

Empty air. Phillipe wasn't anywhere near where Rogers had expected him to be.

Phillipe straightened behind Rogers. He slammed the hilt of his sword into Rogers's nape, then plunged a knife that seemed to appear out of thin air into the man's back.

Rogers gasped and collapsed. Phillipe whirled, saw Caleb watching, and snapped off a grim salute.

In concert, they turned toward the main barracks and waded anew into the fray, assisting their men as they swept on toward the porch, leaving nothing but dead slavers behind them.

Caleb tapped two of their men on their shoulders and, with a hand sign, set them to scout the edges of the fight to ensure no slaver, sensing impending doom, attempted to slip away. It was imperative that no word of Kale and his men's fate reached Freetown.

Rogers falling had marked the turning of the tide, but Caleb and his company were too experienced to let down their guard. As Caleb and Phillipe pushed forward, their men fell in around them, forming an unstoppable wave. Together, they put paid to the last of the slavers.

All except Kale.

His back to the raised front of the barracks' porch, the man was a dervish, keeping a semicircle of Caleb and Phillipe's men at bay with a pair of flashing blades.

With Robert's description of Kale's potential menace etched in his brain, Caleb had warned their men that unless they had an easy and definitely lethal shot at Kale, they were to hem him in but not engage.

As Caleb and Phillipe joined their men, the circle drew back fractionally, leaving the pair of them standing shoulder to shoulder facing Kale.

They'd halted at a respectable—respectful—distance. Kale took stock of them, his blades now still.

The slavers' leader was shorter than Caleb, shorter than Phillipe, but Kale was the very epitome of wiry, and the way he held
himself, at ease but on the balls of his feet, poised to explode
into action, with his curious twin blades—slightly curved like
elongated scimitars—held firmly and perfectly balanced, but
with loose, supple wrists, screamed to the initiated that he was
lethally fast.

Fast, fast, *fast*.

There was a flatness in his wintry eyes that stated he'd killed
so many times it had become all but instinctive—a part of his
nature.

From the corner of his eye, Caleb saw Phillipe's jaw set, then
Phillipe reached to his other side—to Reynaud, who under-
stood the unspoken command and placed his loaded pistol in
Phillipe's hand.

Kale had tracked the movement. He sneered. "What? No
honor in your *justice*?" He spat the last word, but not at Phillipe. Kale's gaze had fastened on Caleb, and the challenge was
clearly directed at him.

Caleb met Kale's gaze. In the art of manipulation, Caleb knew
beyond question that he could give Kale lessons, but…that wasn't
the point here. He knew he was being goaded, that Kale wanted
to fight him, believing he, Kale, would win, and that doing so
would somehow win his freedom, at least from immediate dispatch. In situations such as this, for men such as Kale, surviving even an hour more meant an hour's more chance to escape.

Or to take others with him on his journey from this world.
A revenge of sorts.

If Caleb had been operating as he usually did, he would have
responded immediately, and he and Kale would fight; he'd never
walked away from a challenge—or from a fight—in his life.
However, this time…what was right?

Head tilting, Caleb continued to regard Kale while weighing
the pros and cons. He'd lectured his men against taking undue

risks; shouldn't he hold himself to the same standard regardless of Kale's baiting?

But what of that sticky wicket called leadership? How he dealt with this situation would inevitably impinge on his standing with his men, and with Phillipe's, too.

More, Kale had questioned—had maligned—justice. Not Caleb but the concept of justice they were there to serve.

Didn't that demand some answer? Not just on his part but on behalf of their whole company?

Didn't Kale's challenge speak to and question the validity of why they were there, and more, the justification for what they had done—the lives they'd already taken that day?

Beside him, Phillipe shifted, darting a glance at his face. "Caleb...we are judge and jury here. Curs such as he have no claim to the honor of a fair fight in lieu of sentence."

Who said I intend to fight fairly? Kale certainly won't.

Kale's pale gaze hadn't left Caleb's face. Phillipe might as well not have spoken for all the reaction Kale gave.

But Caleb's steady regard was something Kale found more difficult to tolerate. His lip curled in a sneer. "What, son—cat got your tongue?"

Caleb smiled. "No. I'm merely debating the irony of engaging with vermin such as you over the value of justice."

Kale blinked—then he exploded into action. Blades swinging, he launched himself at Caleb.

Phillipe cursed and stepped back, smoothly bringing the pistol to bear. Startled, all the other men leapt back.

But Caleb had seen Kale's muscles tense. Without a blink, he'd whipped up his sword and a shorter blade and slapped Kale's slashing swords aside.

Then it was on. Caleb could not—dared not—take his eyes from Kale's. He tracked the man's whirling blades by the infinitesimal shifts in Kale's attention; Caleb didn't fall into the trap of trying to keep both blades in view.

In less than a minute, Caleb was wishing he'd let Phillipe shoot the bastard; Kale was beyond lethal—and he was a better swordsman than Caleb. He was no slouch, but Kale was in a class of his own.

Unfortunately, the time for justice via pistol had passed. He and Kale were moving too quickly for even a marksman like Phillipe to attempt a shot.

Although Kale knew that, he also knew that with Phillipe standing just out of reach with the pistol in his hand, Kale wasn't leaving the circle alive.

That realization was etched in Kale's face; it infused his fighting with a snarling, animalistic fury and a nothing-to-lose strength, which, combined with his precise fluidity, made his strikes difficult to predict, much less counter.

Playing defense wasn't Caleb's strong suit, but he forced himself to do it—to concentrate on keeping Kale's blades at bay and letting the man batter at him, trying to break through.

He was justice—he represented justice—and Kale could try as hard as he wished to break through his guard and triumph. But he wouldn't. Caleb wouldn't let him.

Caleb was taller, stronger, had a greater reach—and most telling of all, he was younger than Kale.

If Kale couldn't break through his defense…eventually, justice would triumph.

He was watching for the moment that realization worked its way into Kale's conscious mind. It did, and Kale blinked.

Then he lashed out with one foot, aiming for Caleb's groin.

But Caleb had already danced aside.

He had far longer legs. Before Kale could recover, Caleb stepped in and smashed his boot into the side of Kale's knee.

Kale screamed and teetered.

Moving like a dancer, Caleb pivoted behind Kale and ruthlessly slashed down on first one, then the other of the man's wrists. Kale screamed again as he dropped both swords.

Caleb reached for Kale's shoulders, intending to push the man to his knees—

"Aside!"

Caleb flung himself to the left as Phillipe's pistol barked.

Kale crumpled, then fell.

Caleb had landed on his side; as he pushed to his feet, he saw the stiletto that had tumbled from Kale's now-lifeless hand.

Caleb snorted. "I believe," he said, resheathing his sword and long knife, "that justice has been served."

Phillipe shook his head at him, then handed the pistol back to Reynaud. Then Phillipe bent, picked up Kale's twin blades, and ceremonially presented them, hilt first across his sleeve, to Caleb. "And to the victor, the spoils."

Caleb grinned. He reached out and closed his hand around one hilt and with his chin gestured for Phillipe to take the other. "I believe that's the pair of us. Thank you for intervening."

Gripping the second blade, slashing it through the air to test its balance, Phillipe lifted one shoulder. "It seemed time. You'd played with him long enough."

Caleb laughed, then, smile fading, he looked around at their men. "Injuries?"

Unsurprisingly, there were more than a few cuts and slashes, of which Caleb and Phillipe had their share. Only three gashes were serious enough to warrant binding. They had lost no one, and for that Caleb gave mute thanks. The fire had gone out. Working together, they lifted the dead aside, then they restoked the blaze, boiled water, and tended every wound.

Once that was done, Caleb climbed to the barracks' porch and, his hands on his hips, surveyed the camp. He grimaced. "I hate to break it to you all, but we need to clear this up."

Phillipe had climbed to stand beside him. On the voyage to Freetown, Phillipe had read Robert's journals and so understood Caleb's direction. He sighed. "Sadly, I agree. We need to make

Kale and his men disappear." Phillipe gestured. "*Poof*—vanished without a trace."

"With no evidence of any fight left, either." Caleb looked at their men. They would feel the effects of the battle later, but for now, they were still keyed up with energy to spare. "Right, then. We need to leave this camp looking as if Kale and his men have just walked out and away. Here's what we'll do."

It took them four hours of hard work, but finally, the camp lay neat and tidy, silent, and oddly serene, as if waiting for occupants to arrive. They'd carted the bodies into the jungle along the unused track to the east, then found a clearing a little way off the track and buried all the bodies in one large grave. Caleb had fetched Robert's journal from his pack, along with the sketches Aileen Hopkins, who had joined Robert on his leg of the mission, had made of certain slavers; by comparing those with the dead men, Caleb felt certain that, as well as Kale, they'd removed not only the large leader of the slavers in the settlement—Rogers—but also the one Aileen had dubbed "the pied piper," the slaver with the melodious voice who was key to luring children from their homes with promises of gainful employment. As the last body was tipped into the grave, Caleb had shut the journal. "With any luck, we've completely exterminated this particular nest of vermin."

Once all was done, Phillipe paused beside Caleb at the edge of the now-peaceful clearing and scanned the area; they'd even groomed the dust with palm fronds, and not a hint of the fight remained. "All in all, a good day's work."

Caleb agreed. "So Kale has mysteriously vanished, and no one is likely to guess to where, much less why."

After one last glance around the clearing, he turned and fell in beside Phillipe. They made their way into the jungle. No one had even suggested spending the night in the slavers' camp. Instead, they'd set up a makeshift camp in the clearing where they'd left their packs and supplies.

Caleb walked into the clearing to find crude tents already erected and a fire burning brightly beneath the cook pot. Aromas much more enticing than the charnel scent of death rose on the steam. They all sat—all but slumped. They checked wounds, then when the meal was ready, everyone ate.

Largely in silence. There were no songs around the campfire, no tall tales told. They'd all killed that day, and while they were accustomed to an existence in which life was too often cut short, as the energy of battle ebbed and left them deflated, they each had their own consciences to tend, to appease and allay.

The fire burned low, and quietly, with nothing more than murmured good nights, they settled on their blankets and reached for sleep.

Tomorrow, they would embark on the next stage of the mission.

Tomorrow, they would take the path to the mine.

Two

"John told me at breakfast that he doesn't know how much longer he can drag his heels over opening up the second tunnel."

Katherine Fortescue glanced at her companion, Harriet Frazier; the pair of them had elected to stretch their legs in a stroll around the mining compound during their midmorning break from their work in the cleaning shed.

Of course, the real purpose of their stroll was to facilitate communication; while they walked, they could talk freely, with no one likely to overhear their exchanges.

The "John" to whom Harriet referred was her sweetheart, Captain John Dixon, the erstwhile army engineer who had been the first of their company to be kidnapped from Freetown. When Dixon had refused the mercenary leader Dubois's invitation to plan and implement the opening of a mine to exploit a newly discovered pipe of diamonds for unnamed backers, Dubois had merely smiled coldly—and the next thing Dixon had known, Harriet had joined him in his captivity.

The threats against Harriet that Dubois had used to force Dixon to acquiesce to his demands were, quite simply, unspeakable. Harriet carried a fine scar on her cheek that Dixon still regarded with sorrow and remembered horror. But Harriet bore the mark with pride. In her eyes—indeed, in the eyes of all the captives now there—Dixon had only done what he'd had to, what he'd been forced to do to ensure he and Harriet survived.

And he and all of them continued in that vein, using that as their touchstone; if they didn't survive, they couldn't escape.

Despite their carefully cultivated appearance of being resigned to their lot, every man, woman, and child of their company had banded together, and all were unswervingly committed to escape.

Escape first; retribution could come later.

Katherine had long grown accustomed to keeping her features composed; she and Harriet maintained unconcerned, outwardly unperturbed expressions as they paced slowly around the well-worn clockwise circuit that would take them from the cleaning shed, where they worked at chipping heavy concretions of ore from the rough diamonds extracted from the mine that had eventually been constructed, past the eastern end of the long, central, main barracks building in which Dubois and his band of mercenaries worked and slept when they weren't on guard, either at the gates of the compound, pacing the perimeter, escorting groups of captives to fetch water from the nearby lake, or perched in the high tower that stood at that end of the long building.

Shading her eyes, Katherine glanced up at the pair of mercenaries on lookout duty in the tower. "Given how our output from the shed has been dwindling," she murmured, "I can—sadly—see John's point." She glanced at Harriet. "Let's meet tonight and see how the others feel. There's only so long we can put Dubois off without damaging our own position."

The "others" were the de facto leaders of their small community—the officers who had been kidnapped, plus Katherine and Harriet. Katherine had been taken because, as a governess, she had experience managing children, but another of her skills was fine needlework, and Dubois had quickly recognized the sharpness of her eye and the quality of her work in the cleaning shed; he had effectively made her the spokesperson and leader of the women and children.

So she spoke for both groups, and Harriet was one of her deputies among the six women, most of whom had been taken for their ability to do fine work.

As she and Harriet continued their promenade, the hems of the drab, featureless gowns they'd been given to wear stirring fallen leaves, Katherine contemplated—as she was sure every one of their number did these days—the delicate balance they were striving to maintain. "I wish there was some easier—more obvious and less stressful—way we could manage this."

Harriet grimaced, then smoothed her features into a mask of unconcern. "It's a constant juggle. I know it weighs heavily on John."

"And he's doing a wonderful job—we wouldn't have any hope if it wasn't for him." Katherine laid a hand on Harriet's sleeve and lightly squeezed. "We all understand the dilemma. We have to keep giving Dubois diamonds enough to appease his masters— whoever the blackguards are—while at the same time holding back as much as we can to stave off the time when the deposit is exhausted and they decide to shut the mine."

None of them harbored the slightest illusion about what would happen once a decision to close the mine was made. They would be killed. Lined up and shot—or worse.

Given the atrocities Dubois and his men had committed against one young girl early in the life of the mine, and the threats Dubois occasionally made when using one of the women or children to reinforce his control over the kidnapped men, *worse*, in this case, would be horrific. So horrific none of them dwelled on the prospect.

That was the other reason Dubois had arranged to have women and children added to the mine's captives. Quite aside from their necessary contributions to the work, they were the perfect pawns with which to ensure the men's compliance.

As the location of the mine dictated that Dubois's impressed workforce had to be European and, given his source was Freetown, that meant mostly English, he'd realized he would need an effective means of controlling said workforce. Dubois was all about effectiveness and control—he was coldhearted, ruthless, and appeared to possess not a single scruple or finer feeling in his large, powerful frame.

Because the mine was located within one of the native chief's lands, Dubois and his masters did not dare kidnap natives—not of any tribe. But the chief did not care about Europeans; in his eyes, they were not his concern. So Englishmen from Freetown it was. In addition, kidnapped English were also more useful in that all those taken had some training in skills required for the mine.

Captain John Dixon had been targeted because he was an expert sapper—an engineer skilled in the construction of tunnels. Several of the other men had carpentry skills; others were laborers used to wielding picks, and all of the women had some talent Dubois or his masters had deemed useful. The children hadn't needed to be anything but children—quick and healthy, with small hands and keen vision.

They even had several men and women with medical and nursing experience, which had proved useful in treating the occasional injury. Mining was inherently unsafe, and accidents had occurred, but the compound contained a decently equipped medical hut.

Katherine cynically acknowledged that the one helpful aspect of Dubois's rule—absolute and unchallengeable as it was— was that his single-minded quest for effectiveness and efficiency meant he considered keeping his workforce as hale, healthy, and able as possible to be in his and his masters' best interests.

So regardless of his threats—which not a single one of them doubted he would carry out without a blink if they pushed him to it—he ensured that their needs were met so that they could continue to work and produce the raw diamonds his masters sought.

That was what Dubois was being very well paid to ensure—

that the mine was properly exploited and the raw diamonds dispatched in secret to Amsterdam on behalf of his masters.

Just who those masters were, no one had yet learned. However, although Dubois was French and his band of mercenaries hailed from every quarter, the general consensus among the captives was that the blackguards behind the scheme were Englishmen.

Katherine dwelled on that for several seconds, then shook the thought aside. Time enough to focus on whom to blame after they'd escaped.

She and Harriet rounded the base of the tower, passing the supply hut and, beside it, the large kitchen with its wide, palm-frond-covered overhang beneath which three small fire pits with cook pots suspended above them were watched over by Dubois's huge cook. The man was the grumpiest individual Katherine had ever met, perennially scowling at everyone—even Dubois.

They continued circling the mercenaries' barracks, on their left passing the long barrack-like building in which all the women and children slept, followed by the compound's double gates, as usual propped wide open with a pair of guards lounging, one to each side.

The roughly circular compound was crudely but effectively palisaded by planks lashed together with thick vines and wire. It appeared rather rickety in places and wouldn't be impossible to break through, but if they escaped and fled, where would they go?

The simple fact that they had no real clue where they were and how far it might be to any form of safe harbor, along with the knowledge of the hideous retribution Dubois would unquestionably inflict on those left behind should any of them successfully flee, ensured that they continued apparently acquiescent in their captivity.

They were anything but, yet circumstances and Dubois had forced them to be pragmatic.

They couldn't escape unless they got everyone out all at once and until they knew in which direction safety lay and how long it would take them to reach it.

Skirting the captives' communal area—a circle of logs surrounding a large fire pit—Katherine and Harriet walked slowly past the long building where the men slept and on past the open maw of the mine. Unless dispatched on some other chore, all the male captives labored inside the tunnel, now more than fifty yards long, that had been hacked, inch by foot, more or less straight into the side of a steep hill that rose abruptly from the jungle floor, as if some elemental force had thrust it upward. The hillside above the mine entrance was relatively sheer.

As she and Harriet passed the mine, they both looked inside. Although lanternlight played on the walls, glinting off the roughly hewn planes, none of the men were presently visible; they would all be farther down, hacking out the remnants of the original deposit, or with Dixon supposedly examining the second pipe—a rock formation associated with diamonds—that Dixon had, thank the Lord, discovered to the right of the original find.

If he hadn't found that second pipe, the mine would already be on its last legs, and they would be facing death.

That new deposit had given them a second wind, as it were, in that it held out the chance of surviving long enough to figure out some way to escape.

That it was up to them to save themselves was now accepted by all. Initially, they'd waited, simply surviving, in the expectation that help would arrive in the form of a rescue party sent from the settlement.

It had seemed inconceivable that this many adults, women as well as men, many with positions and connections in the community, let alone the small army of children, could be snatched from one place without any hue and cry being raised.

But weeks and then months had passed, and no rescue had come.

With their hopes dashed, for a while, they'd grown dispirited and despairing.

But they were English, after all. They'd rallied.

And grown increasingly resolute in their determination to survive and, eventually, escape.

They hadn't yet figured out how to do it, but they would.

Katherine never wavered from that stance, because to do so would mean that there was no hope, not for her or any of the ragtag group of children she now considered as being in her care.

Part of that group lay ahead, mostly older girls crouched by a pile of ore that the boys, both younger and older, plus the few younger girls, had fetched out of the mine. That was the role the children played. The boys and young girls darted in and around the men as they worked, grubbing out and collecting all the rock pieces as they fell from the walls and loading the rock into woven baskets. They then lugged the filled baskets outside and upended them onto the pile the older girls were sorting.

The girls sat or crouched in the shade cast by a crude movable awning Katherine had persuaded Dubois to provide and steadily worked their way through the pile of ore dumped before them. The diamonds came out of the mine heavily encrusted with a mixture of ores. The girls examined each clump of broken rock, searching for the signs they'd been taught signified that a diamond lay within. They tapped the rock, listening for the sound, then searched for the lines where diamond met ore. The girls sorted and, eventually, passed the potential diamonds to the women, who more carefully cleaned each find using small chisels and hammers to tap off the encrustations, ultimately rendering the raw diamonds small enough and light enough for transport.

The captives had heard that the cleaned stones were sent to Amsterdam via ships passing through Freetown harbor.

The rocks the girls discarded they threw into another pile. Closer to the compound's perimeter, a massive pile of discarded rocks testified to the amount the men had already hacked out of the earth, that the children had gathered and sorted.

Katherine and Harriet paused beside the girls, responding with gentle, encouraging smiles as several glanced up.

One of the older girls, fair haired and pale skinned, asked Katherine, "Will you be around later?" She pointed to the already large pile of discarded ore. "We'll be getting through a good amount today."

Katherine nodded; it was part of her Dubois-decreed duties to check over the discarded ore for any obvious diamonds the girls might have missed. "I'll be back this afternoon."

The sound of approaching footsteps had Katherine and Harriet turning to see who was coming their way. Hillsythe, a tall, loose-limbed, brown-haired man, was walking from the medical hut in company with Jed Mathers, one of the carpenters. Hillsythe was a gentleman and, regardless of the rough clothes he now wore, was a commanding figure in their small community. He was also one of those with some degree of medical training, and Jed had a bandaged wrist.

As the pair drew level with Katherine and Harriet, Hillsythe slowed, then halted. He nodded at Jed. "Avoid using that hand for at least the rest of the day. Grab one of the boys to help you."

"Aye. I'll do that." Jed dipped his head respectfully to Katherine and Harriet, then continued on his way to the mine.

Hillsythe lingered. His gaze on Jed, he murmured, "We're going to have to move forward into the second tunnel soon. There's too little of the first deposit left."

"So I understand," Katherine said. "I assume the principal question remaining is how we manage output from the second pipe once Dixon opens it for mining."

Hillsythe inclined his head, both in agreement and in unconsciously elegant farewell. "Tonight, then. As usual after dinner."

Katherine stood with Harriet and watched Hillsythe trail Jed back to the mine. Dixon had been the only officer Dubois and his masters in the settlement who were managing the scheme had intended to snatch. Because of his expertise, Dixon had been a necessity. What the schemers hadn't counted on was that other officers would be dispatched to find Dixon. First had come Lieutenant William Hopkins, who'd been followed by Lieutenant Thomas Fanshawe, both navy men, and finally Hillsythe—who didn't have a rank and wasn't army or navy, yet was transparently someone of military background.

Initially, Dubois had been exceedingly unhappy about having more officers foisted upon him; he was far from a fool—he knew danger when he saw it. However, from Dubois's point of view, the advent of Hopkins, the first officer to arrive after Dixon, had instead proved to be an unlooked-for bonus. The disconnected rabble of other men—many sailors or navvies snatched off the docks—had recognized the authority Will Hopkins carried as naturally as a cloak. Although he was only in his late twenties, Will's grasp of command was innate, and the men had responded.

And Will had been clever enough to see that playing to Dubois's liking for efficiency and smooth operations would, in the short to medium term, be to the captives' advantage.

That had been the start of the charade they'd all, bit by bit, started to play for Dubois's benefit. Just how much of their carefully constructed façade of appeasement and acquiescence Dubois actually believed, Katherine—and the others, too—would not have wagered on, but as long as his camp ran smoothly and he met his masters' targets, Dubois appeared content to leave them be.

According to Hillsythe, Dubois was the epitome of a successful mercenary. He wouldn't have reached the age he had, with the absolute control over his men he transparently wielded, without knowing how to best manage an operation like this. Efficiency and effectiveness were Dubois's watchwords; as long as the work was done as he wished, he cared not a fig for anything else.

Under Dixon, Hopkins, and Fanshawe, the male captives had

come together and formed a cohesive company, divided into four units under the three officers and Hillsythe. In addition, Hillsythe acted as their strategist. It was he who, once he'd learned the ways of the camp and Dubois, had sounded the alarm over the dwindling first deposit and had suggested that Dixon excavate more widely, searching for another.

If it hadn't been for Hillsythe's foresight, they would already have been in dire straits.

Subsequently, when Dixon had succeeded in finding the second pipe and they'd all heaved a sigh of relief, Hillsythe had again seen opportunity and had suggested that Dixon—with the full knowledge of all the captives—become increasingly spontaneously "helpful" to Dubois in matters relating to the mine. Hillsythe had explained that a man of Dixon's background—an engineer with a true passion for his work—might believably have his initial loyalties eroded by his excitement over exploiting a second and even more fabulous diamond pipe.

Dixon had been reluctant, but they'd all seen the potential benefit and had urged him to try it.

With Hillsythe's guidance, Dixon had tried being "helpful" over issues that didn't really matter to the captives.

The result was that, having now accepted Dixon's "conversion," increasingly, Dubois trusted what Dixon told him about the mine. That had helped enormously in dragging out the opening of the second tunnel. At this point, Dixon couldn't tell how extensive the second deposit was, so they'd decided to stretch out the mining of the first pipe for as long as possible—as long as a supply of diamonds adequate to appease Dubois's masters was coming out of it—before opening the second pipe for mining.

Dixon had bought them the time by claiming a need for more careful and extensive testing around the second pipe so that when they hacked into the hillside, they didn't unnecessarily risk either damaging the pipe itself or bringing down the hillside on top of it and them. Dubois had accepted the rationale and allowed the delay.

But now that the first deposit was almost mined out, they would have to start on the second. Dubois and his masters wouldn't countenance the output of diamonds falling too low, and no one wanted to risk Dubois receiving an order to cull their company on the grounds that such a number was no longer required.

That was the sort of horrific act of which they all knew Dubois was fully capable.

Strangely enough, while everyone else had given up any hope of rescue, Hillsythe still entertained the expectation that someone would, at some point, come for them—that relief in some guise would eventually arrive. He didn't make any point of it and nowadays rarely spoke of it, yet Katherine sensed that his quiet, unstated confidence still survived.

Which left her wondering about something Hillsythe had never explained—namely, who had sent him after Fanshawe.

As Hillsythe vanished into the mine, a pattering of feet drew her attention to a young boy who came pelting toward her from the direction of the kitchen. She turned with a welcoming smile. "Diccon." As he skidded to a halt before her, she reached out and finger-combed his pale golden hair back from his forehead. "Are you off, then?"

"Aye." Diccon held up the basket he carried. "And I'll be sure to be back before the sun starts down."

She kept her smile in place, but saw the shadow that passed through Diccon's pale blue eyes. "I know you will. Off you go, then."

She and Harriet stood and watched as, with a last fleeting grin, Diccon raced off toward the compound gate. Although tall for his age, he was only seven. Long and lanky, thin and bony, he'd been delivered to Dubois with a group of other children snatched from the Freetown slums. But Diccon hadn't been able to bear the dust in the mine; he'd coughed himself into fits, and his health had quickly deteriorated.

When Dubois had contemplated killing the boy, deeming him a useless burden, Katherine had argued that Diccon wasn't useless—he just couldn't go into the mine. Instead, she'd pointed out that if Dubois wanted his captives to perform at their best and not fall ill unnecessarily, then all the children, and the adults, too, could do with more fruit—and there was plenty of fruit in the surrounding jungle. Fruit Diccon could fetch. Dubois had considered, then he'd agreed to let Diccon ramble for fruit every day, as long as he returned each afternoon before dusk.

Dubois had looked Diccon in the eye and had stated that if Diccon failed to return, Dubois would kill two children—Diccon's closest friends.

That was the cause of the shadows in Diccon's eyes. He enjoyed rambling in the jungle and had grown adept at finding fruit, berries, and nuts, but he worried all the time that something might happen to keep him from returning, and the deaths of his friends would be on his head.

It was just like Dubois to unnecessarily place such a Damocles' sword over an impressionable boy's head. No one in their right mind would imagine Diccon—who was by no means unintelligent—would attempt to run away. Where to? He would die in the jungle if he didn't come back.

Her gaze on Diccon's departing figure, Harriet sighed. "What I wouldn't give to spend a day now and then out in the jungle."

Katherine thought, then arched her brows. "Why don't I ask his highness?"

Harriet glanced at her. "Do you think there's any chance he'll agree?"

"He might if I phrase the request correctly." She paused, then added, "I've noticed he's particularly fond of those large nuts Diccon brings in. Dubois keeps them all for himself."

With Harriet, she turned, and they continued to the cleaning shed. It was time to return to their day's labors. As they reached the steps that led up to the door, she made up her mind. "I can't see any reason not to ask. I'll suggest that one of us can accompany Diccon out each day, and that we'll work an extra half hour each day—all of us—to make up for it."

Harriet's face lit. "That sounds perfect. And Lord knows, Dubois knows that none of us are fool enough to try to run away."

Katherine pulled a face. "We don't even know in which direction to run."

She opened the door and went in. Harriet followed, and they resumed their places on stools about the long raised table that ran down the middle of the shed.

Mary Wilson looked up from the rock from which she was carefully chipping away aggregated ore. She flashed a smile at Katherine and Harriet, then looked back at her work. There were six women in total, all presently in the shed, and they'd banded together into a tight-knit, supportive group. They'd had to. While Katherine was the most confident and assured in dealing with Dubois, the others had backed her up on more than one occasion. Despite their disparate backgrounds—Katherine a governess, Harriet a young woman of good family searching for a position after coming out to Freetown following Dixon, Mary a shop assistant and part owner of a shop, Ellen Mackenzie another young woman who had arrived in the settlement looking for honest work, and Annie Mellows and Gemma Halliday, expert needlewomen who hailed from the slums—they'd all grown comfortable in the others' company.

They'd come to trust each other.

A guard had come in fifteen minutes before Katherine and Harriet had left for their walk; the other women had gone for their walks, two by two, earlier. The guard was still there, leaning against one wall, bored and idly watching them.

Ten entirely uneventful minutes later, he stirred. A large male of indeterminate origin, he drawled, "Later, ladies." Then he moved to the door and left, letting the panel slam shut behind him.

All six women looked up. Mary met Katherine's eyes.

After a moment of straining her ears, Katherine nodded. Mary slipped from her stool, went to the door, and carefully eased it open enough to look out.

There was a grin in her voice as she reported, "He's swaggering off to the barracks."

They never knew when a guard might look in on them—and never quite trusted in them leaving and not hovering, hoping to hear something incriminating to report to Dubois. But this one had, as most of them did, taken himself off.

After shutting the door, Mary returned to her stool and hopped up again. She looked at Katherine. "Any news?"

"I've decided to ask Dubois if we—one by one, one each day—can join Diccon on his forays. Just to break up our days."

"Ooh!" Gemma grinned. "I like the sound of that."

They fell to discussing the pros and cons and how best to present the argument to Dubois. Katherine glanced at Harriet, but as she had, Harriet chose not to mention the issue of opening up the second tunnel.

Time enough to broach that later, after the leaders' discussion that evening, when, no doubt, they would learn the hard facts.

★ ★ ★

Charles Babington stood on the worn planks of Government Wharf. Lounging in the shadows cast by a stack of cotton bales offloaded from some other vessel, he watched the Macauley and Babington inspector and the port's customs officer as they peered down into the open hatch of *The Dutch Princess*, a merchantman bound for Amsterdam.

Impatience rode him, edged with desperation. His intended, Mary Wilson, had vanished too many weeks ago, and there seemed nothing of any substance that he could actually do. Robert Frobisher had given him hope, but Frobisher had vanished and had surely returned to England long since. Whether Frobisher had succeeded in advancing his mission—which might just result in Mary being found and returned to Charles and her uncle—Charles did not know. Short of writing to Frobisher, there was no way Charles could see to learn more.

And he had no idea where Frobisher, or even his brother Declan Frobisher, actually lived. A letter to the Frobisher Shipping Company in London or Aberdeen might, eventually, reach Robert. Perhaps.

But Charles had volunteered to do what little he could to en-sure no diamonds—or gold if that was what was being mined, but his and the Frobishers' money was on diamonds—slipped out of Freetown in some ship's hold. He had the ability to order searches of the cargo of any ship bound for England or for ports nearby on the Continent. Amsterdam, long the home of the world's diamond trade, was just such a port, and so together with all other Amsterdam- or Rotterdam-bound vessels, *The Dutch Princess*'s cargo hold was being searched by a gang of excise men.

Charles's presence was not required—indeed, he had no real business being there—but the sense of helplessness that dogged his every waking moment had driven him to the wharf—just in case.

Just in case the search party stumbled on a cache of uncut diamonds.

The captain, a burly man who looked more English than Dutch, stood by the side of the open hold, his massive arms crossed over his broad chest. He'd been watching the searchers, but as if he'd felt Charles's gaze, he glanced at him.

After a moment of staring, the captain uncrossed his arms, spoke to the inspector, then made for the gangplank. He swung down to the wharf and strode toward Charles.

Charles didn't straighten from his slouch.

The captain halted in front of him. "Babington, am I right?"

Charles inclined his head. "You have the advantage of me—I don't believe we've been introduced."

The captain showed his teeth. "I'm the captain of the ship you're holding up." He glanced back at the activity on his deck, then looked out over the harbor. "Not sure I'll get out in time now." He brought his gaze back to Charles's face. "So what's this search in aid of?"

Charles's smile was thin. He met the man's gaze with every evidence of boredom. "It's just routine. Macauley sometimes gets bees in his bonnet, and nothing will do but that we have to go out and catch whatever beggars he imagines are violating our license." The Macauley and Babington Company held the exclusive license to ship goods to England from Freetown.

The captain humphed. "Bloody nuisance is what it is." He looked toward his ship.

Charles followed the man's gaze and saw the inspector and the customs officer walking to the gangplank, the excise men falling in at their heels.

"Finally!" The captain glanced back at Charles. "So with your permission, I'll be on my way."

Charles hid a grimace and nodded. "Fair weather and good winds."

The captain tipped him a cynical salute and tramped back to his ship.

Charles watched him go and wondered, not for the first time over the past month he'd been authorizing such searches, whether Frobisher's information had been accurate. Whether there was an illicit diamond mine in operation, or if there was, whether it might be in a very different location and not shipping its stones out of Freetown at all. Thus far, not a single search had found even a whiff of contraband.

On the deck, the captain started calling orders. Sailors jumped to the wharf and cast off the ropes. Charles saw one of the crew approach the captain, but there was nothing more to be seen or done. Pushing away from the bales, Charles straightened. Staring at the worn planking, but not really seeing it—seeing instead Mary's sweet face—he followed the inspector from the wharf and headed back to his office.

On the deck of *The Dutch Princess*, now a-flurry with preparations to set sail, the captain glanced over his shoulder. He watched Babington leave the wharf, then turned with a snort.

His first mate halted beside him. "So what was that about? Anything we need to be concerned over?"

The captain hesitated, then said, "Babington made out it was just routine, but I'm not sure I buy that, not with himself being here to watch."

The mate rocked on his heels. "Do you think they know?"

"Nope. If they did, we'd be in more trouble." The captain glanced around, but there appeared to be no one watching them. "Not that hard to send a cutter to keep an eye on us, but I doubt they will. Keep an eye peeled, just in case."

"Aye, aye." The first mate debated, then asked, "So we're still going for the pickup?"

"We most certainly are. We'll take her out and across to the north shore. Give it a few hours for the tide to swing, and to make certain no one's got their eye on us, then we'll head down the estuary."

The first mate nodded and pulled on his long nose. "Always wondered why they set it up for us to pick up the goods on our way out, given we have to turn to do it." The mate grinned. "Guess I understand now."

The captain grunted and headed for his wheel.

Minutes later, *The Dutch Princess* eased from her moorings and sailed out of Freetown harbor.

Three

Caleb paused to pull the neckerchief from about his throat and wipe the sweat from his brow. This was the second day of their trek along the path leading—originally, at least—north from Kale's camp. They'd followed the well-trodden path more or less north for most of yesterday, but in the last hours before they'd halted for the night, the track had veered to the east.

Today, the path had started to climb while angling more definitely eastward. And they'd started to come upon crude traps. Phillipe had been in the lead when they'd approached the first; he'd spotted it—a simple pit—and they'd tramped around it without disturbing the concealing covering. From then on, they'd kept their eyes peeled and found three more traps, all of varying design, clearly intended to discourage the unwary, but it had been easy enough to avoid each one.

If they'd needed further confirmation that they were on the correct path, the traps had provided it. But there hadn't been another for several miles.

Caleb glanced around and saw nothing but more jungle. His internal clock informed him it was nearing noon. He couldn't see the sky; the damned canopy was too thick. Accustomed to the wide expanses of the open sea, he was getting distinctly tired of the closeness of the jungle and the dearth of light. And the lack of crisp fresh air.

Phillipe had been walking with Reynaud in the rear; he came forward to halt beside Caleb. "Time to take a break." Phillipe pointed through the trees. "There's a clearing over there."

Caleb fell in behind his friend, and their men fell in behind him. They trudged ten yards farther along; the track remained well marked by the tramp of many feet. The clearing Phillipe had noted opened to the left of the path. Their company shuffled into it. After divesting themselves of seabags, packs, and weapons, they sprawled on the leaves or sat on fallen logs, stretching out their legs before hauling out water skins and drinking.

Luckily, water was one necessity the jungle provided in abundance. They'd also found edible fruits and nuts and carried enough dried meat in their packs to last for more than a week. If not for the stifling atmosphere, the trek would have been pleasant enough.

Phillipe lowered himself to sit beside Caleb on a fallen log. With a tip of his head, he indicated the jungle on the other side of the path. "We've been angling along the side of these foothills for the last hour. The path's still climbing. I've been thinking that, following the inestimable Miss Hopkins's reasoning, the mine can't be much farther. The children who were taken—certainly the younger ones—would be dragging their feet by now."

Caleb swallowed a mouthful of water, then nodded. "I keep wondering if we've missed a concealed turn-off, but the traffic on the path is as heavy as ever, and it's still going in the same direction."

They'd been speaking quietly, and their men had, too, but Phillipe glanced around and murmured, "I think, perhaps, that when we go on, we should keep talking to a minimum."

Caleb restoppered his water skin. "At least until we've found the mine. The jungle's so much thicker here, we could turn a corner and find ourselves there. We don't want to advertise our presence, and we definitely don't want to engage."

Phillipe's long lips quirked wryly. "No matter how much we might wish otherwise."

Caleb grunted and pushed to his feet. Phillipe followed suit, and three minutes later, their party set off again, tramping rather more quietly through the increasingly dense jungle.

Fifteen minutes later, their caution proved critical. Caleb caught a fleeting glimpse of something pale flitting about a clearing ahead and off the path to their right. Phillipe was in the lead. His eyes glued to the shifting gleam, Caleb seized his friend's arm and halted. Their men noticed and froze.

Phillipe shifted to stand alongside Caleb, the better to follow his gaze. The intervening boles and large-leafed palms made following anyone's line of sight difficult.

Caleb couldn't work out what he was seeing—a gleam of gold, a flash of...what?

Then the object of his gaze moved, and Caleb finally had a clear view. "It's a boy," he breathed. "A golden-haired, fair-skinned boy in ragged clothes."

"He's picking those berries," Phillipe whispered. After a moment, he added, "What do you want to do?"

Caleb scanned the area. "As far as I can tell, he's alone. I can't see anyone else, can you?"

"No. And I can't hear anyone else, either."

"If we all appear, he'll take fright and run." Caleb considered, then shrugged off the pack he'd been carrying and handed it to Phillipe. "Keep everyone here until I signal."

Accepting the pack, Phillipe nodded.

Caleb made his way quietly toward the boy, dodging around trees and taking care not to alert his quarry. The lad looked to be about eight, but woefully thin—all knees and elbows. He was wearing a tattered pair of dun-colored shorts and a loose tunic of the same coarse material. It had been the bright cap of his fair hair, gleaming as the boy passed through the stray sunbeams that struck through the thick canopy, that had attracted Caleb's attention.

The boy was circling a vine that had grown into a clump, almost filling one of the small clearings created when a large tree had fallen. The bushy vine bore plump, dark-red berries that Caleb and his company had already discovered were edible and sweet. His attention fixed on his task, the boy steadily plucked berries and dropped them into a woven basket.

Despite the boy's bare feet, the basket suggested he hailed from a group of some kind; from the features Caleb glimpsed as the boy moved about the bush, the lad was almost certainly English.

He had to be from the mine.

Caleb reached the edge of the clearing. He hesitated, then said, "Don't be afraid—please don't run away."

The boy jerked and whipped around. He grabbed up the basket, his knuckles turning white as he gripped the handle.

His blue eyes wide, the boy stared at Caleb.

Caleb didn't move other than to slowly display his hands, palms open and clearly empty, out to either side.

The boy was poised to flee.

If he did, Caleb doubted he could catch him, not in this terrain. "I've been sent to look for people—English people kidnapped from Freetown." He spoke slowly, clearly, evenly. "We think they're being used as labor for a mine. We're searching for the mine." He paused, then asked, "Do you know where the mine is?"

When the boy didn't respond, Caleb remembered that the mine was conjecture and rephrased, "Do you know where the people are?"

The boy moistened his lips. "Who are you?"

He wasn't going to run—at least, not yet. Caleb was usually relaxed with children, happy to play with them, to join in their games. When convincing children of anything, he knew the literal truth was usually advisable; they always seemed to sense prevarication. "I've come from London. People have been searching for those kidnapped, but we've had to do it bit by bit—carefully. To make sure the bad people who are behind the kidnapping don't get wind of us coming to help." *And kill all the kidnapees.* He stopped short of voicing that truth.

The boy was still staring at him, but now he was studying him, his gaze flitting from Caleb's face over his clothes, his sword, his boots.

"I'm going to crouch down." Moving slowly, Caleb did. If he'd stepped closer to the boy, he would have towered over him—too intimidating. And laying hands on the lad from a crouch would be that much harder.

Sure enough, as Caleb settled on his haunches, the boy noticeably relaxed. But his gaze remained sharp; although he constantly glanced back at Caleb, watching for any threat, he started scanning the shadows behind Caleb. "There are more of you, aren't there?"

"Yes. I asked them to stay back so we didn't frighten you." Caleb paused, then offered, "There are twenty-four more men back on the path."

The boy blinked at him. "So there's twenty-five of you all together. All armed?"

Caleb nodded.

The boy frowned; he seemed to have lost his fear of Caleb. After a long moment of calculation, the boy shook his head. "That's not going to be enough." He met Caleb's gaze. "There's more mercenaries than that at the mine, and they're all fearsome fighters."

So there is a mine. And it is nearby. Caleb tamped down his elation. "We're not the rescue party. We're the advance scouts. Our mission"—and he could almost hear his eldest brother, Royd, groaning over him telling a boy, a young boy he didn't know anything about, such details—"is to locate the mining camp and send word of it back to London. Then the rescue party will be dispatched, and they will have the numbers to put paid to the mercenaries."

The boy studied Caleb's face, searching his eyes as if to determine whether he spoke the truth—then the lad smiled gloriously. "Cor—they're *never* going to believe me when I tell 'em, but the others are going to be in alt! We've been waiting ever so long for anyone to come."

The excitement in his voice was infectious, but… Caleb waved both hands in a "keep it quiet" gesture. "Before you tell anyone, you need to remember that our mission must remain secret. The mercenaries at the mine must not learn that we're here." Caleb locked his gaze on the boy's eyes. "If the mercenaries realize rescue is coming, it could be very dangerous for all the people kidnapped."

The boy's delight faded, but after a second, he nodded. "All right." He looked at Caleb, then glanced out into the jungle again. "So what're you going to do now you've found us?"

"I'm hoping you can take us closer to the mine—to some place from where we can see it but not be seen ourselves. Can you do that?"

"'Course!"

"But before we get to that, I want to hear what you can tell me—us—about the mine and the encampment." Caleb swiveled and glanced behind him, then looked at the boy. "What's your name?"

"Diccon."

"I'm Caleb. And if it's all right with you, Diccon, I'd like to call my men closer, so we can all hear what you say."

Diccon nodded.

Caleb rose—slowly—and beckoned his men to join them. They tramped through the jungle following the route he'd taken, leaving as little evidence of their passing as possible. Each man nodded at Diccon as they reached the clearing. They all sidled in, trying not to crowd Diccon despite the limited space. Several hunkered down, including Phillipe.

Caleb did, too, again bringing his face more level with Diccon's. "Right, then. This mine—does it have a fence around it?"

That was all he had to ask to have Diccon launch into a re-markably clear and detailed description of the camp—more like a compound—that surrounded the entrance to the mine. Crude but effective outer walls, with huts for various purposes. Mention of a medical hut had Caleb and Phillipe exchanging surprised glances.

Diccon's description wound to a close; he'd mentally walked in via the gate, then taken them on a clockwise tour describing every building they would pass.

"That's extremely helpful," Caleb said, and meant it. "Now—how many mercenaries are there?"

"Hmm." Diccon's features scrunched up. He had set down his basket, and from the way his fingers moved, he was counting. Then his face cleared. "There be twenty-four there right now, plus Dubois, and six are off taking the latest batch of diamonds to the coast for pickup."

Caleb blinked. "So it's definitely diamonds they're mining."

"Aye," Diccon said. "Thought you knew that."

"We'd guessed it, but until now, we couldn't be certain." Caleb tilted his head. "You said the mercenaries take the diamonds to the *coast* for pickup—not Freetown?"

"Nuh-uh. At least, we—all of us in the compound—don't think so. Far as we've been able to make out, they take the strongbox toward the settlement, but the pickup is somewhere on the estuary, see? That way, no one in Freetown knows."

Phillipe shifted, drawing Diccon's attention. "The six who've gone to the coast—do they go and return via that path?" He pointed at the path they'd been following, which lay not that far away through the palms.

A pertinent point. Caleb looked at Diccon—and was relieved to see the boy shake his head.

"That path just goes to Kale's camp." Diccon's eyes grew flat, and his expression shuttered. "You don't want to go that way."

"Kale's not there anymore," Caleb said. "He's…left. Along with all his men."

"Yeah?" Diccon studied Caleb's face, then his eyes grew round as the implication registered.

Before he could ask the eager questions clearly bubbling on his tongue, Phillipe intervened. "Which route do the mercenaries take to the coast, then?"

"There's another path—well, there's several leave the compound. One goes to the lake where we get our water, and there's this one, where all of us came in from. Then there's another that divides into two not far from the gate. Those who go to drop off the diamonds take the northwest branch, and we reckon it also eventually leads to Freetown. They *could* get to Freetown through Kale's camp, but Dubois—he's the leader—he mostly sends his men to get ordinary things like food and stuff that we know must come from Freetown when they go to drop off the diamonds."

Caleb nodded, a map taking shape in his brain. "You said that path divides into two—where does the other branch go?"

"Far as we know, it leads dead north. We think there's nothing but jungle that way, all the way to the coast." Diccon paused, then added, "Maybe some natives. There's a chief that owns this land, see, and Dubois pays him to let the mine be. We think he—the chief—lives that way. That's why the track's there, but no one from the mine uses it."

Phillipe caught Caleb's eye. Caleb nodded fractionally. That little-used path sounded like the one they should fall back along. He refocused on Diccon. "Tell us more about the mercenaries."

"Well, like I said, there's thirty of them all up, including the cook and his helper, who are just as fierce as the others. And there's Dubois. He's in charge, and they all mind him. He has two…lieutenants, I suppose you'd say. Arsene—he's Dubois's second-in-command—and Cripps is the other. The mercenaries are all big and tough, and they carry swords, lots of knives, and some have pistols. The ones on the tower and the gates have muskets."

Caleb slowly nodded. Direct observation would be best. But first… "How is it you're allowed out by yourself? You are by yourself, aren't you?"

Diccon's face fell. "Aye. I'm no good in the mine, see. I just cough and cough. Dubois, he was going to kill me—he said I was useless, and he wasn't going to waste food feeding me. But Miss Katherine spoke up for me." Diccon straightened. "She said I wasn't useless and that I could help fetch fruit and berries, and nuts, too, so that the cook could properly feed all us children. And the adults, too. She said that way, we'd all stay healthy and work better—and Dubois went fer it."

Consulting his mental list of the females kidnapped, Caleb asked, "Miss Katherine—is she Miss Fortescue?"

"Aye. That's her. But all us children call her Miss Katherine. She's in charge of us."

And was clearly a lioness if she'd spoken up and saved Diccon.

Diccon heaved a disconsolate sigh. "I wish I could run away, but Dubois said that if'n I ain't back by sundown every day, he'll kill two of me mates." The boy's face paled. "So I don't even dare be late back. He's a devil, Dubois is."

"You believe him?" Phillipe asked the question gently.

Diccon looked him in the eye. "We all believe Dubois's threats. Even Mr. Hillsythe. He says Dubois is one of those villains who enjoys killing, and that we none of us should ever doubt he'll do exactly what he says."

Caleb caught Phillipe's eye. Hillsythe was Wolverstone's man. If that was his assessment of Dubois, they'd be well advised to pay it due heed. "All right." Caleb returned his gaze to Diccon. "I think it's time we took a look at this camp—but first…" As he rose, he glanced at the assembled men, then he looked back at Diccon. "We need to find a place to camp that's close enough to the mine for us to keep watch and study it, but far enough away that no one from the camp is likely to stumble across us. I thought perhaps somewhere along that path to the north—the one no one uses."

Diccon nodded. "I know just the place. There's a good-sized clearing a little way down that track."

Caleb laid a gentle hand on the boy's shoulder. "Can we get to it without going closer to the camp?"

"O' course—I can lead you." Diccon's happy grin returned, and he swiped up his basket. "I know all the places round about. I can go where I like around the camp, and the berries and fruit and nut trees grow everywhere."

"Is it likely anyone from the camp might hear us?" Phillipe asked.

"Nah." As Caleb let his hand fall from Diccon's shoulder, the boy turned and beckoned. "We're still well out, and the trees and leaves and all keep sound in. You often can't hear someone until they're quite close."

Caleb signaled to his men to follow and, with Phillipe on his heels, fell in behind Diccon.

When they reached the path from Kale's camp, Diccon beckoned them onward. "I'll take you through the jungle and around until we hit the other path."

He proved as good as his word, leading them unerringly on a tacking course around jungle trees and more dense pockets of vegetation. He waved them to caution as they approached another path. When Caleb put a hand on Diccon's shoulder and leaned down to breathe in his ear "What?" the boy tipped his head back and whispered, "This is the northwest path they use to drop off the diamonds and go to Freetown. I don't think they'll be on their way back yet, but..."

Caleb released his shoulder with a pat. "Good lad. Always play safe."

They crept to the edge of the path and strained their ears, but heard nothing. Swiftly, they crossed over the beaten track and plunged back into the jungle. Ten yards on, Caleb glanced back and could see nothing but jungle foliage. Finding a guide had been a stroke of luck. Without Diccon to lead them, they would have been stumbling around—very possibly into the mercenaries' clutches.

But Fate had smiled and sent the boy to them.

When they came upon the next path, Diccon walked confidently on to it. "That place I told you about—the nice clearing—is just along here." He led them down what was clearly a very much less well-traveled track. There were small saplings springing up, and vines laced across the path. Phillipe muttered, then told the men to work on keeping their passing as undetectable as possible. So they avoided the saplings and ducked under the vines, all of which Diccon whisked light-footed around.

Then he turned off the path onto a narrow animal track. Fifteen yards on, it descended into a clearing that—as Diccon had promised—was perfect for their needs. Big enough to comfortably house all of them and with a tiny stream trickling past on one side.

"Here you go." Grinning, the boy spun, holding his arms wide.

Caleb grinned back. "Thank you—this is just what we need."

Phillipe smiled at Diccon and patted his shoulder as he passed. "You're an excellent scout, my friend."

The other men made approving noises as they filed into the space.

Diccon positively glowed.

It took only a moment for Caleb and Phillipe to organize the establishment of their camp, then, summoning their quartermasters—Caleb's Quilley and Phillipe's Ducasse—they presented themselves before Diccon.

The boy looked at them expectantly.

"First question," Caleb said. "Have you got enough fruit in your basket to satisfy the cook?"

Diccon lifted the floppy basket, opened it, and examined the pile of fruit inside. "Almost." He looked up and around, then pointed to a small tree with dangling yellow fruit. "If I got some more of those, I'd have enough."

Two captains and two quartermasters dutifully gathered several handfuls of the ripe fruit.

Diccon smiled as they filled his basket, then he clamped the handles together and looked at Caleb. "More than enough."

"Excellent. What we need next," Caleb said, "is for you to lead us to a place where we can see into the camp, all without alerting any guards. Do you know of such a spot?"

Diccon snapped off a salute. "I know just the place, Capt'n." He'd heard Caleb's men using his rank.

"In that case"—Caleb gestured toward where he assumed the mine must be—"lead on."

Diccon did. He lived up to their expectations, leading them first along the disused path again, then cutting left into the untrammeled jungle. He looked back at Caleb and whispered, "This will be safest. We're moving away from the other paths and into the space between that northward path and the one leading to the lake. The mercenaries take some of the men to the lake to fetch water every day, but they do that in the morning. There shouldn't be anyone at the lake now."

Caleb nodded, and they forged on, increasingly slowly as Diccon took the order to be careful to heart.

Eventually, he halted behind a clump of palms. Using hand signals, he intimated that they should crouch down and be extra careful while following him on to the next concealing clump.

Then he slipped like an eel through the shadows.

Caleb followed and instantly saw why Diccon had urged extra caution. The compound's palisade lay ten yards away, separated from the jungle by a beaten, well-maintained perimeter clearing—a cleared space to ensure no one could approach the palisade under cover. The compound's double gates were five yards to their right. And the gates stood wide open with two armed guards slouched against the posts on either side. Both guards' attention was fixed on the activity inside the camp, but any untoward noise would alert them.

Given the gates were propped open, Caleb surmised that the real purpose of the guards—and, indeed, the fence, the gates, and the guard tower in the middle of the compound—was to keep people in; the mercenaries had grown sufficiently complacent that they didn't expect any threat to emerge from the jungle.

Well and good.

They watched in silence for more than half an hour. Caleb noticed that heavily armed guards appeared to be patrolling randomly through the compound, but the attitude of all the mercenaries was transparently one of supreme boredom. They were very far from alert; the impression they gave was that they were perfectly sure there would be no challenge to their authority.

Against that, however, he saw some of the captives—he had no idea which ones, but both male and female—walking freely back and forth. More, some met and stopped to chat, apparently without attracting the attention of the guards.

Curious.

Then he noticed Diccon peering up at the sky. The sun was angling from the west. Remembering the boy's concern over returning in good time, Caleb tapped him on the shoulder, caught Phillipe and the other men's eyes, then tipped his head back, into the relative safety of the area behind them.

Diccon retreated first. One by one, the rest of them followed.

They gathered again well out of hearing of the guards on the gates. Caleb dropped his hand on Diccon's shoulder and met the boy's gaze. "Thank you for all your help. Now, we have to tread warily. Who is the person you trust most inside the camp?"

"Miss Katherine."

Caleb blinked. He'd expected the boy to name one of the men, but his answer had come so rapidly and definitely that there was no real way to argue with his choice. Slowly, Caleb nodded. "Very well. I want you to tell Miss Katherine all we've told you. Can you remember the important bits?"

Diccon nodded eagerly. "I remember everything. I'm good like that."

Caleb had to grin. "Excellent. So tell Miss Katherine, but no one else, and see what she says. Then tomorrow, when you come out, go and look for fruit in this area—between our camp and the lake. Behave as you usually do and gather fruit, and we'll come and find you. We'll be waiting to hear what Miss Katherine, and any others she thinks fit to tell, say."

Diccon's face brightened. "So I'm like...what is it? A courier?"

"Exactly." Phillipe smiled at the boy. "But remember—the mark of a good courier is that he tells only those he's supposed to tell. Not a word of this to anyone else, all right?"

Diccon nodded. "Mum's the word, except for Miss Katherine."

"Good." Caleb released the boy. "I would suggest you circle around and come in from some other direction."

"I'll go to the lake and walk in from there—that way, if you keep watching, you'll see where that path comes out a-ways to the left."

Caleb's approving smile was entirely genuine. "You're taking to this like a duck to water." He nodded in farewell. "Off you go, then."

With a brisk salute and a grin for them all, Diccon melted into the jungle; in seconds, they'd lost sight of him.

"He is very good." Phillipe turned toward the gates. "But I'll feel happier when he's back inside where he belongs." He waved toward their previous hideaway. "Shall we?"

They returned to the spot. Five minutes later, Diccon appeared out of the jungle to their left. He passed their position without a glance and, basket swinging, all but skipped back through the gates. He headed to the right, vanishing into an area of the compound that from their position they had no view of.

Caleb consulted his memory. "He must have gone to deliver his haul to the cook—he said the kitchen was that way."

He'd barely breathed the words. Phillipe merely nodded in reply.

Sure enough, ten minutes later, they saw Diccon, no longer carrying the basket, cross the area inside the gates, right to left. He appeared to be scanning the far left quadrant of the compound—but then he whirled as if responding to a hail from somewhere out of their sight to the right.

Even from where they crouched, they saw his face light up. Diccon all but jigged on the spot, clearly waiting...

A young woman appeared. Brown haired, pale skinned, she moved with a grace that marked her as well bred. Smiling, she came up to Diccon and held out her hands. Diccon readily placed his hands in hers, all but wriggling with impatience and excitement.

Closing her hands about the boy's, her gaze on his face, the woman crouched as Caleb had done.

Immediately, the boy started talking, although from the way the woman leaned toward him, he was keeping his voice down.

"Miss Katherine, obviously." Caleb scanned all of the area around the pair that he could see, but there were no guards or, indeed, anyone else close enough to hear the exchange.

As Diccon poured out his news, Caleb saw the woman— younger than he'd expected by more than a decade; he'd had no idea a governess could be that young—start to tense. Clearly, she'd realized the import of what the boy was telling her—and she believed his tale.

That last was verified when she glanced out of the gates—not directly at them but in their direction.

Immediately, she caught herself and refocused on Diccon again.

But Caleb had seen that look, had caught her expression.

However fleeting, that look had been a visual cry for help that had also held a flaring of something even more precious—hope.

By some trick of the light, of that moment in eternity, he'd felt that hope—fragile, but real—reaching out to him, something so indescribably precious he'd instinctively wanted to grasp it. To hold and protect it.

Then she'd clamped down on the emotion, but he no longer harbored the slightest concern that the adults in the camp wouldn't believe Diccon's tale. She—Miss Katherine—did, and even though Caleb had yet to exchange so much as a word with her, he felt certain a woman brave enough to stand up to a mercenary captain in order to save an urchin's life would have the backbone to carry her point with the English officers in the camp.

Diccon finished his tale. Her gaze fixed firmly on his face, Miss Katherine slowly rose to her feet. Then she released one of his hands, but retained her clasp on the other. Drawing him around, she set off with a purposeful stride, heading in the direction of the mine. In just a few paces, she and Diccon had passed out of their sight.

They continued to watch for several minutes, but no alarm was raised, and there was nothing of particular interest to see.

Caleb frowned. He leaned toward Phillipe and whispered, "We need to see *into* the compound—we need a much more comprehensive view."

"I was thinking the same, and it just so happens"—without raising his arm, Phillipe pointed, directing Caleb's gaze upward—"the compound is nestled into a curve in the hillside, and if you look very closely just there…"

Caleb looked. His eyes were accustomed to reading ships' flags at considerable distance; he quickly picked out the rock formation Phillipe had spied. "Perfect." Caleb grinned. He glanced back at Quilley and Ducasse. "We've plenty of time before the light fades to find our way to that shelf."

They did and discovered it to be the perfect vantage point

from which to survey the compound. The rock shelf was wide enough for all four of them to sit comfortably, sufficiently back from the edge that the shifting leaves of trees growing up from below screened them from anyone on the ground. They spent another half hour observing the movements of the guards and the captives, thus confirming and acquainting themselves with the uses of the different structures in the compound. Diccon had given them an excellent orientation, but it seemed that most of the adult males were down in the mine and not presently available to be viewed.

There was a large circular fire pit in the space between the entrance to the mine, the barrack-like building that from Diccon's description was the men's sleeping quarters, and the large central barracks that housed the mercenaries. Ringed with logs for seats, the fire pit was situated well away from all three structures. A small fire burned at the pit's center, doubtless more for light and the comfort imparted by the leaping flames than for warmth, and the women were already gathering about it. Miss Katherine sat with five others, but from the relaxed postures of the other women, she had not—yet—shared Diccon's news. Instead, she glanced frequently toward the entrance to the mine.

"She's waiting for the men to join them," Phillipe said. "She's waiting to tell whoever's in charge."

Caleb nodded. "I wish we could stay and identify who that is, but we should get down and back to our camp before night falls."

Night in the jungle was the definition of black; scrambling about on an unfamiliar hillside above an encampment of hostile armed mercenaries in the dark would be the definition of irresponsible.

Phillipe pulled a face, but nodded, and the four of them rose and scrambled back onto the animal track along which they'd climbed up. Once they reached the jungle floor, despite the fading light, they skirted wide through the deepening shadows. Giving the open gates of the compound and the well-armed guards a wide berth, they made their way back to their camp.

Four

The next morning, Caleb, Phillipe, and two of Caleb's men, Ellis and Norton, returned to the rock shelf as soon as it was light. Light enough to see their way, and light enough to observe the activity in the compound.

Caleb settled on the granite shelf. "Let's see if we can establish their routine." From the pocket of his lightweight breeches, he drew out a pencil and a small notebook.

Phillipe, not an early riser, grunted. But he sank down beside Caleb, drew up his knees, rested his chin upon them, and focused his heavy-lidded gaze on the compound far below.

Over the course of the next hours, they watched the camp come awake. The guards changed at six o'clock. Shortly after, the captives straggled out of the barrack-like huts in which they'd slept and tended to their ablutions in the lean-tos built against the sides. Some hung laundry on lines strung at the rear of the long huts. Eventually, each crossed to the awning-covered open-air kitchen on the opposite side of the compound to the mine to fetch their breakfast, then carried their plate and mug back to the large fire pit and settled on the logs to eat.

The mercenaries also breakfasted, in their case under another palm-thatched awning erected in front of the guard tower, close by the kitchen. From their position on the rock shelf above and to the rear of the compound, Caleb and his men could get no clear view of the mercenaries as they broke their fast.

Caleb grunted. "I would have liked to get a look at this Dubois and his lieutenants." They all knew that the mercenaries they'd seen thus far were followers, not leaders.

In contrast, they were fairly certain who among the male captives were the leaders—the officers.

"That's Hopkins—the one just joining the other three." Caleb focused on the four men who sat together at the side of the fire pit closest to the mine. "I met his sister in Southampton. They share that same odd-colored hair."

"I'm fairly certain," Phillipe said, his eyes narrowed on the group, "that the lean, brown-haired one will prove to be Hillsythe. He looks like I imagine one of your Wolverstone's men would look. Which leaves the other two as Fanshawe and Dixon."

"That matches their bearings," Caleb said. "From the way they hold themselves, they must be either army or navy."

They watched, but gained no further clues as to who was whom among the captives. Caleb made a note of their number. "I make it twenty-three men all told, six women, and twenty-four children."

Phillipe stirred. "Most of the children are young—less than ten or so. There are only five who are older—four boys and that fair-haired girl."

"I think," Caleb said, studying the girl, "that they must be the ones Robert and Aileen had to allow to be taken."

Phillipe nodded grimly. "I read that in Robert's journal."

After the meal, the captives dispersed. The men headed for the mine in groups, followed by most of the children. A few of the children, all girls, went to an awning-shaded work area closer to the rear of the compound—closer to the base of the cliff from which the men watched. The girls picked up small hammers and started to take rocks from one pile, tapping each, then sorting them into two piles, one much larger than the other.

After a moment of studying them, Phillipe offered, "I think they're sorting the raw ore into the chunks that might have diamonds and those that most likely don't."

Caleb grunted.

On quitting the fire pit, the women carried the tin plates and bowls back to the kitchen, then they retreated to a hut that sat directly behind the long central barracks that housed the mercenaries. An armed guard patrolled the area before the hut's door, but as with all the guards, including the pair who had climbed to the tower and the fresh pair of guards who had slouched into position on the recently opened gates, he appeared utterly confident and clearly expected no threat.

Sitting on Caleb's other side, Norton humphed. "It's as if the guards think they're just there for show."

Miss Fortescue was the last of the women to enter the hut—the one Diccon had dubbed the cleaning shed. There was something in the way Katherine Fortescue held her head that effectively conveyed her complete disregard for the mercenaries about her. It wasn't as overt as contempt but was a subtle defiance nonetheless.

Regardless of his absorption with jotting down everything useful he could about the camp, Caleb had spent long minutes drinking in every aspect of the delectable Miss Fortescue. For despite the privations of her captivity, she was enchanting, with her brown hair shining and with features that, as far as Caleb could make out, were striking and fine, set in a heart-shaped face. As for her figure, not even the drab, all-but-shapeless gowns that all the women had, apparently, been given to wear could hide her nicely rounded curves.

Regardless of the situation, his interest in Miss Fortescue was a real and vital thing—definitely there and, quite surprising to him, distinctly stronger and more compulsive than such attractions customarily were. Why a woman he'd never even met should so effortlessly capture his attention—fix his senses and hold his focus—he couldn't explain.

"I haven't been able to count all the mercenaries yet," Phillipe said, "but Diccon's number of twenty-four in camp at the moment, plus Dubois, seems about right."

Reluctantly eschewing his thoughts of Katherine Fortescue, Caleb jotted the number in his notebook, then looked down at the compound once more.

Four of the male captives—none of them the officers, all of whom had vanished into the mine—had hung back in a group to one side of the mine entrance. As Caleb watched, two mercenaries ambled out from the central barracks and, each holstering a pistol, walked to join the group.

Nearing the four captives, one of the mercenaries waved the men to a cart parked nearby. Two large water barrels and four large cans for filling them sat on the cart. The four men fell in; they lifted the cart's axle and started the cart rolling across the compound toward the gate.

Caleb watched the men angle the cart through the gate, then turn in the direction of the lake. "Hmm."

The animal track they used to reach the rock shelf, if followed in the opposite direction, ultimately led down to the lake. On the previous day, they'd joined and later left the track halfway up the hillside and hadn't noticed the proximity of the lake, but that morning, a glimmer of light off the water had flashed through the trees and drawn their collective eye. They'd made a brief detour; they hadn't wanted to be there when the men with their guards came to fill the compound's barrels. They'd lingered only long enough to fix the scene in their minds. The lake was fed by a stream rushing down the hillside; it was small, but from its intense color, it was reasonably deep. A short, narrow wharf jutted out along one bank, no doubt built to facilitate drawing water for the camp; on all the other banks, dense vegetation crowded the shoreline.

Caleb, Phillipe, Norton, and Ellis continued to watch the compound, but captives and mercenaries alike seemed to have settled to their morning's duties. The only people coming and going were the children who occasionally emerged from the mine, lugging woven baskets filled with loose rocks that they added to the pile the girls were sorting, then returned to the mine.

Letting his thoughts about the lake slide to the back of his mind, Caleb spent some time drawing a detailed map of the compound, marking in all the buildings and structures and noting the position and direction of the tracks, including the animal track leading to the rock shelf, plus the location of their camp in the jungle clearing and the position of the lake.

After a moment, working from memory, he added a crude sketch of the lake itself. He studied the sketch for several minutes, then glanced at Phillipe. "Those weapons we took from Kale and his men." They'd gathered all the weapons before burying Kale and his crew, and had searched and removed more from the buildings in the slavers' camp, then they'd bundled the weapons up and brought them along in case of future need. "There are far more than we could ever use ourselves. What about creating a cache nearby—somewhere those in the compound could get to when the time to fight arrives?"

Phillipe lightly shrugged. "Why not? Better than just discarding them when we leave—no sense wasting good weapons." Briefly, he studied Caleb's eyes, then faintly smiled. "Where were you thinking of burying this cache?"

Caleb grinned. "The lake. There was a mound just beyond the end of the wharf." He pointed on his sketch; Phillipe, Norton, and Ellis leaned closer to look. "If we buried the cache there, it would be easy for those in the compound to get to. And they only send two lackadaisical guards with four men—that's not bad odds."

Phillipe nodded. "That's also an easy place to describe to those in the compound."

"And as we're only talking of a month," Caleb said, "two at the most, before a rescue force arrives, then even with light wrappings, the powder should still be useable."

Norton pointed down into the compound. "There are the

men bringing back the water barrels." They watched the men haul the now-laden cart through the gates.

"The guards have returned, too," Phillipe noted, "so from what Diccon told us, the lake should be safe for us to visit from now through the rest of the day."

"Perfect." Caleb glanced at Ellis. "Go back to camp and tell Quilley to take three men, wrap up the excess weapons and ammunition, and go to the lake and bury the lot behind the mound at the end of the wharf. Go with him and make sure he chooses the right spot."

"Tell Ducasse to take two of my men and help," Phillipe said. "More hands and it'll be done that much faster."

Caleb endorsed the order with a nod.

Ellis snapped off a salute and scrambled off the ledge, heading for the track down the hillside.

Caleb, Phillipe, and Norton settled to watching the compound again.

After some time, Phillipe said, "I take it we're watching for Diccon to leave."

Caleb nodded. "We came upon him about noon, and he'd already half filled his basket, so I would expect him to leave fairly soon."

"I saw him go into the kitchen," Norton said. "He helped the women take the plates and bowls back, but he didn't come out again."

"Ah, but there he is now." Phillipe sat up and nodded down at the compound.

Caleb watched as the skinny figure of Diccon, readily identified by his bright mop of hair, skipped out from under the palm-thatched overhang shielding the kitchen. He was swinging two baskets, one from either hand. But instead of heading for the gates, Diccon circled the guard tower. Caleb frowned. "Why two baskets, and where is he going?"

They had their answer in another minute. Diccon went to the

cleaning shed. He climbed the steps to the door and knocked. The door opened, and he waited a moment. Then he backed down the steps, and Katherine Fortescue joined him.

Caleb blinked. He watched as Miss Fortescue took one of the baskets, then, side by side, she and Diccon headed for the gates.

The guards saw them coming and didn't react in any way; they watched the pair walk out of the compound and into the jungle.

Caleb stared at Diccon and his Miss Katherine as, heads high, they blithely marched on. Then they disappeared from view. He frowned. "That seems just a tad too good to be true."

Phillipe looked faintly grim. "The boy said nothing about anyone else coming out with him."

It fell to Caleb, as commander of the mission, to weigh every factor that might prove dangerous to their men. That Miss Fortescue might have told Dubois what Diccon had told her...

He didn't want to believe it, but...he grimaced. "Let's watch and see if anyone else follows them."

But no one did. No one seemed to have any interest whatever in the whereabouts of the pair who had, supposedly, gone foraging.

After thirty minutes, Caleb looked at Phillipe.

Phillipe looked back and shrugged. "I would point out that women make excellent traitors, but...who knows?"

Caleb grunted. He stuffed his notebook back into his pocket, then rolled to his feet. "I don't see Miss Fortescue as a likely traitor, but as matters stand, I can think of only one way to find out."

★ ★ ★

By the time Katherine had put seventeen of the large nuts she'd agreed to gather for Dubois and his men into her basket, her nerves were jumping. From the moment she'd grasped the implications of what Diccon had told her regarding who he'd met in the jungle the previous day, she'd been trapped on a peculiar seesaw of emotions—vacillating dramatically between cynically weary disbelief and the burgeoning of unexpected hope. Up, then down, almost to the rhythm of her breathing.

Despite their resolution to find some way to escape, every one of the captured adults had long ago given up all hope of rescue—of someone from outside arriving to save them. As the days, then weeks, then months had rolled past, they'd lost all faith in anyone from the settlement mounting a mission to save them from the fate they all knew would ultimately befall them.

None harbored any illusions about the end Dubois and his masters had in mind for them.

But Diccon had said that the men—the mysterious captain and his crew—had come direct from London, and if Diccon had understood correctly, they were part of a long-running push to rescue all those taken.

She'd discovered that learning of a possible route to freedom after one had believed all such possibility extinguished could be unsettling. Indeed, distinctly unnerving.

She dropped another nut into her basket. Unable to resist the impulse, she cast a searching glance around, but saw and heard no hint of anyone approaching. Diccon had insisted that they had to come to this part of the jungle—between the lake and the track north—and go about collecting fruit and nuts, and then the men would come and find them.

Yesterday, once Diccon had poured out the sum of his discovery, she'd immediately seen the potential danger and had sworn him to secrecy—only to discover that the mysterious Captain Caleb had been before her. She wasn't sure whether to be encouraged or concerned by such foresight; had he acted for the same reason she had, or had he had some ulterior motive?

Regardless, she'd immediately wanted to take Diccon to speak with Dixon and Hillsythe, the de facto leaders of the captives, but as Diccon could not go into the mine and there'd been guards hovering by the entrance, she'd had to wait until after the evening meal before she'd been able to engineer a suitably private meeting.

Dixon and Hillsythe had listened to her condensed version of Diccon's tale, then had called Diccon over. After she'd convinced Diccon that his Captain Caleb—the only name Diccon had been given—wouldn't mind him repeating his story to Dixon and Hillsythe, they'd taken Diccon over his report again. Hillsythe in particular—to this day, Katherine did not understand exactly what his background was—had focused on the captain; with a sense of suppressed but building excitement, Hillsythe had asked Diccon to describe the man. Hillsythe had been well-nigh transformed by Diccon's reply; clearly in the grip of some heightened anticipation, Hillsythe had called Will Hopkins and Fanshawe over and had Diccon repeat his description of the captain to them.

"Frobisher." Will had breathed the name, then glanced at Fanshawe. "A Captain Caleb who looks like that and who has led a crew here on a clandestine operation…that *has* to be Caleb Frobisher."

His eyes alight, Fanshawe had nodded. "And if it is he…*damn.* This is really happening." Enthusiasm of a sort Katherine hadn't heard for months had colored his tone. Fanshawe had met Hillsythe's, then Dixon's eyes. "There really *is* a rescue underway."

Despite the excitement in his eyes, Hillsythe had swiftly said, "We need to keep this to ourselves—at least until we learn more." He'd glanced at Diccon. "You, too, Diccon." Hillsythe had paused, then added, "As matters stand, you're a vital cog in this, m'lad—you're our only way of maintaining contact with those outside."

That had been Katherine's cue. "Actually," she'd said, "I asked Dubois this morning if one of the women, taking turns, couldn't be allowed to go out with Diccon. We bargained—you know how he is. But the upshot is that he agreed as a trial to let me go into the jungle with Diccon in return for me bringing back those nuts he's particularly fond of."

Dixon had grinned. "It seems our luck's finally turned. For once, matters are falling our way."

Hillsythe had nodded. "That's excellent—an unlooked-for advantage." He'd looked at Diccon. "That doesn't make your role any less important. Miss Fortescue can be our mouthpiece, the one more able to tell the captain all he needs to know, but she and we all will be depending on you to guide her to the captain and his men and get her back again, too. No one knows the jungle around about anywhere near as well as you do."

Katherine had smiled at Hillsythe. That had been exactly the right thing to say.

They'd sent a happy Diccon back to join his friends. The four men had looked at each other, then Dixon had said, "Frobisher—assuming it's he—said he and his men were the scouting party." He'd looked at Katherine. "Katherine, my dear, we need you to go out and learn what the situation really is before any hopes are raised."

She'd understood perfectly. To have lost all hope, then have it handed back, only to have it snatched away again...that would be beyond cruel. She'd nodded. "Of course. I'll go out with Diccon tomorrow and meet with...Captain Frobisher and learn all I can."

So here she was, collecting nuts by rote, but... "Where the devil is Frobisher?" she muttered.

She bent over to pick up yet another nut—and a frisson of awareness swept over her nape. She abruptly straightened and looked around, searching through the shadows beneath the trees.

And he was suddenly there, walking out from the shadows, materializing from the gloom. She swung to face him and swiftly took in all she could see—all her senses could glean. The confidence in his easy stride, his lean, clean-cut features, his square chin, and the thick, dark locks that overhung a broad brow. His relaxed expression contrasted with the sword that rode on his hip—so very comfortably, it seemed. He was at least six feet tall and broad-shouldered, all lean muscle and masculine grace, then her gaze rose to his face, and she noted the network of lines at the corners of his eyes that she'd noticed many sailors bore. Then her gaze skated down over his strong nose and fastened on his mouth.

On a pair of mobile lips that looked like they curved readily...

And there her gaze remained as he halted before her.

Stop staring!

With an effort, she managed to haul her gaze to his eyes. The lines at the corners crinkled as he smiled.

She felt her temperature rise and feared it showed in her cheeks. But great heavens! Smiles like that—on men like him—should be outlawed.

"Good morning. Miss Fortescue, I believe?"

His voice was deep, slightly rumbly, and ruffled her senses like an invisible hand.

She managed a nod. "Ah...yes."

So eloquent! She nearly shook her head in an attempt to shake her wits back into place. Instead, she forced herself to look aside, to glance at Diccon; he'd drifted away searching for fruit and berries.

He'd heard Frobisher's voice and came running up.

She caught the boy to her, draping a protective arm over his shoulders. "Diccon told us you had come to learn more about the camp so that a rescue could be mounted." Reminding herself of Frobisher's supposed purpose helped her stiffen her spine. She raised her gaze to his eyes once more. "Is that so?"

He inclined his head, but his expression hardening, he lifted his gaze from her face and scanned the vegetation about them. Then he returned his gaze to her eyes, and all trace of the light-hearted gentleman had vanished. "Forgive me for asking this, Miss Fortescue, but I must. Don't rip up at me." He lowered his voice. "Are you truly free of Dubois? Free to talk, free to take back what I say to your colleagues at the mine?" He paused, then, his blue gaze locked on her eyes, he asked, "Can I trust you?"

"Yes." The word came spontaneously, and she realized she meant it on every level. How odd. She didn't trust others all that easily. Fate and hard-won experience had taught her bitter lessons she'd never forgotten. But there was something about him—this man who had, against all hope, walked out of the jungle to meet her—that spoke to her and reassured her at some level she didn't comprehend. She nodded and repeated, "Yes. You can trust all of us." She gestured in the direction of the camp. "We've worked together for months. If we had any who might have been tempted to collude with Dubois and his men, we would have known long ago."

She glanced at Diccon and realization dawned. "But if it's my coming out with Diccon that has worried you, I had already asked Dubois for permission for the women, one a day in rotation, to go out with Diccon. Dubois agreed to a trial, but with only me being allowed out and that only for an hour, and only to collect these nuts"—she gestured to the contents of her basket—"that he particularly enjoys. He very likely hopes his conditions will drive a wedge between me and the other women by making me appear to be favored." She grinned cynically and glanced up at Frobisher. "That's how he thinks. Unfortunately for Dubois, it was another woman's idea—I just offered to ask."

He frowned. "I need you to tell me about Dubois—about how he manages the camp and all of you."

She hesitated, her gaze on his face. His handsome face, but this time, she looked beyond the glamour. "First…will you tell me your name, please?"

He met her eyes, then he stepped back and swept her a bow. "Captain Caleb Frobisher, of Frobisher Shipping Company, sailing out of Aberdeen." Despite his level tone, as he straightened, he waggled his brows at her.

She nearly laughed in surprise, threw him a mock-disapproving look instead, but the silly byplay reassured her. "Hopkins and Fanshawe thought that was who you were."

"Ah, of course. I don't know them personally, but they would know my older brothers."

She peered into the shadows behind him. "Diccon said you had twenty-four men with you."

Caleb grinned down at Diccon, who had remained beside Katherine and was staring up at Caleb with rapt attention. "That's correct, but most are busy burying some weapons in a cache by the lake, and others are watching the compound or guarding our camp. I only brought one man with me—a friend, another captain, who I'm grateful saw fit to join me in this mission." He returned his gaze to Katherine's face. "With your permission?"

When she nodded, he waved to Phillipe to join them.

Phillipe walked out of the jungle. Caleb performed the introductions—and discovered he wasn't all that happy to have to watch Phillipe bow over Miss Fortescue's hand and press a kiss to her knuckles.

He knew it was just Phillipe's way, yet...

But on retrieving her hand with no more than a polite smile, Miss Fortescue immediately returned her bright hazel eyes to Caleb's face. "Weapons?"

He felt oddly mollified. "Indeed." He looked at Diccon. "Perhaps you'd better gather more fruit so that you can go back with Miss Fortescue. She only has another twenty minutes or so left."

Diccon flashed Caleb a swift grin. "All right. Will you still be here?"

"Yes." Caleb looked around and spotted a fallen log; he pointed to it. "We'll be over there."

"Right-o!" Diccon smiled at Miss Fortescue. "There's a big berry bush I passed yesterday nearer to the lake. I'll be back in no time."

"I'll wait for you." Miss Fortescue watched Diccon run off, then she looked at Caleb. "Sadly, there's no need to protect him.

He told us he thought that you and your men had killed Kale and his slavers. Is that correct?"

Caleb kept his gaze on Diccon's dwindling figure. "We didn't just kill Kale and his crew—we wiped all sign of them from this earth." He looked back and met Miss Fortescue's pretty hazel eyes without apology. "That's where the weapons come from."

Her gaze remained steady on his face. "Once that news is known in the compound, you'll be feted as a hero. For all of us, Kale was the instigator of our captivity."

Caleb hesitated, then said, "He might have been the one who arranged your kidnappings, but the instigators…sadly, they're closer to home." He saw the questions leap to her eyes, but forced himself to wave them aside—to wave her to the fallen log. "You don't have much time, and there's a lot of information we need, as well as news we should impart."

She nodded and accompanied him to the log. He reached for her hand—felt the delicate bones under his larger, stronger fingers; he gripped gently and handed her to the log. She drew in her skirts and sat, with an unconscious grace that would have done credit to a ton drawing room.

Rather than sit beside her—he wasn't at all sure that would be a good idea, Phillipe's presence notwithstanding—Caleb sat on the ground facing her, and Phillipe fluidly sat alongside him.

The instant they'd settled, she asked, "What do you need to know?"

Caleb thought of all they'd seen and noticed about the captives. "How does Dubois run the camp?"

She held his gaze. "By intimidation."

Phillipe frowned. "How so? We haven't seen any sign of aggression from him toward any of those he holds."

"He doesn't need to convince us of anything." Miss Fortescue's slim fingers twined, then gripped. "Let me tell you the tale those who were the first to be brought to the compound told me."

In an even tone, with no real inflection, she proceeded to tell them of an act of violence, of viciousness, that made them both pale under their tans and tied their stomachs in knots. Caleb literally felt nauseated.

She concluded, "That girl was the only captive lost to us." She paused, then went on, "Dixon, Harriet Frazier, Hopkins, and Fanshawe, as well as several of the men and quite a few of the children, were here at the time. Subsequently, if there's the slightest sign of resistance, Dubois will pick some scapegoat and make threats—quietly, calmly, and utterly cold-bloodedly. And every one of us knows he'll carry out those threats to the letter if we give him the excuse. Beneath his outwardly controlled demeanor lurks a monster."

Her expression bleak, she met Caleb's gaze. "That's how he controls us. He never threatens the one he wants to cow, but whoever he believes that person is closest to—that person's emotional Achilles' heel."

"Like he threatens Diccon with his friends' lives?" Caleb asked.

She nodded. "Exactly. So we do what we must to survive—to keep all of us alive. We do what he asks, exactly what he asks… but no more than that." She straightened her spine and lifted her chin. "But that doesn't mean we're not actively fighting him— we just fight in a different way."

Caleb had to admire her quiet dignity. "How so?"

"We've been trying to work out a way to escape, all of us together, but how to deal with the mercenaries is a problem we've yet to solve. In the meantime…we let Dubois believe he manages the mine, but in reality, in that respect, we manage him. He's truly complacent over his hold on us—and in the way he thinks of it, that's understandable enough. He's clever and intelligent, and used to succeeding, but like many people who are very sure of themselves, he doesn't appreciate what he doesn't know."

She looked from Caleb to Phillipe, then returned her gaze to Caleb's face. "In this case, what Dubois doesn't know is how a mine really operates. His understanding of that is very limited. Once Hillsythe arrived…he saw it and explained how we could use Dubois's lack of real knowledge against him and so manage how fast the diamonds are mined." She paused and drew in a breath. "We all know that once the diamonds run out, the mine will be closed, and we'll all be killed. Even the children understand that—they might be young, but they're from the slums, and when it comes to survival, they're very quick. So we manage the output from the mine with a view to eking it out for long enough for us to find some way to escape."

Caleb nodded decisively. "That's going to fit nicely with our mission. We're here to learn the location of the camp and ensure that gets back to London. Whatever else we can learn of the mine, of Dubois and his men and the overall operation, will assist mightily in formulating a viable rescue mission, which, as I understand it and now fully expect, will be the next stage."

She frowned. "This rescue force will come from London?" When Caleb nodded, she asked, "Why? Why hasn't anyone from the settlement come to find us? Why can't the soldiers from the fort or the men from the navy ships come to free us?"

Caleb grimaced. "That's what I alluded to earlier—the villains closer to home. We know there are several—more than one, most likely more than two—people in positions of authority in the settlement who are actively involved in this." He met her gaze. "Lady Holbrook was one. She's now fled the colony, but we know there are others still in place. The naval attaché, Muldoon, plays an active part, but who his coconspirators are is at present unknown, so we can't afford to raise a force from the settlement. By the time such a force reaches here…to be blunt, it's likely all the captives in the compound will have been executed, any evidence in the compound destroyed, and Dubois and his men will be long gone."

She'd paled slightly, but her expression hardened, and she nodded. "I understand. That makes sense of the silence until now."

Caleb hurried to add, "That's not to say that those kidnapped have been forgotten by their friends in the settlement. Rather, because of the activity of the villains and their associates, said friends have been unable to get anything done. For instance, the Sherbrooks haven't forgotten you, but their pleas to Governor Holbrook were turned aside, Holbrook having been duped by his wife." Concisely—and speaking ever more rapidly—he gave her a severely edited account of his brother Declan's mission, followed by that of his brother Robert, the sum of what they'd discovered, and the conclusions that had been drawn. "So, you see, it's imperative that we get news of the mine's location plus as much information about Dubois's operation as we can back to London, so that an effective rescue can be launched with all speed from there."

She nodded. "I cannot tell you how...*heartening* it is to know that there are people who care and who are working to free us. That someone—some group—understands the situation and is truly committed to getting us out of this jungle alive." She hesitated, then more quietly said, "We'd almost lost hope, but this news will give everyone heart again."

"That's all to the good," Caleb said, "but please make sure everyone understands that even with us sending word as fast as any ship can go, it's going to be weeks yet before any rescue force can reach here."

"How long, exactly?"

He frowned. "I suspect it'll be at least a month."

Phillipe snorted. "Even with your family's ships, it'll be more like six weeks."

Caleb caught Katherine's gaze. "Do you think you and the others will be able to stretch the mining out that long?"

She sat straighter. "Obviously, we'll have to. I'm sure with rescue pending, we'll manage somehow."

Phillipe looked at Caleb. "You should check the list of the missing."

"Ah—yes." Caleb drew his notebook from his pocket and flipped it open. "These are the people known to have gone missing from Freetown. Obviously, we haven't got all the names, but by the same token, we don't know if all these people were kidnapped for the mine." He read down the list.

Katherine confirmed each and every name. When he came to the end, she reiterated, "All of those people are at the mine and still alive. As I said, the only one lost was that young girl. She was called Daisy. None of the others who were kidnapped know her full name. Of course, we've had accidents and injuries, but Dubois is motivated to keep us alive and functioning so we can continue to produce diamonds as swiftly as possible, and his current difficulty in getting more men—let alone replacements—ensures he continues to treat us well." She lifted a shoulder. "Essentially, he can't afford not to."

Phillipe shot Caleb a glance. "That's what's behind the medical hut."

When Katherine nodded, Caleb said, "Diccon will be back any minute. Is there anything more—any insights you can share—that will help us better understand what's happening in the camp?"

She hesitated for only a heartbeat, then said, "There's a stalemate of sorts operating at the moment, holding everything in check. Dubois is under increasing pressure to produce more diamonds more quickly—as we interpret it, to mine out the deposit as fast as possible, so that those behind the scheme can order us all killed and protect themselves from any risk of exposure."

Caleb grimaced. "That's almost certainly correct."

"Against that, however—and you need to understand that Dubois never cares if we overhear his discussions with his men—we know he, Dubois, has been stymied in pushing ahead by a lack of more men. He's been calling for more for weeks, but Kale hasn't been supplying as many as Dubois needs." Her lips curved with satisfaction. "And now, of course, Kale won't be supplying any more at all."

Phillipe pulled a face. "We'll have to see how that plays out. Dubois doesn't strike me as the sort to let Kale's disappearance stop him for long."

"No," she admitted with a dip of her head. "But it will slow things down even further, which is all to our good. Dubois doesn't dare push us—the workers he already has—too hard for fear of accidents and injuries, which will only result in lower production. So he's caught—he has to simply wait for more men. That helps us keep production from the mine at what we hope will be a safely low level."

Diccon appeared, sliding through the palms.

They all rose. Caleb felt a flaring impulse to reach for Katherine Fortescue's hand; he thrust both his hands into his breeches pockets instead. "Last question—I assume all those held captive have elected a leader. Who is it?"

"We actually have two—Dixon and Hillsythe. Dixon manages the mine, and Hillsythe plots our way. The others—their lieutenants, I suppose—are Lieutenants Hopkins and Fanshawe, and I speak for the women and children."

Caleb spared a smile for Diccon, but immediately returned his gaze to Katherine Fortescue's face. "If there's any way to do it, I would like reports from Dixon and Hillsythe. They'll know what's needed, and such reports would be invaluable."

She nodded. "I'll ask." She paused, then added, "Given the reports will have to be done in secret, they will almost certainly take more than a day to prepare." She met Caleb's gaze. "I'll come out again the day after tomorrow. If Dixon and Hillsythe have the reports ready, I'll bring them then."

"Thank you." Caleb bent and picked up her basket. He handed it to her. "One thing—please stress to everyone concerned that at no point should they do anything to arouse suspicion."

She nodded and turned to Diccon. She took his hand, then

glanced at Caleb. "Thank you." Her gaze moved briefly to include Phillipe, then returned to Caleb's face. "I'll see you in
two days."

She turned away, and she and Diccon started toward the compound.

Caleb and Phillipe watched them go, then once the pair were
far enough ahead, started trailing behind.

They halted deep in the jungle shadows, well concealed from
the guards on the gate, and watched Katherine Fortescue and
Diccon walk stoically back into captivity.

After a moment, Phillipe stirred. "She told us quite a lot. Dubois sounds…dangerous."

"Hmm. And this bind he's in—more production on the one
hand, no ability to achieve it on the other. That must be frustrating, yet he doesn't seem to have lashed out."

"Which only proves my point," Phillipe said. "Dangerous.
Any man can play the bully. A sadistic bully who can control
himself…that's something else again."

Caleb grunted and turned away. "Let's get back to the camp.
I'd better start writing my own report, because heaven knows,
these people need rescuing."

★ ★ ★

After seeing Diccon on his way to the kitchen with his basket full of berries, Katherine reined in her giddy, rather scattered thoughts, mentally girded her loins, hefted her basket, and
climbed the steps to the mercenaries' barracks.

She walked along the narrow porch to the single door, which
lay toward the left of the front of the long building and was presently propped open. Dubois's "office" lay beyond the door in
the space at the end of the single room, separated from the bunk
beds by a communal area with stools and low tables where the
off-duty mercenaries lounged and played cards. Out of ingrained
courtesy, she tapped on the door frame, waited for a heartbeat,
then calmly walked in. She spared not a glance for the other

mercenaries sprawled at their ease but fixed her gaze on Dubois's desk and the man himself, leaning back in his chair behind it.

There was a wide window set in the side wall of the barracks. Through it, Dubois could see the entrance to the mine. He appeared to be staring moodily at that sight, but as she approached, he turned to study her.

By anyone's measure, he cut a commanding figure, with a powerful physique, thick dark hair, and even features. He had oddly pale hazel eyes; she often thought that cold steel had somehow got mixed into the hue. Hazel eyes weren't usually chilling, but Dubois's gaze certainly was.

"Miss Fortescue." Dubois didn't smile, yet she detected amusement in his tone. Much like a cat viewing a potential mouse. His gaze fell to the basket. "I take it your foraging was successful?"

"Indeed." She placed the basket on the desk. "Here are your nuts. I quite enjoyed my time beyond the palisade, but I confess I hadn't expected the atmosphere beneath the trees to be quite so oppressive." She frowned as if somewhat chagrined. "I suspect I had better not indulge again tomorrow—not so soon." She forced herself to meet his gaze. "Perhaps one of the other women might take my place and fetch nuts for you tomorrow?"

Dubois's lips eased. He reached out and pulled the basket toward him. "I don't think that will be necessary. I believe I will be quite content with nuts delivered every second day." He looked steadily at her. "By you." He paused for a beat, then stated, "Thank you, Miss Fortescue. That will be all."

Katherine suppressed a derisive snort. She contented herself with a tiny, haughty inclination of her head, then she turned and left the room.

The man made her skin crawl. His habit of trying to bait her—and the others who were well born, too—by subtly lording it over them added another layer of grating irritation.

But they had all long ago resolved not to react—not to play

the mouse to Dubois's cat. As he enjoyed the hunt so much, he tended to let them go—the better to taunt them the next time.

Descending once more to the dust of the compound, she drew in a deep breath—and finally allowed everything she'd learned in the jungle that morning to surge to the forefront of her brain.

Rescue was on the way. They hadn't been forgotten.

She felt hope, real hope, bubbling up inside—a startling, entirely unexpected upwelling of an emotion she'd thought excised from her soul.

She remained where she was, staring unseeing out of the gates while she considered who she should speak with first, what was most important to be communicated, and how best to achieve that.

Over and above all other considerations, she resolved that, whatever steps she and subsequently the other captives took, they would need to ensure they did absolutely nothing to jeopardize the safety of Captain Caleb Frobisher and his men—for all their sakes.

Five

Katherine spoke with Hillsythe that evening during dinner. By the looks Dixon cast them from where he sat across the fire pit, he was itching to join them, but Harriet had claimed the place by his side, and as Hillsythe had informed Katherine, he and Dixon had agreed that it was better for the three of them not to be too openly sharing news; the other captives would notice and expect to be told.

She certainly wasn't about to chide the pair for their caution. They needed to handle the information she'd brought back with care.

That said, once Hillsythe had heard all she had to report, he appeared to be having as much difficulty as she in cloaking his excitement.

"I'd been hoping for something like this. Now you've confirmed that it is, indeed, Frobisher who's found us...*well!*" Hillsythe looked at his plate to hide his enthusiasm.

Katherine searched for the words with which to ask what her curiosity wanted to know. "I have to admit that I don't quite understand why you, and the others, too, place such confidence in a name." When Hillsythe looked up, she widened her eyes at him. "Does 'Frobisher' really convey so much?"

Hillsythe grinned, a fleeting expression that took years from his apparent age; of them all, the group's captivity—the responsibility of assisting them all to weather it—had weighed most heavily on him. "The Frobishers are well known in certain circles. Frobisher Shipping is a private company, but the family has a long—generations-long, as I understand it—association with the Crown and its more covert agencies. That's why Fanshawe and Hopkins, being navy, recognized the name and the man, but Dixon, being army, didn't—I explained the connection to him later."

"You recognized the name, too."

Hillsythe dipped his head. "Although I haven't crossed their paths before, I've heard of the exploits of others of his family."

Katherine primmed her lips. Hillsythe had never let fall— not to anyone—just what arm of government he worked for, although all the captives were sure his superiors would be found somewhere in Whitehall.

Hillsythe continued, "The crucial point about it being a Frobisher who has arrived is that the family being involved means that news of our plight has reached the highest echelons of government. He's confirmed he's been sent to scout out the camp and send the intelligence back to London so that an effective rescue mission can be launched—and given the level of power the Frobishers serve, that means an effective rescue *will* be launched." Hillsythe sighed. "We can finally have faith that rescue is on the way."

Katherine heard the confidence in his tone. She wanted to embrace the news as he had, yet as the hours since she'd been in Caleb Frobisher's company had passed and the reassurance conveyed by the warmth in his blue eyes and the comforting strength of his presence had faded, she'd started to question whether believing so wholeheartedly in the abilities of him and those who had sent him to successfully rescue them all wasn't just a touch naive.

As if sensing her doubts, Hillsythe went on, "That Caleb is the third of his brothers to collaborate in locating us is, of itself, heartening. That means those arranging this rescue mission understand the dangers—that there are, as we suspected and Caleb has now confirmed, villains in the settlement in positions of authority such that they would learn of any 'official' rescue and shut down the mine and dispose of us before any relief could reach us. Our would-be rescuers have acted with all due care, and as the Frobisher name attests, those would-be rescuers are people with the capabilities and resources to carry off such a mission successfully."

Hillsythe fixed his gaze on the flames of the small fire cheerily burning in the fire pit. "Trust me—we now have every reason to believe we will be rescued. Consequently, what we need to concentrate on now is, first, giving Frobisher and his masters every assistance we can and, second, surviving until the rescue force arrives and frees us." Hillsythe raised his gaze to look at Dixon on the other side of the circle. "I'll tell Dixon, Fanshawe, and Hopkins. We should tell Harriet, too—can you do that?"

"Yes, of course." Katherine hesitated, then asked, "What about the others?"

Hillsythe weighed the question, then murmured, "Let's keep it to just the six of us—and Diccon—for now. At least until we know that the necessary intelligence is on its way to London and cannot be stopped, and we get as firm an idea as possible of how long it'll be before rescue arrives—will it truly be six weeks, or might it take longer? Frobisher is the only one who can give us a sound estimate, and we'll need to work on strategies to ensure that we keep the mine producing steadily for at least that long."

"I jockeyed Dubois into decreeing that I should go out only every second day—I thought if I went out every day, as he originally trapped me into doing, then after a week passes and he sees no trouble brewing between me and the other women, he might change his mind and stop me going out altogether. Then we would have to rely on Diccon to make contact with Frobisher, and that might not be wise if we have critical information to pass back and forth."

Hillsythe nodded approvingly. "Good thinking. And if we need to make contact on your off days, we still have Diccon as a fallback courier." He thought, then added, "Those reports Frobisher asked for—Dixon and I will have them ready so you can deliver them on your next outing. In the meantime, we can all put our minds to thinking of what we need you to ask Frobisher. Once we get him those reports, we need him to take them back to London as soon as humanly possible." Hillsythe's gaze swept all those—adults as well as children—sitting on the logs about the fire pit. "We simply can't know what might happen with the mine, so the sooner rescue arrives the better."

Katherine merely nodded; there was nothing she could think of to add to that. Rescue—even once on its way—still had to reach them before the diamonds ran low.

"I wonder..." Hillsythe's gaze grew distant, almost dreamy. "Caleb said two of his older brothers, Declan and Robert, had captained the earlier legs of this mission. In light of that, I wonder if the oldest Frobisher brother—Royd—will be tapped on the shoulder to lead the rescue party."

Katherine studied Hillsythe's expression. "Will that be a good thing?"

Hillsythe's rare smile lifted his lips. "Very likely an excellent thing. I've never met Royd Frobisher, but in my circles, tales of his exploits abound. Him taking on the likes of Dubois...that would be something to see."

It had grown late. The children had been sent off to the barracks they shared with the women, while the women gathered any plates and mugs left about the logs. Katherine stood and shook out her skirts. She felt...different. More alive, more determined to remain so—buoyed on a slowly building wave of hope.

Hillsythe rose, too. He paused to murmur, "Remember—no word to anyone but Harriet." He glanced at the others now drifting away, and his hard-edged expression softened. "This is news for rejoicing, and I'd like to tell everyone immediately, but we shouldn't risk it. I suppose making such judgment calls is what leadership is all about." He met Katherine's eyes. "Once we've got confirmation that the necessary information has departed these shores, that will be the time to spread the good news."

She let her lips curve reassuringly and nodded. With a murmured good night, she went to find Harriet.

★ ★ ★

At that same moment, Caleb was sitting with Phillipe and all their men on logs arranged about the center of their camp. A small lantern, turned very low, sat on a flat rock where a fire would have been had they been able to risk lighting one. With the compound so near, even shrouded in black night, chancing a fire was too great a risk; even a faint breeze could carry the smell of smoke to the guards, and then they would come looking.

"So." Phillipe tossed the husk of a nut to join the small pile building up around the lamp. "We will spend tomorrow observing the mine, and I will write up a report on the best way for a rescue force to approach the area, while you write one on the compound itself, those inside, and possible considerations for mounting an attack-cum-rescue. Then on the day after tomorrow, the lovely Miss Fortescue will deliver the reports from inside the camp. And *then*"—Phillipe glanced sidelong at Caleb—"we'll retreat to our ships, and you and *The Prince* will ferry all that information back to London."

Caleb kept his gaze fixed on the lamp, but felt his face harden as he strove to mask his distaste for that path. Yet that was the mission he'd seized and taken on.

Responsible captains abided by the rules—by the unwritten demands of their mission's imperatives.

Responsible captains didn't rewrite missions to suit themselves. Yet...

Unable not to, he lifted his gaze and scanned the faces of his and Phillipe's men. The light was dim, yet he could still plainly see their disaffection—their uncomfortableness over simply doing what they'd been sent to do and no more.

The *more* that they could do.

Caleb didn't need to glance at Phillipe to know what his friend thought. In such circumstances, he could guarantee that Phillipe would think as he did. Feel as he did.

Act as he did.

In this case, Phillipe and his men as well as Caleb's crew would all abide by whatever Caleb decided.

It was his call. His responsibility.

He closed his eyes, searching for inner guidance—and remembered some of the tales he'd heard of Royd's exploits.

Faced with this situation, if Royd were in his shoes, what would Royd do?

Phrased like that, the answer came in the next heartbeat.

Caleb felt his features ease. He opened his eyes, swept the group, then looked at Phillipe. "Our mission is to get the information back to London. But it won't take all of us to accomplish that task."

Phillipe merely arched his brows, inviting Caleb to continue down that path.

Looking at his men, Caleb said, "Once we've collected all the information London will need, if we're where we think we are, even going directly north to the estuary, it'll take at least two days to get the information back to *The Prince*. After that, it'll be three weeks to get to London. Then realistically, it will take another three weeks minimum for any rescue force to reach here—and that's assuming they're ready to set sail within days of our news reaching Whitehall." He scanned the faces. "That's more than six weeks, very likely more than seven, that those held captive in the compound must survive."

Various scenarios, various arguments, flowed through his mind. "As I see it, there's nothing—no orders or mission considerations—that require all of us to leave and escort the information to London." He glanced at Phillipe. "*The Prince* is fastest, so she should take the packet, but there's no reason *The Raven* has to follow."

"No, indeed." Phillipe's dark eyes glinted with amused approval—and encouragement.

"Against that," Caleb continued, "we cannot know what might happen at the mine over those crucial seven weeks. Miss Fortescue told us that Dubois is already under pressure to mine faster, to get as many diamonds out as quickly as possible, presumably so the mine can be closed and the captives eliminated, thus concealing all evidence of the scheme as well as the identities of the villains behind it.

"So"—he drew a deep breath—"given the ultimate intent of our mission is to rescue the captives, in the circumstances in which we now find ourselves, I believe our correct way forward is to send the information back to London with an escort capable of ensuring it gets through, while the rest of us remain here—in readiness should something go wrong at the mine such that the captives need us to intervene. And if nothing adverse occurs, we'll be here, in position to join the rescue force when it arrives."

Approving murmurs broke out all around.

Caleb cocked a brow at Phillipe.

Phillipe grinned and nodded. "An excellent summation of the current state of affairs. And as we all know, those who survive are those who adapt to changing circumstances—to what they find on the ground."

Ducasse, Phillipe's quartermaster, who had been talking animatedly with Carter, Caleb's bosun, turned to Caleb. "The boy said there were only twenty-four *canaille* in the compound. There are twenty-five of us. Why can't we take the compound and free the captives ourselves?"

Carter leaned forward to ask, "Do we really need to wait for the rescue force?"

Caleb sobered in a blink. "Yes. We have to wait. If it was just us against the *canaille*"—he used Ducasse's highly appropriate description—"and the captives were safely screened from any clash, that would be one thing. But from everything we've heard about this Dubois, at the first hint of an attack, he'll lead his men to seize the women and children. He'll hold them as hostages and force us to surrender." Caleb shook his head. "We can't go that route."

"I agree." Phillipe met Ducasse's eyes, then looked around the circle. "By all accounts, this Dubois is not a commander we should even poke."

Caleb nodded. "For instance, even though it's tempting, we will not attack this group of six who took the diamonds to the coast and have yet to return. Removing them will alert Dubois that someone is out here—that, most likely, someone knows about the mine. He will then tell his masters, and they might decide to preemptively shut down the mine—which is the opposite of what we want."

Ducasse frowned. "But won't it be the same later, even when the rescue force arrives?"

"Once we have more men and resources, we'll have more options, but you're correct in that to take the compound, we're going to need an effective diversion—one that distracts Dubois and his men long enough for us to get between them and the captives." Caleb pulled a face. "I've no idea what such a diversion might be, but that's something we should use our time here to plan."

"What we need to do at this point," Phillipe stated, "is to keep things as they are, as far as possible exactly as they are, until the rescue force gets here. All we do should work toward that goal."

"So we wait and we watch"—Caleb gave his words the weight of an order—"and we only intervene if something occurs that threatens the captives." He looked around the circle and saw understanding and agreement in all the men's faces. "We'll set our initial mission on course for completion, but as many of us as possible will remain here, both to continue to scout and prepare for the eventual storming of the compound

and also to act as the captives' last line of defense—as extra protection until the rescue force arrives."

★ ★ ★

The following morning, as they had the morning before, Caleb
and Phillipe and two of their men scrambled into position on
the rock shelf before the compound woke for the day.

Caleb observed the same pattern of activities; he jotted down
the more relevant—such as the movements of the guards and
male captives—then turned his attention to putting the finish-
ing touches to his diagram of the compound.

More than an hour later, Phillipe jogged his elbow.

When Caleb glanced his way, Phillipe nodded toward the
compound's gate. "The boy's leaving, but no one's with him."

They watched for ten more minutes, but no one—mercenary
or captive—made any move to follow Diccon.

Phillipe caught Caleb's eye. "Shall we?"

Caleb nodded, tucked away his notebook, and got to his feet.
"He might have news for us."

They found Diccon in the area between their camp and the
lake. He was circling a large berry vine-cum-bush, swiftly picking berries. His face lit when he saw them. "I hoped you'd come.
I didn't want to go to your camp in case you had guards."

Caleb smiled and ruffled the boy's hair. "They know who
you are." He crouched and looked Diccon in the eye. "Do you
have any messages for us?"

Diccon nodded. "From Capt'n Dixon and Miss Katherine.
Capt'n Dixon said as he and Mr. Hillsythe would need until
tomorrow to do their reports for you—they have to be careful
about getting the paper to write on, but he said they'd have everything ready for you by then."

Caleb nodded. "Good. And Miss Fortescue?"

"She said as she would bring the reports out to you tomorrow—that she'd come out with me like she did yesterday. Du-

bois agreed to let her collect nuts again tomorrow, but wouldn't let any of the other women take her place today. He's like that."

Caleb dropped a hand on Diccon's shoulder and rose. He exchanged a glance with Phillipe, then smiled down at Diccon. "It's nearly noon, and there are plenty of fruit trees around our camp. Why don't you come back with us and have something to eat?" The boy was little more than skin and bones, and they had a good supply of jerky.

Diccon grinned and nodded. He fell in between Caleb and Phillipe, and they made their way back to the camp.

Both Caleb and Phillipe settled down to finalize the reports they'd been writing, pulling together all they'd learned. Diccon flitted in and out of the camp, stopping to chat with the men who were scattered in groups, some tending weapons, others preparing various fruits to go with the dried meats they would all later eat.

After a while, Phillipe glanced up from his scribbling. He watched Diccon skip off to another fruit tree, then murmured, "Once Dubois's men come back from the coast, from wherever they handed over the diamonds, we should try that path for ourselves. If it eventually leads to the settlement as the others suspect, we can fetch more supplies."

Caleb grunted an agreement. "If we're going to remain here for the next seven or so weeks, we'll need more food, especially as we can't light a fire and can't hunt, either."

Hornby, Caleb's steward, was in charge of meals. He summoned them all to the bounty he and several others had prepared—fruit, nuts, and dried mutton.

Caleb mumbled around a mouthful of the chewy meat, "At least it doesn't have weevils."

Phillipe just pulled a face, but Diccon smiled sunnily and reached for another strip.

Two hours later, Diccon declared he had enough fruit in his

basket, and after exchanging farewells with all the men, he wandered off to return to the compound.

Eventually, Caleb and Phillipe swapped their reports and read over each other's efforts.

Caleb reached the end of Phillipe's precise description of the various possible approaches a rescue force might take to reach the compound, along with the pitfalls and advantages of each route. "This is as good as it could be. I can't see anything you've missed." He placed the report on the satchel he was using to collect all the documents destined for London. "It'll all depend on what sort of force they deploy—and if they work with Decker or not."

Phillipe nodded and handed back Caleb's report on the compound. "That's thorough, but there are two connected points I can see another commander wanting to know—the structure of that palisade and the strength or otherwise of the gates."

Caleb grimaced. "I thought of that, but I can't remember well enough to comment. Can you?"

Phillipe shook his head. "But we have time." He started to get to his feet. "And I've had enough of sitting. Let's go and see what we can make of things now, and when the light fades, perhaps we can risk slipping closer to confirm how the planks are held together."

They took two of Caleb's men with them. They returned to the same spot Diccon had first led them to, not far from the gates. From the cover of the palms, they studied the way the planks were lashed together and squinted at the hinges. Caleb mouthed, "We need to get closer."

Phillipe nodded, then pointed to the guards slouching at either side of the gates and signaled that they should wait until the light faded before venturing closer.

Eventually, as the day dimmed and a short twilight took hold, the guards on the gate straightened, slung their muskets over their shoulders, and tugged and lifted and finally swung the gates closed.

Caleb waited for a minute, then, in a crouch, slid from behind the concealing palms and swiftly crossed the cleared space to fetch up in the shadow of the wall. He was still five yards or so from the gate. He paused to study the construction of the planking palisade, confirming that, as they'd thought, the planks were lashed together with ropes made of jungle vines. No nails or other metal fixings, except for the occasional piece of wire used to bind two planks. That said, the rope lashings were thick, plentiful, strong, and tight. Using a machete to hack through the bindings enough to break in would take time—and would create some degree of noise. Quietly slicing the bindings with any smaller, more covert tool would take forever.

Phillipe slipped into the deeper gloom by Caleb's shoulder. He looked at where Caleb pointed at the lashings; he grimaced expressively, then with a tip of his head, he directed Caleb to the gate.

They crept along, careful to create not even a whisper of sound. They reached the nearer gatepost and hunkered down beside it. Both of them examined the junction between the gate and the post supporting it. A long piece of solid giant bamboo, five or so inches in diameter, had been used as the hinge, lashed into position with so much vine the hinge appeared fully wrapped in rope.

While it might appear more fragile than a metal hinge, breaking through the gates if they were locked into place—for instance with cross beams—would take explosives.

Even as they stared at the hinge, feet shuffled on the other side of the gates, then a chorus of grunts was followed by a huge thump. The gates rattled, then settled.

"That's done, then," one of the guards said. Hands slapped solid wood.

Phillipe glanced up at the gates, then looked at Caleb and mouthed, "Two beams."

Caleb nodded. Breaking into the compound at night was not going to be easy—not unless he and his men prepared the way. Luckily, they had time.

They'd discovered what they'd come to learn; ready to return to the jungle, he swiveled.

"Wish Dubois wasn't such a fiend for having it all his own way."

Caleb shared a glance with Phillipe, then both of them eased back against the wall. Caleb put his ear to one side of the hinge, while Phillipe rested his head against the palings of the gate.

On the other side of the gatepost, two guards were, apparently, still on duty. Now the gate was closed, they'd elected to slouch together and chat as they idly watched the compound.

"*Huh.* I've worked with the devil long enough to know there's no getting around that. It's his way or you're out." The second guard sounded older, more experienced.

"I can't see his point. Why's he so finicky? It's not as if the women, nor even the girls, are working at night. No reason they couldn't entertain us then."

"Don't even think it. The last man who did...no doubt the leopards have picked his bones clean by now."

"But...why? I can't see the sense in it."

"Then watch and learn. Those women and children—they're not just here for the work they do. They're here to make all our lives easier. They're here to keep the men in line." After a pause, the older mercenary went on, "If we take and use even one of them, that hold Dubois has—the promise that all the women and children will remain untouched as long as the men behave—that'll be gone. And then they'll all riot, and if it's you who's done it, then if the men in the mine don't slit your throat for you, Dubois will—after he flays you alive. I've only seen him lose his temper once—and I never want to see that again."

The mercenary paused, then went on, "Trust me. Meddling with Dubois and his ways isn't worth it. I've worked with him on more'n ten jobs, and every one's been a piece of cake. Money for the taking. When you've been in this business as long as I have, you appreciate the captains who can deliver jobs like this one. Boring as all hell it might be, but it's as easy as pie and pays damn well."

A sly note crept into the man's voice. "And there's always the fun at the end—when Dubois walks out and lets us do as we please with all the captives he no longer has reason to keep alive."

"He'll do that?"

"Oh, yes. Why do you think so many of us have stayed in his company for so long?"

The younger man cackled. "I didn't know that. Something to look forward to, then."

Their expressions grim, Caleb and Phillipe exchanged looks, then Caleb tipped his head toward the jungle. Silent as wraiths, they left the wall and, shadows among shadows, slid back into the palms and trees.

They collected their men, but didn't speak until they were nearly back at their camp.

"In addition to a structural description of the palisade and the gates"—Caleb spoke over his shoulder to Phillipe, who was following him down the narrow track—"I'm going to add a few lines to my report about the need to keep Dubois alive and in charge right up until the moment we attack."

Phillipe grunted. "Sadly, I'm forced to concur. And we'd better pass the word to all our men that, regardless of any opportunity or temptation that might present itself, we should not kill Dubois."

"Not until later." Caleb's tone signaled that he was already making plans for a confrontation once the need to keep Dubois alive had passed. Once the rescue force had arrived and taken control of the compound.

As he led the way into the clearing and their makeshift camp, he stifled a sigh.

Phillipe sensed his disaffection and shot him a questioning glance.

Caleb grimaced. "I would so much rather be free to simply remove Dubois and go in with swords swinging. What with having to juggle so many lives, all in the same balance, and trying to help and improve things without making anything worse, this mission is"—he blew out a breath—"a hell of a lot more complicated than I'd expected."

★ ★ ★

When Katherine walked into the jungle alongside Diccon the next morning, she was, once again, prey to conflicting emotions. The anxiety she'd felt as she'd set off toward the gates with Diccon skipping by her side—the fear that something would somehow alert Dubois or his mercenaries to the reports she carried folded and stuffed into a hurriedly sewn pocket in her gown—evaporated as the cool shadows of the jungle enveloped her.

Eagerness took hold.

She wanted to find Frobisher and his friends and hand the documents over; the need to have them depart and take the information back to London so that an effective rescue force could be dispatched burned fiercely inside her.

And yet...

Contrarily, she felt she would be losing a chance—letting something she couldn't even name slip through her fingers—when she, however metaphorically, waved Frobisher and his men goodbye.

Stupid, really. She'd met him only two days before. Had spent only half an hour in his company.

But he'd given her hope. He'd made her feel that rescue could and would happen, and that there was a life waiting for her, for them all, once they left the compound.

That belief in a future was precious, even if she didn't know what her future might hold. Just the conviction that she would live to see it—to make mistakes and also triumph as she made her way on through life—was a gift of incalculable worth.

A godsend, really, for all the adults, given that, despite their wishes, despite their talk, they had all, in their hearts, started to lose all such hope.

She let Diccon lead and simply followed. He stopped here and there to gather fruits and berries. When she saw a nut tree of the right type, she paused to collect whatever unbroken husks she could find. She dropped the nuts into her basket, then straightened.

A rustle had her whirling.

Frobisher stepped from the jungle, the other man—Lascelle—beside him.

Just seeing Frobisher made her smile. "I've got the reports." Hauling her bedazzled gaze from his answering smile, she reached for the slit seam at her side, above her waist and below her breasts, and carefully withdrew the folded reports from their hiding place.

She saw Frobisher's eyes widen and hurried to explain, "They've never searched us before, but we didn't want to take the chance."

He grinned. "Ingenious." He took the sheets she held out.

As he looked down and unfolded them, she stepped closer, to his side. "Dixon said he wrote down everything he could think of that might be relevant about the mine itself. Hillsythe—his is the finer hand—said his report was by way of a situational report and that you'd know what that meant."

She watched Frobisher's face as he scanned the documents, then he handed them to Lascelle and met her gaze.

"Thank you—and thank Dixon and Hillsythe. Combined with our own reports, these are exactly what London needs." He hesitated, then said, "We have one question we hadn't thought to ask—when the mercenaries carry the diamonds away, does anyone know where on the shoreline they rendezvous with the ship?"

"They go west," she said. "Hillsythe overheard that they rendezvous with a tender on the eastern tip where the river to our west meets the estuary."

Lascelle had been reading the reports more closely. "It's here—in Hillsythe's report." He glanced at Frobisher. "That must be the river Robert and his lady used to reach the estuary. That should mean our ships are moored sufficiently farther east to be out of sight of the vessel the tender must come from."

"Good." Caleb met Katherine's hazel eyes. "Our ships are tucked away more or less north of here."

She smiled, but there was a fragility behind the expression, caused by what he had no clue—but he wanted to know. The smile faded as she said, "You must be keen to return to your vessels and rush back to London."

Caleb paused—hesitated. Not over any question of trust but because something inside him wanted to keep her cocooned and far from harm...in the circumstances, there was no sense in that. He glanced briefly at Phillipe—who nodded almost imperceptibly—then looked back at her. "We're going to send the reports—the ones you brought as well as ours—along with our maps to London on our swiftest vessel."

"Which is his," Phillipe helpfully stated. He handed the refolded reports to Caleb.

"True." Caleb shot his friend a "you're not helping" look, took the reports, then met Katherine's now-wondering gaze. "But we and as many of our men as we can spare from our ships have decided to remain."

Her eyes widened. "You're staying?"

He nodded. "Our mission was to get the information required to those in London, and once my ship gets under way, that mission will be essentially complete. So we'll be free to do whatever we wish, and we've decided that there's no reason we shouldn't linger here, in the jungle, near enough to help all of you in the compound should anything go wrong between now and whenever the rescue force arrives." He shrugged. "If nothing does go wrong, then we'll be here to add our numbers to the attack on the compound. Whoever comes in as leader will be glad of extra men—especially men who've had time to become acquainted with the terrain."

If her face—her expression—was any guide, she was debating flinging her arms around his neck and kissing him…

He hoped she would, but then she managed to rein in her exultation. Enough to ask, "Are you sure you want to risk it? You don't have to, you know."

"Yes, we know," Phillipe replied. When she glanced his way, he grinned. "But we like to live dangerously."

Truer words were never spoken.

But Katherine Fortescue didn't grin back. She studied Phillipe, then turned her oddly searching gaze on Caleb. The quality of her regard forcibly reminded him that she'd been a governess to small children. After several silent moments, she gravely said, "I won't try to dissuade you, because no words can adequately convey what the knowledge that you've chosen to remain, more or less to keep watch over us, will mean to all in the camp. We assumed you would leave. That was one of the reasons that we, the leaders—Dixon, Hillsythe, Fanshawe, Hopkins, Harriet, and I—decided against mentioning your presence to any of the others. Because of how much hope now means to us. Telling the group that someone came and has taken information back to London so that a rescue can be mounted—just that would have been a powerful positive. But knowing that, in addition, you and your men have elected to remain to assist us? *That's* going to buoy everyone enormously. It's going to make everyone feel that we're no longer struggling on all by ourselves."

Her expression grew a touch grim. "Especially as, increasingly, we're getting the impression that the mining will not just roll along as it has been—not for much longer."

Caleb frowned. "Has there been any change since last we spoke?"

"Yes and no. It's more a case of degree. The diamonds in the first tunnel are nearing an end, but Dubois is pushing harder and harder for increased production via us opening another tunnel to mine a second deposit of diamonds Dixon has found. Thus far, we've held off. But the pressure on Dubois to increase production is coming from outside—from what he calls the 'backers of the enterprise.' Given the way he uses that term, we're not sure that those are the people in the settlement. They could be others, located somewhere else."

Caleb shot a questioning glance at Phillipe.

Phillipe nodded. "Hillsythe covered that. He thinks the people in the settlement are not the backers, but that the backers are some other group entirely."

Caleb arched his brows. "People with money. That would make better sense given the likely cost of hiring Dubois and his crew."

"And for months," Phillipe added.

Caleb looked at Katherine. "About telling the others. Of course, tell the three officers and Hillsythe, and the women you can trust to keep the information to themselves, that we will remain here, in our camp—ready to be summoned should anything go wrong and our assistance be needed."

She considered him, then said, "Our group—all the captives in the compound—have grown very close. We're one big family now—we've had to become that to survive. And trust is an important aspect of such a bonding. So I will agree to tell those you mentioned, and then together we'll decide whether or not to spread the news throughout the company. As I explained, hope is what you and your men represent, possibly in ways no one who has never endured the sort of captivity we have would understand. Withholding that hope from the others…" Slowly, she shook her head. "That's not something I can agree to do. If Hillsythe, Dixon, and the others think we need to continue to restrict the information, I will keep my counsel, but"—her expression softened—"I really do not expect they will. We've learned that including everyone works—as I mentioned yesterday, we've had no defectors. No one siding with or assisting our captors, not in any way."

She didn't ask it of them, but after studying the calm certainty in her hazel eyes—a calm steadiness she allowed him to see—Caleb inclined his head. "Very well. We'll leave it up to you and the others to decide. We are, as you pointed out, all in this together."

Phillipe had shifted to look at Diccon. "What about the children?" He arched a brow at Katherine. "Some of them, surely, are too young to understand."

Her lips twisted. "You'd be surprised by what they understand."

Although he'd been picking berries throughout, Diccon turned and looked Phillipe in the eye. "I won't tell. And neither will the others. Not even the youngest ones. We all know the guards at the camp are bad—rotten to the core, more like. We don't tell them nuthin'." He paused, then added, "Truth be told, they always assume we know nuthin', so they never do ask, anyways."

"Actually," Phillipe said, "I'm revising my position." He looked at Caleb. "We need to let everyone, including all the children, know that we're out here—and they need to be told where our camp is."

Caleb mentally shifted his perspective, saw, and grimaced. "You mean in case something happens, because we can't say who will be able to get free and summon us."

"Or run to us for protection," Phillipe said.

"Exactly." Katherine nodded. "If something happens, and

some get free and flee into the jungle, there's no reason they'll run your way, not unless they know you're here."

Caleb heaved a sigh. "All right. I'm convinced." He met Katherine's gaze. "Tell everyone—all the captives."

She smiled. "You won't regret that. Every one of us knows that, as matters stand, our lives are limited by how long the mine stays in operation. You and your men being here holds out the hope that, if something goes wrong and the worst befalls us, some of us might yet make it out alive, and not one of us will do anything—anything at all—to jeopardize that chance."

He had to accept that.

He helped her fill her basket with the large hairy nuts Dubois had sent her to collect. Phillipe chatted with Diccon and picked the ripe fruit the boy couldn't reach.

Then Caleb and Phillipe walked with the pair back toward the compound. At Katherine and Diccon's insistence, Caleb and Phillipe halted on the disused path well out of sight of the gates, but they watched the pair walk on hand in hand until they passed out of sight.

★ ★ ★

Katherine carried the full basket of nuts into Dubois's office. Her mind was full of Caleb Frobisher, Lascelle, and their men, and their decision to remain in the jungle, under conditions that were far from salubrious, to act as hidden protectors for a group of captives none of whom they personally knew.

Some men had honor. Some men had courage.

Some men stepped up and instinctively defended women, children, and those weaker than themselves—those under threat.

Dubois was standing beyond the end of his desk, deep in discussion with his second lieutenant, Cripps. She managed not to sniff disparagingly. She had no wish to stop and converse so took advantage of Dubois's distraction to set the basket on his desk, direct a vague nod his way, and leave.

As she quit the room, she felt Dubois's gaze on her back. And as always, her skin crawled.

Dubois continued to lend his ears to Cripps's comments while his curiosity, piqued by something in Katherine Fortescue's demeanor, tried to identify just what he had seen—and what it might mean.

"I've been having the men in the mine watched, like you asked, and there really seems no way for them to increase production without having more hands on the job." Cripps snorted. "Adult hands, too—those older boys Kale sent us, while better than nothing, can't wield a pick like a man."

Dubois grunted noncommittally. He was well aware that one of his greatest strengths lay in his observational skills—his ability to pick up tiny signs that revealed a person's true concerns and deepest fears. Concerns and fears he could then exploit. Yet he couldn't imagine what might have occurred to cause Miss Fortescue to feel anything new. Perhaps he was overextrapolating and it was just that time of the month for her.

He refocused on Cripps.

Just as the large, heavyset Englishman concluded, "So as we need to increase production, what are we going to do for more men?"

Dubois arched his brows. "I take it you have a suggestion?"

"It's been a week since Kale's last delivery. Let me go and visit him and find out why he hasn't come up with more men for us." Cripps cracked the knuckles of his left hand. "And put a little pressure on him to get off his lazy arse and get us the men we need."

Dubois considered, then mused, "Lazy is not a term I would have applied to Kale. However, it appears that something has disrupted his supply to us, so…yes."

He circled his desk and dropped into his chair, then looked up at Cripps as he came to stand, ruddy faced and eager to be doing, before the desk. "You can't leave until Arsene gets back."

Dubois wasn't about to run a compound of this size without at least one of his lieutenants by his side, and Arsene had taken the last shipment of diamonds to the coast and was to have gone on into Freetown for various mundane supplies after that.

"But he should be back any time now," Cripps said.

Dubois nodded. Resting his forearms on the desk, he clasped his hands and turned his mind to Kale. What might be in the devious bastard's mind—whether Kale was playing some deep game or if the lack of supply was due to some factor beyond the master slaver's control. Dubois stated, "As soon as Arsene returns, take three men and pay Kale a visit." Dubois sat back in his chair and looked at Cripps. "I want you to ask *politely* what his problem is."

Cripps frowned. "Politely?"

Dubois smiled thinly. "Indeed. At least initially. It's entirely possible that it's not Kale who's dragging his heels in this. He has his own crew to keep busy—I doubt it would be his choice to sit in the jungle twiddling his thumbs." Dubois paused. When he continued, his tone had turned steely. "It's possible that the lack of supply of useful workers stems from some difficulty caused by those in the settlement. If so, I want to know."

Cripps studied his face. "And if that's the case?"

"Then," Dubois said, "it might be necessary for us to exert pressure on different people entirely."

Six

"Take care, you old codger." Caleb clapped his steward, Hornby, on his hefty shoulder. "And tell Fitz I'm counting on him to get you and that information to England as fast as the winds allow."

Frederick Fitzpatrick was Caleb's lieutenant and would captain *The Prince* on the run to Southampton.

"Aye, Capt'n." Hornby stepped back and snapped off a salute. "I'll tell him, and you may be sure I'll see these papers into your brothers' hands in London, like you ordered. But as for takin' care, I'm thinking it's you and this lot that'll need to exercise all due caution." With a dip of his gray head, Hornby indicated the men gathered behind Caleb and Phillipe—those who had volunteered to remain with them and keep watch over the captives in the compound.

Caleb had delegated Hornby, who had sailed with him for nearly a decade, to carry the vital documents along with Caleb's orders back to *The Prince* and thence to London. Caleb's bosun, Carter, and one of his midshipmen, Johnson, were also returning—under orders, for they would be needed aboard for *The Prince* to sail at maximum speed.

Also returning along the path leading northward, the one they hoped would eventually lead to the southern shore of the estuary near the spot where *The Prince* and *The Raven* waited, were Reynaud, Phillipe's bosun, along with four of his midshipmen. Phillipe sailed with a smaller crew than Caleb, and they'd agreed that, as *The Raven* would remain in the estuary as their ultimate means of escape, the ship needed to be well manned and thus well defended should any unexpected attack eventuate.

The entire company had walked a mile along the northbound track to see the group returning to the ships on their way. They'd halted at a point where the track descended sharply through a series of switchbacks to say their farewells.

"We'll be careful." Grinning, Phillipe clapped Reynaud on the back, then caught Caleb's eye. "Well, as careful as we ever are."

Hornby snorted as he turned and stepped down along the path. "That's what I'm afraid of."

"Farewell!"

"Adieu!"

"God-speed!"

The goodbyes came from multiple throats in a blend of accents.

His hands on his hips, Caleb stood and watched the small procession wend its way down the track. Phillipe waited by his shoulder, similarly watching their men depart.

The group who remained at their backs—Caleb's quartermaster, Quilley, and nine seamen, and Phillipe's quartermaster, Ducasse, and four others—turned and, in twos and threes, ambled back to the camp.

When they were alone, Caleb murmured, "Seeing those papers off to London is essentially mission complete—and we achieved that far more easily and straightforwardly than I'd imagined. Yet this situation is so much more complex."

"And very far from over." Phillipe turned back up the track.

Caleb joined him. As they strode toward their camp, Caleb's mind, rarely still, wandered—assessing, considering. They'd instituted a roster of men, two at all times through the daylight hours, to keep watch on the compound from the rock shelf above. Caleb jogged Phillipe's arm. "Let's go to the lookout and see what we can see."

They did. After settling beside the two men who had resumed their duties after the short excursion to see the others on their way, together with Phillipe, Caleb studied the activity in the compound, occasionally exchanging some comment or pointing out something of note.

After nearly an hour of observation, Caleb, sitting with his knees drawn up and his arms looped around them, said, "Now that I've read Dixon's and Hillsythe's reports, I can see what they're doing."

His gaze fixed on the compound, Phillipe nodded. "Keeping the pace of the work very steady and just fast enough to placate Dubois."

"Or to be explainable in terms of not having more workers." Caleb paused, then went on, "There's a lot of different, intersecting pressures and balances operating down there."

"Meaning?" Phillipe prompted.

Caleb sorted through the thoughts gradually clarifying in his mind. "For instance, that Dubois takes such good care of the captives. The medical hut, the fact he does not apply any physical coercion, any beatings or physical incentives to work harder."

"That's because they've gulled him into believing they're already working as hard as they can."

"No—not as hard but as *efficiently* as they can. That's Dubois's goal—the tack he insists on adhering to. He needs people to work day after day. He can't afford to push them harder and have them collapse, because he doesn't have a ready supply of replacements." Caleb paused, then went on, "And that testifies to how clever Dubois really is—that he's seen that, appreciated the necessity, and despite the fact that going easy on his captives would almost certainly not be his preference, he's rigidly adhered to what is necessary to achieve his aims. To deliver on the contract he presumably has with his masters."

"And," Phillipe added, "he's strong enough to enforce his direction on his men. From what we heard yesterday, treating the captives well is certainly not what they would prefer, either."

They continued to watch for another hour; all they saw only confirmed their earlier conclusion. The captives were walking a tightrope, but thus far they'd succeeded. As long as balance was maintained—as long as the captives kept diamond production at a level sufficient to appease Dubois's masters—there was no reason the present situation couldn't continue until rescue arrived.

The only fly in that ointment was the backers' insistence on increasing production.

Eventually convinced they understood the situation to that point, Caleb and Phillipe rose and scrambled back down the animal track to the lake. They bathed in the cool water, then, refreshed, ambled back through the jungle toward their camp, giving the compound a wide berth.

Caleb glanced toward the mine. "I've been thinking—just in case any of us stumble and get caught by the guards, we should have an agreed story, one that will account for any or all of us being here." He met Phillipe's eyes. "That's the one true danger I can see in us remaining here—if any of us get caught and Dubois realizes why we're really here."

Ducking under a hanging vine, Phillipe nodded. "That we were sent and haven't just chanced on the mine."

"We can't risk alerting the bastard that London knows anything about him or the mine."

"Agreed."

They walked into their camp and made for the logs about the central pit. Caleb glanced around, noting that several men were absent. He looked at Quilley. "Where are the others?"

Quilley grinned. "Martin brought his crossbow. He brought down a goat. He, Ducasse, and three of the others have hauled it all the way back to where we said goodbye to the others. We figured that far out, a fire wouldn't be a problem. They're going to butcher the animal and cook the meat, then bring it back here." Anticipation lit Quilley's face. "They should be back by suppertime."

"Excellent!" Phillipe rubbed his hands together. "We could do with some fresh meat."

Caleb sat and stretched out his legs. "With that to look forward to, let's put our minds to inventing our tale."

Phillipe sat on the next log. "Indeed. You're right. This is not the sort of situation in which a wise commander should leave anything to chance."

★ ★ ★

Late in the afternoon in a tavern in Freetown, three men gathered about the table in the rear corner of the taproom. They'd met there so often in recent months that the other denizens now viewed them as regulars; the barman pulled the pints they favored as soon as he saw each of them coming through the door.

As usual, Muldoon was the last to sit down at the table. He set his foaming tankard on the scarred surface and looked across the table at the man who always arrived first. "Have you heard anything from Kale?"

The first man frowned. "No. Why?"

Muldoon shot an inquiring look at the third of their group, but Winton shook his head. "Because"—Muldoon looked back at the first man—"I've been trying to get hold of him. Or, at least, his man here."

"Rogers?" When Muldoon nodded, the first man's frown deepened. "He's almost always in the settlement, except when he's delivering men to Kale."

"Which he shouldn't be doing as we haven't set him onto any new victims." Muldoon expelled a tense breath. "And now that we have some, I can't raise him. A merchantman came in yesterday with an excess of hands. The captain's putting off at least four—all young and strong, perfect for Dubois's needs."

"Can't you send Kale a message?" Winton asked.

"I tried, but there's no one at the house in the slums. The boy I sent said it was empty, as near as he could tell."

"That's odd." The first man raised his pint and took a long sip.

"Very odd," Muldoon agreed. "And dashed inconvenient. Dubois wants more men, and we have more men, but Kale's not here to nab them."

A long silence followed as all three men considered the situation. Finally, the first man stated, "We can't do without Kale. At least, not easily."

"I know." Muldoon stared into his tankard. After several more seconds, he said, "One of us will have to go to his camp and find out what's going on."

The first man set down his mug. "I can't go. Holbrook would have a fit."

"Well, I certainly can't," Muldoon replied. "Not with Decker back in port."

He and the first man turned their gazes on Winton, sitting at the small table's end and staring into his beer.

Winton felt the weight of their regard and looked up. Then he looked appalled. He waved his hands. "Don't look at me. My uncle would read me the riot act—which, I remind you, is another thing we don't need. Not if we want to keep Dubois supplied with the necessary equipment."

Muldoon grimaced. "True enough." He looked at the table in front of him. He traced one of the scars that marred its surface. "So what are we going to do?"

Several seconds passed, then the first man spoke. "Undoto might have some idea of where Kale is, or if he's gone somewhere and how long he'll be away."

Muldoon met the first man's gaze. "Are you volunteering to ask Undoto?"

The first man smiled thinly. "I'll do it." He drained his mug and set it down, then looked at Muldoon. "You keep your eye on those four likely lads. I'll call on Undoto and see what I can learn." He glanced at Winton, then looked at Muldoon and tapped his palm to the table. "Meet back here tomorrow, and we'll see where we are."

★ ★ ★

That evening, Katherine sat with the other leaders of the captives about the fire pit to discuss recent developments and decide on their immediate course. The rest of their company, presently all gathered around the pit, their faces lit by the leaping flames, were talking animatedly, most with smiles wreathing their faces.

Earlier, speaking to smaller groups here and there, she and the other leaders had shared the news of the impending rescue and of the small protective force now camped nearby. The effect on everyone had been every bit as intense as she'd anticipated— hope was a heady elixir, and after such a prolonged abstinence, they were all but drunk.

At her suggestion, to account for their transparent delight, the group as a whole had adopted the story that they were celebrating the betrothal of two of their number—Annie Mellows and Jed Mathers—which was true enough. The pair had, indeed, decided to marry, and even if they couldn't yet, they'd decided to declare their intentions—a statement of their plans for their future and, by extension, their dogged belief that they would live to see that future. Annie and Jed had agreed to allow their news to be used as an excuse for the company's high spirits.

Hopkins—who had employed his boyish charm to befriend several of the guards—put the story about. Subsequently, the guards laughed cynically from the shadows, but as far as Katherine could tell, the excuse had held up. Neither Dubois nor his men appeared to be suspicious; they certainly weren't lurking, hunting for any other source for the captives' sudden upwelling of joy.

Sitting beside her, Hillsythe surveyed the chattering group. "Let them have their evening. Tomorrow will be time enough to buckle down again."

Fanshawe, Hopkins, and Harriet nodded in agreement.

"Indeed," Dixon said. "But what *we* need to decide tonight is whether or not we open up the second tunnel or, alternatively, if we want to risk trying to engineer more delays."

"Take us through the arguments again," Fanshawe suggested. "Things change so often, I, for one, lose track."

Dixon grunted. "The situation as of now is that output from the first tunnel is winding down. We're still getting diamonds out, but only just enough, and given the backers are pressuring Dubois to *increase* production, we can't afford to allow overall production to drop away—as it will if we don't open the second tunnel and start to actively mine the second pipe *soon*. In short, if we want to keep production at a safe level, I believe we've held off as long as we dare."

"Am I correct in thinking," Hillsythe said, "that if we move now, we'll have enough diamonds coming out of the first tunnel to tide us over while we open the second—so that we won't have any sudden drop in output to further irritate Dubois and tweak the attention of the backers?"

"Yes and no." Dixon glanced at Fanshawe and Hopkins. "We might be cutting it fine if we banked solely on output from the first tunnel, but we should have enough ore hidden in our stockpile to cover the switch from the first tunnel to the second, at least as far as Dubois and his masters are concerned."

Fanshawe didn't look thrilled, but nodded.

"There's enough in the stockpile to supply several days' full production," Hopkins volunteered.

"To remind us all of the context," Harriet said, "if we had opened the second tunnel earlier, overall output would have soared, which is why we've held off and held off, until production from the first tunnel is starting to decline."

Dixon nodded. "While soaring output would have made Dubois and his backers very happy for several weeks, after that, output would almost certainly fall away, possibly dramatically enough to trigger closure of the mine. Avoiding that scenario remains our paramount goal, and the only sure way to achieve it is to keep production steady at a level as low as Dubois and his backers will swallow."

"Indeed." Hillsythe glanced at their fellow captives, still happily chattering. "And now we know that rescue is coming, stretching the mining out until relief can reach us is a finite and imperative goal. Frobisher and his men turning up has given us a strong incentive to succeed—a vital one, in fact."

There were murmurs of agreement from the others.

"What does Dubois know about the second deposit?" Hopkins asked.

"At this point, only that it's there," Dixon replied. "I haven't told him that it's a much denser deposit with many more diamonds than the first pipe. In order to delay mining it, I invented all sorts of structural obstacles." He shrugged. "Some were real, most weren't, but they've served their purpose."

The first tunnel ran more or less straight into the heart of the hill. It had just grazed the upper end of a pipe of diamonds, and they'd had to dig deep into the side of the tunnel in order to bring out the ore-encrusted stones. The second tunnel would run more or less perpendicular to the first, opening off it to the right about ten yards inside the mine entrance. "All I've done so far," Dixon went on, "is to put in an exploratory shaft. I convinced Dubois that by doing the minor excavations necessary to plot a tunnel that ran along the pipe, rather than grazing the end as we did with the first pipe, then ultimately, getting the bulk of the diamonds out of the second pipe will take much less time."

Fanshawe nodded. "You convinced him to go slow now in order to mine faster later."

Hillsythe straightened. "But with the first deposit waning, it's time to convert your exploratory shaft into a working tunnel so our teams can switch from mining the first deposit to mining the second, all the while keeping the level of production steady."

Katherine looked at Fanshawe and Hopkins. Each led a team of six men; those two teams performed the bulk of the heavy mining, wielding pickaxes for most of each day. Hillsythe managed a crew of four slighter, wiry men who oversaw the children and effectively controlled the amount of ore that went out of the mine to the sorting piles. Hillsythe also managed the three burly carpenters in Dixon's team when they weren't actively assisting the engineer with his structures. The carpenters kept a close watch on the tunnel supports that kept everyone safe.

"It's evidently time we took that step." When they all nodded in agreement, Hillsythe looked at Dixon. "So what do you need to open up the second tunnel?"

"That," Dixon said, "is where complications arise." He looked around their group. "Opening the second tunnel will require more men and more supplies—more timber, more nails, and so on. The supplies Dubois can doubtless get, but the men?"

They all knew Dubois had been pressing for more men to be kidnapped for weeks. Katherine glanced around and confirmed no guard was close before adding, "And now Kale's vanished, so there will be no more men—at least not from that quarter."

Hillsythe met her gaze. "Kale's disappearance is going to disrupt the supply of men until Dubois finds out and works out another route through which to source what he needs. That's going to take time."

"Exactly." Dixon looked grim. "That's my point. With the output from the first tunnel declining, Dubois not having the men needed to open the second tunnel means time *we* may not have."

"Ah." Hillsythe looked struck. "I see what you mean by complications."

They all did. While Dubois might understand that he didn't have enough men to keep production from the first tunnel up while simultaneously opening the second, there was no guarantee that his masters would—that they wouldn't instead see any dip in overall production as reason enough to close the mine. And kill all the captives. Once such an order was given, Dubois would simply shrug and carry it out—no appeals to rationality would be entertained.

Eventually, Hillsythe stirred. "You were correct in your opening statement—we need to make a decision now, tonight, on what direction we take with the second tunnel." He looked at the others' faces, meeting each one's eyes. "Although our decision might prove critical—might end up being one of life and death for us—the only way we can make it is based on the facts before us." He paused, then looked at Dixon. "I vote for you to tell Dubois that you're ready to open up the second tunnel and give him your requirements. For my money, trying to delay further might land us in even worse straits and, more, might prick Dubois's suspicious nature, which we've been so very careful to lull."

Katherine compressed her lips, then said, "I agree, for much the same reasons. We can only judge by what we know today, and as I understand things"—she glanced at Hopkins and Fanshawe—"we have enough ore held back to cover the slack when the carpenters and others move to help Dixon, at least somewhat."

Fanshawe nodded. "Somewhat." He, too, looked around at the others' faces. "Our original purpose in building our stockpile was to give us a cushion of at least several days when the deposit was finally mined out. A few days to do whatever we might to escape. But that was before Dixon found the second pipe and before Frobisher and his crew arrived. Although the second pipe, too, will eventually run out, as you say, we can only base decisions on what we're faced with today." He nodded again, more decisively. "So I vote for opening the second tunnel, too, even though that will run down our cushion and, unless and until we can replenish the stockpile, will leave us with little to fall back on when the second pipe runs out—we have to pray the rescue force reaches us before that happens."

Hopkins grimaced, but he nodded, too. "I agree. We have to take the risk, open up the second tunnel as expeditiously as possible while using the stockpile to cover the drop in production, and pray the rescue force reaches us in time."

Harriet and Dixon both added their votes to the consensus to open the second tunnel, making the decision unanimous. "There's also the fact," Dixon said, "that by us moving forward—apparently cooperating—then any further holdup generated by a lack of men or supplies is going to focus Dubois's attention on his supply lines and not on us."

Fanshawe grunted. "For all his many faults, he's never yet proved stupid enough to hold us liable for things beyond our control."

"So we're agreed." Hillsythe straightened, easing his back. He looked at Dixon. "We'll leave it to you to inform Dubois."

Dixon huffed. "I'll see him first thing and let you all know if there are any unexpected ramifications."

"Actually"—Hillsythe glanced at Dixon, then looked at Katherine—"our discussion raised two questions that we really ought to push to answer. First"—he addressed her—"what is Frobisher's best guess as to how long it will take for the rescue force to reach us? Can he put a date on it?"

She widened her eyes. "He said at least six weeks, but that struck me as an off-the-cuff estimate. I forgot to ask last time, but when next I see him, I'll ask if he can be more definite."

"Do. The second and connected question"—Hillsythe looked at Dixon—"is whether the second deposit is rich enough to allow us to mine sufficient diamonds fast enough to keep Dubois's backers happy and yet last until our rescuers arrive."

Dixon pulled a face. "*That*, indeed, is the ultimate question. And I won't be able to answer it until we get the second tunnel fully open. We'll need to extend it the full length of the deposit, which we haven't yet done even with the exploratory shaft, and

I suspect we'll need to go down a level, too, to access the far reaches of the pipe."

The others all nodded.

The small fire at the center of the log circle was burning low. Most of the company had started to drift away to their respective huts, to their hammock beds.

Katherine exchanged glances with the other leaders, but no one seemed to have more to say. They all rose.

"Onward, then," Hillsythe murmured. With a nod for Katherine and Harriet, he turned away.

Katherine glanced around, then, leaving Harriet whispering with Dixon, headed toward the women's and children's hut.

As she passed through the shadows cloaking the compound, her mind juggled two entirely separate facts. Dubois wanted more men to work the mine. Caleb, Lascelle, and their men were only yards away in the jungle.

What if…?

She didn't think anyone else had thought of that, much less the horrendous implications. Quelling a shudder, she determinedly banished the thought from her mind, feeling very much as if even thinking of both facts at the same time was akin to inviting some malignant fate to notice. And act.

★ ★ ★

Undoto, preacher extraordinaire and reluctant slavers' accomplice, was expecting the knock on his front door. Indeed, he'd expected it rather earlier. He opened the door wide, a practiced smile on his face—and froze.

A single figure cloaked in black and wreathed in shadows stood on Undoto's porch.

Instinctively, Undoto's gaze swept over the man—by height and stance, he knew it was a man—and in the faint light, he saw the pistol the man held in his hand, the barrel trained unwaveringly on Undoto's chest.

"Good evening, Mr. Undoto." The voice was cultured, an

Englishman's voice. "If you wouldn't mind stepping outside for just a moment, I have a matter I would like to discuss with you."

His gaze fixed on the pistol's barrel—intensely aware of his sons and daughters already asleep in the front room of the narrow house—Undoto drew in a tight breath and, outwardly calm, stepped outside. Then he closed his already sweating palm about the doorknob and pulled the door shut behind him.

"Excellent." The man had stepped back.

Peering through the dimness, Undoto saw that the man had a black scarf wound loosely about the lower half of his face. A dark, wide-brimmed hat pulled low on his forehead effectively screened his eyes.

"I regret the pistol." The man tipped up the barrel, then slid the weapon beneath his cloak, presumably into the pocket of his coat. "It was necessary to get you alone."

Undoto didn't relax. "You wanted to discuss something?"

"Indeed. We have an acquaintance in common—namely, Kale. Although I believe you generally deal with his lieutenant in the settlement, Rogers."

Undoto reluctantly nodded. "I know of them."

The man's cold smile colored his tone. "Let's not play games. You work for them. You select marks, and they oblige by snatching them up. Which is all well and good. Ultimately, we work for the same people. However, we need to contact Kale and have been unable to do so. Do you know where he is?"

"No." Undoto fought to suppress a frown. After a second's hesitation, he volunteered, "I expected Rogers to call this evening—I thought you were him. Him and his men. I gave a sermon today, and they always call after that to learn if I spotted any likely pickings."

"And did you? Spot any likely pickings?"

"Two sailors just in off a merchantman and looking for work."

The man nodded. "Indeed. They sound like two of a group

we noted. We tried to send word to Kale's base in the slums, but no one's at home. Do you have any idea how to contact him?"

"No. He—or rather Rogers—always comes to me."

"Do you know where Kale's camp is?"

Undoto hesitated. He did know, but... "It's out to the east. Other than that..." He slid his hands into the pockets in his robes and shrugged.

The man shifted, then stilled. Several seconds ticked by, then the man looked out at the street and said, "It seems we have a shared interest in locating Kale. I strongly suggest you make every effort to contact him. If you do happen to see him, tell him to get in touch with those who've most recently paid him."

The man's tone had grown progressively more clipped. He looked at Undoto. "I'll return in two days to see what you've learned. I believe we have a mutual interest in keeping our interaction discreet."

"Perhaps," Undoto said. "But you have the advantage of me— you know my name. You know my face. I don't know yours."

The man looked directly at him, then evenly replied, "And for all our sakes, that's the way it needs to be." With a swirl of his cloak, he went quickly down the steps. "Good night, Mr. Undoto."

Undoto watched the man walk briskly up his garden path, turn into the street, and stride away.

Undoto stared after him as the minutes ticked past.

Other than the moment with the pistol, which he had subsequently put away, the man hadn't uttered a single threat.

Yet the promise of one hovered in the humid night air.

Eventually, Undoto turned, opened his door, and went inside.

★ ★ ★

The following day in the late afternoon, Muldoon, Winton, and their colleague met in the tavern once more.

Immediately all three were settled with pints in their hands, the first man—who, as usual, had been the first one there—related his conversation with Undoto. He concluded, "I'm sure Undoto knows where Kale's camp is. He'll go—for his own sake, he needs to know what's going on with Kale." He took a sip of his ale, then said, "I'll give him another day—I'll call on him tomorrow night and see what he's learned."

Muldoon and Winton exchanged glances.

Muldoon looked at his tankard, then turned it between his hands. "So Undoto has also lost touch with Rogers. I was hoping that the empty nest in the slums simply meant they'd changed locations and hadn't got around to mentioning it, but that Rogers and his crew didn't call on Undoto suggests otherwise."

Winton swallowed. He moistened his lips and murmured, "What are we going to do if Kale's gone and taken his men with him?"

None of them attempted any answer.

Eventually, the first man drained his mug. "There's no point speculating until we know what's happening with Kale. Undoto will bring us news. There's no sense scrambling until he does."

Seven

Katherine walked briskly out of the compound's gates two mornings later. Diccon skipped ahead; the boy was, she felt, better at hiding his excitement than she was. It took effort not to openly search for Frobisher even while she was still within sight of the guards on the gates and the tower.

As the jungle closed around her and she followed Diccon deeper into the shadows, she lectured herself on the subject of keeping her unruly reactions suppressed. Why Frobisher so easily provoked such responses, she had no clear idea; no other man had ever captured her awareness as he so effortlessly did. And the strength of her reactions—those impulses she hadn't felt before and consequently had no experience subduing—only made dealing with him, even simply viewing him, in a businesslike way all the harder.

As distractions went, he was shaping up to be her Achilles' heel.

Diccon halted at a clump of berry vines. The boy's calm patience as he set to, picking berries and dropping them into his basket, was instructive. She spotted a nut tree nearby and went to look for fallen nuts.

While she searched the carpet of leaf mold, her mind—for the moment free of Frobisher—returned to the problem she'd spent the previous day wrestling with. In the early days of the mine, the men had realized that some of the children had a knack for telling which lumps of freshly mined rock contained diamonds and which most likely did not. They'd worked with those children to separate some of the diamond-bearing rocks while still within the mine—before the ore was taken out to the sorting piles. As the guards had quickly grown complacent and entered the mine only occasionally to run their bored gazes over the workings, the men and children had managed to dig and conceal an alcove-like hole in which to hide their bounty.

That hidden alcove now held their cushion of ore to tide them through any unexpected shortfall—that was the stockpile they would have to draw down in order to open the second tunnel without risking a dramatic fall in production.

It had occurred to her that there were other points in the mining process at which they might hold back some of their product. Once the second tunnel was fully open, no doubt the men and children would gradually replenish their stockpile inside the mine. It was harder to see where the children might hide any diamond-bearing rocks while sorting, which was performed in plain sight in the compound under the gazes of the passing guards, albeit hidden from those in the tower by the movable awning. So harder, but not impossible.

The cleaning shed was a different matter. Guards patrolled outside, and although they randomly came in from time to time, as the women ignored them, the guards rarely stayed for long. She was more or less in charge and felt sure the other women would be glad to assist in creating their own stockpile of cleaned stones. Stripped of the other minerals clumped about them, the raw diamonds still looked like rocks, but they were much smaller and would be easier to hide…if only she could think of a place in the cleaning shed in which to hide them.

The shed was much like the other buildings, with plain plank walls and floor, and palm-thatch on the roof. The long table that ran down the middle of the room, the stools the women perched on, and a plain bench across the end wall were the only pieces of furniture.

She'd checked the floor, but it was raised above the ground, and the area beneath it was visible to anyone who looked. The walls contained no crannies large enough and were only one plank thick. The roof—the thatch—might, however, be a possibility. She would need to examine it more closely.

Diccon called. She looked up and saw him beckoning her on. She straightened, hoisted her basket, now a quarter full, to her hip and followed him deeper into the jungle.

Where was Frobisher? Diccon had insisted that they should just go about their collecting until Frobisher and his men came to them. Which was all very well, but she could remain out of the compound only until midday, and she had messages from Dixon and Hillsythe, and their question to ask, as well as information the women had overheard to pass on. When Diccon halted by a fruit tree, she hunted and found another nut tree. After dropping her basket to the ground, she plonked her hands on her hips, then sighed and started looking for nuts.

Caleb halted with Phillipe in the shadows nearby. They'd been in the camp when one of the men on watch had come running to tell them that the lady and the boy had come out of the compound and headed into the jungle between their camp and the lake.

The man hadn't waited for long enough to be certain the pair hadn't been followed. Phillipe had urged caution, and Caleb had agreed.

They'd located the pair fifteen minutes ago. They'd watched and then circled them, searching for any guards who might have trailed them. And found no sign of anyone.

Caleb relaxed. "They're alone."

Phillipe nodded. "This Dubois—he plays very strange games."

Caleb humphed and moved forward. He made no effort to mute his approach. Miss Fortescue—Katherine—heard him. She turned his way—and her expectant expression dissolved into one of smiling welcome.

He felt a warmth blossom somewhere inside him. He all but

swaggered up, returning her smile with one of his own. "Good morning."

"Hello." She stared at him for a moment, then blinked and looked away. "I...have several messages." Her tone turned brisk and matter-of-fact. "Dixon and Hillsythe asked me to outline how the work in the mine is progressing, which will explain the importance of a question we hope you can answer." She looked past him to Phillipe and nodded a greeting, then glanced back at Caleb. "And there are a few other bits and pieces that perhaps you should know."

"Of course—but first, we thought it might be best if we take you to our camp. Diccon found the spot for us, so he knows the way." With a gesture, Caleb invited her to follow the boy and Phillipe, who had already started through the trees. He bent and picked up her basket. "But if others in the camp ever need to send for us, more of you need to know where to find us."

She nodded. "Yes, of course."

As they wended through the trees in Diccon and Phillipe's wake, Caleb added, "Although we're approaching from an angle this time, the clearing we use is just off the path that leads directly north—the one that's virtually unused. We can fill your basket from trees around the clearing, then you can walk directly back to the compound on that track."

"Good." She tucked an errant strand of hair behind her ear. "That way, I'll be certain of the way."

They reached the camp, and she glanced around, then at his invitation, sat on one of the logs about the empty fire pit. She accepted a mug of water from Ellis, one of Caleb's men, with a grateful smile. Caleb took a moment to hand over Katherine's basket to Foster and Collins, two of his men who were happy to have something to do to fill their time.

"Now." He let himself down beside her. "What do you have to tell us?"

Katherine was determined to keep her senses in line; she

schooled her features to what she thought of as her governess look—severe and slightly intimidating. Or at least, as intimidating as she could appear; she doubted it would have much effect on Frobisher or Lascelle. "The first thing I need to explain is that we—all those at the mine—have been managing the ultimate output. Early on, we realized that if the output fell too low, there was a good chance the backers—whoever they are—would deem the mine too great a risk for too little reward and order it shut and all of us killed." With her hands cupped about the cool mug, she drew breath and continued, "To avoid that—or at least stave it off—whenever the men hit a vein with more diamonds than usual, they held back some of that ore and hid it inside the mine. That's become our stockpile—if the output falls, we feed more out. If the output rises, we keep more back."

"And Dubois and his men have no idea of this?" Lascelle asked.

She shook her head. "They've never realized." After a second, she went on, "The problem for us is that there are a lot of elements at play that influence the output from the mine itself. Some of those elements are under our control, but others aren't. In the latter category are the mining supplies—timber, nails, tools, and so on—and also the number of men at the mine. Those two elements, in particular, used to be under Dubois's control via Kale and presumably others in the settlement." She looked at Frobisher. "But now you've eliminated Kale, you've disrupted the supply of both elements, and Dubois is having to…"

"Re-establish his supply lines?" Frobisher suggested.

"Exactly. But another element in all this has been Dixon opening up the second tunnel—that's been under our control, even though, again, Dubois doesn't realize that. Up until recently, our plan for that was straightforward—we assumed that it would be best for us to delay opening the second tunnel for as long as we could to ensure the life of the mine was as long as possible—the better for us all to remain alive long enough to devise some way to escape." She paused, then went on, "But that's now changed, because output from the first tunnel is declining. So in order to keep production at levels acceptable to the backers—to keep them from closing the mine—we now have to open up the second tunnel."

She grimaced. "We can and will do that—but we've now got other problems restricting the output from the mine, namely the lack of mining supplies and the lack of men."

Lascelle laughed—a cynical, world-weary sound. "So you actually need Kale back."

She met Lascelle's gaze. "I think we all know that no one would ever wish to have Kale back." She glanced briefly at Frobisher. "I told you that you and your men would be heroes in the camp for putting paid to Kale, and trust me, you are. No one regrets his passing." She brightened. "And as it happens, we have a way around our problem. It's that stockpile I mentioned earlier. We'll feed out enough stones to keep the output sufficiently high while the men work to open the second tunnel and get it into full production. Once we have that done—and Dixon believes the second deposit holds more diamonds than the first—we should be able to continue mining, we hope for at least some time."

She looked first at Lascelle, then turned to fix her gaze on Frobisher's face. "And that brings me to the question to which we in the compound truly need an answer. What is your best guess as to when the rescue force will reach us? Can you give us a date?"

Caleb blinked. She'd explained the situation so clearly, he could instantly see the connections—and the importance of his answer. His gaze on her eyes, he nodded slowly while his mind raced. "We worked out a rough guess before, but let's see if we can be more accurate." He glanced at Phillipe. "Our men should have reached the estuary by now."

Phillipe nodded. "I would think we can be confident that, one way or another, *The Prince* will slip past Freetown and Decker tonight." He met Caleb's eyes. "Your men won't dally, and in the circumstances, it will have to be at night."

"Indeed. So that's *The Prince* on the open sea tonight." He paused, then grimaced. "I can't see Fitz getting the old girl into Southampton in less than twenty-one days—and that only if the winds blow his way."

"Let's say twenty-three days to Southampton." Phillipe frowned. "From there, how fast will the news reach your brothers in London, and more pertinently, how quickly will they be able to alert those required to authorize the dispatch of the rescue force?"

Caleb thought through what that was likely to entail. Eventually, he offered, "Four days minimum."

Phillipe glanced his way. "Four days to sailing?"

Caleb paused, then said, "The rescue force will have to come on several ships—it can't be just one, not given the distance and the urgency."

"You think they'll use your family's fleet?"

"As much of it as is available in Southampton or London, or even Bristol. Altogether, that would do it." Caleb felt his expression clear as the most likely scenario coalesced in his mind. "The thing is, I'd wager heavily that the first ship here will be Royd's."

Phillipe snorted. "Unquestionably."

Caleb glanced at Katherine. "Royd's my oldest brother and the operational head of Frobisher Shipping."

"And," Phillipe put in, "more pertinent to this discussion, Royd's *Corsair* is unquestionably the fastest ship of that class on the waves."

"From what I've gathered," Caleb said, "Royd can make the run from Southampton to Freetown in twelve days or less."

"That's twenty-three, plus four, and now twelve." Katherine had been keeping track. "That's thirty-nine days at least for the first ship to reach Freetown."

"I think it's safe to assume," Caleb said, "that in terms of raw diamonds or any message being dispatched to the backers, or of any instruction from those backers reaching Freetown and eventually the mine, those thirty-nine days will bring an end to traffic in either direction." He met Phillipe's eyes, then looked at Katherine. "My brother will contact Decker—the vice-admiral of the West Africa Squadron. Decker will, however grudgingly, listen to Royd, and Royd will get Decker to blockade the estuary, halting all vessels going in and out and allowing only our vessels carrying the rescue force to pass."

"So." Katherine blew out a breath. "Let's say forty days. Forty days is the minimum that we absolutely must keep the mine producing at acceptable levels."

"Preferably more than that to allow time for the rescue force to reach here," Phillipe warned.

"We have ten more days to the end of this month," Caleb said. "So to be safe, you need to plan for the mine to run smoothly into and preferably through the first week of September. So aim for the seventh of September."

"Thank you." Katherine nodded briskly. "Having a firm date is going to be very helpful, not just for planning but for morale, too. Speaking of which"—she glanced from Caleb to Phillipe— "we've now told everyone—all of our company—about your presence and the impending rescue. I cannot tell you how thrilled and...*uplifted* everyone is. It's made a great difference—we now all feel more confident we can see this through and survive."

"That's the ticket." Caleb smiled encouragingly. "We need to stay focused on getting everyone out alive." He paused, then asked, "Is there anything else you can tell us? For instance, about the group of Dubois's men who returned yesterday and the other group that left this morning?"

"Indeed." Katherine sat straighter and proceeded to report on all the captives had learned once Dubois's first lieutenant, Arsene, had returned to the camp. "The guards talk to each other and never care that we overhear. After handing over the diamonds,

Arsene went on to Freetown, and he brought back food and similar supplies, as he usually does. Then this morning, Dubois's other lieutenant, Cripps, left with a group for Kale's camp—apparently they've been sent to find out what's going on, and Dubois hasn't assumed it's Kale who's the problem. It'll take Cripps at least three days to go there and return. But according to the guards, Dubois is already thinking about directly contacting those in the settlement for more mining supplies and more men."

Frobisher's eyes had narrowed. "So Dubois knows who in the settlement is involved."

"Some of them, at least. But none of us have ever heard any names. It's possible the guards don't know either, just Dubois, and maybe Arsene and Cripps."

Frobisher nodded. "Tell us more about the guards." He met her gaze. "What their rosters are like—how long they stay in any one place or patrolling any one area. How often they do, and so on."

As clearly as she could, she outlined the pattern of the guards' usual behavior.

When she concluded, Lascelle grimaced. "They're well placed, and much of their movements are random."

Caleb glanced at Katherine. "That makes it harder to plan an attack." He paused, then, realizing that midday was approaching, he rose and held out his hand to her.

She glanced at it, then, delicately, rested her fingers across his palm. He gripped lightly, helped her to her feet—then had to force himself to release her slender fingers.

She shook out her skirts, then slanted him a smile. "Thank you—it is time I headed back."

Phillipe went off to find her basket.

Caleb didn't want her to leave. "We're going to use our time here—our enforced inaction—to learn as much as we can about the compound itself and how it operates, with a view to planning various ways of attack. Possibly even taking some first steps—making preparations."

He paused as Phillipe returned, bulging basket in hand. Caleb frowned. "She's never going to be able to carry that."

Phillipe grinned and bent to tip some of the nuts out into a pile. "The men got carried away."

"Incidentally," Caleb said, reclaiming Katherine's attention, "before I forget, we've hidden all the weapons we took from Kale's men in a cache near the lake. There's a mound just beyond the wharf—the weapons are in a covered pit on the other side of that mound."

Her eyes had widened. "I'll tell Hillsythe and the others. That's likely to be a real boon."

"We thought that when the weapons are needed, the men sent to fetch the water would be able to overpower the guards and retrieve them."

"I see." She accepted the now more reasonably filled basket from Phillipe.

Caleb reached over and relieved her of it, then gestured for her to precede him down the narrow path that led back to the track to the compound. "Diccon has wandered on. I'll walk with you part of the way."

He pretended not to see Phillipe's grin.

Katherine inclined her head, smiled a farewell to the other men scattered about the clearing, then started off along the path.

Caleb followed at her heels, occasionally reaching past her to hold back looping vines. They were nearly to the track when he finally gave in to the prodding of his baser self—that self who wanted to give her a reason to come out into the jungle again and spend an hour with him. "Regarding our plans, it would be helpful if Dixon and Hillsythe could confirm that you will be able to stretch the mining into September. That would take one concern off our list. But also, please ask if there's anything we can do to assist—such as intercepting further supplies. Or will that only make matters worse?"

She reached the track, stepped into the wider space, and turned to face him. She was frowning. "I can't venture answers to either question as yet, but I'll ask." She met his gaze. "I don't dare push Dubois by attempting to come out earlier than two days hence, but if you have any urgent message to send us, Diccon can be counted on to act as a courier." Her smile bloomed again. "He's quite taken with the role."

Caleb returned her smile.

Swinging her basket, he walked on by her side until they reached the point where going farther would risk being spotted by the guards.

He halted. When she halted and looked at him, he handed her the basket.

Speaking was too risky, but as she reached for the handle, she mouthed a gently, rather shyly smiling "Thank you."

Her fingers brushed Caleb's—a touch that traveled all the way to his toes, via all regions between.

He released the basket, nodded in farewell—then he stood in the dappled shadows and watched her walk away.

★ ★ ★

By the time Katherine reached Dubois's office, she felt thoroughly distracted, her mind awash with considerations of the potential obstacles likely to be encountered in stretching the mining into September, and the even more concerning—anxiety-producing—prospect of Frobisher and his men doing something to assist with that, and Dubois—fiend that he was—realizing they were there, close by in the jungle somewhere, and...

She walked into Dubois's office and did her level best to haul her mind from that thought.

But Dubois was not sitting behind his desk. She glanced around and saw him at the rear of the communal area, speaking with Arsene. Although Dubois had doubtless noticed her, he gave no sign of having any interest in talking to her—which suited her to the ground.

She walked to the desk, set the basket upon it—sent up an errant prayer that one day, Dubois would choke on one of the nuts—then turned and, without glancing his way, left the office.

As usual, she felt his gaze on her back and steeled herself against her instinctive shudder.

Dubois stared after Katherine Fortescue—and wondered why his instincts were pricking. She had never shown signs of intransigence or rebellion, even though she clung to her so-very-English, proper and faintly haughty façade. That had never bothered him, yet there was now something in her...what was it? Her aura? Whatever it was, it was stirring instincts he knew well enough never to ignore.

"So if Cripps has no luck getting useful answers out of Kale," Arsene said, summarizing their discussion to that point, "you want me to take a few men and seek out Winton directly and tap him on the shoulder, so to speak."

His gaze still fixed, unseeing, on the empty doorway, Dubois nodded. He started to walk to his desk—to the window behind it—knowing Arsene would follow. "We may as well try for Winton himself—a direct line to the commissariat in the fort would be most efficient." He rounded his desk and continued to the window. "But if you can't easily approach Winton without risking his cover, then try Muldoon—he's easier to find alone in suitable surroundings." Dubois halted just inside the window, where the shade cast by the overhanging thatch would conceal him from those outside. "Just remember, we mustn't risk exposing any of them. Not while we still need them."

Katherine Fortescue hadn't returned to the cleaning shed, nor to the children crouched under the awning, sorting the pile of fresh ore. She was presently waiting—he thought faintly impatiently—at the entrance to the mine.

Unaware of Dubois's distraction, Arsene asked, "What about

the other one? The one we aren't supposed to know of? If I can't get to Muldoon, should I try him?"

"No." Dubois knew who that man was and agreed with the assessment that he should not be approached—not unless their scheme fell completely apart. "He's too vital to this operation to risk. If you can't get to Winton, you'll be able to find Muldoon—just stay in Freetown until you do."

Arsene grunted.

Dubois added, "Regardless, this is all speculative. We'll wait until Cripps gets back and we learn what's going on with Kale."

From the corner of his eye, he saw Arsene dip his head. Dubois waved, and the big man lumbered off.

Dubois continued to watch Katherine Fortescue.

Two minutes later, she was joined by Dixon, then a moment later, Hillsythe appeared.

Katherine Fortescue started talking.

Dubois watched. He might have thought that the discussion merely concerned some aspect of the mining—such as the roster of children who scrabbled in the mine and carted rock to the ore pile. Miss Fortescue had proved to be something of a champion for the brats—which, of course, was what had got her kidnapped in the first place; she knew how to keep the blighters in line and encourage them to work.

He might have thought she was arguing with the other two over the children or something similar—had it not been for her animation. For the way her expressive hands moved, and the energy that seemed to have infused her slender form.

It took him several long moments of narrow-eyed scrutiny before he identified what element about Miss Fortescue was so strongly triggering his internal alarms—but finally, he had it.

Hope. Somehow, from somewhere, for some unknown-to-him reason, Katherine Fortescue now had hope.

Dubois didn't like that.

★ ★ ★

It was midafternoon, and the heat trapped beneath the jungle's canopy was approaching stifling, when Undoto walked into the clearing that he'd visited only once before. He'd been brought to Kale's Homestead to be reassured that those kidnapped would not escape and carry tales of his perfidy back to the settlement.

He hadn't wanted to come back—to see the brutal evidence of the fate he was guilty of delivering people up to.

But today...

Puzzled and frowning, he halted before the fire pit and looked around. The place appeared as he remembered it, exactly as he remembered it, except with no people.

And no sound.

Everything looked normal—but deserted.

His senses prickled, not in the way they would if someone was watching, if someone was there, but in mounting alarm that where he'd expected to find people, there was, in fact, no one.

No one at all.

His ears strained. His eyes searched—for some hint, some clue.

There was nothing there—and nothing to explain the emptiness.

Something was wrong. Very wrong.

Carefully, cautiously, his senses flaring, he paced past the fire pit, then, placing his feet carefully, slowly climbed the steps to the porch of the main hut.

He halted before the door. And waited. Listening.

Nothing stirred.

He hauled in a breath, held it, and reached out, closed his hand about the latch, lifted it, and pushed the door wide...

He stared into the gloom. Even in the low light, it was apparent the place was empty. Swept clean and tidied.

His senses screamed that everything was far too neat.

He shifted, peering this way and that, then stepped to the threshold and looked further.

Everything about the hut that had been Kale's permanent barracks was as Undoto had expected—except it was empty. He could see no personal possessions; every surface was clear. Everywhere he looked was spick-and-span.

Abruptly, he stepped back onto the porch. He turned away from the still-open door and looked over the camp, this time more critically surveying the scene.

It was all too neat. Too clean. Too tidy.

No one lived there anymore.

No one lived.

He was off the porch and striding for the path leading back to the settlement before he'd done more than register that thought.

Beneath his breath, Undoto muttered a curse.

Whatever had happened to Kale, he was no longer at his homestead.

★ ★ ★

Undoto didn't slacken his pace until he was once again within the settlement. Surrounded by dwellings, by close-packed humanity. He drew a deeper breath and forced himself to calm. Yet no matter which way he considered the matter, something had gone very wrong with Kale's enterprise.

But that wasn't anything to do with him.

When the mysterious man called again, he would tell him what he'd seen. But there was nothing more he could do.

Nothing more he *would* do.

He was finished with this.

★ ★ ★

The following morning, Katherine settled in her usual place about the long table in the cleaning shed, picked up her favorite hammer and small chisel, selected a clump of ore from the basket in the middle of the table, and knuckled down to work.

She'd been the first one through the door. Gradually, the other five women filed in. They greeted each other with smiles and nods, but once the first flush of comments had been exchanged, they all focused on their task, and a comfortable silence fell.

Katherine steadily worked on a hand-sized clump of aggregate, yet even as she concentrated on chipping the mineral encrustations bit by bit off the underlying diamond, she was aware of a niggling impatience in her soul. Despite her wish to see Frobisher again—and she was in no way sure that she trusted that compulsion, that it wasn't a symptom of some silly infatuation or obsession of which she would later feel thoroughly ashamed—she was, she told herself, grateful for the reprieve.

She needed to work out some way to screen her interest in him—especially from him.

Aside from all else, now was not the time for any flirtation with romance.

Could any place be less suited to fostering gentle affection?

Yesterday, before she'd left ostensibly to pick nuts, she'd found herself mentally bemoaning the drabness of her gown and the lack of sufficient pins to properly style her hair.

Such idiotically missish thoughts had no place here. Not while they were stuck in this compound.

Here, survival had to be their only thought.

And not going out into the jungle every day was clearly the path of wisdom. She was confident she'd done nothing to alert Dubois to the presence of the group outside the palisade, but there was no need to tempt Fate by visiting too frequently.

Besides, Dixon, Hillsythe, and the other men were still working on the answers they wanted her to take back to Frobisher.

To Caleb.

She frowned as she turned the name over in her mind, silently hearing it, trying it on her tongue.

Then she realized and tried to shake the distraction away, but somehow, the name had got stuck in her mind. Stuck and attached to the feeling that enveloped her whenever she was with him, beside him, in his company.

Safety. Support. Protection.

A sense of being embraced by a type of care she'd never before experienced with any other man. A shield and sword freely offered.

If he'd been a knight in shining armor and she'd been some gentle maiden, she could imagine she might have felt this way.

She finished cleaning her first raw diamond of the day, set it aside, and reached for the next clump of ore.

She might try to hide how she felt, might try to argue that the feeling would go away, would fade as the exigencies of their situation came to bear on them both. Yet...

Somewhere inside, she had to own to a somewhat cynical thought that it truly was just like Fate to, after all these years, choose such fraught and difficult circumstances—with her a virtual slave in the impressed workforce of a mine in the darkest depths of an African jungle—to finally remember her existence and send love her way.

Lips setting, she positioned her chisel in a tiny crack in the rock—and struck the head sharply with her hammer.

★ ★ ★

Caleb lounged on the rock shelf high above the compound and moodily stared down at the guards in the tower. The sun was westering, bathing the compound in golden light, making it relatively easy to identify each guard. He, Phillipe, and their men had started taking note of those who were more alert, more likely to react effectively to any incursion, and those who were close to somnolent.

It was a small thing—a minor weakness—but given all they'd learned of Dubois and his command, it might well be the only weakness they and the rescue force had to exploit.

For Dubois was proving to be an unexpectedly canny and frighteningly competent leader of mercenaries. His experience showed in many ways, such as his refusal to leap to conclusions over Kale, that he had already had other ways of both getting to

Freetown and contacting people there independent of Kale, and his care in never stretching his resources—his men—too thin, even when, as far as he knew, the compound was not under any sort of threat.

Bad enough, but Dubois's method of managing people—through a mixture of intimidation and fear verging on terror, not for themselves but for others—marked him as being in a different class. A more dangerous enemy.

On multiple counts, Dubois was the sort of mercenary one didn't want to meet, much less have to defeat.

Caleb shifted restlessly. He'd always found inactivity difficult to bear, and in the past, he would have been off searching for ways to poke at Dubois, anything to move the action along. But in seizing this mission, he'd sworn himself to a different standard—to be the epitome of responsibility and eschew all recklessness.

Unfortunately, responsible boredom wasn't proving any more palatable than boredom usually was.

He sat straighter, stretched his back, then relaxed again. He refocused on the compound, on the figures moving purposefully about their business. And took a large mental step back— far enough to view the entire scheme, of which the compound was the beating heart, dispassionately.

A few minutes later, Phillipe scrambled onto the rock ledge. He let himself down beside Caleb and focused, as Caleb was, on the scene below. "Anything happening?"

"Nothing down there, but…it's just occurred to me. The backers—the mysterious men who wield the power of life and death over the captives." Caleb paused, ordering his thoughts, then went on, "Dubois used the term, and our friends in the compound picked it up. In his report, Hillsythe said that, based on Dubois's comments, he believes the backers are not those in the settlement but another group, located elsewhere."

Phillipe nodded. "As you said, given the cost involved in hiring a mercenary of Dubois's caliber along with his men, for an exercise like this"—he tipped his head toward the compound—"one that runs for months on end, then it's obvious these backers must have money. Dubois would have demanded a significant initial payment in cash, as well as ongoing payments."

"Exactly. And of those in the settlement we know to be involved—Muldoon, a naval attaché, a man called Winter obtaining mining supplies, Lady Holbrook, now departed, Undoto, a priest, and that still-mysterious man somewhere in Holbrook's office—not one is at all likely to have access to the necessary funds."

Phillipe stared down at the compound. "So what does that tell us?"

"I'm not sure," Caleb admitted, "but Hillsythe also wrote that the nature of the pressure being brought to bear on Dubois—demands that show no understanding of the difficulties of doing even simple things in a settlement and country like this—also suggests that the backers have no direct or personal knowledge of this region but, instead, are located far away." He shifted, drawing his legs up. "Now we know the mine is a diamond mine, then presumably the raw stones are being shipped to Amsterdam. And thence presumably to our backers—or more likely, they'll get the money raised when the cut and polished stones are sold."

"Which means the backers are most likely in Europe. And as Freetown is a British colony..."

"What odds the backers are English?" Caleb snorted. "Indeed." After several moments, he went on, "I'm trying to think of how we unmask the backers. And I note that everyone throughout has used the word in the plural, so let's assume we're trying to trace a group of wealthy—"

"And therefore very likely powerful and influential—"

"Englishmen." Caleb felt his features harden. "I can't believe they don't know what's being done here, that the enterprise they've paid to establish is using English men, women, and children as slave labor, and that when they—the backers—decide to close the mine, all those people will be killed."

Several seconds passed in silence, then Phillipe murmured, "It is often the case that the wealthy and powerful possess fewer morals than the common man. I have often observed it. But as wealthy and powerful as they must be, these backers will doubtless have covered their tracks—even following the trail of the diamonds and money back will almost certainly lead nowhere."

Phillipe paused, then went on, "For now, my friend, we need to remain focused on protecting the defenseless down there"—he nodded at the compound—"and to do all we can to facilitate their rescue. As for the backers…we will need to leave hunting them to others."

Caleb snorted. He didn't argue—couldn't argue. He did, however, mutter, "At least for now."

★ ★ ★

Muldoon was, as always, the last of the trio to set his tankard on the tavern table and sit down.

The instant he had, the first man stated, "I called on Undoto last night. He'd been to Kale's camp." In blunt, unadorned terms, the man repeated Undoto's description of what he had found at Kale's Homestead.

"No one?" Muldoon stared. "Where the devil have they all gone?"

The first man swallowed a draft of his ale, then set down his mug. "More pertinently, where is Kale, and what is he up to?"

"Up to?" Winton stared at the first man. "What do you mean—up to?"

The first man's face hardened. "I mean is he playing some game with us? Is he truly gone, or does he just want more money? Or has he actually decamped for some reason?"

"And if so," Muldoon said, "what was that reason, and is it something we should be concerned about, too?"

"Exactly." The first man looked at Muldoon. "I've heard and

seen nothing that would suggest any repercussions from Kale's crew's previous stumbles—the kidnapping of Frobisher's lady and the one you sent them to take—Miss Hopkins. Have you?"

Muldoon shook his head. "Nary a whisper. If something's happened to Kale—if someone has scared him off—then I can't see how it could have anything to do with his work for us." He paused, then added, "That might be it, you know. Kale worked for whoever paid him. Perhaps someone else offered him another job, in some other place, and he and his men have gone off to take it."

The first man grimaced. "Sadly, that's all too possible." After a moment of studying the table, he went on, "Regardless of whether he's gone off or been scared off, it appears Kale is no longer in our picture, which means we have no way of contacting Dubois short of one of us going all the way to the mine." He glanced at Winton, then looked back at Muldoon. "Something I suspect none of us want to do."

Muldoon snorted. "You have that right. However, Dubois knows who we are and where we are. I think we can be reasonably certain that he'll be in touch."

The first man nodded. "That's true, but while Dubois making contact with us will re-establish communication, the significantly more important issue is how we supply him with the men he needs to open up the second tunnel and, also, the mining supplies he'll continue to need."

Muldoon swore and set down his tankard with a thump. "This is all so frustrating! Dubois is desperate for more men, and at last we have more men ready to be picked up—but now Kale's vanished and not here to do the kidnapping and delivery."

"What's truly frustrating," the first man said, his words clipped, "is that without Dubois getting those extra men, he won't be able to open the second tunnel—not without moving men from the first tunnel and lowering overall production at precisely the time we've promised our backers that we'll *increase* production."

His expression grim, Muldoon nodded. "We're finally poised to meet our targets—and get our final payments from our damned backers—and out of the blue *this* happens."

A minute passed in tense silence, then Winton ventured, "We're not going to have to kidnap men ourselves, are we?"

The first man humphed. "I'm sure Dubois will agree to take on that task—for more cash. He refused to at the outset because Kale was better placed to carry out that side of things, and Dubois would rather not risk operating inside the settlement. But with the entire scheme now resting on him getting more men, I'm sure he'll see his way to overcoming his reluctance."

Muldoon snorted in cynical agreement. After a second, he added, "We'll have to pay Dubois more to send his men to fetch the mining supplies directly from Winton here, too." Muldoon spun his tankard between his hands. "I can't see any way around that."

"Not if we're to meet the demands of our infernal backers." The first man drained his mug and set it down with a disaffected *clunk*. "Which is to say, not if we want to see a penny more of the money they've promised us."

"At least the stones are still getting out," Winton said. "The backers can't complain about that."

Another silence fell, this one longer and weighted with welling unease.

Eventually, the first man said, "There's nothing we can do at this time. We'll need to wait for Dubois to contact us, and proceed from there."

"As best we can." Muldoon continued to stare at his tankard. After another fraught silence, he said, "I'd still like to know where Kale went and why."

The first man said nothing. Neither did Winton.

Yet uncertainty hovered over them all.

Eight

A flicker of unease stirred in Katherine's mind as she walked toward the gates, the basket she'd just fetched from the kitchen swinging from her hand.

Diccon had gone ahead. All had agreed that he should keep his distance from Frobisher's camp, at least for today, when Katherine herself was due to return and give Frobisher the answers to his questions.

In response to that vaguest of vague premonitions—the sort one felt over tempting Fate one step too far—as she neared the gates, she mentally cataloged all the guards she'd seen.

All were at their usual stations. Not one showed the slightest interest in her and her mission—supposedly to fetch more of Dubois's favorite nuts.

She passed through the gates and walked into the cool of the jungle's shadows—and told herself not to be silly. Nothing had occurred to alert Dubois to Frobisher and his men's existence. Instead, that spark of anxiety almost certainly sprang from her own concern over the man and his friends—her determination that they should not come to harm through their espousing of the captives' cause, and that nothing she or the other captives did should result in such harm.

Indeed, if she hadn't agreed to return with the answers Frobisher had wanted, she wouldn't have risked venturing out today—or at least, she wouldn't have ventured in his direction. Unfortunately, avoiding him today would contravene her "do nothing to cause him and his men harm" dictum; if having agreed to come, she didn't arrive, she wasn't at all sure he wouldn't grow concerned on her account and do something rash. Like coming too close to the compound looking for her and getting captured.

Her feet followed the path to his camp without conscious instruction. As she walked through the prevailing gloom, she rehearsed the answers she'd come to convey. First, that if there was no further change other than more mining supplies eventually arriving, and specifically, no more men were added to their impressed workforce, then based on what Dixon had seen of the second deposit, he was confident that they would be able to stretch the productive life of the mine into September. As for Frobisher and his men doing anything directly to assist the captives, she'd been relieved when all the men, and Harriet, too, had reacted very much as she herself had; they'd all agreed there was no assistance Frobisher and his crew might render them that would be worth the risk of alerting Dubois to their presence.

She smiled and took the fork onto the disused path. Frobisher and his men simply being there had raised the confidence of all the captives and bolstered their inner strength—their determination to hold on until the rescue force arrived and to aid in their own liberation.

In a situation such as they, the captives, were in, hope wasn't an insubstantial thing.

★ ★ ★

Caleb and Phillipe made their way as quickly as they dared down the animal track and on toward their camp. They'd spent the morning lolling on the rock shelf, observing the routines of the guards and the captives, confirming that, day to day, very little in the compound changed.

They'd seen Diccon leave as he usually did, but no slender brown-haired young woman had walked out with him.

Caleb had frowned and sent Ellis to rendezvous with Diccon and learn whether Miss Fortescue was intending to meet with them that day. As it transpired, Diccon had headed for the area near the lake, so Ellis had been back in fifteen minutes with the news that it had been decided that Miss Fortescue would come out later, separately, to their camp, and that Diccon should keep his distance.

"A wise precaution," Phillipe had opined. "No sense in risking both couriers at once."

Caleb had nodded and continued watching.

Ten minutes ago, they'd seen Katherine Fortescue come out of the cleaning shed. Unhurriedly, she'd rounded the base of the guard tower and the end of the mercenaries' barracks and had gone into the kitchen.

Caleb had scanned all the guards in sight, but none had shown any signs of especial alertness.

Katherine had ducked out from under the kitchen's awning and, apparently carefree, had walked to the gates.

Caleb, Phillipe, Ellis, and Norton had continued to watch, searching for any suggestion of pursuit, but of course, there had been none. Not one of the guards had done more than yawn.

Eager to get down to meet with Katherine, who had, indeed, walked off in the direction of their camp, Caleb had tweaked Phillipe's sleeve. They'd left Ellis and Norton on watch and headed down.

Caleb finally reached the flatter going of the jungle floor. Grinning in anticipation, not least of seeing the lovely Katherine again, he tacked through the palms on a more or less direct route to the camp.

★ ★ ★

Katherine kept her ears peeled as, her pace deliberately unhurried, she neared the side track to Frobisher's camp; she half expected him and his friend Lascelle to appear out of the jungle to greet her. She'd stopped at a tree along the disused path to gather nuts, just in case any guards had thought to follow her, but she'd seen no one. Eventually, she'd picked up her basket and walked on.

Regardless of her concerns—or perhaps because of them—she wanted to see Caleb again. Just seeing him would be enough; she just needed to know he was safe.

She halted at the mouth of the narrow track and glanced back the way she'd come. All lay silent and unmoving in the jungle dimness. Reassured, she started down the track. Even if Caleb and Lascelle weren't as yet in the camp, some of their men would be. She could wait with them.

The narrow track wended this way and that, as all tracks through the jungle did. Eventually, it led over a lip and dipped via a series of natural steps formed by the gnarled roots of trees down to the floor of the clearing.

She reached the lip and started down the more densely shadowed tunnel enclosing the steps. As she neared the bottom, she heard the tramp of footsteps approaching the clearing from the opposite side.

She stepped off the last root-step and into the clearing proper—just as Frobisher, with Lascelle at his shoulder, stepped into the clearing.

She smiled and knew the gesture was too bright, too brilliant—too revealing.

Frobisher met her eyes, saw her smile. His expression started to lift, to light in response—but then his features froze.

He froze.

Lascelle did, too.

She glanced around and saw that every man in the clearing had frozen, some even in the act of rising.

"Thank you, Miss Fortescue."

The words—*that voice!*—sent ice streaking down her spine.

Before she could react—before she could whirl and face the monster behind her—an arm like steel clamped around her waist and jerked her back against a body like rock.

Her nerves shrieked.

Her stunned gaze fell on the tip of a dagger that suddenly appeared pressed against her right breast. Her scrambling wits informed her—screamed at her—that Dubois was holding the wicked-looking blade in the hand above her waist. That he'd followed her—somehow—and she hadn't known. Caleb hadn't known.

And now the monster had her...

Even as her panicking mind caught up with that reality, Dubois raised his other arm—his right—and leveled the pistol he held at Caleb's chest. The sound of the pistol cocking rang through the clearing.

Thudding footsteps came racing toward the clearing, approaching along the same path as Caleb and Lascelle had arrived on.

Two men burst into the clearing—running into Lascelle and pushing him and Caleb forward.

"Dubois and his men—" The breathless warning cut off as the newcomers realized they were too late. Panting, they slowly righted themselves, their gazes fixing, like those of every other man in the clearing, on Dubois.

For one hysterical moment, Katherine felt as if she'd become invisible—then she realized the action was deliberate. Every man in the clearing did not want Dubois's attention on her.

She could have told them that was a vain hope.

Sure enough, Dubois stated, in that tone of voice she'd long ago learned to hate, "Let me tell you what is going to happen. If you give me and my men the slightest trouble—show the faintest hint of resistance—I will slice Miss Fortescue's so-lovely face."

He shifted his hold, and the dagger flashed—a whisker from her cheek.

She squeaked in sheer terror and instinctively pushed back, but with Dubois behind her, his shoulder against her head, she didn't gain so much as an inch of distance from the silvery blade.

Her heartbeat thudded in her ears. Her breathing came in shallow pants. Every iota of her awareness had focused on the dagger's blade—on the horrible promise it made.

Dimly, as if from a distance, Dubois's hateful voice penetrated the fog of panic shrouding her brain. "Once—one deep, scarring cut for every little instance of resistance on your part. Just think of how she will look if you try to fight. And if you try to escape, I make you this promise: Once we have you captured again— and we will succeed in that—I will tie you up and tie her to a post, and inch by inch, I will strip the skin from her body—"

"Enough!" Caleb held up a hand in surrender. He met Dubois's pale eyes. "You've made your point. What do you want us to do?"

For an instant, a depraved soul stared back at him—a monster denied his next feeding—but then Dubois blinked, and the pragmatic mercenary captain was back.

"Disarm. Every last weapon. Every last blade. Any weapon discovered later will earn Miss Fortescue a cut—on her breasts."

Caleb clamped his jaw shut. Slowly, he withdrew his sword and crouched to lay it on the ground before him. He stripped the knives from his belt and pulled out those hidden in his boots. As he did, his mind raced—assessing, sorting through his options, searching for the best way forward.

This was what he was good at—what he was renowned for. Conquering the unexpected, especially when the unexpected appeared to be invincible.

The problem, his reckless brain informed him, was that in this case, he needed Dubois to continue to believe that he—Dubois—*was* invincible.

With an inward sigh, Caleb straightened. He glanced around at his and Phillipe's men. "Every weapon as instructed."

He didn't think any of them would be fool enough to attempt to conceal anything, but Dubois might appreciate hearing Caleb's capitulation repeated. Giving the man everything his warped heart might wish for was, at present, Caleb's best way forward.

Aside from Dubois, Caleb counted at least six mercenaries with muskets trained on him and his men. Two stood on the track above Dubois, their guns leveled over his shoulders. The others had fanned outward, forming an arc of firepower to back up Dubois's threats.

To Caleb's mind, Dubois and his internal monster needed no support.

When the last blade had fallen to the scattered leaves covering the clearing's floor, Dubois jerked his head at one of his men.

The man set aside his musket and walked into the clearing. He swiped up a loose canvas sheet, laid it down, and quickly collected all the weapons, efficiently checking the pistols to ensure they were unprimed before tossing them onto the heap, too. Finally, he gathered the edges of the sheet, creating a clattering bundle he then hoisted over his shoulder.

Dubois said, "Take those back to the armory."

The man grunted and set off, cutting through the jungle rather than interfering with Dubois's or the other mercenaries' lines of sight.

That still left far too many men—far too many muskets—to consider any action, even if Caleb managed to separate Dubois from Katherine. Besides, his reckless and whirring brain informed him, joining the captives might actually prove the wiser long-term course.

Before he had a chance to examine that unanticipated thought, Dubois refocused his pale gaze on him.

"Is this all of your men?"

"Yes."

Dubois held his gaze for a long moment, eyes narrowing as if by staring he might detect a lie.

He couldn't, of course; Caleb had spoken the truth. This was all of his men in this area.

Sadly, Dubois wasn't convinced. "If I discover you've lied to me, I will force you all to watch as my men take turns in raping Miss Fortescue, and then I'll take my knife to her..." He paused, no doubt for effect. "Have you ever seen anyone flayed alive?"

Caleb clenched his jaw. Hearing the threat was bad enough, but the way Dubois delivered it, with a sort of chilling eagerness as if some part of him was relishing the prospect, made the conjured vision utterly vile. Without inflection, Caleb reiterated, "These are all the men I have in this jungle."

Dubois waited for a heartbeat, then calmly asked, "Where did you come from, and what brought you here?"

Excellent questions to which Caleb had answers prepared. But he knew better than to just trot them out. Instead, he thought of Royd and attempted to look haughtily uncommunicative.

He knew he was clearly marked as the leader of this band—the one all the other men would take their cues from. He wasn't the heaviest or largest man of their company, but he was the tallest bar Phillipe and, at least to most people's eyes, appeared the most physically powerful and therefore the most dangerous.

That was deceptive, because Phillipe was infinitely more dangerous.

But Caleb hadn't had to exchange so much as a glance with his friend for Phillipe to stay in a secondary role; they'd played this "sleight of man" more times than either could count and knew the value of concealing Phillipe's true talents.

So Caleb kept his lips firmly shut, kept his gaze—not precisely challengingly but levelly—fixed on Dubois, and waited for the man to respond. He'd already concluded that, as Dubois desperately needed strong men for the mine, he wouldn't kill any of them—not unless they gave him sound reasons to do so, which they wouldn't. Caleb was already looking forward to joining the others in the compound.

He wasn't looking forward to what he knew would come next, but consoled himself with the truth—it was necessary. Dubois would never be comfortable having Caleb in the compound if he hadn't had a chance to establish his authority. It was better to get that little ritual out of the way here. Phillipe and their men would know what he was doing. Katherine wouldn't, and he was sorry for that, but he could explain and apologize later.

Once they were both back in the compound and free to associate.

His reckless side thought that a fitting reward for him taking this tack.

Sure enough, when he continued to keep mum, Dubois gave a soft—rather pleased—grunt. He removed the dagger from Katherine's breast, grasped her arm, and shoved her at the mercenary who had descended to stand at his shoulder.

"Hold her." Without taking his gaze from Caleb, Dubois handed over the dagger as well.

Once his man had taken the blade, Dubois stepped into the clearing and walked, slowly, toward Caleb.

Caleb watched him come.

Dubois halted before him, not quite a yard away. He was shorter than Caleb by several inches, but more powerfully built.

Dubois transferred his pistol to his left hand—then in an explosion of movement, he viciously backhanded Caleb across the face.

Caleb had seen the blow coming; he had to fight not to duck. He did turn his head at the last moment, avoiding the worst of the force behind the blow. But Dubois wore a heavy ring; it tore across Caleb's right cheek.

Katherine cried out.

As he righted his head, Caleb caught a fleeting glimpse of her, white-faced and struggling futilely against the mercenary's hold—and told himself not to wink.

Then Dubois plowed a fist like a rock into Caleb's gut, then stepped to the side and slammed his linked fists across Caleb's nape, all but felling him and driving him to his knees.

Head hanging, Caleb gasped. He let himself fall forward, but caught himself on his braced left arm; his right arm was clutched—not entirely for effect—across his bruised stomach. He felt ridiculously proud of himself. Chanting "responsibility" in his head had worked—had stopped him giving in to instinct, blocking the blows, and striking back.

He was the youngest of four brothers; the one thing the other three—and their friends and his—had taught him was how to fight, especially hard scrabble, outside the rules. They had also—unintentionally—taught him how to fake injury and weakness; there was some benefit in being the youngest, and he'd been quick to claim it.

Every one of his men would by now have guessed his tack, even if they might not understand his reasoning. Phillipe had jerked, once, but then had grown deathly still, holding against the instinct to intervene. Or retaliate.

From the corner of his eye, Caleb watched Dubois's heavy boots move as the mercenary—who walked surprisingly lightly on his feet—circled him, watching for any sign of him fighting back.

When Caleb made no such move but continued to labor to breathe, Dubois halted on Caleb's right, locked his fingers in Caleb's hair, and hauled Caleb's head up.

Dubois's gaze bored into his eyes. "I'll ask again. Where did you come from?"

Caleb let the air saw as he drew it in and came upright on his knees to ease the tension on his scalp. "The coast north of here. We were put off a ship—a merchantman—in Freetown. We hired a fishing boat and followed the estuary shore east, just to see what we could find." He paused to artistically draw a deeper breath, then went on, "There's a native village north of here. They told us about a slavers' camp hidden away up here, so we thought we'd come and take a look—see if there was anything worth plundering." A doctored version of the truth.

He shifted his gaze to Katherine; the rest of their invented tale was a calculated risk. "We came across her two days ago. She said she needed to talk to others, but there might be money in it for us if we took a message to the settlement for her." He gave a slight shrug, "No skin off our noses to see what she came up with—we saw your defenses, and we weren't about to mount any noble rescue."

Dubois chuckled, a chilling sound. He released Caleb's hair. "What was the name of the ship you left in Freetown?"

Caleb opened his mouth to answer—

"Not you." Dubois's gaze shifted to Phillipe. "You."

Phillipe didn't hesitate. *The Aberdeen Rose.*

"And what class of ship was she?" Dubois swung around and pointed at Quilley.

"Three-masted freighter."

"And how many oars were there in this fishing boat you hired?" Dubois jabbed a finger at Norton.

"No oars. Single mast and a jib."

Thank heaven they'd rehearsed their tale. That Dubois was smart enough to check their veracity by asking them all for different details…again, Caleb reminded himself of just how canny the man was, how dangerous to underestimate.

Dubois even thought to ask Ellis, "How much did the fishing boat cost to hire?"

Ellis blinked, then looked at Caleb. "I don't know. It was the capt'n who arranged it."

Which, of course, was the correct—and convincing—answer.

Dubois turned away and ordered two of his men to search the packs and seabags for any stray weapons, money, and powder. Also any documents; Caleb shared a quick glance with Phillipe and knew a moment of abject relief that, after much debate, he'd tucked Robert's diary into the satchel he'd dispatched to London.

No forgotten weapons were discovered.

Finally satisfied, Dubois looked down at Caleb, then kicked his nearest shin. "Get to your feet."

With becoming slowness, as if every joint hurt, Caleb did. Phillipe grasped his elbow and helped him up.

More or less upright, but hunching so his eyes were lower than Dubois's, Caleb looked hesitantly at the mercenary captain. "Now what?"

Dubois's smile was that of a delighted jackal. "Fate, my friend, has clearly smiled upon me. You and your men are the answer to my prayers—you are precisely what I need to deliver on my contract."

Nine

Katherine stumbled along, her arm in Arsene's unbreakable grip. She couldn't think—could still not get her wits to function. The sensation of helpless witlessness, of her awareness being somehow adrift, felt the same as when she'd first found herself in Kale's clutches.

The compound's gates loomed ahead. She and Arsene were in the lead. Caleb's men followed, two by two, carrying their packs and seabags, with the mercenaries, muskets still in their hands, flanking the column.

Caleb and Lascelle walked at the rear of their men, with Dubois trailing behind—no doubt gloating.

She hadn't had a single clue that he'd followed her, not until he'd spoken.

Had he followed her?

Or had he already been in the jungle when she'd left the compound? She hadn't seen him that morning, but that wasn't unusual. Now she thought of it, Dubois had enough men in the compound for the group with him to have been in the jungle since daybreak; if they'd left before it was light, none of the captives would have known.

But why had Dubois thought to follow her? What had she done that had made him so suspicious?

They passed through the open gates. The guards on either side grinned widely, called greetings to their fellows, and made various ribald comments about the new captives.

Just inside the compound, Arsene jerked her to a halt by one of the gateposts. The heavyset mercenary held her securely, close beside him, and still openly brandished Dubois's long dagger. Arsene called orders to the mercenaries to march the captured men to the fire pit and have them sit.

Several of the men glanced at Katherine as they passed; to her surprise, rather than glaring or staring sullenly at her, most sent faint smiles—clearly meant to be reassuring—her way.

There she stood, wracked by guilt over having led Dubois to them…and they smiled at her?

Still stunned, still unable to think clearly, she raised her gaze and looked beyond Caleb's men—at her fellow captives. Many had heard the unexpected tramp of feet. The children had slowed in their busy backing and forthing and then stopped to watch. Several of the women had come out of the cleaning shed and around the barracks to see. Some children with their wits about them had darted into the mine and spread the word, and men were starting to gather at the entrance to the mine; Katherine saw Dixon, then Hillsythe and Hopkins, appear and join them.

The look on everyone's face was closed. Katherine might not yet be able to think, but she could still feel. Despite the universally impassive expressions—showing no hint that their owners had known Caleb's men were nearby—she could feel the deflation, the puncturing of their newly acquired hope.

The deadening sensation settled in her gut, then spread, insidiously dragging her emotions down. To have regained hope, only to have it snatched away…

No. We mustn't think like that.

If they did, they'd die, here, in this hellhole. They couldn't give up, not now, not ever.

She dragged in a deeper breath, straightened her spine, and lifted her head.

Harriet, standing across the yard by the corner of the barracks, her arms crossed over her waist with her hands clutching her elbows, hunched as if trying to protect herself against a blow, saw.

A second passed, then Harriet straightened; she released her elbows, lowered her hands, and stood tall, too.

The change was subtle, but person by person, it rippled through the watching crowd, and the atmosphere transmuted into one of silent yet steadfast cohesion and support.

Everyone waited to see what happened next.

Caleb's fifteen men had finally trudged past, steered by the flanking mercenaries toward the fire pit. Caleb himself, his cheek marred by the long gash Dubois had inflicted and moving with less than his customary grace, walked past, Lascelle at his elbow. Fleetingly, Caleb met her gaze; she stiffened, steeling herself to bear his condemnation…instead, that brief glance seemed… *apologetic?*

She blinked. Obviously, her wits had yet to regain their customary facility.

Dubois halted beside Arsene; he watched Caleb and company move into the compound with transparent satisfaction. "Seventeen strong men accustomed to hard labor." Dubois turned and looked her in the eye. "How can I possibly punish you, Miss Fortescue, when you have single-handedly accomplished what Kale and so many others have signally failed to do and given me the men I need to accomplish my task here?"

Oh, yes. Dubois was gloating. She retained enough sense to keep her lips firmly shut and evince no reaction.

Dubois studied her face, then smiled. He looked back at the men about the fire pit. "I wonder how our new recruits, and even more, perhaps, those already here, will view you being the instrument of my salvation." Dubois's cold smile widened. "It will be amusing to see."

He surveyed the scene for a moment more, then said, "Meanwhile"—he nodded at Arsene to release her—"if you please, Miss Fortescue, come with me."

He set off for the fire pit. She dallied as long as she dared; she handed her basket to Arsene, settled her gown, shook out her skirts, then followed. She knew what Dubois had intended—having her trail at his heels like his lapdog as he approached his new captives. Those were the little games he played, but along with the others, she did her best to deny him—or at least thrust a spoke into his wheel.

Caleb's crew was now sitting in a partial circle about the fire pit.

Dubois halted at the edge of the circle of logs, taking up a position behind Caleb—a position that underscored his control, wordlessly declaring that Caleb was now under his command, his inferior.

As she stopped two paces from Dubois, she saw Caleb's shoulders tense, but he didn't twist around to look up at Dubois. The other men glanced at Caleb, then lifted their gazes to Dubois.

Coldly, dispassionately, Dubois surveyed them, then stated, "You are here to work, to assist in our mining operation." Imperiously, he beckoned Dixon forward. "Captain Dixon will see you settled into your new accommodations." He looked at Dixon. "There's space aplenty, I believe."

His features tight, Dixon nodded.

"Excellent." Clasping his hands behind his back, Dubois spoke, ostensibly to the newcomers, but in reality reinforcing his edicts more generally. "You will start work tomorrow morning alongside your compatriots. During the rest of today, Captain Dixon will assign you to the appropriate teams. I suggest you use the time to familiarize yourself with the work you will be expected to perform and with the camp's routines. For myself, I demand but one thing of you—that you work hard, consistently, and perform the tasks allotted to you to the best of your ability. I care for nothing else—and as those already here will attest, I am prepared to allow a great deal of leniency just as long as you meet my requirements."

He paused, then, his voice subtly altering, menace sliding beneath his smooth tones, stated, "You have already heard what I will do should anyone cross me, and I'm sure those already here will confirm that I am a man of my word. Unless you wish to have such an outcome on your conscience, I would advise you to take my, and their, warnings to heart."

Dubois allowed several seconds to pass in silence, giving his words—his threats—time to sink in and take hold, then he glanced down at Caleb, then turned to Katherine. "Miss Fortescue, as a measure of my welcome, perhaps you would take the gallant captain to the medical hut and tend his wound."

Caleb finally swiveled on the log to look up at Dubois, then at her. A coldly calculating expression on his face, Dubois smiled at Caleb, then stepped back and waved in invitation. "We wouldn't want infection to set in. I need you hale enough to work, and it's not really possible to amputate a cheek."

His expression entirely unresponsive, Caleb returned Dubois's gaze for an instant, then he smoothly shifted and got to his feet. Reminding himself of what he shouldn't know, he switched his gaze to Katherine; she was, he was pleased to see, holding up well. "Which way?"

She glanced once at Dubois, then gestured past the central barracks. "Over there." She moved to walk around the circle.

Caleb stepped over the log on which he'd been sitting and, ignoring Dubois, in three long strides, reached her side. Behind him, he heard Dubois instruct Phillipe and their men to go with Dixon. Thus far, all was proceeding smoothly; they were inside the compound, and no one had got hurt. Well, except for him, and a cut cheek, bruised stomach, and sore neck were hardly anything to moan about. He met Katherine's eyes. They were close enough for him to risk a quick, reassuring smile. "Lead on."

She saw the smile; a puzzled look filled her eyes, but she faced forward and kept walking.

His expression once more impassive, he matched his pace to hers and glanced around, taking in the relative distance between the buildings, their elevations off the ground, and other minor but potentially useful details, marrying his previous view from the rock shelf above with his new perspective.

He studied the large, central barracks into which the mercenary carting their weapons had lugged them. Presumably, Dubois's armory was—wisely—located close to his and his men's beds.

Katherine led him around the cleaning shed to the medical hut—a large single hut located to the rear of the compound below the face of the hill that contained the rock shelf; other than the hut's roof and a sharply angled view of the left wall, they hadn't been able to see much of the structure from their lookout. Like all the other huts in the compound, the walls were built of roughly hewn planks, with a roof of thatched palms supported by a framework of beams fashioned from the boles of large palms and trees. The façade proved to be wide, with a decent-sized window on either side of the door, which had a set of three wooden steps leading up to it; in common with the other huts, the medical hut was raised several feet above the ground.

After directing a single, faintly frowning glance at him, Katherine led the way up the steps, opened the door, and went inside.

Caleb followed, scanning the area within before pulling the door shut behind him. It was dim and cooler inside. The narrow central hallway ended in a door. Two other doors opened into the rooms on either side.

Katherine had paused in the doorway to the right. She pointed at the door at the end of the hall. "That's the storeroom, and"—she indicated the door opposite and the room into which she intended to go—"we have two treatment rooms." She walked into the room.

Caleb trailed behind her, looking around. "I didn't see any guards about."

"There aren't any. They rarely come this way."

He glanced back toward the main door. "Will any follow us? Perhaps wait outside, close enough to hear what we say?"

As she walked across the room, she shook her head. "The lack of close guarding is part of Dubois's strategy to impress on us how insignificant any plotting we might do will be." She glanced back. "And to this point, he's been correct. He allows us to talk and plot freely, but he knows nothing will come of it—beyond our own disappointment, of course."

"Hmm. A man of strange but seemingly effective ways." He halted just inside the room. Taking in the amenities, he let out a low whistle. "You'd be lucky to find this level of medical care in Freetown."

She'd crossed to a cabinet against the wall beside a plain examination table. She gave an inelegant snort. "It's just another example of Dubois's little games. He accommodates us—sometimes to remarkable levels, as he has here—in matters that either don't impinge on his goal or, as is the case here, that actively support said goal. He wants us all hale and hearty and able to work at full capacity, so he gives us *this*." She gestured at the many well-stocked cabinets and the comfortable-looking netted bed. "So we can't complain, but there's always a point to Dubois's generosity."

"I'll bear that in mind." He continued toward her. "I can understand his tack, but it's hardly the usual one a mercenary captain takes."

She was opening drawers and pulling out ointment, gauze, and swabs, and tossing everything on the table. "You'll find plenty of instances of Dubois's strange ways as you go about the compound."

He halted two feet away.

She laid her hands on the table. He saw her chest rise as she drew in a deep breath, then she swung to face him. Her eyes locked with his. "I am so terribly sorry you and your men were captured. I can't imagine what you and the others think of me, and I cannot apologize enough."

He studied her face. "You didn't tell Dubois we were out

there." He made the words a statement; he couldn't imagine that wasn't the truth.

Her eyes flared. "Of course not! I would *never* have betrayed you in such a fashion."

"Well, then. All's well."

"No, it isn't!" She stared at him uncomprehendingly. "I'm to blame for all of you being captured. That's a dreadful thing to have to say, and…" She gestured. "I'm sorry."

He compressed his lips, regarded her for a moment, then offered, "If it makes you feel any better, if any blame is to be apportioned, then we ourselves should shoulder some of it. We were watching the compound from a rock shelf up on the hill." With a tip of his head, he indicated the rise of the hill behind the hut. "But we didn't catch any hint of Dubois and his men leaving the compound to follow you. My men only caught a glimpse as they fell in behind you, shadowing you as you went down the northbound track. They—Dubois and his men—must have left the compound in the early hours, before our watch commenced."

She stared at him for several seconds, then said, "That doesn't really excuse me—I must have done something to alert him." She paused, then, her gaze steady on his face, on his eyes, her twisting fingers locking together at her waist, she said, "I don't want you or your men to believe that I had any active hand in your capture, and I need to apologize—*profusely*—because it must have been something I inadvertently said or did that brought Dubois down on your heads."

She was so earnest, her expression so open, her eyes so lovely, her gaze so beseeching in the low light.

Caleb finally let his expression relax, let his smile fully surface; she'd said they were alone, that there were no guards to overhear. "Don't fret. None of us think any the worse of you." He tilted his head and kept his tone reassuring. "Dubois has obviously got strong, well-honed instincts. He guessed. You can't stop a man like him from picking up on tiny little things, putting them all together, and then guessing."

She considered him uncertainly, then caught her lower lip between her teeth.

Sheer lust shot through him—he wanted to tug that lush lip free with his teeth. He shifted, swinging around and leaning back against the table's edge, slouching enough to bring his face closer to level with hers, and wrestled his wits into line. "Truly, I mean that. You need to shrug this off—to stop feeling guilty"—and from the responsive spark in her hazel eyes, guilt was what she truly felt—"because it's unnecessary, and"—inspiration struck—"giving in to it will mean Dubois wins." He fixed his gaze on her eyes. "We don't want Dubois to win, do we?"

She regarded him levelly for several seconds, then softly said, "Why do I get the feeling I'm being…led?"

He grinned, honestly delighted. "Because when it comes to manipulating people, Dubois could take lessons from me. Trust me—I grew up in a large family, and I'm the youngest. In such circumstances, being able to manipulate others is a necessary survival skill."

She nearly choked on the laugh she tried to suppress. She attempted a frown, but it was a dreadfully weak effort. "Are you always this…irrepressible?"

He smiled happily. "More or less." Then he blinked and sobered. "But right now, we need to concentrate." Because if they didn't, his baser self would be only too happy to take charge of this conversation and try to seduce her. She was so much more potent a magnet for his senses at close quarters and in private. He dredged up a serious look. "I didn't pick up any telltale signs, but do you think Dubois guessed that all of you in the compound knew we were out there?"

"Your story made it sound as if I would have spoken with others, but I might not have." She turned back to the supplies she'd assembled and started laying them out neatly on the table.

"Regardless, given the way Dubois's mind works, that point is most likely moot. He's captured you and solved his big problem in one fell swoop, and marching you all in like that also allowed him to paint himself as even more omnipotent in the eyes of those already here. I'm quite sure he's now celebrating. With any luck—and if experience is any guide—he'll focus on that and not worry overmuch about the circumstances of your being out there in the first place."

"Good."

Valiantly ignoring the slavering of her senses, witless things, Kate—no, she was Katherine these days—reached beneath the table and pulled out a stool. She set it between them and tapped the seat. "If you'll sit down, I'll clean up that cut and then see what we can do for your other injuries."

He obligingly sat, his long legs bent, his thighs splayed to either side.

To reach his face, she had to step between those long, lean, powerful thighs. All but holding her breath, she tried to block the impact of his shoulders and well-muscled chest—and all the rest of him—from her mind as she edged still closer and dabbed the long gash with a cloth wetted with a prepared herbal tincture. At least using the cloth, her bare fingers didn't touch his skin.

He hissed in a breath, but clamped down on the impulse to pull away from her touch.

"I'm sorry—it stings. But we've learned to use this for cuts in this climate. It's so easy to get an infection."

He made a hmming, noncommittal sound and then remained silent, allowing her to doctor his face.

The silence, the lack of other distraction, allowed her mind, her senses, to wander....

Which was really not a good thing.

She frowned slightly, then turned to set aside the wash solution and damp cloth, now pink with his blood. She picked up another cloth and turned to dab the long gash dry. And tried not to focus on the thick fringe of his long, sooty lashes. Tried not to notice the strong patrician curve of his nose and the intriguingly mobile, inherently flirty line of his lips…

She set her teeth and stated, "I can't see how there can be anything good in this situation." She set down the cloth and picked up the pot of ointment. "You and your men have been stripped of your weapons, and you're now captives with the rest of us, forced to work in the mine…how can any of that be good?"

She looked at his face in time to see those distracting lips curve.

"Because now we're on the inside of the palisade and can actively help everyone here."

Gently, she dabbed ointment along the cut. Her fingertips tingled. Ignoring the unsettling sensation, she silently prayed he wouldn't scar; on a face like his, that would be a crime against womankind.

Unaware of the direction of her wayward thoughts—thank heaven!—he went on, "That was one of the problems I could foresee over attacking the compound once the rescue force gets here. There are too many mercenaries and not enough able-bodied men *inside* the palisade. Now the odds are much better. We've just succeeded in adding seventeen experienced fighters to our forces within the compound, and all without tipping our hand to Dubois."

His lips lifted in a grin.

Satisfied with her ministrations to his face, she turned to set the ointment down.

"Of course, Dubois doesn't know that we're anything more than itinerant, opportunistic merchant-sailors. That's why I had to let him hit me."

She blinked. Slowly, she turned to stare at him. "You *let* him hit you?"

"Of course." He looked faintly offended that she'd thought anything else. When she continued to stare uncomprehendingly, he consented to explain. "Dubois is slow. He's powerful, but—at least compared to me or Phillipe—he's slow. It's a long time since he's been on any training ground, so he doesn't recognize that he is, but I saw each blow coming and had plenty of time to react. If circumstances had been different, I would have had some fun, then ultimately knocked him out. But I had to let him hit me instead, so that he felt he'd established his position as top dog, so to speak. He could tell that I was the one in charge—the captain—so it was me he had to put down. Now he thinks I'm slow, and because I am the leader of our group, he'll assume all the others are even more so. That's the way a mercenary's mind works in measuring his opposition."

He looked at her as if his reasoning was perfectly transparent. He'd been able to avoid the blows, but instead, he'd taken the beating in order to get him and his men safely into the compound.

And he'd thought of all that on the spur of the moment.

She opened her mouth and managed an "Oh."

His insouciant grin bloomed again. "So, you see, all is, indeed, well."

She had to shake her head at him. "I cannot believe you're so…indefatigably *cheery* about this. When I brought you in here, I expected you to be, if not furious, then at least angry—at least *grumpy*."

His grin deepened. "That's me. Indefatigably cheery."

"Be serious." She could barely believe she was having this conversation. She found herself calling on her governessy voice. "Why are you accepting this so readily? Don't tell me you had this all planned out—an option ready to put into place on the off-chance Dubois came upon you."

He paused, then, sobering, said, "Seriously, then… I see men like Dubois—and situations like this—as a challenge. Something I can pit my wits against." He shifted on the stool, as if the effort of being serious didn't come easily. "Worthy opponents, even.

Or at least, worthy targets. The man certainly needs to be removed from this earth."

"There's nothing worthy about Dubois, but bringing him and this enterprise down would certainly rate as exceptionally worthy."

"So if we're talking of good deeds and worthy actions, then all the steps that lead to success…"

She had to smile; how could she not? Again, she shook her head at him—this time in wonder. "How can you just…rationalize it all away? Just shrug aside the difficulties, reset your direction, and plow on with barely a pause?"

He shrugged. "I just can. What can I say? It's an innate talent." He met her eyes, and although his were clear, she got the distinct impression that he, the man he was, had at least two personas— the irrepressible adventurer he so often outwardly seemed, and the man of significantly deeper thoughts of whom she'd thus far caught only glimpses. Both were real, both genuine facets of his character, but he flipped from one to the other, using the former as a shield to deflect attention from the depths of the latter.

Before she could see—grasp—more, he blinked, and the moment was gone.

"We need to keep focused on the end game here," he stated, "and not get tangled up in minor issues along the way."

Truer words… She scanned all she could see of him. "You don't have any other cuts, do you?"

"No." He gently palpated the right side of his jaw, then somewhat tenderly massaged his lower ribs. "But if you have something to ease bruises, I wouldn't say no."

She nodded and told herself she could handle this. "He hit you on the back, too. Best take off your shirt." *And let me look.* She swallowed the words and turned to search the cabinet for the bruise ointment.

When, pot in hand, she turned back, she couldn't stop her eyes from widening, then she lowered her lashes and paid attention to loosening the lid of the pot. Finally mustering enough courage, she drew in a breath, held it, and, with the browny cream on her fingers, allowed herself to look—at the finely sculpted abdomen now revealed to her gaze.

The only factor that saved her from staring in utter fascination was the discoloration marring the muscled expanse. She focused on that and swiped the cream delicately across his skin. It flickered—was he ticklish? Again, her fingertips tingled; she applied more pressure, smoothing the cream over the bruise, then gently rubbed the ointment into his skin.

Caleb set his already aching jaw and directed his gaze upward and across the room—anywhere but at the delectable female ministering so seriously and carefully to his hurts. When she drew back to swipe more ointment onto her fingers, he surreptitiously shifted on the stool. Why had he thought this a good idea? It was tantamount to torture. But he'd had no notion his attraction to her would be anything like this strong. Yes, he was interested in her, in the way any man with eyes would be interested in such an appealing and pretty female, but this? It felt more like some sort of ravenous hunger than anything so mild as interest.

He tried to think of things powerful enough to haul his mind, his senses, away from the circular motion of her fingertips over his skin, the pressure reaching to the muscle beneath—and much further. Things like his mother. Or his aunt Gertrude.

Then she finished and stepped back, taking her touch with her—and suddenly he wanted it back.

Before he could embarrass himself by saying so, she circled him. She halted at his back. "This bruise is even worse."

She started to smooth on the ointment, then she rubbed it in. He closed his eyes; it was an effort to hold his head upright and not drop it back—he hadn't realized how tense the muscles between his shoulders had been, not until she set about her gentle massage…he bit back a groan. He closed his fingers about the front edge of the stool and endured. And fought not to growl with pleasure.

The moment was a small slice of unexpected bliss in what had turned into a day of disruption and having to walk with care. Until he and his men were firmly established in Dubois's mind as just part of the company Dubois had successfully held captive for so long, they would need to tread warily.

After ministering to his back, Katherine shifted to his side and, with delicate strokes, smoothed salve over his bruised jaw; he cravenly kept his eyes shut throughout.

At last, she patted his shoulder. "All done. That should ease the hurt, and the bruises will fade more rapidly."

He opened his eyes and saw her heading for the cabinet.

He wasted no time in reaching for his shirt and pulling it on. He stood and tucked the tails into the waistband of his breeches and forced his mind to the task at hand. "I take it Dubois rarely has guards stationed outside the buildings—we noticed that while watching, but weren't sure if there were guards posted inside. We only rarely saw any going in and out, usually into the cleaning shed and occasionally into the mine."

She shut the cabinet and turned to face him. "Yes. That's right. As I said, it's part of Dubois's system of managing us."

"So all his guards are—more or less—on the gates, patrolling the perimeter, in the tower, or at their ease in their barracks." He arched his brows at her.

She nodded. "At most, only two will be anywhere else, but even that is probably only for an hour or so each day." She paused, then asked, "Why?"

"It's useful to know where the beggars are likely to be—and in fact, tactically speaking, that the guards are not generally close to the captives is something of a weakness." He grinned at her. "Something for me to bear in mind for when the rescue force gets here."

"Ah. I see." Then she clasped her hands before her, drew in a breath, and parted her lovely lips—

He reached out, tugged her right hand free, smoothly raised it to his lips, and brushed a kiss across her knuckles. "Pax, Katherine—I may call you that, mayn't I?" When, rather stiffly—or was it dazedly?—she inclined her head, he smiled. "We need to accept what's happened and go forward—all right? No further apologies necessary on anyone's part."

Katherine found herself nodding…then he released her hand, and the vise about her lungs eased, and she managed to drag in another breath and haul her wits from where they'd gone. She studied him for a moment more. "Do you always get your own way?"

His grin was unrepentant. "Usually."

Of course, his tone made everything seem all right. She watched as his gaze grew distant—and realized he was already doing as he'd said and moving forward. "Come." She turned to the door. "I'll take you to the men's hut. Your friends will most likely be there."

"You know," he said, as he fell in beside her, "I'm actually looking forward to working out the ways to ensure that Dubois lives to regret ever having set eyes on me, let alone so arrogantly bringing me and my men into his compound."

There was that deeper persona again, lending strength, determination, and a visceral edge to what could have been light words.

As they left the medical hut, with him pacing, alert and observant, by her side, she felt a buoyancy, a lightness, she hadn't felt for months. His impact; he was such a *positive* sort of person—and exactly the sort of man all those in the compound had needed to appear.

Dubois had been wrong. Fate hadn't smiled on him.

It had smiled on the captives and sent Caleb Frobisher to rally them.

Ten

In the early evening, the expanded company of captives gathered about the fire pit. Katherine had wondered if Caleb's men would embrace captivity as blithely as he, and as far as she could see, they were, indeed, cut from the same cloth. As if very little in life could throw them off their stride.

Several of his men had volunteered to trim logs to add to the circle, the better to accommodate the increased number. Now, as they all sat and ate watery goat stew, she pondered what she'd seen over the past hours—specifically how Caleb's men, including Lascelle, reacted to Caleb's unwaveringly positive lead.

He seemed like a cat—fling him any which way, and he landed on his feet and immediately looked for ways to improve his and his men's position. From their calm-but-ready-to-respond attitudes, his men had expected to see him reacting exactly as he had and was; they clearly viewed his behavior—both in allowing Dubois to hit him, and his subsequent recovery, his resilience—as nothing out of the ordinary. At least, not for him.

She glanced around the circle of fire-lit faces and saw hints of her own curiosity about him and his actions in the expressions of all those who, like her, had been under Dubois's rule for months. She looked at her plate. Caleb and his men's capture had doused the hope their presence outside the compound had raised. But perhaps, as he'd suggested, it was *better* that he and his men were inside rather than outside the palisade. And perhaps that earlier hope hadn't died but was in the process of transforming and growing even stronger.

Seated between Hillsythe and Phillipe, Caleb was grateful for the stew; the events of the day had left him famished. While he ate, he rapidly reviewed all he'd learned about the compound since entering it—the interiors of the medical hut and the men's hut, the quick tour he and Phillipe had taken of the mine—integrating that with their earlier information.

When his tin plate was empty, he did as the others had and set it down by his feet. He glanced swiftly around. There was no guard hovering; there were two ambling around the inner perimeter, two lounging on the barracks' porch, and three up in the tower, but not one was close enough to overhear the exchanges about the fire pit.

Caleb looked at Hillsythe; Dixon, Fanshawe, and Hopkins sat beyond him. "I find it curious that Dubois allows such free and unsupervised association."

Hillsythe smiled wryly. "He does it for the same reason he does almost everything—because, all things considered, it works to his advantage."

When, with a questioning look, Caleb invited further explanation, Hillsythe went on, "There is no easy way out of this camp—the palisade is secure, the guards patrol randomly, and the tower is always manned. We have no weapons—pickaxes and a few shovels are no match for countless blades, much less muskets. But even more than that, Dubois ensures we do as he wishes—that we work as he wishes and don't even attempt to escape—via a standing threat."

"I told them about Daisy." Katherine spoke quietly from where she sat with the other women a little way around the circle.

Hillsythe's features hardened. "So you know the basis of that threat. In allowing us to...well, fraternize freely, Dubois encourages us to form bonds, to become a community, so that we care about each other. That, for him, is crucial, because it gives him the strings—more like a net—to control us. If a man proves intransigent, Dubois threatens the most appropriate woman or women. If the women are difficult, he threatens the men or the children. If the children don't fall into line, he threatens the adults. So the closer we all grow, the better for him—the easier his job. Consequently, he allows us to talk and interact freely."

"But surely," Phillipe said, "that also means you—we—can plot freely as well."

"True, and I'm sure he's aware of that. But until now"—Hillsythe glanced at Caleb, then looked past him at Phillipe and the rest of their men—"there's been no real chance of us plotting to any great effect. And even now, at least as Dubois will see it, nothing about that has changed. As long as we have no access to weapons, and as long as he has such ready access to so many viable hostages, he knows we can't—won't dare—do anything. He's utterly confident about that."

"More," Dixon put in, "he *delights* in allowing us the freedom to talk and plot, as all that does is emphasize how hopeless our situation is and how little he fears us."

Phillipe nodded. "He treats your ability to overthrow his rule with contempt."

"Exactly." Fanshawe leaned forward. "It's just another element in his strategy—another way to drive home that we live inescapably under his thumb."

Caleb arched his brows. "Such arrogance—such complacency."

"Which," Hillsythe pointed out, "has thus far proved well founded, but I take your point. If the situation changes sufficiently, such complacency becomes a weakness."

Caleb smiled. "Megalomania-induced blindness—that could be decidedly useful." After a moment of weighing that, he glanced at Hillsythe, Dixon, Fanshawe, and Hopkins. "Am I correct in assuming that, in terms of defending the compound, Dubois's attention is focused outward—that he believes that if any attack comes, it'll come from outside the palisade and not from inside?"

Hillsythe thought before replying, "Provided nothing disturbs his current view of us, then yes." He met Caleb's eyes. "We take pains to ensure that nothing we do makes him suspicious of us or focuses his attention on us—in case worse comes to worst and we're forced to attempt to escape."

Caleb considered Hillsythe, then let his gaze travel around the circle. Eventually returning his gaze to Hillsythe, his voice low, Caleb said, "There's one aspect I still find hard to believe. Are you sure you have no collaborators? If I were Dubois, I would want at least one."

Hillsythe's grin was sharp enough to cut. "That was our conclusion, too." He glanced at Dixon. "So we gave him one." Hillsythe—with Dixon's somewhat bashful assistance—went on to explain the role they'd invented and developed for Dixon, that of an engineer seduced by the challenge of operating a diamond mine under such difficult circumstances.

"I'm not much good at charades, and it's not a role I like," Dixon said, "but as I was the one whose work allowed the mine to open in the first place…" He grimaced. "I've done my best with it."

"He feels guilty," the woman Caleb had learned was Harriet Frazier, Dixon's sweetheart, murmured, a gentle, affectionate glance at Dixon softening the statement. "So he does what he can to atone. Mind you, if anyone should feel guilty, it's me for being the hostage Dubois used to force John to open the mine, but it doesn't help to wallow, so instead, we all do whatever we can to keep us all alive."

"Indeed. No one here has anything to atone for," Hillsythe said, his gaze on Dixon. "And our stratagem worked." Hillsythe turned to Caleb. "Dubois knows no more about mines and mining than the average civilian, and he assumes that there's really not all that much to know—that it's all relatively obvious and straightforward."

Caleb nodded. "His natural arrogance at work again."

"Indeed. Consequently, I suggested to Dixon that if he played the role—that of an engineer who's grown obsessed with working this mine—correctly, then Dubois would gradually come to rely on his advice, and then to trust it. To accept that whatever Dixon tells him about the mine is true. And Dubois would assume that if the rest of us did anything to either damage the mine or adversely impact the mining, then Dixon would almost certainly complain."

"And so it's proved." Dixon's tone suggested that he was as surprised as anyone that his subterfuge had worked. "Mind you, I—and indeed, we all—strive to do nothing to overstep. Nothing that might jar Dubois's perceptions and stir his suspicions."

Fanshawe put in, "We're walking a tightrope of sorts, so we know to tread warily, but Dixon's 'managing' of the mine has allowed us to exert some degree of control over how quickly the deposits are depleted."

Caleb nodded slowly, slotting the information into the picture taking shape in his brain.

Hillsythe captured his gaze. "I'm hoping that all we've said has convinced you that it's safe to talk—to share the information you've thus far held back." Hillsythe held Caleb's gaze steadily. "No one here will speak out of turn—not even the children. We're all in this together—we will live or die together—and everyone here knows that." His expression hardened. "And none of us are likely to trust Dubois."

Caleb glanced swiftly around the company. He and those he'd been conversing with sat around one segment of the log circle; the six women sat in a group beyond Hopkins, and all the rest were jumbled together in loose groups. Many of the children were chattering among themselves, but most of the adults had their eyes on him.

He turned back to Hillsythe. "What do you want to know?"

Hillsythe had his question ready. "Tell us about this rescue—about what's happened until now."

Caleb drew a deep breath, then complied. As everyone there knew the settlement, the geography was one thing he didn't have to describe; as he summarized Declan and Edwina's adventures, then Robert and Aileen's, and the conclusions drawn from their findings, even the children fell silent and listened. Caleb was aware that, beside him, Phillipe kept an eye out for any guard drawing near enough to hear, but none did. Dark rumbles erupted when he named the known conspirators—Undoto, Lady Holbrook, Muldoon, and the supplier, Winter.

By the time Caleb reached the end of his recitation, including the removal of Kale and his men and the cache of weapons now hidden by the lake, everyone about the fire pit—even the children—understood why no relief had been forthcoming from the settlement, and that in order to be rescued, they had to keep the mine active and productive—sufficiently so that the mysterious backers, whoever they were, did not order the mine shut—at least into early September.

Silence ensued. Caleb gave them a moment to absorb and assimilate, then stated, "So now we all know where, together, we stand." He looked around the circle, briefly meeting each pair of eyes. "Our next phase must be working out how best to assist in our own salvation—how to ensure that the mining continues until the rescue force arrives, and when it does, that the attack on the compound is successful."

Murmurs rose as some started thinking aloud, and others added suggestions.

Katherine watched Caleb encourage even the children to offer their thoughts, then—so gently it was almost imperceptible—he steered the speculation to focus on his stated objectives.

She noted she wasn't the only one appreciating his performance; Hillsythe—and Lascelle, too—were watching with understanding and quiet approval. By inviting everyone into the discussion, Caleb had made everyone an active participant, included in the whole. He'd honored the togetherness they'd worked so hard to establish—and strengthened it.

Eventually, however, he raised his voice slightly and—it seemed effortlessly—reclaimed control. "I think we're in agreement that the most crucial issue we have to address is ensuring that the mine remains in operation until the rescue force reaches us." He glanced around; unsurprisingly, no one argued. "However, as I understand things, us"—with his gaze, he included Lascelle and his men—"joining you, while positive in one way, is going to mean we need to go carefully in terms of opening up and mining the second tunnel without depleting the deposits too soon." Caleb looked at Dixon. "We're the extra men Dubois wanted. How best can we manage having seventeen more men working each day, yet minimize the impact on the depletion of the deposits and the life of the mine?"

Dixon thought, then grimaced. "My suggestion will be to use you and your men to fully excavate and shore up the second tunnel—that needs to be done before we can start actually mining from that pipe. That will keep all seventeen of you, plus myself and the three carpenters, occupied without adding to the mining itself." He glanced at Hillsythe, then at Fanshawe and Hopkins on his other side. "As planned, we'll eke out what we can from the first tunnel meanwhile and bolster the output to reasonable levels by drawing down our stockpile."

Dixon returned his gaze to Caleb's face. "We can't risk the backers getting cold feet. The stockpile won't last all that long, but it should be sufficient to allow us to switch to mining the second pipe without dropping overall production too low— low enough to trigger the closing of the mine. And as far as I can tell, the second pipe is richer, meaning denser in diamonds, than the first. My only reservation is that the way the pipe runs through the rock means I can't yet tell how far it goes—how big the overall deposit will be."

"Let's play safe and work on a worst-case scenario," Caleb

said. "Based purely on what you currently know of the second deposit, will we be able to generate enough diamonds to keep Dubois and the backers happy until early September?"

Everyone fell silent as Dixon calculated, then he refocused on Caleb's face. "Given the extra men, it will be very, very close. Possibly too close. But our more immediate problem is that the backers are expecting output to increase, and now Dubois has the extra men he knows were needed, he'll expect the same."

Caleb nodded, apparently undismayed. "In that case, until you have information that revises the size of the second deposit upward, we should assume we need to keep production down in some believable way—not so low it will trigger the closing of the mine but enough to stretch the mining out for as long as possible." He looked around the circle. "In a nutshell, we need to keep production at the current level and find believable excuses for it *not* increasing even when the second tunnel is opened."

"So," Lascelle said, "as of tomorrow, one group prepares the second tunnel for mining, and the others continue to mine the first tunnel and produce diamonds at the current rate. All as Dubois would expect. *Bon.*" He held up a long finger. "But while we are doing that, we think of ways—unexpected and unforeseeable accidents, breakages, whatever will work—to ensure that even when the second tunnel is open and, with all the men available to work, the output would be expected to rise…" Lascelle spread his hands. "Things happen, and the best that can be done is to keep production at the current level until said things are fixed." He looked at Caleb. "That's the plan, yes?"

"Yes." Caleb nodded. So did Hillsythe and Dixon. Caleb looked around the circle. "Any suggestions of ways to slow things down that Dubois will accept?"

People glanced at each other.

Katherine hesitated, then said, "It's not the actual mining, but this might have the same effect. What about our hammers and chisels?" She looked at the other five women. "We've been using the same ones since we got here. Surely some chisels must be blunt by now? And the hammers—the heads might come loose from the handles."

From across the circle, Caleb grinned. "That's the sort of thinking we need. It doesn't have to be something that affects the mining itself, as long as it allows us to keep the amount of diamonds that get carried out of the compound to a level that's just barely acceptable."

Several of the girls who worked on the sorting piles suggested that they could easily create another stockpile by hiding some of the ore they would otherwise send on to the cleaning shed. Someone else suggested breaking some of the lanterns used to light the tunnels. Another pointed out that although they now had more men, they had yet to get more picks and shovels; until more arrived, even if the second tunnel was opened, the actual mining could only go so fast.

"All excellent suggestions." Caleb looked past Hillsythe at Dixon. "Captain Dixon knows more about the mining process than anyone else." Caleb arched his brows at Dixon. "If I could suggest, Dixon, that you continue to 'manage' the production? And if anyone thinks of further suggestions, they should bring them to you, and that the rest of us should leave it to you to coordinate any happenings, so to speak." He glanced around the circle, inviting everyone to agree. "We don't want to have too many things happen at once, and by the same token, we need anything we do to have the maximum—best for us—impact, and the effect of any particular action might change as we mine further." Returning his gaze to Dixon, he arched a brow.

Dixon looked grateful. He nodded. "I'm happy to take charge of that."

Katherine saw Hillsythe cast a penetrating—assessing and approving—look at Caleb.

Caleb felt Hillsythe's gaze; he turned his head and met the man's eyes.

Hillsythe hesitated, then murmured, "That was well done. A wise and sensible move."

Caleb grinned. "Unlike Royd, I have no difficulty sharing command."

Hillsythe snorted in an effort to smother his laugh.

Still grinning, Caleb looked back at the faces lining the circle. "I'm increasingly impressed by how cohesive your company already is. That makes working together much easier."

Hillsythe's expression sobered. "Shared burdens, shared enemies. Both bind men—and women and even children—together."

Caleb nodded. Raising his voice a fraction—enough to be heard around the circle, but nowhere near strong enough to carry to the nearest guards on the barracks' porch—he said, "There's one other thing we all need to put our minds to." Talk ebbed; when everyone was looking expectantly at him, he went on, "Lascelle and I realized this a few days ago, when we viewed the compound from a rock ledge toward the top of the hill behind us. Seeing the compound from above made it clear that there's no obvious point of attack—no real strategic weakness. The palisade and the gates are sound." He looked around the circle. "For a rescue to have any chance of succeeding without massive casualties within the compound, we're going to need a diversion inside the palisade. Something big and effective—sufficient to claim Dubois's attention and that of all the guards."

"And it would be best," Phillipe put in, "if this diversion did not, initially, appear to be part of any attack. So preferably, it needs to look like an accident."

Sober now, Caleb nodded. "We know what this diversion needs to do, but we've yet to come up with any notion that might work."

Frowns now ringed the circle; the announcement had brought everyone back to earth.

Suddenly, one of the guards in the tower called down to those on the barracks' porch; exactly what was said wasn't clear. In the porch's shadows, the two mercenaries stirred, then stepped down to the compound's forecourt and loped toward the gate. On reaching the now-barred gates, the guards spoke—presumably to whoever was on the other side—then, satisfied by whatever response they'd received, the guards unbarred the gates and swung them open.

Four of their fellows tramped through.

Hillsythe leaned toward Caleb. "That's Cripps—Dubois's second lieutenant—in the lead. Dubois sent him to see what was going on with Kale."

His gaze on the burly mercenary, Caleb nodded.

The guards on the gates shut and barred them again, then fell in behind Cripps and his party.

The captives watched without comment until the small troop followed Cripps into the barracks, and the guards resumed their positions on the porch. Caleb noticed the flare of a lamp being lit in the window along the side of the mercenaries' hut; from what he'd gathered from Katherine, the lamp sat on Dubois's desk.

Gradually, all the captives turned back to the fire pit, to the small fire that was dying to red embers within the central hearth. From the looks on most faces, everyone was retreading their earlier conversation about the need for a diversion—something Cripps and his men's arrival had underscored.

Eventually, Hopkins caught Caleb's eye. "We've a month to come up with something effective before any rescue force can reach us."

Caleb inclined his head. "True." He allowed his voice to take on a steely note. "But we need to have our diversion worked out and everything in place before they do."

★ ★ ★

Dubois had been leaning against his desk in relative darkness, the better to observe the captives about the fire pit. Not that he'd seen anything to alert him; he'd expected the young captain to be the center of attention. No doubt the young man was responding to questions and describing the world beyond the jungle. Dubois would have preferred that the newcomers not reawaken thoughts of life before the compound in the minds of those already there. However, he considered that inevitable, and he felt more than confident enough of his hold on his captives—his hold *over* his captives—to shrug the point aside.

Especially when the young captain had brought a crew of sixteen hale and hearty men with him.

Smiling at the thought of Fate's beneficence, as Cripps had entered the building, Dubois had quit the window and the view and moved to light the lamp on his desk.

He'd wanted light by which to read Cripps's face, to glean everything he could about Kale's odd behavior. Sinking into the chair behind the desk, he fixed his gaze on Cripps as his lieutenant drew himself up in an approximation of attention. "What did you find?"

Arsene came ambling up to halt to one side of the desk; he, too, fixed his gaze on Cripps.

Cripps returned Dubois's regard, but deferentially. "As near as we could make out, Kale and his men have done a bunk. They've disappeared."

Dubois limited his frown to his eyes. "Define 'disappeared.'"

"There was nothing at their camp. The place looked like they'd tidied up and cleared off. No sign anyone's been there for days—perhaps not for a week."

Dubois exchanged a glance with Arsene, then looked back at Cripps. "Had they left in a rush?"

Cripps shook his head. "Didn't look like it. All nice and neat."

"No sign of any fight?" Arsene asked.

"No." Cripps paused, then said, "It looked to us all as if Kale and company had packed their bags and walked off. Back to the settlement, most like." ·

Dubois tapped his finger on the desk. "Why would Kale up

and leave? What would induce a man like him to walk away from steady employment?"

"More money," Arsene promptly replied.

Cripps nodded. "That was my thought, too."

Arsene sniffed. "Kale always was an unreliable bastard, and his men, especially those in the settlement, had been growing restless because those calling the shots had given them so little to do in recent weeks. So few people to seize."

Dubois nodded. "Kale was being paid by the person, delivered to us here, so I can sympathize with his predicament."

Arsene shrugged. "So someone made him a better offer—"

"Or he learned of some action where he and his men could make more." Cripps gestured in a what-can-you-expect fashion. "So off he's gorn."

Slowly, Dubois nodded. "I agree that's the most likely scenario." But was it the right one? Instinct skittered, not exactly pricking but uneasy; what were the odds of Kale disappearing and the young captain and his crew turning up outside the walls within a week?

Dubois quashed the impulse to turn and stare out of the window at the group still no doubt gathered about the fire pit. It had to be coincidence. Kale wouldn't have been driven off by the captain and his crew; indeed, if Kale had found them lurking in the jungle, Kale would have captured them and brought them to the mine.

The young captain's reactions were far too slow for him—or any of his men, who presumably would be no better than he—to have faced Kale and won. Even Dubois had a healthy respect for the slaver's skill with a sword.

No—there were no grounds on which to make any connection between the sailors' arrival and Kale vanishing. The latter would have been Kale's decision.

Dubois focused on what came next. "With Kale gone…" He narrowed his eyes. "As we've managed to secure enough men to meet our needs without Kale's help, we no longer need his particular expertise. The only additional difficulty his disappearance leaves us facing is the collection and delivery of our mining supplies."

Dubois looked at Arsene, then at Cripps. Then he leaned back in his chair. "We're not going to wait to see if Kale returns. As far as I'm concerned, he's dealt himself out of this scheme, and we'll proceed on the assumption he won't be back. But now that we have our extra men and Dixon is ready to open up the second tunnel, we need more picks, shovels, and a lot more nails, and whatever else Dixon has on his list." He paused, then went on, "The last I heard from those in the settlement, they were pressing hard for us to increase production to appease their backers. I gather there was a degree of urgency involved."

He smiled coldly. "Given that urgency, when we tell them what they need to do—the equipment they must provide and the extra money they'll need to pay—no doubt they'll swiftly oblige." He looked at Arsene. "Take four men and go into the settlement by our usual route. There's no point using the route via Kale's camp—it's longer, and we don't need to waste the extra hours."

Arsene came to attention. "And once in the settlement?"

Eyes narrowing, Dubois debated, then said, "As we discussed, contact Winton at the fort, but only if you can do so discreetly. If you can't reach him, then speak with Muldoon—you know where to find him. Whoever you speak with, get them to arrange to have the supplies Dixon's requested—" Dubois broke off and flipped through a stack of papers. He withdrew one, glanced at it, then handed the sheet to Arsene. "That's Dixon's latest list. Tell Winton or Muldoon that if they want more diamonds for their precious backers, they need to have everything on that list delivered to you at our usual haunt as soon as humanly possible, along with an extra cash payment—the usual amount for our trouble. As soon as you have everything, return here."

Arsene hesitated, then said, "I know I asked before, but now that things have changed, if for some reason I can't get hold of Muldoon or Winton, should I approach our man in the governor's office?"

Dubois considered briefly, then shook his head. "No. Not at this point. He remains the hardest to approach covertly and..." Dubois grimaced. "Given the mounting urgency from the backers, given that Fate has sent us the men we need to meet their demands, then experience suggests that if anything's going to go wrong, now is the time. And if anything unexpected occurs, we need that gentleman in the governor's office to alert us to any impending threat. He's also in the best position to deflect any threat, at least long enough for us to learn of it and cover our tracks." Dubois met Arsene's gaze. "So no—don't risk tapping him on the shoulder."

Arsene nodded, accepting the edict. "If we can get the supplies and cash in good time, we should be back in five days."

★ ★ ★

The next morning, Caleb, Phillipe, and their men gathered about the fire pit with the other captives to indulge in a breakfast of what appeared to be ship's biscuits and tea. The children were served bowls of thin gruel, which they devoured with indecent haste and unwavering attention.

Sipping hot tea from a tin mug, Caleb watched Katherine Fortescue and the other women. They'd sat together as they had the previous evening, heads close as they animatedly discussed what he gathered were the suggestions for delay that they planned to pass on to Dixon.

He glanced at the other men, many of whom also had their heads together, quietly talking. Reviewing the conversations he'd overheard the previous night while they'd rested surprisingly comfortably in hammocks strung between the poles that held up the roof of the men's hut, Caleb murmured to Phillipe,

"It appears we negotiated the reversal of yesterday reasonably well. Everyone's focused on what comes next."

Phillipe's lips curved. Sipping from his mug, he met Caleb's eyes. Lowering the mug, still smiling, he murmured back, "I never doubted it would be so. It's your special skill."

Caleb blinked. "It is?"

His question was entirely serious, but before he could pursue an answer, Dixon, Fanshawe, Hopkins, and Hillsythe joined them. Two sat on either side of Caleb and Phillipe and sipped from their mugs, then Dixon said, "I told Dubois several mornings ago that we were ready to begin properly constructing the second tunnel. I've had the carpenters framing the entrance, but we'll soon run out of timber, bracing, and nails. Meanwhile, as someone pointed out last night, we don't have enough pickaxes and shovels to increase the number of men wielding them."

Dixon looked toward the barracks. "I usually consult with Dubois every morning. As I suggested last night, I'm going to tell him that I could best use you and your men in opening up the second tunnel—he's keen to see that happen. However, until he provides more picks and shovels, he's going to have to make a choice—do we use the tools for mining diamonds from the first tunnel or to dig out the second tunnel so we can subsequently mine the second deposit?"

Caleb nodded. "One's productive, one's not." He paused, then asked, "One pertinent question we haven't yet touched on. Do you know how Dubois gets paid? Is it in his and his men's best interests that the mine operate for longer—or does it not matter to them either way?"

The other men looked at Hopkins, who replied, "Apparently, Dubois got a large payment at the start and is in line to get another at the successful end of the scheme—for which you should read when he's successfully killed all of us—but he and his men also get additional payments every week."

"Excellent." Caleb looked at Dixon. "So Dubois has a financial incentive to keep the mine operating for as long as the diamond output holds up and the backers don't call an end. Therefore he's going to get us those tools as fast as he can, so there's least chance of the mine prematurely closing."

"That would be my reading of things, too," Dixon said. "He already knows what we need. I gave him a detailed list yesterday after you lot arrived. But as to what we do in the interim, I'm going to suggest that in order to keep diamonds coming out while also making some headway on the second tunnel, we include you and your men as a separate team, but because of the lack of tools, we work in shifts. That way, the men on each shift will be less tired and more productive—or at least that's the line I'm going to try and sell him."

All the other men, including Caleb, nodded.

"That seems reasonable all around—from our point of view as well as Dubois's..." Hillsythe's gaze sharpened on the shadows of the barracks' porch. "Hello—where's Arsene off to?"

They all looked, then Hopkins rose. "I'll find out."

Hands in his pockets, he ambled up to one of the guards by the gate.

He returned before Arsene and the four men with him had reached the gate. Hopkins sat again and said, "Apparently, Arsene is off to the settlement to fetch the mining supplies Dixon requested."

Before they could comment, Dubois appeared on the porch. He looked across at the fire pit and imperiously beckoned.

Dixon rose. "Wish me luck," he said, and went.

Hillsythe shrugged. "We may as well wait to hear what Dubois decides."

Caleb nodded. He glanced around the circle; as usual, his gaze snagged on Katherine Fortescue and refused to budge. Giving in to temptation, he rose and walked to where she sat in the center of the line of six women. She—they all—looked up as he approached.

He smiled winsomely, then crouched so he wasn't towering over them. To his surprise, he realized Phillipe had followed at his heels. Caleb caught Katherine's eye. "I wonder, Miss Fortescue, if you would mind introducing us?"

That got him—and Phillipe, who crouched beside him—smiles from all the women.

Katherine obliged and introduced each woman—Harriet Frazier, Ellen Mackenzie, Gemma Halliday, Annie Mellows, and Mary Wilson. Caleb exchanged smiles and nods with each one in turn, but on reaching Mary, a sweet-faced young woman with soft brown hair, he lingered. "You're Charles Babington's lady."

Mary blushed. For a moment, she appeared tongue-tied, but then rather breathlessly said, "Thank you for mentioning Charles and his search for me last night. Until then, I thought—" She broke off and dragged in a tight breath. Then her eyes lit, and a soft smile wreathed her face. "I thought he must have forgotten me."

Caleb's smile was sincere. "He most definitely hasn't. He's doing all he can to assist in the rescue, and he was moved to do that because of you."

Taking pity on Mary's blushes, he shifted his gaze to Katherine and Harriet, although he directed his question to the group as a whole. "What, exactly, do you do in the cleaning shed? You mentioned chisels and hammers."

Katherine allowed Harriet and the others to explain how they spent most of their days chipping away at the ore-encrusted diamonds, removing as much of the various minerals aggregated around the stones as they could, ultimately converting the rocks—or diamonds in the rough—into raw diamonds, smaller, lighter, and much easier to transport.

Caleb appeared to note her silence. When the others finished their description, he glanced at her. "You also deal with the children, don't you?"

She felt ridiculously pleased that he'd remembered. "I take

breaks during the day to check on the children, and they know to fetch me if there's any problem. Their tasks are to fetch the rocks out of the mine—most of them are involved in that. A small group of girls then examines and tests each piece of ore, discarding the lumps that are just rock and keeping aside the lumps that might contain diamonds—those are the rocks that ultimately are brought to the cleaning shed. Annie and I"—she tipped her head at the other woman—"usually go in the afternoon to check the day's discards to make sure no obvious diamonds have been missed."

He glanced swiftly around.

Alerted, she did the same, but there were no guards close. She looked back at him as he asked, "That's what the children meant when, last night, they spoke of creating another stockpile?"

She nodded. "It would be easy enough to do, but everything would be out in the open—there for any guards to see if they took it into their heads to look."

"How likely is that?" He looked at all the women, inviting their input.

The others shrugged or grimaced. Harriet rather darkly said, "Sadly, with them, you never can tell."

Katherine stated, "The children are the most vulnerable in all ways, and their work is the most exposed. Unless there's no other option, I would suggest we don't involve them in anything…covert."

Caleb met her eyes, read the determination—the protective instinct—in the hazel depths, and nodded his agreement. He glanced at the other women. "Is it possible for Lascelle and me to look in on your work in the cleaning shed? We need to understand the details of what you do, and the children, too—and perhaps we might take a look at your tools."

The women all readily agreed.

He looked at Katherine. "Is it likely any guard will stop us, or that our coming to the cleaning shed will raise eyebrows, so to speak?"

She shook her head. "The men—Dixon, and others, too— stop by often enough to check this or that. Or just to talk. No guard will stop you entering, but a guard occasionally patrols outside and sometimes comes inside—we can never predict when they might appear."

Caleb inclined his head. "Duly noted."

The sound of footsteps approaching from the barracks had them all turning. Dixon was striding back to the fire pit, his stride as well as his expression signaling unhappiness.

"Excuse us." Caleb rose.

After nodding politely to the women, Phillipe joined him, and they returned to where the other men, who had also seen Dixon approaching, were waiting to hear his news.

Dixon halted facing the group—Hillsythe, Fanshawe, Hopkins, and several others as well as Caleb and Phillipe—and blew out a frustrated breath. "The damned man's learning. He's insisted the men working the first tunnel continue as they have been, keeping up the production of ore to at least the same levels as before." Dixon glanced at Hillsythe. "To do that, we'll need to start feeding out ore from our stockpile."

Hillsythe nodded. "And?"

"And he's agreed that I should use Frobisher and all the newcomers to work with the carpenters and go as far as we can with opening up the second tunnel with the timber and supplies we currently have. He accepts that we'll need more supplies to fully open the second tunnel, but he says they should arrive within five days."

Hopkins nodded. "Once Arsene and his boys get back."

"Exactly." His hands on his hips, his expression grim, Dixon drew in a deeper breath. "In the meantime, however, rather than agreeing to shorter shifts, Dubois wants us all—or rather every pick and shovel—in use for every minute from our morning start until midnight."

Fanshawe softly swore.

Hillsythe looked bleak. "He's extending the hours—which means he'll be expecting more diamonds."

"Which," Dixon said, "will run down our stockpile that much faster."

Caleb frowned. "Not necessarily." He caught Dixon's eyes. "Did Dubois specify that all the picks and shovels should be used by those in the first tunnel, or does he also want us to use some to start opening the second tunnel?"

Dixon's expression grew distant as he retrod his recent conversation. Then he focused on Caleb. "He didn't specify—not in so many words—and I could easily interpret his orders as meaning the latter."

Caleb grinned. "There you are, then." He looked at Hillsythe. "We just need to ensure that the crew working on the second tunnel—an unproductive endeavor in terms of diamonds at this point—have sufficient picks and shovels in use to account for the output from the first tunnel *not* going up." He looked around the circle of men. "That said, I suggest we keep overall output steady, as we'd planned. We don't want to give Dubois or the backers reason to complain about falling output—we just need to set the scene so that it's obvious why we won't be giving them *increased* output."

There were murmurs of agreement all around.

Then Hopkins said, "That solves the immediate problem, but there's a larger prospective one raised by this change to longer hours." He glanced around the circle. "What happens when Arsene gets back with more picks and shovels? We all know Dubois won't reduce our hours back to what they were, so how will we account for production not escalating dramatically then?"

Other men had come up to join them. Now more or less all the men in the compound, all of whom worked in some capacity in the mine, stood in a loose group around their leaders. Caleb took stock of the expressions on the faces of all those who had been there for months; he saw and sensed the men's deflation and the anxiety rising beneath it. He stirred, drawing everyone's attention, and evenly stated, "That's where those other suggestions we discussed last night come in." He caught and held Dixon's gaze. "For instance, all work in the mine is under lanternlight, so what happens if the oil runs low, or even out?"

For an instant, the company stared at him, then Hillsythe snorted and clapped him on the shoulder. "You're right. You'll have to excuse us—I can see we've got into the habit of accepting reverses too tamely." Hillsythe looked around at the men. "This is the difference a fresh pair of eyes and a different attitude makes. We're not going to let any obstacle throw us off our path, not now—so we'll simply find a way around whatever difficulty Dubois wishes on us."

Hillsythe brought his gaze back to Caleb. "In answer to your question, the lamp oil is brought in not with the mining supplies but with the mundane supplies, so it's unlikely Arsene will bring any back with him, not on this trip. And it's at minimum a three-day round trip for mundane supplies—food, lamp oil, that sort of thing."

Rapidly calculating, Caleb nodded. "So there's no real problem for us in doing what Dubois wants now—sharing out the picks and shovels so everyone can do their part and both tunnels get worked on. We know we can cover the expected production for that amount of work. When the extra picks and shovels arrive, that will be the time for the oil to run out. Perfectly understandable given that we'll be running lanterns for longer hours and in two tunnels where before there was only one."

"True." Dixon had regained his equanimity. "You're right. We can manage this."

Caleb grinned. "And we'll just keep tacking as necessity demands."

As the men dispersed, heading for the entrance to the mine, the atmosphere was a great deal more settled, more confident, than when Dixon first broke his news. Along with the other women and some of the children, Katherine had waited to hear the outcome; she was glad she had.

She rose, shook out her drab skirts, then, with the other women, stepped over the logs and headed for the cleaning hut. The impact Caleb Frobisher was having on the captives' morale was, quite simply, critical. Lascelle and their men understood and expected it of him. Hillsythe had realized and was standing ready to support and actively foster his influence.

The others—Dixon, Fanshawe, Hopkins, and all the other men—had yet to fully grasp the significance of the catalyst that had appeared in their midst, but even they were moving forward.

Under Caleb's direction, they were, step by small step, transforming into a force that might—just might—have a real chance of surviving into September and thereafter through the action that would determine their fate.

Eleven

Later that afternoon, Caleb and Phillipe, who had spent most of their day helping the carpenters wrestle beams into place in the entrance to the second tunnel, were freed to take a break while the carpenters prepared more struts.

Pausing beside Phillipe in the shadows of the mine entrance, with his neckerchief, Caleb wiped the sweat and dust from his face, then he nodded toward the cleaning shed. "I'm going to see what the ladies do. Coming?"

Phillipe grunted and fell in beside him.

As they crossed the compound, both instinctively scanned the area, registering the position of the pair of mercenaries ambling about the perimeter.

Phillipe softly said, "They may look bored—I've no doubt they are. But they're too well trained to be taken lightly."

Caleb cast a swift glance up at the tower—and saw a mercenary idly watching them, his musket held lightly in his hands. "Dubois isn't the sort of captain to allow any but the best to join his company. And everything we've seen of him and of them screams 'experienced professional.' They are not going to be easy to overcome."

Several paces later, Phillipe murmured, "But we do love a challenge."

Caleb laughed.

They reached the cleaning shed. Caleb led the way up the three wooden steps, pushed open the door, and walked inside.

Halting two paces inside the room, he blinked. Phillipe shut the door, then paused beside Caleb, their gazes drawn to the narrow glass panes set into the roof, one on either side of the ridgeline. They'd noted the long windows from the rock shelf, but the significance had, until that moment, escaped them.

The long, narrow rectangles allowed natural light to fall along the length of the high table that ran down the middle of the rectangular shed. Around the table, the six women perched on high stools; they'd all glanced up as Caleb and Phillipe had entered, swiftly smiled, then returned to their tasks.

Their finicky, painstaking chipping of the mineral encrustations from the raw diamonds.

Caleb and Phillipe approached the table. Phillipe slowly circled it, studying the women's work. Caleb halted beside Katherine.

Katherine glanced at him to find his gaze fixed on the rock she held in her hands.

He felt her gaze, but didn't shift his. He nodded at the rock. "Please. Show me."

She returned to her task, slowly turning the raw stone until the light caught the line where ore met diamond. Holding the rock at the right angle, she positioned it in a small vise bolted to the table and cranked the vise closed. Once the rock was secured, she picked up her chisel, positioned the sharp edge with precision, then she raised a small, heavy-headed hammer and struck the head of the chisel sharply.

Rock splintered away, leaving a section of dark, odd-appearing stone beneath.

She heard Caleb let out the breath he'd held.

"That's the raw diamond?" He pointed at the dark face.

She nodded.

He glanced at the other women, all engaged in the same work. Looking back at her as she loosened the vise and took the stone back into her hands, he waved at the vise, chisel, and hammer. "Are these all the tools you use?"

"Yes." She glanced at him. His skin was grimy with dust from the mine; it coated him in a fine layer. Sweat trickled in rivulets from his hairline, yet he still looked like a god to her. A tousle-haired god with vibrant blue eyes; there was a feeling of *aliveness* about him she found impossible to resist. She watched his dark brows tangle in a slight frown and added, "We don't need anything more."

He grimaced, glanced around, then murmured, "That makes it harder to engineer breakdowns." He held out a hand. "Let me see that chisel."

She handed it over. Lascelle appeared by Caleb's side; together they peered at the fine metal edge at the end of the chisel.

Lascelle said, "The metal's of reasonable quality, but it should be possible to either blunt or damage it." He looked at the rocks they were working on. "What's being chipped off here looks to be relatively soft or brittle. I'll see if I can find some denser granite amid the rocks in the mine—we should be able to use that to blunt, if not chip, the chisels."

"A few of the other men have worked with blacksmiths," Gemma volunteered. "Perhaps they might have some idea of how best to do it so it looks…well, natural."

"And not like sabotage—an excellent notion." Caleb handed the chisel back to Katherine and picked up her hammer. He held it up and smiled. "This is easier. We should be able to loosen the head from the shaft readily enough." He looked across the table at Harriet. "If I might borrow your hammer?"

Eager to see what he intended, Harriet handed over her hammer. All the women watched as Caleb crouched. He and Lascelle murmured and pointed, then Lascelle held Harriet's hammer upside down, and Caleb swung Katherine's hammer sharply downward, striking the head of Harriet's hammer a swift, solid blow.

The men rose. Lascelle held up Harriet's hammer so all could see and wiggled the head; it was just a touch loose. He met Caleb's eyes. "A few strikes and it'll be too loose to use."

Caleb nodded. "So that's a possibility, although we'll have to make sure we make it look as if the tools are falling apart purely due to the work." He looked at Katherine, then glanced around. "Where do you put the stones once you've cleaned them?"

"The strongbox is over there." She pointed to the wooden box lined with tin, sitting open on the bench against the shed's rear wall.

"They don't lock it?" Caleb wandered over to examine the box.

"Why bother?" Harriet replied. "It's not as if raw diamonds will be of any use to us."

Caleb glanced back.

Through the soft light spilling from above, down the length of the shed, Katherine met his gaze. "Except if we thought to hold any back." She glanced at the door, then looked at the other women. "I was thinking that if there was some place in here where we could hide a small cache, it might help with managing the output at some point."

Immediately, all the women glanced around—at the floor, the walls, the roof.

Caleb and Lascelle turned to study the bench.

Katherine grimaced. "I've looked, but I couldn't see any spot in which we might hide any stones."

Caleb swung about and looked at the table. He walked back to Katherine. To her surprise, he set both hands about her waist and gripped; strong fingers and palms clasping her firmly through the thin cotton of her drab dress, he lifted her from her stool as if she weighed nothing and set her gently on her feet to one side. "If I may?"

She blinked. She would have been shocked if she hadn't been so stunned. So distracted, her wits sent spinning, flung adrift by the warmth—the startling heat—of his touch, and by the way her skin, her flesh, had responded.

Without waiting for an answer—for which she was infinitely grateful given she could barely breathe let alone speak—he shifted her stool aside, ducked down, swung onto his back, and stared up at the underside of the table.

Lascelle crouched beside him and ducked his head to look under the table, too. After a moment, he grunted. "It's the same as the bench—the construction's too simple to hide anything there."

Caleb grumbled an agreement and started to wriggle out from under the table—then he stopped, reached out and seized Katherine's stool by one of its legs, and tipped it to look underneath. A big grin split his face. He pointed to the underside of the seat. "There!"

Lascelle fluidly rose, took the stool, and upended it.

Caleb rolled from under the table, got to his feet, and joined his friend.

Lascelle ran his fingertip around the roughly square space between the tops of the four legs. "A square of canvas tacked in place would work."

Caleb looked at the women's tools. "You have chisels and hammers to hand—it would be a simple enough matter to ease out a tack, put stones in, then hammer the tack back into place."

"If we did it neatly on every stool," Lascelle said, "as if it was a part of the construction for some reason, then even if someone spotted it, it wouldn't immediately register as odd."

Caleb nodded and looked at Katherine. "Leave it with us—we'll get the canvas patches and put them in place."

The sudden patter of feet up the steps of the hut heralded the arrival of two grimy urchins. They pushed through the door, then halted and grinned at everyone. "We're ready for inspection, Miss Katherine!"

Katherine smiled at the pair. She took care to have an encouraging smile for the children at all times; sometimes, it was difficult, but today... With Caleb and his positive ideas infusing the atmosphere, her expression was genuine as she set aside her tools. "Let's have a look, then, shall we?"

Annie pushed back her stool and stood; she usually helped Katherine with the chore of checking the day's discards.

"I'm due for a break." Harriet set down her tools and stretched her back. "I'll come and help."

"I'll add my hands, too," Gemma said. She grinned at the children. "More hands make light work, as they say."

The children grinned back. Their gazes were openly curious as they passed over Caleb and Lascelle, but as Annie, Harriet, and Gemma approached, the pair turned and led the way out of the hut.

Caleb swiftly strode to the door and held it open. Annie, Harriet, and Gemma left. As Katherine paused on the threshold, he asked, "Is it all right if we come, too?" With a tip of his head, he included Lascelle, who had come to stand beside him. "We're trying to get a clear idea of every step in the process prior to the stones being taken out of the compound."

"Of course." Katherine managed to keep her smile within bounds. As she passed him and stepped outside, she added, "Occasionally, some of the men stop by, just to cheer the children along." She went down the steps, then slowed; when Caleb and Lascelle fell in beside her, she added, "Adults tend to forget how sensitive most children are—often they hide it, but they do get dragged down with worrying. We try to keep their spirits up."

Caleb nodded. "I'm used to children."

She might have doubted the comment—in her experience, most men didn't know all that much about interacting with children—but Caleb proved a natural. Almost as if he hadn't left his own childhood so very far behind. Or perhaps he simply retained clear memories of happy and carefree times.

With so many willing hands and educated eyes, checking the pile of discards generated that day didn't take long. Caleb asked, and several of the girls who worked the pile demonstrated how they distinguished the likely diamond-bearing clumps from the rest.

Plainly genuinely intrigued, both Caleb and Lascelle tried their hands at doing the girls' job, an endeavor that set the children giggling and left them more relaxed than Katherine had ever seen them.

As Caleb and Lascelle, both laughing at their fumbling attempts, too, surrendered the tools and rose to their full heights, emboldened, one of the boys who had come out to dump another basket of rock onto the pile for sorting fixed a searching gaze on Caleb's face. "How's the second tunnel going?" The boy hesitated for a second; when Caleb simply looked at him, the boy more urgently asked, "Are there goin' to be enough stones to see us through 'til"—he darted a glance around, but there were no guards near—"they come to get us out?"

Katherine studied Caleb's face. She expected him to offer the boy the usual generic reassurance adults gave children in fraught situations; instead, he surprised her.

He crouched so his face was closer to level with the boy's and held the boy's gaze, his own gaze rock steady. But when he spoke, his voice was pitched to reach all those listening, the women as well as the children. "We won't be certain until Captain Dixon has a chance to properly examine the second deposit, but at the moment, all the signs are good. As for the second tunnel, the reason we"—he tipped his head to include Lascelle—"are outside is that together with the carpenters and the good captain, we've put all the timbers the carpenters had ready for today into place, and so the carpenters are off preparing more. Which means we're moving forward faster than expected, and as matters stand, that's all to the good."

Smoothly rising, he laid a reassuring hand on the boy's thin shoulder. "So at the moment, all is going well, and you and the others"—with a flick of his gaze, he included the women and children, all of whom were hanging on his words—"can be sure that even if there are minor hiccups, we'll all work together to make certain that, in the end, everything is as we need it to be."

The boy gazed up at Caleb, searching his face, then the lad nodded. The children watching seemed to take that as a sign; a subtle sense of relief rippled through the small crowd.

Another boy piped up, "I heard tell you're a capt'n, and he"— the boy dipped his head at Lascelle—"is one, too. And there's Capt'n Dixon. So who's in charge?"

Caleb nodded encouragingly, as if the question was especially astute. "An army has only one commander-in-chief, but it has many actual commanders—many generals, colonels, and majors as well. The armies that win are those that fight together. In this case, we have four captains—Hillsythe ranks as the equivalent of a captain, too—and several lieutenants." With an elegant wave, he included Katherine and the women. "And, of course, these ladies. That leaves our combined force with a nice number of leaders—a good number to manage things going forward. It gives us a strong structure for our forces, and like an army that wins, the most important thing we have in our favor is that we are, indeed, all working together—all doing our parts to get to our shared goal."

Katherine surveyed the children's faces. It seemed that had been exactly the right thing to say; the children looked reassured, more confident—as if they felt safer, or at least more certain of surviving.

Jed Mathers came up, strolling with two of the other men. He parted from them and, smiling, came to join Annie.

Annie greeted him with a warm smile. She directed a quick look at Katherine, who grinned and nodded.

With a wave to the other women, all of whom smiled, Annie went off to walk with Jed.

"Now." Gemma bustled up and dropped two empty baskets— the woven baskets the children used to ferry the ore from the mine—beside the small pile of reclaimed ore, the ore the girls had discarded but that the women considered worth a closer look. "We need to get this lot over to the shed."

Several of the girls gathered around and helped load the small pile into the two baskets.

"Allow us." Lascelle stepped in to pick up one basket, and Caleb gripped the handles of the other.

Caleb watched as Katherine and Gemma confirmed that the children should tidy up their tools and take themselves off; although the light was still good, it was, apparently, the end of the children's day.

Katherine glimpsed the question in his eyes as she turned toward him and the shed. "They can't work much longer without starting to make mistakes. Dubois saw the sense in having them work only through the hours during which they perform well. If he pushes them harder, we—the women—just end up redoing the sorting, which takes us away from cleaning the stones."

Caleb nodded; he hefted the basket and fell in beside her. Together with Lascelle and the other women, they walked back to the shed. The men followed the women in and, at Harriet's direction, set the baskets down at the end of the long table.

Slipping onto her stool, Harriet caught Katherine's eye and waved her away. "Except for just now, you've been in here all day—it's your turn for a break. Go for a walk. We can handle the discards."

Katherine hesitated, but the other women added their encouragement. They took care to spell each other—a concession she'd argued hard to gain them and one they took care to consistently exercise. "Very well. I'll take a turn about the compound."

Lascelle saluted the women. "Ladies." Smoothly, he turned to the door.

Caleb sent a grin around the table, swept the women a bow, then turned to trail Katherine as she went outside. He ducked through the door; as he straightened, he saw Lascelle nod to Katherine, then stroll off toward the men's hut. Caleb grinned again. He went down the steps and halted beside Katherine, where she'd paused as if debating which way to turn; she looked up, into his face, as he joined her.

He smiled and tried to keep his delight within bounds. "Do you mind if I join you on your walk?"

Faint color tinged her cheeks, but she replied, "No, of course not." After an instant's hesitation, she added, "I would be glad of your company."

He turned his grin into a grimace. "I would offer you my arm, but I'm filthy." Raising his gaze, he swiftly scanned the segment of the compound he could see. Somewhat to his surprise, he noticed several other groups—men in twos and threes, as well as Jed and Annie—ambling about, hands clasped behind their backs, heads down as they chatted, for all the world as if they were taking the air in some park. "I see it's the local hour for promenading."

Katherine gave a soft laugh.

He looked down at her. "Which way? Do we meekly follow the established pattern"—all the others were moving clockwise— "or strike boldly out on our own?"

This time her laugh was more definite. "Why not? We could set a new fashion."

On the words, she stepped out, heading in a counterclockwise direction toward the mine entrance. As he settled to pace beside her, she murmured, "There is another purpose to our promenades. We check the palisade as we go around. We've noticed a few sections where the vines used as binding are starting to fray."

Caleb nodded. "I see." They neared the mine entrance and swung to pass between the fire pit and the men's hut. "One thing I still find curious is Dubois's…for want of a better term, leniency." He caught her gaze as she glanced up. "Does he really believe the adults need breaks from their toils in order to remain healthy enough to work?"

She looked ahead. They'd walked several paces before she replied, "Our health is just Dubois's excuse—the one he gives if anyone asks."

"And his real reason?"

"Is more to do with encouraging attachments—friendships and relationships, like Annie and Jed. They announced their betrothal a few days ago. To Dubois, that's just another weakness to exploit."

"Ah." Caleb felt his features harden. "That's more the sort of thing I expected from him—a vile ulterior motive. So in his assessment, allowing us to develop affection for each other, on whatever level, adds more ammunition to his arsenal and consolidates his control over us."

She inclined her head in wordless agreement.

They paced slowly past the gate and the pair of guards lounging to either side, then diverted to pass along the front of the women and children's hut. Once they were out of range of the guards' hearing, his gaze on the kitchen and storerooms ahead of them, Caleb debated, then decided he might as well take the bull by the horns. "Would you rather I kept my distance?" He felt her gaze, surprised, strike his face and looked down to meet it—openly, without any screen, without the slightest guile. "I'm not going to dissemble. I'm interested in you, and I hope, in time, you'll come to be interested in me in the same way. But will that—my interest in you—increase the danger you face...?" Lost in the warm hazel of her eyes, he paused, then forced himself to say, "For instance, as it did in the jungle the other day?"

She held his gaze for a moment longer, then swiftly searched his face. Then she looked forward. They walked on in silence for several minutes, skirting the front of the open-air kitchen and the large supply hut beside it.

Katherine felt awash on a tide of emotions. She couldn't disbelieve the evidence of her own eyes, could not doubt the sincerity of the message she'd read—been allowed to read—in the vibrant blue of his. His "interest" was real; the recognition had set her heart beating significantly faster. Her lungs felt constrained, her breathing restricted, as if she were wearing stays cinched too tight instead of no stays at all.

But his question was genuine, too. And so she'd swallowed the impulse to brazenly assure him that his interest was entirely reciprocated and she most definitely returned his regard.

His question was pertinent—the danger he alluded to clear and present.

And yet...

This was not a situation she'd ever dreamed of facing. Again, she felt as if Fate was challenging her in order to test her true worth.

In the end, as they passed sufficiently beyond the base of the guard tower so no one could overhear their words, she drew in a deep breath and said, "We can never predict the future."

She glanced sideways and saw that he'd bent his head and was pacing alongside, his hands clasped behind his back. She sensed he was listening to her with the same focused attention she'd come to expect of him. "We—here and now—cannot be certain how much future we might have. And although I understand Dubois's reasoning, and that he sees affections and relationships as weaknesses, in my experience, affection, and relationships based on that, can bolster one through the worst of times." She tipped up her chin. "In my view, relationships don't make one weak." She gestured, searching for the right words to explain her view. "They may create a...vulnerability one wouldn't otherwise have, but even purely in the sense of shared purpose, of having shared goals, they give one so much more." The right words suddenly glowed in her mind. "They give one a reason for living. A reason and a future to fight for."

"Indeed." From the corner of her eye, she saw his dark head nod. His deep voice held a conviction she hadn't expected as he went on, "I agree. Relationships are like internal armor— they impart strength, an inner fortitude, and courage. Potentially boundless, limitless courage. But your description is exactly right—relationships give one a future to fight for."

He glanced at her then, met her wondering gaze.

For an instant, she felt weightless, as if she'd pitched into some emotional void, and then he—his blue eyes, the solid certainty she saw in them—caught her and steadied her.

She felt breathless again. Pulling her gaze from his, she looked forward. How could this be happening—and so very quickly? She wasn't fool enough to pretend not to recognize what *this* was. No long, gentle courtship with glances exchanged across a drawing room and a protracted period of meeting each other in social company, no extended preliminaries; they were simply here, already talking about a relationship.

And it was already a reality taking shape between them.

No wonder she felt giddy.

Yet…something in her responded to him. To his honesty in reaching so directly, clear-headedly, and openly for what he wanted. For not dissembling and playing society's games.

"I believe," she said, and wondered where the words that burned the tip of her tongue truly came from…from some inner self she'd long been aware of, yet only now—with him, in response to him—had that inner self emerged, "that when Fate deigns to offer something one wants, it's better to take what's offered when it's offered, rather than let the chance slide by in the expectation—the assumption—that the chance will come again. Because taking Fate for granted is never a wise move, and she might not let that particular chance come your way again."

She glanced at him. "So my considered opinion is that, if Fate offers us a chance we want, we should seize it regardless of any potential repercussions." She waited until he met her eyes to brazenly ask, "What do you think?"

The smile that curved his lips, that lit the brilliant blue of his eyes and made them sparkle, was the definition of irrepressible.

"As anyone who knows me will attest, I'm the very last person to play cautious."

Reading his expression, she accepted that as truth, yet still, she arched her brows. "Not even in this? Many men would not agree."

"*Especially* in this." His jaw firmed. "And I am not like many other men."

That was certainly true; there was an openheartedness to Caleb Frobisher, and a readiness to meet life and whatever life threw at him with a grin and the confidence to succeed come what may, that was, if not unique, then rare.

Regardless of their surroundings, despite the murkiness of any potential future, feeling blessed by Fate, Kate—*Katherine*—accepted the challenge, took the plunge, and disregarding the dust covering his clothes, she slid her hand into the crook of his arm and felt steely muscles tense beneath her touch. "So," she said, shaking back the wisps of hair that had come loose from her bun to dangle about her face, "tell me who Caleb Frobisher is."

He studied her face for a moment, then he shifted his arm into a more comfortable position and closed his other hand over hers on his sleeve. "Did I mention I'm the youngest of four brothers?"

"How much younger? And what do the other three do?"

They strolled on, circling the compound a second time while he answered her questions, and she answered a few of his.

Twelve

For the next three days, little of significance changed within the camp. The men labored in the mine. Those working in the first tunnel kept the actual mining to a steady pace, the lack of escalation excused by the limited number of picks and shovels. Meanwhile, Caleb, Lascelle, and their crews worked alongside the carpenters widening and shoring up the second tunnel—again restrained by the even more limited number of picks and shovels that could be spared to them.

More, after the first day, the lumber started to run low. By the end of the second day, those working in the second tunnel could no longer move ahead due to a lack of the large beams necessary to frame the tunnel. They busied themselves putting in supporting struts and braces along the first yards, while Dixon champed at the proverbial bit, frustrated because he wanted to push farther so he could size the deposit and reassure them all.

Given the limitations caused by the lack of implements and lumber, the captives saw no need to use any of the delaying tactics they'd explored and assessed. Dixon, assisted by Hillsythe, Fanshawe, and Hopkins, had evaluated the possibilities put forward and decided on a shortlist of those actions most likely to support their cause. At Caleb's suggestion, they took advantage of the days before Arsene returned to make any preparations necessary to put their delaying tactics into effect.

Arranging for the lamp oil to run low was high on their list. They needed a place to secrete oil—somewhere out of sight of the guards. The dim far reaches of the first tunnel, beyond the area still being mined, was the obvious place. In between using their shovels to scoop shattered rock into the children's baskets, those wielding the shovels—assisted by the children who kept their eyes peeled for any guards—slipped into the shadows at the rear of the tunnel and dug a pit. Shovel full by shovel full. Once it was deemed deep enough, they refilled the pit with sufficient loose rock to hide its existence. But by initially using large slab-like rocks propped at angles, creating spaces between, then covering all with smaller fist-sized rocks, they left plenty of space for oil, when poured through the upper level, to pool in the depths of the pit.

By the morning of the third day, when the leaders had inspected the pit and congratulated everyone concerned, the company was feeling ready for the challenge to come, buoyed by the simple fact of having taken some definite action toward their own relief.

Also during those three days, Caleb, Lascelle, Jed, and two other men who'd been apprenticed to blacksmiths in their youth stopped by the cleaning shed whenever they were free. As long as no patrolling guards were near, they worked on the women's chisels and hammers, taking care to weaken only a few and each in a different way. They also didn't want the tools to fail too soon—another issue they had to juggle. They worked out their best approach and did what they could, but couldn't go too far.

More covertly yet, Caleb, Lascelle, Hillsythe, Fanshawe, Hopkins, and Dixon concluded that they might eventually need something akin to a small disaster to slow production down. Something along the lines of weakening the second tunnel and causing a cave-in, but that was such a desperately dangerous proposition they decided to keep the notion strictly to themselves.

"The problem," Caleb said, as he strolled beside Katherine in the softer light of the late afternoon, an exercise that had quickly become a part of their daily routine, "is that from what Dixon's seen of the second deposit, he's convinced it's going to yield many more diamonds per foot of tunnel, and they'll be larger, too, and hence more valuable."

Her arm twined with his, Katherine frowned. "Isn't that good? For us, I mean."

"Good as far as it goes. Whoever's behind this enterprise, they, and certainly our mysterious backers, are in it for the money. They're greedy for wealth, and the second tunnel looks set to offer them that and more. So opening up the second tunnel and demonstrating that there's untold wealth there for the taking will be the most effective way of keeping the mine open. If we present it correctly—*and* keep production up—they'll argue and fight to keep the mine operational and everyone here alive."

"To keep us working and producing the diamonds."

"Exactly. Dubois might be a cold-blooded killer, but he's consistently demonstrated that he's pragmatic to the nth degree—as long as he needs us to work the mine, he'll do whatever is necessary to preserve his workforce, meaning us, in sound and effective condition." He paused, then admitted, "Truth be told, that he is so amazingly devoid of the usual weakness that afflicts mercenary captains—namely seizing short-term gains rather than holding out for long-term riches—makes him more of a threat in my eyes. That quality of cold calculation is, no doubt, what has allowed him to thrive in this business for so long—and why his men obey him without question."

She huffed a cynical laugh. "It's ironic, isn't it? Without Dubois, we wouldn't be here, and yet now we are here, it's because of him that we are, relatively speaking, safe."

Caleb snorted.

Arm in arm, they strolled on, then she glanced frowningly at his face. "You said that the second tunnel having more diamonds was somehow a problem. How so?"

He grimaced lightly. "Dixon's uneasy over the size of the deposit. He can't yet see far enough to even guess how many diamonds the second pipe contains, and how spread out they are, which is the critical factor in determining how long it will take us to mine out the deposit. And in terms of us surviving until the rescue force arrives, *that* is the critical question. Dixon equates the likelihood of discovering a third pipe as akin to lightning striking twice, so effectively, the second pipe is all we have to see us through. An added complication is that once Arsene returns with the extra picks and shovels and more timber, the work will ramp up—those working on the first deposit will soon mine it out, although we're hoping that by then, we'll have the second tunnel fully open."

Caleb paused to draw breath. "And *that's* the point at which we'll know whether lasting until September is going to be a simple exercise or whether we'll have to manufacture delays. Not having enough of a deposit to stretch the distance output-wise is one potential scenario. Another is that the diamonds are there in sufficient quantity, but are too concentrated and too easy to mine, so the output will escalate, and again, the deposit won't last long enough. Both those scenarios will require us to act, either to slow the mining itself in some believable way or, in the second case, perhaps to allow the mining to proceed, but to hide the diamonds so we can feed them out at a slower rate."

"Yet it could be that the second deposit is both large enough and spread out enough that mining it will take more than enough time."

"True. But that's the best-case scenario."

Katherine glanced at him. "And you're not inclined to place your faith in the best-case scenario?"

He pulled a face. "Let's just say that I'm more comfortable making contingency plans."

She smiled, but all levity faded as she envisaged how anything other than the best-case scenario might play out. "As long as the backers are satisfied with the flow of raw diamonds, Dubois is unlikely to concern himself. Which in turn means that as long as we can keep the number and quality of the diamonds sent out to the coast sufficiently high, he's not going to be overly exercised by any temporary holdups."

Caleb nodded. Several paces on, he mused, "I'm sure Dubois knows, or at least guesses, that we're plotting and planning, but as long as we don't test him—as long as we make no overt bid to escape and keep working, and the diamonds going out satisfy his masters—he really doesn't care. His men maintain absolute control over the perimeter, and while that's in place, he knows there's no point worrying about what we might be up to. We can't get out, and he has immediate access to effective hostages should we ever attempt a challenge. As far as he can see, we're no threat and never will be. All of which is true. For us, there is no way out of here *unless* some force attacks from outside—and even then, with so many hostages, Dubois believes he'll always have the upper hand."

"Still," she murmured, "if we're forced to act to influence production, we can't afford to have him guess that we're doing so."

"That we're manipulating him?" Caleb's grin took on an edge. "No. We need to ensure he never has any firm evidence of that. He might suspect, but he won't act on suspicion—he still needs us to keep working the mine. As long as there's nothing overt— as long as we do nothing that forces him to confront the reality that we're managing him—he'll leave us be."

"But if he does find out…" She shivered.

Caleb unwound their arms, looped his arm about her, and drew her against his side.

The medical hut was near; he steered their steps in that direction. He glanced at her and caught her eye. "There's no sense worrying—we all know the score, that we have to keep our activities hidden."

He guided her into the dense shadow at the side of the hut, then halted, leaned his shoulders against the plank wall, and drew her to stand before him.

Resting her hands lightly on his chest—an innocent, all but absentminded touch he felt to his marrow—she studied his face. Then in a transparent bid to lighten their mood—to turn to a happier subject—she demanded, "Tell me about your home. Does your family live in Aberdeen?"

He grinned. "No." Settling his hands comfortably about her waist, he held her gaze. "Our business—the shipping company—operates out of Aberdeen, but home is a manor house at Banchory-Devenick. That's about two miles west..." He paused. Her eyes had widened, her brows rising. "What?"

"I know the place—not the house but the village." She held his gaze. "I was born not far away."

"Oh? Where?"

Katherine studied his eyes, drank in the uncomplicated interest that was evident even through the shadows. She tended to keep her background private, but it was no real secret, and she wasn't ashamed of any of it. "Fortescue Hall. It's just outside Stonehaven—on the coast about fifteen miles south of Aberdeen."

His eyes flared. "You're a local!"

She couldn't help but smile at his open delight. Yet she felt forced to continue, "Although I was born at the Hall, my father was a younger son, so we lived in a house in the town, in Arbuthnott Place. And later, after he died, my mother and I moved to a small cottage on Mary Street."

There was nothing deficient about Caleb Frobisher's understanding; his features sobered and the expression in his eyes grew more intent. "Your father left debts?"

His tone held no pity, just a simple wish to know.

She nodded. "My mother had broken with her family in order to marry him, and although my grandmother—my father's mother—always stood ready to help, my mother refused to live on charity. She was a gifted needlewoman, so she became a sempstress specializing in fine embroidery, mostly, of course, for the local gentry." Which had ensured that she, as the daughter of their sempstress, was forever excluded from the social circles into which she'd been born.

She drew in a breath and lifted her chin. "When Mama died, I had the option of living as a poor relation with any of several connected families, but I decided I was too much my mother's daughter." She smiled somewhat wryly at her memories and met his gaze. "I saw an advertisement in *The Times* for the position of a governess with a family located in Freetown, so I went to London and applied, and ultimately, that's how I came to be here. Dubois decided he needed someone to oversee the children, so he asked Kale to get him a governess."

For one instant, his expression was—unusually for him—difficult to read, then he grimaced. "On the one hand, I wish Kale had chosen someone else. On the other"—his blue eyes held hers—"if he had, I wouldn't have met you."

And I would never have met you. She could feel the connection between them—new, growing, still fragile, yet quite tangibly there... "Truth be told, I'm not sorry Kale seized me—there've been times I've been glad, even grateful, that I've been here for the children."

"Like Diccon."

She nodded. "Although I had no siblings, I grew up with tribes of cousins, which is why I chose to be a governess—because I liked children and knew how to deal with them."

She lowered her gaze to her hands, to where they rested splayed on his chest. Through the thin linen of his shirt, she could feel the warmth of his body impinging on her fingers and palms, seducing her senses. If they'd been in some more normal place, she would have felt compelled to break the illicit contact— and step free of his grasp, away from the hard hands that rested gently yet firmly about her waist.

But they were here, and this was now, so she looked up and met his eyes. "Tell me about your brothers—about you and them."

Caleb smiled easily and proceeded to entertain her—and distract himself—with long-forgotten tales of the Frobisher brothers' exploits. "Royd was always the leader, of course—and often there were far more in the group than just us four."

There were so many tales to choose from, he rattled on, seeking to draw her smiles, and even more her laughter, yet his nerves were alive in a way they'd never been before, and something—a web woven of primitive instinctive interest and some more fundamental need—had wrapped about them and now held them.

As if they were trapped in that moment in time, in a place far removed from either of their homes, and so very far from the comfort of family—and there was some degree of visceral understanding they each had of the other that made each unique to the other…

Here. Now. Together in this place.

When he came to the end of his latest tale, he felt as if the weight of the moment had reached a peak that demanded he act.

His eyes remained on hers, her gaze locked with his. They'd been speaking not just with words but with their eyes for long minutes.

So it seemed natural, expected—certainly anticipated—when he slowly lowered his head…

At the last, she pressed her hands more firmly to his chest and stretched up—and their lips met.

It was a gentle kiss, innocent and almost heartbreakingly tentative…at first.

Then he angled his head slightly and settled his lips over hers, and she kissed him back—and for an instant, his head spun.

But her direction was clear, and he was only too happy to oblige—to sup at her lips, to explore their contours. And when he found her lips pliant and plush, just begging to be parted, desire ignited like a leaping flame, and he pressed in.

And savored.

And only just remembered in time that he shouldn't go too

far too fast—that he couldn't simply plunge in, ravage, conquer, and seize.

Even if her untutored enticements made him feel like a chest-beating barbarian.

Yet her encouragement was plainly there, openly tendered, and that, in itself, made him feel unexpectedly humble—as if she and Fate had conspired to gift him with something indescribably precious.

Here, in the depths of the West African jungle, while held captive by violent men, and with their survival nowhere near assured...

Perhaps Fate hadn't changed her spots all that much.

Katherine felt giddy. She wasn't sure she was even breathing, but couldn't spare any mind to care, not with her senses whirling and darting this way, then that, wanting to absorb, to experience and remember every tiny detail of this—their first kiss.

Not her first kiss, and certainly not his, but in that instant of feeling drawn into the exchange, all but drowning in the compulsion to go forward, she'd made her decision and knowingly taken that step—just as he had. In that moment, she'd sensed a tide, a pressure quite unlike anything she'd previously felt—as if this kiss was meant to be. As if she needed it. As if, for her—and for him, too—this kiss was a vital part of their way forward.

Ridiculous, some long-buried kernel of conservative caution informed her. How could she be so sure when she'd only met him mere days ago?

Yet she was.

Experience—not just since her mother had died and she'd been alone, but even before that—had taught her to trust her judgment. That the one thing in life she could rely on was herself and that inner knowing.

So she leaned into him, gave herself up to his hold, and slid her hands up the solid planes of his chest. She curved her palms over the heavy muscles of his shoulders, then reached farther to feather her fingers over his nape, then into the thick, tumbled locks of his dark hair.

The fall of the silky locks over the backs of her hands was a sensuous caress that made her shudder.

Want bloomed—a new flame within her.

She noted it—that burgeoning need—and sensed that he did, too.

To her surprise, she felt a small shudder rack him.

Then his lips firmed.

And without thought or hesitation, she met their demand, and the siren she'd never known lived inside her rejoiced.

But almost immediately, she sensed him pause—then, very clearly, he took control and eased them both back...

Until their lips parted.

Until, from under weighted lids, their gazes met and held.

Their breaths mingled, their breathing not as steady as it had been.

As her heart slowed, he murmured, "Enough." *Not here.*

She held his gaze. "For now." *Later.*

★ ★ ★

The cavalcade that marched into the compound late the next day was impressive in its way.

A long row of native bearers swung through the gates two by two, each pair supporting a bundle of long, roughly dressed timber beams on their shoulders. Others carried pallets on which rested all manner of other mining supplies, while Arsene and his men hefted heavy packs, no doubt weighed down with nails and the rolls of metal strips used to anchor the bracing.

Caleb stood with the other men in the shaft of afternoon sun flooding the mine's entrance. They watched as the bearers halted and let the timber tumble from their shoulders to the ground. Under the direction of one of Arsene's men, the pallets were set down in front of the supply hut.

"That's an awful lot of everything," Dixon said.

Fanshawe muttered, "Dubois is clearly taking no chances on any of those items running out again."

At that moment, Dubois emerged from the barracks. He paused on the porch to survey the scene, then descended to speak with Arsene, who'd halted not far from the steps.

The guards who'd been idly patrolling the perimeter ambled up to stand by the fire pit—between the captives and the natives—as the latter approached Dubois and Arsene.

Dubois paid off the bearers, then the band—at least twenty strong—turned and, eyes forward, strode for the gates. Only as they stepped out of the compound did a few of the bearers cast furtive—unhappy, even worried—glances at the captives. But then they were gone, vanishing into the jungle, presumably marching back to some village.

"Dixon!" Arsene called from across the compound.

Caleb and the other men looked and saw Dubois retreating into the barracks.

Arsene beckoned. "Bring the men and store these supplies."

As Caleb followed Dixon across the compound, he whispered to Hillsythe, walking alongside him, "No doubt Dubois wants us to see that he's brought in more than enough to keep us going."

Hillsythe nodded. "And therefore there's no excuse for us not simply getting on with mining the second pipe. With Dubois, there's always a message."

They reached the packs and the pallets. The jumbled timber lay nearby.

After a word with Arsene, Dixon set one group of men under Fanshawe and Hopkins to stack the timbers in an organized way between the gates and the men's hut. Then Dixon and the others hefted the packs and the heavier packages off the pallets and carried them into the supply hut.

While he unpacked bundles of long nails and stacked them on one of a row of crude shelves, Caleb studied his surroundings; he'd been inside the hut only once, to fetch a lantern, and hadn't had a chance to assess what possibilities the hut and its contents might offer.

Although Arsene watched them unburden the pallets, he didn't bother venturing into the stifling atmosphere of the hut. Through the open door, Caleb could see him and his men loosely gathered in the shade cast by the barracks, keeping nothing more than a vague eye on the hut and the men inside.

On the other side of the hut, Jed Mathers and several others were unwrapping and stacking picks and shovels. Jed paused to study a short-handled shovel. "Be damned if this isn't brand new." Raising his head, he looked at Dixon. "Weren't the others—the ones we already have—secondhand? Like from some store that resells things after others are finished with them?"

Jed glanced at the shovel, then held it out to Dixon. "Here. Take a look."

Frowning, Dixon reached out and took the shovel.

Jed released it, then turned to survey the small mountain of new tools—including pickaxes, shovels, and numerous pry bars of various sorts. "This *all* looks brand new. Must've cost Dubois and the backers a pretty penny an' all."

Dixon, frowning even more deeply, turned the shovel over, then looked along the shaft—and swore.

"What?" Hillsythe asked.

Dixon studied the shaft for a moment more, then he raised his gaze and looked at Hillsythe, then at Caleb and Phillipe. "I'd noticed the army stamp on most of the tools before, but they were used, so I assumed they'd come from some mining store's secondhand stock, and in a place like Freetown, the fort would be the principal source of used tools. But these bear the army stamp"—Dixon held up the shovel, then handed it to Phillipe, who was closest—"and as Jed said, they're brand new. And there's no reason I can think of for Fort Thornton to have ordered any huge number of such tools, only to send them out as surplus. That makes no sense. Major Winton would never make such a mistake—not when things have to be brought by ship all the way out here."

"Wait—Winton." Caleb frowned. After a moment, he said, "Major Winton's the commissar at the fort, isn't he?"

Dixon nodded.

"My soon-to-be sister-in-law," Caleb said, "heard that the supplies came from someone named Winter, but she was gagged and had a canvas sack over her head at the time."

"You think she misheard Winter for Winton?" Hillsythe look struck, then he glanced at Dixon.

Whose frown was now black. "*Not* Major Winton." Dixon's tone was adamant. "The major is old school, and a more solid man you won't find." Dixon paused, then drew breath and went on, "*However*, the major has a nephew—one William Winton. A spineless wonder, if ever I saw one. He's greedy, and I can readily see him being two-faced. But more to the point, he's the major's assistant." Dixon looked around at their faces. "William Winton is the assistant commissar at the fort."

Hillsythe sat on a stack of boxes. "So we have Winton in the fort and Muldoon in the navy office."

"And someone in the governor's office who we've yet to identify." Caleb had been keeping an eye on Arsene and the guards. "We need to keep unpacking. Let's table this for later."

The others all glanced through the doorway, then with grunts returned to their labors.

Later, as Dixon, Caleb, Phillipe, and Hillsythe followed the other men back to the mine, and Fanshawe and Hopkins joined them, they returned to the subject of William Winton and the fact that their tools and all mining supplies appeared to be coming directly from the fort's commissariat. Dixon explained that Winton had to have ordered extra supplies specifically to support the mine. "Which means he's pulling the wool over his uncle's eyes, and as the major got him the post—it's one a civilian can hold—this is going to fall hard on the major."

"What a way to repay someone for doing you a good deed," Phillipe murmured.

Snorts of agreement came from all around.

They reached the mine and went inside, but halted in the area just inside the entrance. They all looked at each other, then Dixon said, "With the first deposit on its last legs and our stockpile of ore running down, too, we don't dare delay completing the shoring up of the second tunnel so we can start mining the second pipe—and with all that timber, there's no viable excuse to do so, anyway."

His expression grave, Hillsythe nodded. "But once the second tunnel is open, now we have all those tools and all the mining supplies we could ever need, Dubois will expect production to increase."

Dixon paused, clearly calculating, then said, "We can increase by a small amount, but until I properly assess how far the second pipe reaches, we'd be unwise to mine without restraint."

Caleb met Hillsythe's gaze. "It looks like we need to start being inventive sooner rather than later."

★ ★ ★

After all the captives had gathered for the evening meal and had shared the latest news, Caleb and Katherine went for a stroll around the compound. The evening perambulation was an exercise Dixon and Harriet had pioneered, and one Annie and Jed also frequently indulged in, seizing the quiet moments in the cooler evening air to share insights, reactions, and feelings, and above all else, to bolster each other's spirits.

Tonight, all three couples had grasped their chance, leaving the rest of the company about the fire pit. Each couple struck their own course, ambling arm in arm between the huts, avoiding the occasional perimeter guards, and pausing here and there as inclination took them.

Dixon's discovery of the source of the supplies had been touched on only briefly about the fire pit. Caleb elaborated, explaining that they now believed that "Winter" had really been "Winton," referring to the younger man of that name known to be second-in-charge in the fort's commissariat.

After digesting that, Katherine asked, "Given the large amount of mining supplies Dubois has brought in, what are the implications for us stretching the mining out long enough for the rescue force to reach us?"

Caleb grimaced. "We still can't tell." Through the shadows, he met her gaze. "As you heard, we've little choice but to make a good show of working the mine at increased efficiency, with all the men working for the next three days." That consensus had been discussed and adopted before they'd left the group. "Unfortunately, the first deposit is almost mined out, and increasing output even by only a small amount—which we have to do in response to having more men working and for longer hours— will run down the stockpile to almost nothing."

He glanced ahead. "However, by the end of those three days, we'll have the first level of the second tunnel fully open. We've done the exploratory work, and the entrance and first stretch are already shored up. As soon as it's safe, we'll have men mining the second pipe—and the first call on the results will be to replenish the stockpile. And by then, Dixon should be able to give us a firm answer as to what we face."

They continued strolling. Leaning on his arm, Katherine looked ahead. "I haven't been in to see the new tunnel yet— where does it start?"

"The opening is about ten yards down the first tunnel, on the right. The second tunnel runs at roughly ninety degrees to the first—more or less parallel to the ridge line."

"So the entrance to the second tunnel lies before the section where they're mining the first deposit?"

"Yes. At the moment, the second tunnel is not that long— not even fifteen yards. Once we have it fully open, it'll be more than forty yards, and Dixon will assess how much of the second deposit we can mine from that run. He's already sure we'll need to extend the tunnel on a lower level to reach all of the deposit, but as the second deposit is richer in diamonds, both in quantity and in size, it's possible we might not need that lower level—not before September."

He glanced at her and smiled. "Best-case scenario is that even with all the men working longer hours, even with us increasing the output from the mine, the mining from the first level of the second tunnel will nevertheless last long enough—until the seventh of September, at least."

"So we'll know in three days."

"Yes." He lowered his voice. "And if we don't get our best-case scenario, then we'll decide when and how to slow things down. Dubois didn't bring in more lamp oil, so running down the oil remains a possibility."

Katherine nodded and walked on by his side. With her arm looped in his, she was very conscious of the muscled strength of him, of his easy, confident stride. Just being physically close to him, as well as hearing his indefatigably positive private thoughts—positive even when he wasn't trying to carry his men with him—gave her heart.

Gave her heart enough to think of the future—of home. Of Stonehaven. Of Banchory-Devenick. Of Aberdeen.

She felt his gaze touch—and caress—her face.

"A penny for your thoughts." When she looked at him, he grinned, rueful and inviting. "Yet even that penny will have to be on tick, for I haven't even one farthing on me."

They'd reached the back of the cleaning shed, out of sight of the mercenaries in the tower, and the patrolling guards had passed them minutes before. She halted in the deeper shadows, drew her arm from his, and faced him. "I was thinking of home." *And you.*

"Ah." He studied her face, but she doubted he could make out much of her expression in the dark. "And?"

Was it madness to hope? So soon? To leap so far ahead? Yet life was for living. She tipped up her chin fractionally. "When we get back"—not if, but when; he'd infected her with his confidence—"our homes are so near, we'll no doubt see each other. In Aberdeen, if nowhere else."

He gazed at her, then, his voice deeper, huskier, he said, "I was hoping for somewhere else." When she waited, he went on, "For instance, your home—and perhaps Fortescue Hall, if your grandmother's still alive. I believe I'd like to meet her. And at Frobisher Manor, too—for I'm sure my parents would love to meet you."

She blinked at him. What he was saying—what she wanted to hear…she stared into his eyes. "We can't talk about this—not yet."

He compressed his lips, then nodded. "It feels too much like tempting Fate."

Thank God, he understood. She stared at him for an instant more—then she reached for him.

In the same heartbeat, he reached for her.

Their lips met—not tentatively this time but in the confident expectation of welcome. His fingers firmed about her waist, and he drew her closer, until her hips met his thighs. She released the folds of his shirt that she'd gripped and slid her hands up the acres of his chest, clasped his nape, and held him to her as she parted her lips and clung tight as he accepted her wordless invitation.

And her senses giddily spun.

Then they resettled and realigned, yet it seemed on a different plane of reality, one where only they existed—him and her in each other's arms—communing in the warm dark.

She might have been a relative novice in this sphere, yet every long, drawn-out exchange had meaning. Each kiss, each slow and utterly absorbing caressing stroke of their tongues, each shift in pressure, took them both on a journey of exploration. His lips were firm and seemed cooler than hers, but then hers seemed so hot, so flushed and swollen. As if the realization had triggered a spreading of the sensation through all her nerves, over all her senses, her breasts caught the fever, then the heated sensation washed in a wave all the way through her. All the way to her toes.

She felt alive, radiant, heated and buoyed on a cresting tide of need. Of wanting.

Desire whispered softly through her mind, trailing seductive tendrils of hunger over her wits, before wreathing through her senses.

The strength of him, latent in his tall frame, in the lean, taut, steely muscles sheathing his heavy bones, should have made her wary. Any other man and she would have shied from being this close—from allowing him to tighten his hold about her waist and urge her closer still.

Any other man and she wouldn't have gone, would never have let him draw her flush against him.

Would never have thrilled to the feel of her breasts compressing against the iron muscles of his chest. Would never have gloried in the heady delight of feeling his erection, rampant and solid, press against her stomach.

She might be a virgin, but she was no wilting flower. Yet with no other man had she ever felt this wanton—no other man had ever made her crave the sensation of his hands caressing every inch of her skin.

All with just a kiss.

A heady, hungry, greedy, wanton, shockingly heated kiss.

He couldn't indulge her—shouldn't, not here, not now—but the fire had been kindled and now smoldered beneath her skin.

Caleb knew it—knew that she was his, and that, somehow, he was and always would be hers. He'd indulged with more women than he could count—his easygoing nature and physical stature had always made attracting the fairer sex a simple matter—but this was different.

So very different he felt as if he was embarking on some voyage—one vital to his future life—with no effective compass.

But the needy sound she made, trapped in her throat, was one sign he recognized. That, and the way she pressed against him, so open in her burgeoning ardor that he couldn't mistake her hunger. Her rising passion.

He wanted to claim it, and her—wanted to gorge and satisfy the hunger she evoked. For one instant, that need threatened to overwhelm him—to take control and drive him. But then he realized the danger and, on a mental oath, wrestled his libido into submission.

Not now. And certainly not here.

How long had they been kissing?

Too long, the tactical part of his brain drily informed him.

Too dangerous.

That thought gave him the strength to ease back—to ease them both back from the exchange. Yet her mouth was a haven of delicious delight, honey sweet and tempting; it required serious effort to haul his senses from their absorption, to convince them to relinquish the heady taste of her.

To draw back from an exchange that spoke so convincingly to the man he was, that lured the daredevil and tamed him.

Claimed him.

Irrevocably ensnared him.

Another minute ticked by.

Finally, he drew breath and raised his head, and their lips parted—reluctantly, overtly so on both their parts.

Through the darkness, lips still parted, their mingling breaths not at all steady, they looked into each other's eyes—as if, despite the darkness, they could see into the other's soul.

He filled his lungs, then, gently, set her on her feet.

He steadied her. Then he breathed deep again and quietly stated, "Just to be clear, my interest in you—this"—with one hand, he waved between them—"has nothing to do with being here—with us being trapped here together. There's nothing incidental, much less casual, about how I feel about you. Had I met you anywhere else—in a ballroom, in some drawing room—the result would have been the same. I would have come after you. I would have sought you out."

She tipped her head, her gaze steady on his eyes, then she equally quietly replied, "I could say the same. I could point out that I've been here for months, yet I've felt no need to kiss any other man. Yet with you…from the first, you were different in my eyes." She paused, then went on, "I don't know where this will lead—this connection between us—but I know I want to find out. With you—together with you."

He held her gaze for a moment more, then he held out a hand. She placed her hand in his.

As one, they twined their fingers, then they turned and, side by side, walked on through the night.

Thirteen

Three days later, and they knew they would have to do something to slow production down if they wanted to live until September.

"You have to admit," Dixon said as the captives sat around the fire pit that evening, "that if we weren't in such a bind... well, it's an amazing sight."

All who had ventured into the second tunnel—and most of the captives now had—had to agree. All now knew how to spot the rough diamonds peppering the rock, and the second deposit was nothing short of spectacular. Hundreds if not thousands of diamonds, a huge number readily visible and for all intents and purposes ripe for the taking.

And all too easily mined.

Dixon had placed the tunnel perfectly, skimming the edge of the gradually downward-angling pipe. The tunnel, therefore, gave access to a long stretch of the deposit. With all the men working extended hours—as they had feared, Dubois had never allowed them to retreat to their previous shorter working day—Dixon estimated that they'd have the bulk out within two weeks.

And then Dubois would start killing the men, and then the children.

Jed looked at Annie. "Won't Dubois wait until everything's finished before he starts...culling us?"

Caleb exchanged a look with Lascelle, then glanced at Hillsythe, who also looked grim. When no one else spoke up, Caleb quietly stated, "No intelligent commander—or captain of mercenaries—would want to have a large group of captive men idle, just waiting for execution. That's a recipe for an uprising, and everything we know about Dubois says he's far too smart to do that. He'll keep the six women to the last"—Caleb paused to draw breath, his mind shying from what, if Dubois's men had their way, would ultimately happen to the women—"but the men and children? He'll start eliminating us the instant we're no longer needed."

The group fell silent as all digested that. No one argued.

"We"—Katherine gestured to the women—"won't be able to process the rock that fast, but that won't stop Dubois or the backers from…"

"Starting to tidy up loose ends," Caleb supplied. "He won't care what you—those left—think. The instant he—and his back-ers—judge that they no longer require our services, they'll move to eliminate us."

"Because regardless of all appearances, just by existing, we pose a threat to them," Lascelle said. "We would be foolish to think otherwise."

Dixon grimaced. "I haven't had a chance to explore a lower level. It's possible we might be able to extend along the pipe and thus extend the mining—"

"For long enough?" Hillsythe asked.

Dixon stared at the mine, then, slowly, shook his head. "I doubt it. Experience tells me the part of the second deposit we've already got open will be the better part of it. We might get an-other week, but that still won't be long enough."

Caleb looked around the circle, took in the expressions—and lightly shrugged. "So as we'd planned, we'll start slowing things down." He was sitting beside Katherine. Across the circle, he caught Hillsythe's gaze. "Starting from now. There's no sense in waiting—we need to keep as many of the diamonds in the rock, unmined, as we can."

Hillsythe nodded. "We've got quite a bit of stretching to do, so we need to start as soon as possible." He paused, then said, "We've worked hard to keep Dubois reasonably happy—there's no reason for him to imagine that any hiccup in production is deliberately caused by us. We need to preserve that fiction."

Fervent murmurs of agreement came from all around.

"So," Fanshawe said, "what's it to be? The oil?"

Everyone, including all the children who were huddled in groups on the logs around the pit, was listening, waiting. The acknowledged leaders of the men—Dixon, Hillsythe, Caleb, Lascelle, Fanshawe, and Hopkins—all exchanged inquiring looks.

Then Caleb shifted on his log and looked at Katherine. "It might be preferable to open our campaign with a hiccup that isn't in the mine itself." He arched his brows at her, then shifted his gaze to Harriet, seated beyond her. "What about the problems with the women's tools?" He glanced around the circle. "Bad cleaning tools will leave the rocks too encrusted for easy transport—more or less blocking getting them to the ship." Caleb looked at Hillsythe. "And having Dubois focus on the cleaning shed and a blockage in production of the final raw diamonds means he won't be focusing on the output of the mine itself, which means we can appear to keep working, but manage how much we do and hold back as much of the ore as we can to replenish the stockpile we've run down."

"Another buffer against the future." Hillsythe nodded. "That will, at least, give us a few days up our sleeve."

When the diamonds eventually ran out.

Caleb looked around the circle, brows raised, inviting further discussion, but apparently everyone agreed. "Right, then," he said. "As we've touched on many times, the problems have to look realistic and not staged—nothing to make Dubois suspicious."

Katherine and Harriet exchanged a glance, then Katherine addressed the circle. "We think we can be ready by the middle of the morning tomorrow." She glanced at Caleb. "Will that be soon enough?"

He met her gaze. "I believe I speak for us all in saying: Take your time. It has to look good—good enough to fool Dubois."

Later, much later, when he was escorting her back to the women's hut through the darkness, she tightened her fingers on his and murmured, "I just hope this works and that nothing goes wrong."

He gripped her fingers back, then raised her hand and kissed her knuckles. "Courage, my love. I have confidence in you."

★ ★ ★

The following morning, Katherine collected Harriet's hammer—now with its head so loose it spun on the handle—and Mary's and Ellen's chisels, which now had edges that were brittle, cracked, and chipped; the women had worked with the two erstwhile blacksmith's apprentices to make the damage look authentic, as just wear and tear. Tools in hand, she drew a breath, mentally girded her loins, and left the cleaning shed; summoning a bothered frown, she strode swiftly—purposefully—to the barracks.

With Caleb's words of encouragement from the night before repeating like a mantra in her mind, she climbed the porch steps and headed for Dubois's office.

He was sitting behind his desk. He looked up when she knocked on the door frame, then beckoned her in. "What is it?"

Clinging to her façade of feminine aggravation—as if beset by some unforeseen irritation—she walked to the desk and plunked the tools down before him. "These." She waved at them in exasperation. "We've used them for as long as we can, but they're now close to useless." Looking up, she met his gaze. "You cannot expect us to clean the stones with these. We asked Dixon for replacements, but he said there aren't any in the supply hut."

She folded her arms and all but glared at Dubois. "So what do you want us to do?"

Dubois looked down at the tools, and a faint frown appeared on his rarely expressive face. He reached for the hammer.

She drew in a breath and stated, "We can carry on with the tools we have, but obviously not at the same pace. Of course, the other tools are also showing signs of wear, but they're not as bad—yet."

Dubois studied the loose hammerhead, then looked at the chisels. "It would have been useful to know this earlier."

Katherine suspected he was speaking to himself, but nevertheless, she frowned as if perplexed. "Earlier when? No one's asked us about the tools. If they had, we would have said."

His gaze still on the worn tools, Dubois muttered something under his breath. Then he set down the hammer and pushed back his chair. "Show me."

Katherine inwardly sniffed at the brusque order, but swung on her heel and led the way to the cleaning shed. As she entered, she cast a swift glance down the room; four of the other women were working diligently using those tools still fit for the task, while Harriet sat and watched. Katherine caught Harriet's eye, then stepped aside and let Dubois stride past.

He immediately went to the table. He stopped beside Annie, closest to the door, and demandingly held out his hand. When she gave him her tools, he examined both closely. Eventually, he dumped Annie's tools on the table and moved on to examine Gemma's. Gradually, he circled the table. His expression increasingly hard and forbidding, he grunted several times, but remained unnervingly silent.

After he'd scrutinized each tool, he walked back to where Katherine waited by the door, her hands clasped before her. He met her gaze, then turned and looked back at the women, who were now all watching him. He grunted. "I will get you more tools. Meanwhile, do the best you can with what you have."

With that, he strode out of the door.

Katherine exchanged a look of burgeoning hope with the other women, then moved to shut the door.

Before she did, they all heard Dubois bellow, "Arsene!"

Katherine and the other women grinned.

★ ★ ★

They had to wait until the afternoon to verify their success.

The women had reported on Dubois's reaction over the short break the captives were allowed at midday. Later, while fetching more nails from the supply hut, Caleb noticed several of the mercenaries who had previously accompanied Arsene to the settlement sitting on the barracks' porch and checking their weapons, traveling packs ready at their feet; after delivering the nails into the mine, Caleb opted to take a short break and go for a walk.

He went first to the cleaning shed to suggest Katherine join him.

They were now an accepted sight ambling together about the camp. This time, they took advantage of a temporary absence of guards in that particular section of the compound and ambled to a halt by the east side of the barracks, near Dubois's window and out of sight of anyone inside the hut or in the tower.

Leaning back against the rough planking, through it, they heard Arsene say, "Perhaps they damaged the tools themselves."

"I don't think so." Dubois's accents were clipped, his tone impatient. "We've had no difficulties with the women to date, and I examined the tools myself—the damage is variable in type and also in degree. If they'd done it themselves, deliberately, the damage would have been more uniform."

Caleb and Katherine exchanged a smug look. They'd worked hard to ensure the damage was sufficiently variable to appear innocent.

Dubois continued, "More, the good Miss Fortescue did not suggest they halt their work, but rather she came to point out that, due to the failing tools, they would be unable to work at full pace. As we've all seen the large amount of diamonds that will be coming out of the second tunnel, she was right to call attention to what will, ultimately, cause a bottleneck and restrict our deliveries of raw diamonds to the ship." Dubois paused, then went on, "If you think it through, in this, she behaved as I would wish her to. She and the women might have continued working, increasingly slowly, until the tools gave out altogether, thus more gravely impacting our ability to send diamonds to the backers."

Arsene grunted, apparently in grudging agreement. "We've had a few pickaxes and shovels break. I suppose it's only reasonable the women's tools, which are constantly in use, might also become damaged."

"Indeed. So I suggest we don't borrow trouble and doubt the women in this. Instead"—Dubois's tone turned calculating—"let's see if we can bend your trip to the settlement to our advantage." He paused, then said, "Make sure you get double the number of tools the women need. And call Dixon in."

Caleb and Katherine exchanged another glance, then they pushed away from the wall—Arsene or whoever went to fetch Dixon might see them—and wandered over to where the older girls were busily sorting through the piles of ore.

From the corners of their eyes, Caleb and Katherine watched the guard who, seconds later, crossed to the mine, presumably to fetch Dixon. While they waited for the guard and Dixon to emerge, Katherine crouched and chatted to the girls.

Caleb stood beside them; his hands in his pockets, he pretended to listen while his mind ranged over the visit Dubois had paid to the mine the day before. Neither Dubois nor his lieutenants entered the mine often. Once or twice a day, one of the guards would randomly wander in unannounced and stroll through the tunnels, but their interest was transparently perfunctory; evidently, Dubois and his crew had long ago decided that the only thing they cared about was what came out of the mine, and they didn't need to concern themselves with what went on inside.

Yesterday, however, their curiosity no doubt piqued by Dixon's report on the second deposit as revealed via the second tunnel, Cripps, then Arsene, and finally Dubois had come to see the sight with their own eyes.

Playing his role of excited engineer to the hilt, Dixon had proudly shown off the diamonds. The other men had paused in their labors and stood back against the opposite wall of the tunnel. The temptation to use his pickaxe on Dubois had gripped Caleb—and he suspected most of the men there—but the presence of several guards with muskets, and the certainty of more outside with the children in full view and, no doubt, orders to shoot should there be any sign of riot, effectively quashed the impulse.

But then while watching Dubois, Caleb had noticed sweat pop out on the man's forehead. He'd looked more closely—and had seen the slow clenching and unclenching of Dubois's fists, and his increasing pallor.

Caleb had glanced at Phillipe, just as Phillipe—having noted the same signs—had glanced in dawning wonder at him.

They'd both looked down the tunnel at Hillsythe; he, too, had been looking at Dubois, a faint frown forming on his face. Hillsythe had felt their gazes; he'd shifted his own to meet them and had nodded almost imperceptibly.

They'd all gone back to observing Dubois.

Later, they'd conferred, and all had agreed it was very likely Dubois suffered from a fear of enclosed spaces or some similar condition, enough to make him panic over being in the mine. His lieutenants might also be affected, which would account for all three rarely entering the mine.

What use such knowledge might be, no one could guess, but it was a weakness—especially in Dubois, who had thus far demonstrated very little by way of vulnerability.

Caleb heard the tramp of boots and glanced across to see Dixon accompanying the guard to the barracks.

Katherine rose. With her gaze, she followed the pair; once they'd passed out of sight around the front of the barracks, she caught Caleb's eye. "There's still no guard on this side of the compound—shall we eavesdrop again?"

They did, and heard Dubois order Dixon to give Arsene a list of anything and everything he could think of—nails, timbers, tools—that might be required to mine out the diamonds in the second tunnel. "As Arsene is going to have to return to the settlement and contact our mining supplier to get more tools for the women, as those are relatively small and light, I want to ensure the trip is worthwhile." Dubois's tone grew colder and harsher—more menacing. "And I do not want your operation to run into any further shortage of tools or other mining supplies."

Caleb and Katherine listened as Dixon, with apparent enthusiasm, threw himself into ordering more of everything.

Dubois must have waved Dixon and Arsene away; Dixon's excited chatter and Arsene's responding grunts slowly faded.

Caleb tightened his grip on Katherine's hand. "Once around the barracks, then back to the cleaning shed."

Dixon and Arsene had halted on the porch, with Dixon still very much playing his role. Neither man muted his voice as Caleb and Katherine strolled past.

They continued their circuit of the barracks. Caleb saw Katherine into the cleaning shed, then returned to the mine. He reached the entrance as Dixon strode up. Together, they walked into the mine's shadows.

The other leaders and several other men were waiting in a group outside the second tunnel's entrance. "Well?" Hillsythe asked.

"It all went off as smooth as silk." Dixon tipped his head back toward the barracks, then he turned, and they all watched as Arsene collected his men and they left the porch. After swinging their packs to their backs and hefting their muskets, the mercenaries headed for the gates.

His hands on his hips, Caleb watched Arsene and his men stride out into the jungle. "Katherine and I eavesdropped. Dubois swallowed whole the idea that the tools had broken through normal wear and tear. He dismissed Arsene's quibbles."

Fanshawe nodded after the departing men. "So how long will they take—how long will the ladies be able to go slow?"

"Given the list I gave Arsene," Dixon said, "I imagine they'll take their usual five days."

"Good." Hillsythe glanced around at all the men. "So we should do as planned and appear to work at our usual pace, but divert as much of the ore as we can to our stockpile."

All the men nodded.

"And," Dixon concluded, "as we discussed, I'll approach Dubois this evening and point out that there's really no sense in having us men working longer hours while the women can't process the ore, at least not as fast as we're sending it out. I'll suggest we adjust our output to keep pace with the women."

"Will he agree, do you think?" Phillipe straightened from his slouch against the tunnel wall. "I wouldn't, were I him."

Dixon grimaced. "It's worth asking. It won't affect the overall output leaving the compound, and to date, that's been Dubois's overriding concern."

"One possibly relevant point," Caleb said. "We heard Dubois tell Arsene to bring back extra hammers and chisels for the women. Is there any chance that, once Arsene gets back, Dubois will order the older girls into the cleaning shed, too—or even order the women to work longer hours, as he's done with the men?"

Hillsythe, Dixon, Fanshawe, and Hopkins all shook their heads.

"He tried some of the older girls once—it wasn't a success," Fanshawe said.

"You can't smash diamonds," Dixon said, "but it's all too possible to unnecessarily shatter them along internal fracture lines.

What the women do is clean the raw stones of nondiamond aggregates. Dubois is under strict orders to send out the raw stones unfractured, in as large a size as possible, so the fracturing can be left to the diamond cutters. That way, they get the most out of each raw diamond."

"When the women are tired, their concentration slips, and so do their chisels, and the fractures mount," Hillsythe said. "So Dubois can't overwork the women, and on top of that, they need to work under natural light. Lamplight's not good enough for what they do."

Dixon nodded. "And the girls aren't as careful as the women, not as adept at sensing where the fault lines are and avoiding them, so it doesn't pay to have them take up cleaning."

Both Caleb and Phillipe nodded their understanding.

"So for the moment," Caleb said, hefting his pickaxe, "we continue working steadily, hold back as much ore as we can, and hope Dubois agrees to allow us to slow down."

★ ★ ★

Unfortunately, in this instance, Dubois proved intractably resistant to Dixon's persuasions.

As Phillipe had foreseen, Dubois was now set on getting all the diamonds out of the mine as rapidly as possible. He insisted that the men continue mining at maximum pace, either breaking rock, shoveling it, or shoring up the next stretch of the second tunnel—with every man working from breakfast until midnight.

Caleb encouraged Dixon to make the best of the situation he could. Consequently, the four older boys who'd worked alongside the men in the mine were sent to clear out the last of the diamonds from the farther reaches of the first pipe. The youngest children continued to gather the ore from under the men's feet, scrabbling and scrambling over the tunnel's rough floor, grabbing all the shattered rocks. They then lugged their laden baskets to where several men helped them rapidly sort and remove some of the diamonds for their stockpile, then continued out to the ore pile.

At the pile, the older girls sorted—joined by those women who no longer had tools with which to work.

By the end of the first day, it was evident to all that Dubois's intention was to run the mining side of the operation to completion—to depletion of the mine—as fast as he could, and if the present lack of cleaning tools meant that resulted in a huge pile of sorted but as yet uncleaned rocks, so be it.

The gathering about the fire pit that evening was decidedly glum.

"So," Hillsythe said, summing up for everyone, "we've created a bottleneck which will soon result in a massive pile of rough diamonds to be cleaned prior to shipping, but Dubois hasn't allowed us to ease back on the actual mining, yet that's what we urgently need to do." He glanced around the faces. "We need to slow down the mining itself."

Poking at the dust between his feet with a branch, Dixon grimaced. "I tried pointing out that it was safer to keep the diamonds in the rock, and that having a huge pile of rough diamonds just lying there was surely tempting Fate. Dubois just stared at me and said he had faith in his men—that they would put paid to any marauders." Dixon sighed and looked up, letting his gaze sweep over the faces before coming to rest on the other leaders. "So that's the outcome—or rather lack of it—from our latest gambit, and I would strongly advise against us trying anything else, at least for a few days."

Caleb pulled a face. He glanced around, taking in the cast-down expressions, then said, "We might have failed to gain what we wanted, but at least we haven't gone backward."

When Hillsythe, Fanshawe, and the others all looked inquiringly at him, he elaborated, "We would have been mining at the same rate—the increased rate—regardless. What we've done hasn't escalated that rate further, and more, we're diverting part of the increased output to the stockpile."

He shrugged. "We aren't in a worse position than we were, and in fact, we've improved our position just a little and will continue to improve it by a small amount—the amount of ore diverted to the stockpile—every day from now on." He glanced around the entire circle, at the too-quiet children, at the women and all the men. "We didn't get the effect we wanted, but we're in a position to"—he tipped his head at Dixon—"in a few days, try another tactic to reduce the actual mining."

Seated beside Caleb, Katherine slipped her hand around his arm and squeezed in support and agreement; he patently needed no encouragement.

Across the pit, she saw Hillsythe's lips curve slightly, and he gave Caleb one of his tiny nods. "Also," Hillsythe said, "we now know there's no benefit in focusing on anything but the mining itself. Nothing else is going to work."

Caleb nodded. "So that's what we'll concentrate on forthwith—slowing down the rate of freeing diamonds from the rock."

★ ★ ★

Later, when Caleb came to fetch her from the tiny porch of the women's hut where she'd taken to waiting for him to join her for their usual late-night perambulation, Katherine felt no overwhelming need to discuss the mine.

She understood Dubois's strategy: Extract all the diamonds from the mine as soon as possible and kill the men, who constituted the greatest threat to his mercenary force as well as to his masters. She didn't need to know more.

They had to find some effective way to slow down the mining.

But that was for tomorrow. For tonight, she needed time and space, and to go to that place she reached only with Caleb.

He strolled up, then held out his hand. She rose from the stool on which she'd been sitting, placed her hand in his, and let him

steady her down the two steps to the ground. Rather than release her, he drew her near and tucked her hand into the crook
of his elbow.

They set out strolling slowly, side by side through the dark.

Not that it was completely dark. Moonlight silvered the scene,
washing over the open ground so the guards on the tower could
still see them.

When they walked and talked during the day, the bustle of the
camp was more than sufficient to drown out their words. But in
the cool of the night, with only the mine itself in operation and
the noise emanating from the tunnel's mouth deadened by the
earth surrounding it, as they circled past the deserted kitchen,
the silence was pervasive enough to force her to whisper. Without looking at Caleb, her voice barely a murmur, she ventured,
"You're very good at making people face forward rather than
getting dragged down, affected by temporary setbacks."

That was one trait he possessed that, again and again, came
to the fore and buoyed the whole company.

He looked at the ground before their feet. After a moment, he
shrugged. "It's just part of being a captain, I suppose."

She could have told him that wasn't true, that there were lots
of men who led yet who did not have the indefatigably positive—ready to engage with life with an iron-clad refusal to even
contemplate taking a step back—outlook that he possessed. That
he communicated so clearly.

Plainly, he viewed the effect he had on others as ordinary and
nothing worth commenting upon. She knew better. Despite the
way in which it had occurred, she'd come to view his joining
the captives as nothing less than an act of God.

And in part because of that, and because of the threat hanging
over them, she wanted to use this walk, this time—these next
moments—to confirm what might be. To explore and define
what lay between them—what it was they had at risk.

What value was theirs to place in the scales of life's balance.

Survival was one thing. Surviving in order to claim a higher prize was something else again; she was ineradicably convinced that the existence of such a higher prize held the power to strengthen their will to live.

To support them through what was clearly going to be a trying time. A demanding time.

She'd read somewhere that wise monks advocated living in the moment—with one's entire being focused on what that moment held, on what could be achieved within it—as the true route to happiness. She was determined to give that philosophy a try, especially as, as far as she'd seen, Caleb's own approach to life held something of that unswerving commitment to the here and now.

Here, she decided, should be the darkness in the lee of the supply hut, where the moonlight tonight did not reach and the angle from the tower meant the guards couldn't see them. As they drew level with the hut, she tightened her grip on Caleb's arm and changed their tack.

He glanced at her, but didn't resist.

She felt his gaze on her face, but didn't meet it.

With a sense of growing calm, of growing certainty, she steered him into the deep shadows. Then she released his arm, turned and put her back to the hut's side, reached up and closed her fist about the knotted kerchief he wore looped about his neck, and brazenly drew him to her.

Directly into a kiss.

He didn't resist. Not in the least. He didn't, however, reach for her, didn't close his hands about her waist and draw her to him.

Instead, he set his hands to either side of her head, palms flat to the boards, bent his head, and with his lips meshing and melding with hers, he let her take the kiss where she would. He met her, matched her, but didn't direct. At her invitation, he savored her mouth, then she boldly returned the pleasure.

And the kiss grew hotter. More intense. More sharply intent.

His lips lured; with artful strokes of his tongue, he beckoned and drew her on, and her hunger swelled, then ignited, transforming into a fiercer force, one that demanded appeasement.

She released the neckerchief and clutched the plackets framing the opening of his light shirt. Fisting her hands in the fabric, she clung as the kiss transmuted into a duel of mating tongues.

And something inside her stirred—some more powerful impulse, a compulsion to seek more of the seductive heat that seemed to emanate from him.

To wantonly bathe in that delicious warmth.

To seize the moment and experience the scintillating frissons of pleasure his touch could evoke.

That something inside her was ancient, knowing. With it flooding her, she simply knew.

Knew what she—and he—needed.

There, in that moment in time.

She came away from the wall, stretched up on her toes, and kissed him passionately. Opened the gates of her inner soul and let all the pent-up yearning out. Let it pour into the kiss.

He straightened, and his hands gripped her waist, then slid farther, and he crushed her to him.

His lips were afire as much as hers were, the passion in their kiss well-nigh scorching.

Then he pivoted and put his back against the wall, hard hands and steely arms locking her tight against him. His lips ravaged hers, more demanding and infinitely more commanding than before, and she gloried and plunged headlong into the tumultuous maelstrom welling and swelling between them.

Caleb's head was whirling—a novel occurrence for him. He'd waited, patiently, to see what she wanted, where she would lead them—he'd never imagined it would be into this.

This whirlpool of want that even now threatened to suck him under.

Sensual greed—to touch her, to take the next step—burned beneath his skin.

Yet there was something he was missing in this—something that might make sense of her tack.

It took more effort than he'd expected, yet he managed, finally, to break from the kiss—not that he succeeded in parting their lips, so heated and yearning, by anything more than a fraction of an inch.

Eyes closed, he concentrated and managed to utter, "Why?"

He waited—could almost sense the battle she waged to corral her careening wits.

Eventually, she murmured, "Because I need to know."

Then she kissed him again—pressed the reality of her wants, her wishes, on him again.

Several heartbeats passed before he succeeded in refocusing his wits, then parting their lips enough to ask, "About what?"

"About *this*." She leaned into him, caught his face between her palms, and threw her all into making him understand...

Oh. Even as realization dawned, he—the elemental male inside him—was moving to meet her. To meet the demands—now quite clear, insistent, and unequivocal—that she was pressing upon him.

A distant part of his awareness instinctively, protectively, scanned for danger, but they were cloaked in darkness, and the patrolling guards rarely if ever marched close to that spot. As long as they made no sound—as long as he kept his lips locked with hers—they would be safe enough.

She leaned in again, pressing against him, the demand in her kiss enough to scramble what wits he'd retained.

He eased his grip on her waist and sent one palm skating upward to brush, tantalizingly lightly, over the swell of her breast.

Katherine stilled—just for an instant, just long enough to savor the sudden scintillating spiking of her senses—then she dove back into the kiss and urged him on.

And he obliged, closing his hand about the soft mound of her breast and gently kneading.

Only a thin, now nearly transparent chemise and the light-weight fabric of the drab dress supplied by the mercenaries separated his hot, callused hand from her skin, from her yearning flesh.

Nerves she hadn't known she possessed came alive.

His long fingers stroked, then the pad of his thumb circled her nipple, and she would have sworn flames leapt beneath her skin.

Her breast swelled beneath his hand, her flesh flushed, heated. Her nipple was an excruciatingly tight bud when his wandering fingers returned to caress it.

Artful, repetitive, and far too knowing, his lazy caresses slowly, step by tiny step, drove her on.

Drove her—the passionate self she'd only just discovered—wild.

Until she had to have more—whatever more entailed—and she needed more now, and she wasn't afraid to beg.

But begging, she realized, had to be accomplished not with words but on this very different plane of communication.

The kiss had turned lazy, too. Despite the effects of his ministrations, despite the compulsive haze overwhelming her mind, she discovered she could still give as good as she was getting. A shift of emphasis, of pressure, a change of intent, and with a nudge, she took control—and the kiss turned sultry.

Hotter, more imbued with welling passion than before.

It was like learning a new language; she hunted for the right expressions to make her needs known.

And realized that the tiller of their engagement, at least at this point, lay—literally—in her hands.

She eased her palms from the beard-roughened planes of his face and boldly set both to his shirt-draped chest. She allowed her hands to rest there for a heartbeat, two, then slowly, with intent, swept them wide, and immediately felt tension invest his muscles and lock his long frame.

With a soft hum in her throat, she set herself to caress, to explore—and through that, to demonstrate her own desires. She located his flat nipples beneath the thin fabric and circled both. Felt the thud of his heart through his rib cage and hers accelerate as she played…

He wasn't slow.

He let her lead, let her show him, let her fill her mind—her senses—with him, then he reciprocated. He raised his other hand from its position at her waist and closed it about her other breast. And proceeded to send her senses into overload, caressing her breasts in concert, kneading, then tweaking, fondling, then petting, ultimately possessing.

Instinctively, her fingers curled, and her nails pressed into the broad muscles on either side of his chest.

Through the kiss, she sensed his sharply indrawn breath—and inwardly smiled.

They took turns—him, then her—at playing on the other's senses. Never had she been party to such an exchange. Some distant—very distant—part of her brain suggested that she ought to be shocked, but she wasn't. She was thrilled, and too honest not to admit it.

More, something in her exulted.

This was right; this was proper. This was as things should be.

At least, between them.

Gradually, however, she sensed him drawing back, retreating from the tumult of the absorbing kiss. Reluctantly, she conceded and eased back from him, allowing their lips to part.

He didn't immediately set her from him, although he released her breasts—with a reluctance to match hers—and returned his hands to either side of her waist.

He held her as she was, pressed wantonly to him, and from close quarters, from under heavy lids, his eyes met hers.

He didn't seem to study her eyes, her expression, so much as look into her soul.

Then, softly, his words a whisper in the night, he asked, "Why? Why did you need to know?"

Somewhat to her surprise, she didn't need to think; her response, the words, leapt readily to her tongue. "Because at some point, we're going to need to fight, and knowing that this might be ours if we survive to claim it…"

She saw understanding bloom in his eyes.

He held her gaze for a heartbeat more, then he nodded. "You're right." There was a whisper of steel in his tone that she hadn't heard before when he confirmed, "Knowing that makes doing whatever we must to survive that much easier."

He paused, then he set her back on her feet, captured her hand, and pushed away from the wall. "Come. I'll walk you back to your hut."

She walked beside him through the night, satisfied that she'd gained the knowledge she'd sought—and, indeed, more.

Fourteen

The men spent the next day with most of them breaking rock in the second tunnel. The resulting amount of rough diamonds and the ease with which they were mined only served to underscore how urgent was their need of an effective way of slowing the process down.

The gatherings about the fire pit at midday and again in the evening were unusually quiet, tending grim.

Later that evening, while working with Dixon to extend the second tunnel onto a lower level in the hope of gaining access to yet more stones, Caleb sliced open his left palm on an extrusion of exposed diamond. He swore and stepped away from the rock face.

"Let me look." Phillipe took one glance and said, "No stitches required, but go and get it cleaned. You can't risk it festering."

Caleb grumbled, but he knew Phillipe was right. Holding the cut closed with the fingers of his other hand, he turned and made his way past the other men in the second tunnel, clambered over the piles of rock they'd left for the children to cart away in the morning, and finally walked out of the mine.

He looked across the compound to the women's hut and saw Katherine sitting on her stool. Even before he set out to meet her, she'd realized he was holding his hand and had quit the porch and was hurrying to meet him.

"What have you done?" she asked the instant she reached him.

"Just a cut. It's not that deep."

She caught his hand. He allowed her to tug it free and examine the wound. She snorted. "Bad enough, especially for here." She seized his sleeve as if afraid he would bolt. "Come to the medical hut and let me take care of it."

He was entirely content to fall in with her wishes. Aside from his mother, no other woman had wanted to take care of his hurts before; it was, he discovered, rather nice.

Her lips set, she all but towed him along.

The medical hut was dark and full of shadows, but she knew where the lamp and tinderbox were kept. He stood in the doorway of the same room they'd used when he'd first come to the compound while she lit the wick, then set the glass in place.

Golden lamplight bathed the scene, making the room appear cozier than in daylight.

Already busy searching in a drawer, she glanced back at him, then frowned and waved him to the bed. "Sit down."

The bed was draped with the usual mosquito netting suspended from a hook above; even the hammocks they slept in in their huts were swathed with the stuff. He crossed to the bed, swept the netting aside, and sat on the edge of the well-stuffed pallet.

Apparently satisfied she'd assembled all she would require, she poured water into a bowl, then set aside the pitcher, tipped liquid from a blue glass bottle into the water, swirled it around, then set aside the bottle, picked up the bowl, and carried it to him. "Here. Balance this on your lap."

He did. Then she crouched before him, took his injured hand between both of hers, and gently dunked it in the water.

He hissed and nearly jerked his hand away, but she'd anticipated his reaction and held tight, keeping his palm submerged. "It'll stop stinging in a minute."

Teeth gritted, he said nothing, but sure enough, the vicious sting faded until it was merely pain. "What the devil is that?" he finally managed to ask.

"Believe it or not, it's a tincture Dubois gave us. The children often get cuts and scrapes. After one of the boys got a badly infected hand, he—Dubois—gave us the bottle. He said it was something the natives used to treat wounds." She glanced up and met his eyes. "Whatever it is, we've found it to be highly effective."

He grunted. He peered down at the cut as she gently bathed it. "Given the pain, it's a wonder the damned thing isn't cauterized."

She chuckled.

After washing and drying the wound, she stroked salve across it—making him shiver. She smiled softly to herself, set aside the pot of salve, then picked up a long strip of gauze. After carefully laying the strip across his palm, she wound the bandage around his hand and tied it off with a tiny knot.

"There." She patted the bandage, then rocked back on her heels and stood. "At least you had the sense to come and get it cleaned straightaway. If you can manage to keep that binding more or less on for more than a day, and avoid putting too much pressure on the cut itself, it should heal nicely."

He grunted again. He watched her tidy and put things away; he would have offered to help, but he didn't know where anything went and suspected he would simply get in the way.

But when everything was neat and she came to smile down at him, he reached out and took her hand. He caught her eyes, saw her brows faintly rise in question, then, holding her gaze, he raised her hand to his lips and brushed a long, slow kiss across her knuckles.

It was her turn to shiver.

His turn to smile. "Thank you."

Then he fell back on the bed and, still holding her hand, pulled and toppled her down. She landed in a sprawl atop him.

Before she could react, he grasped her waist, lifted and shifted her, and settled her over him.

Planting her elbows on his chest and balancing on them, she pushed back the loose hair that had fallen over her face. Then, looking down from a distance of mere inches, she studied his features. Their eyes locked, the moment stretched…then she bent her head until her luscious lips were no more than a whisker from his. "Perhaps," she murmured, sultry and low, "you might think of some way to show your appreciation."

Before he could chuckle, before he could respond, she lowered her head, their lips met and melded, and they both fell into the kiss.

It felt almost as good as coming home—laden with reassurance and the promise of contentment. Of the assuagement of hunger and the joys of simple pleasures.

All the joys of a future assured.

The future they wanted and intended to have. The future they would fight for.

For long moments, they exchanged physical pleasure on one plane and hopes and dreams on another.

Touches, caresses, and the communion of their mouths held their senses spellbound.

Together, they explored.

Holding him to their kiss, Katherine moved sinuously over him, using her body, her limbs, to caress his; she delighted in the tension that hardened his muscles to iron. With growing confidence, she tested his control and found it rock solid, absolute—something she could have faith in.

He returned the pleasure, his big hands roving over her—over all he could reach. He paid homage to her breasts, leaving them swollen and aching. In long, sweeping caresses, he traced the curves of her back, her waist, her hips, then he filled his hands with the globes of her bottom and, with a blatant possessiveness that stole her breath, molded her hips to his.

Then he held her steady and rocked beneath her, the base of his rigid shaft pressing against her mons, and sensation speared through her, sharp, intense, and glorious, and she caught her first glimpse of paradise.

Eventually, they accepted that, here and now, they could explore no further.

They drew back from the engagement, fraction by fraction, until, at last, their lips parted. From beneath weighted lids, their eyes met, held. Their rapid breathing, their thudding heartbeats, impinged on her awareness.

She tensed to lift away, but his arms tightened about her, the wordless message clear.

Her lips curving, she surrendered and tucked her head beneath his chin, and relaxed, boneless, in his arms.

He shifted and settled, his embrace comfortable, protective, and secure, and she seized the moments to wallow in the uncomplicated closeness.

In any other place, at any other time, what she felt for him—what she knew beyond question already existed between them—would have taken months to build to this point, to where they both openly acknowledged the reality.

But the exigencies of their situation had left them no time for niceties. For the usual, slow, getting-to-know-each-other stage. Not for them the customary questioning, the normal hesitancy.

From the moment they'd met, they'd been forced to look and truly see each other, to assess each other's character. And this place had not granted them the time for the polite dance of courtship.

So there they were, knowing what they knew and trying to find their way forward.

After several silent moments, she set her tongue free. "Are we mad, do you think, for pursuing this, when we might be dead in a few weeks?"

"No." Although the rebuttal came instantly, his tone made it clear his reply was considered; he'd already thought of the point. "If anything, I think pursuing this is a testimony to how sane we both are."

She raised her head and looked into his face.

He met her eyes. "We both know *this* is worth wanting. Worth claiming. Whatever the price."

"You're right. I just hope…"

That we survive. That this *isn't doomed.*

Although she didn't say the words, she felt sure he understood.

His arms tightened about her. "All we can do is go forward and do what we need to—to meet each challenge as it materializes. Just as long as we never forget what we want, what our end goal truly is, trust me, we will win through."

She couldn't stop her lips from curving; he could make even her believe triumph was inevitable.

Then she thought further, and her smile faded. "What of the mining?" She studied his face. "It's bad, isn't it?"

He grimaced. He drew his arms from around her, grasped her waist, and lifted her from him.

Side by side, they sat on the edge of the bed. He went to scrub both palms over his face, then realized one was bandaged.

He lowered that hand, with the other reached and took her hand and twined his fingers with hers. "I have to admit, it's worse than we expected. We sink picks into the rock face, and the diamonds all but fall at our feet. In some spots, the rock face has so many diamonds in it, it's crumbling." He paused, then went on, "We're putting what we can into the stockpile, but there's a limit to how much we can secrete inside the mine, especially with Dubois showing greater interest in how much is coming out." He blew out a breath. "We've agreed that we can't afford to wait until Arsene returns with your new tools to try our next tactic. We have to restrain the mining itself—and that's now a matter of urgency."

She frowned. "What about Dixon's lower level?"

"At present, that's the only potential light on our mining horizon. *If* a lower level gives us access to a deposit like that in the upper level, then *if* we slow things down for a while, we might be able to stretch the mining out for long enough without doing anything more."

"Dixon still can't say what the lower level is like?"

Caleb shook his head. "The rock structures at that end of the tunnel are more difficult to break through and then stabilize. He says he won't know either way until we open an exploratory shaft and he can see the extent of the pipe."

She nodded. "So what's our next tactic? The lamp oil?"

"Yes." He glanced at her face. "And we're going to act tomorrow morning—we can't afford to wait."

She met his eyes, then gripped his hand more tightly. "I'll warn the other women and the children before we come out for breakfast."

"Do." He considered, then said, "It won't be that early, but best everyone knows, so they stay out of the way and carry on as if nothing's happening. Dixon, Hillsythe, and I are working on a charade—a way to present the problem to Dubois so he accepts that the oil running low is just one of those things, and not anything planned by us."

Caleb didn't add that the only other viable method of restricting the mining remaining to them was to collapse at least a part of the tunnel. Strictly between themselves, the male leaders felt forced to keep that on their list of potential tactics, but there were so many things that could go wrong with such an action—not least that it might permanently close the tunnels, thus precipitating the very situation they were striving so hard to delay—that they viewed it as a last and distinctly desperate resort.

He glanced at Katherine, but all the men involved had agreed that the fact that they'd even contemplated such an act was best kept to themselves.

He faced forward, heaved a sigh, then pushed up from the bed. He used their linked hands to draw her to her feet. He met her eyes and summoned a gentle smile. "Thank you for your care.

Thank you for your attentions." He bent his head and brushed a kiss across her lips.

Then he straightened and said, "Come. I'll walk you to your hut, then I need to get back."

Into the mine. Back to their planning.

★ ★ ★

The men waited until midmorning before putting their plan into action—before commencing the charade that, they hoped, would convince Dubois that the compound running low on lamp oil was an innocent and understandable accident.

Whatever they did, they could not risk Dubois developing any definite suspicions of them. None of them wished to even contemplate what his reaction might be.

An empty lantern in his hand, Caleb stood inside the mine entrance. Still well within the concealing shadows, he looked out. And waited.

They'd dug the pit to hide the oil a week ago, and every day since, they'd drained oil from the lanterns in the mine. In addition, they'd taken advantage of Dubois's insistence that the men work extra hours to burn all the lanterns on maximum flame for all those hours, further running down the supply.

They'd lined up the excuses, the reasons Dixon would advance for the oil running low. It was helpful that their access to the oil supply was restricted; only Dixon could fill their lanterns, whether for the mine or their huts, including the cleaning shed and medical hut. The other lamps in the compound—all those the mercenaries used as well as those in the kitchen—were filled by whichever mercenary thought of it.

Lots of others had access to the oil supply. Lots of others should have noticed it running low and reported it to Dubois, but no one had.

Which meant Dixon would have to, because the lanterns in the mine had now all but run out.

And although it was tempting to simply sit in the mine in the dark, Dubois would all too soon notice the lack of ore coming out, and then they would have to explain why they hadn't said anything…that wasn't a tack they wanted to take.

Courtesy of a calendar they'd found in the supply hut, they knew today was the fourth of August. That left at least a month before rescue could reach them. A month during which they had to ensure the mining continued.

The scuff of a boot had Caleb glancing around. He watched as Dixon, brushing his palms on his breeches, came to join him.

Caleb briefly studied the engineer. Unlike Caleb, Phillipe, or Hillsythe, Dixon wasn't a man to whom fabrication came easily; playing a part was something he had to work hard to pull off. Caleb gave Dixon a moment, then murmured, "Ready?"

His gaze fixed on the mercenaries' barracks, Dixon nodded. From his breeches pocket, he pulled out a sheaf of papers. "I'll head for the supply hut. Let me get level with the barracks' steps, then call and stop me."

Cripps and two of his men were lounging on stools on the barracks' porch.

Caleb nodded. "Good luck."

Dixon hauled in a breath, held it, then walked briskly out of the mine.

He continued across the compound, striding purposefully past the fire pit and on toward the supply hut, his head bent, his attention on the lists in his hand.

Caleb strode out. The lantern swinging from his hand, he broke into a lope. "Dixon!"

Dixon halted—level with the porch steps and directly under Cripps's and the other two mercenaries' noses—and swung around. He saw the lantern in Caleb's hand and frowned. "Another one?"

Slowing to halt before him, Caleb held out the lantern and shrugged. "All those extra hours, I suppose."

Resigned, Dixon took the lantern. "I'll fill it. Wait here."

Caleb cast a glance at the men on the porch. "I'll wait by the mine."

Dixon nodded and, returning his attention to his lists, continued toward the supply hut.

Caleb didn't risk watching him go but swung around and retreated to the mine entrance. He slouched against the beams framing the tunnel mouth and fixed his gaze on the toes of his boots.

He heard movement in the shadows behind him; head bent, he cast a swift glance behind and saw Hillsythe and Phillipe settling to watch. Apparently, they all felt the need to be there to support Dixon, just in case, but exactly what they might do was one part of the charade they hadn't rehearsed.

As per their plan, after several minutes, Dixon came out of the supply hut, the lantern—its glass reservoir now half full—in one hand. He stuffed his lists into his pocket and, his frown now definite, marched to the barracks.

Dixon went up the steps. He ignored Cripps and his men and went straight to the open doorway; from the first, Dubois had made it plain that he expected Dixon to report directly to him. Dixon knocked on the door frame.

Watching from the mine entrance, Caleb and the others couldn't see inside the barracks, but Dixon remained on the porch. They knew Dubois was inside, most likely at his desk. In what was plainly a response to a question—almost certainly from Dubois—Dixon held up the lantern. "I just filled this." Dixon's words were muted by the distance and barely audible. "Because we're working longer hours, we're running through lamp oil more rapidly, but that's not my point. Has anyone reported that the supply of lamp oil is running low?"

Even from the mine, they heard Dubois's thunderous *"What?"*

A second later, Dixon stepped back and Dubois appeared in the doorway. By the time he stepped onto the porch, Cripps and the other two mercenaries had leapt to their feet. They stood rooted in a stance that, for them, passed for attention.

Dubois's choler had already risen. He cast a single dark glance at the lantern in Dixon's hand, then rounded on Cripps. *"What the devil do you mean by letting the lamp oil run low?"* Dubois flung his hands in the air. "Am I surrounded by incompetents? No— not *just* incompetents—I'm also plagued by impatient backers." Dubois advanced on Cripps and spoke into the man's face, yet his fury was so rabid his grating tones carried clearly. "I told you of the letter Arsene brought back. More diamonds, they want! Send out more on the ships, they demand! This from those who are paying us—and let me remind you, paying us all handsomely. So now at last, after holding them off and sending excuse after explanation, we are finally in a position to send them all the diamonds they could wish for…and we *run out of oil!*"

Dubois's fists clenched and unclenched, then clenched hard again—as hard as his jaw.

Dixon cleared his throat. "Actually, it's not really any person's fault—more a failure in logistical planning." He looked at the lantern in his hand—no doubt so he wouldn't have to look at Dubois's furious face as the mercenary captain rounded on him. Dixon's engineer's tones were calm and even—an expert explaining to those who didn't understand. "It's a combination of things—more men working in the mine, so more lanterns burning. Plus the extension of hours, which means all the lanterns are burning for half a day longer every day." He shrugged. "Hardly surprising the lamp oil's run low. Once the decision was made to extend the hours, the last order should have been doubled."

Caleb pushed away from the frame at the mine's entrance and walked unhurriedly toward the porch.

Dixon hadn't actually said it, but given that Dubois issued all the orders, the implication was that the need for more lamp oil was something he—Dubois—should have foreseen and taken care of. That if fault there was, it was his.

Cripps, for one, understood very well; the relief in his face as he—along with his men—looked at Dubois was transparent.

Caleb reached the porch. His gaze on Dixon, he nodded at the lantern. "Can I have that?" With a backward tip of his head, he directed attention to the mine's entrance, where Phillipe and Hillsythe had come into the open. "We need it to go on."

"Here." Dixon moved to the edge of the porch and handed over the lantern.

Caleb took it. The diversion had given Dubois a chance to breathe in—and swallow his ire.

And also to see that the captives' interest was focused on working the mine and nothing else.

He hadn't underestimated Dubois. The man's gaze had shifted from Dixon to Caleb, and then to the pair by the mine. Dubois considered them for a full second, then he turned to Dixon. "How much oil is left?"

Dixon grimaced. "Not much."

"What can be done with what we have left while Cripps goes to fetch more?"

Dixon considered, then replied, "Because of the longer hours, the lanterns in the mine are running low on a daily basis. The women can't work under lanternlight, so there's two lanterns in the cleaning shed we can take for the mine. I'll check the other huts and see what oil we can draw from there, but I doubt it will be much." He glanced at Dubois. "We can't risk mining under insufficient light—that will lead to lots of unnecessarily fractured diamonds, which your backers won't like. Even opening up the lower level—we need to see what we're doing, or we'll risk bringing the mountain down on top of us and the entire mine."

He paused as if calculating, then offered, "We can keep going, but only at a very much reduced rate. It'll be nothing like full production, at least not out of the mine, but luckily the output from the cleaning shed will ramp up as soon as Arsene returns, so the amount of raw diamonds going out to the ship should be unaffected. Regardless, I'll ensure we stretch the oil out in the best way possible—to yield the most while we wait for more."

That Dubois accepted the assurance with nothing more than a terse nod was a testimony to how well Dixon had managed to play his role over the past months. Dubois in no way liked the situation, but he'd accepted it.

Dubois swung to face Cripps. A muscle in Dubois's jaw flexed; through gritted teeth, he said, "Go to the settlement and fetch more lamp oil. A *lot* more."

"More lanterns would—" Caleb pressed his lips shut and assumed a look of chagrin.

Dubois had glanced at him. Now he smiled like a shark and turned back to Cripps. "And as the good captain suggests, bring back more lanterns as well." He paused, then added, "And more food."

Dubois turned back to survey Caleb. The mercenary captain waited until Caleb looked up and met his gaze before inclining his head. "Thank you for the suggestion, Captain Frobisher."

Caleb frowned, genuinely puzzled. "And the food?"

Dubois's shark's smile returned. "That's to ensure that, once Cripps returns with the supplies, you and your fellows will be in prime condition to continue the mining at maximum rate."

He didn't voice the words, but the warning *No more excuses* rang in the air.

Caleb shrugged. Lantern in hand, he turned and walked back toward the mine. He'd realized that having more lanterns wouldn't make any difference to the mining—indeed, they might even help to continue to run the lamp oil down. And more food wasn't anything to sneer at.

But best of all, his little ploy—his apparent slip of the tongue—had set the seal on Dubois's conviction that there was nothing peculiar about the lamp oil running low.

That the captives, although affected, weren't in any way involved in generating the shortage.

As he neared the mine entrance where Phillipe and Hill-sythe waited, Caleb smiled—the gesture every bit as sharklike as Dubois's.

★ ★ ★

As had become their habit, Katherine walked with Caleb in the cool of the evening, making a slow counterclockwise circuit of the compound. Harriet and Dixon and Annie and Jed were also strolling, and Gemma, Ellen, and Mary were taking the air in a group with five of Caleb and Lascelle's men.

There was an unstated feeling of seizing the comfort of each other's company while they could.

As they neared the medical hut, her gaze on the pair of guards patrolling the perimeter beyond the heaps of discarded ore, Katherine murmured, "Has Dixon made any estimate of how slow we'll be able to go?" She glanced at Caleb's face and amended, "Whether we'll be able to stretch the mining out long enough?"

He shook his head. "He and the rest of us spent all afternoon working out our best way forward and, with that in mind, fig-uring out the best proposition to put to Dubois—meaning the one most likely to support the fiction that the mining is going forward as fast as possible given the lack of oil, but that in real-ity will result in the fewest diamonds taken out of the rock. We decided we should use what little oil remains to keep one sec-tion of the second tunnel—the part closest to the tunnel mouth and most visible to the guards—well lit and operational. That's what Dixon will recommend to Dubois. However, in addition to that and unknown to Dubois, we'll send a party deep into the first tunnel with lanterns turned low—they'll be out of sight and hearing of the guards. There are no diamonds in the rock down there, but we'll use the ore they generate to thin out the diamonds produced from the second deposit. We're planning to divert as many of the diamonds as possible into our stockpile while still sending out a reasonable concentration of stones in the broken rock, enough to keep Dubois or anyone else who checks the output appeased."

She nodded. "I can see that will stretch things out, but will it be for long enough?"

"Probably not by itself. But given what we have in the upper level, Dixon is hopeful that once we open up the lower level, which will allow us to continue mining directly along the pipe, we'll have access to enough stones to see us through. Which is why we've acted to keep the concentration of stones going out of the mine as low as we dare, and also why we've ceased all work on opening the lower level—Dixon feels we'll be better served by putting that off for as long as we can."

He glanced at her, read the confusion in her face, and went on, "There's a physical limit to how many men can work the rock face in the second tunnel. When Cripps gets back and we return to full production, only just over half the men can work the second tunnel at any time. Now the first deposit is all but mined out, there are more men available. If there was more of the diamond-bearing rock face accessible—"

"Dubois would have you all working all of the time." She nodded. "So you need to hold back on opening the lower level until a reasonable amount of the upper level is mined out."

"Or until we're sure we have enough stones between the upper and lower levels to see us into September." Caleb grimaced. "But we haven't yet opened up the lower level sufficiently for Dixon to go down and make an assessment. Once he does, then we'll know where we stand, and hopefully, we'll have reason to feel safe."

She sighed and looked ahead. "It will be a huge relief to be able to feel safe."

"Indeed." They'd circled around the cleaning shed. The guards who had been skirting the ore piles had moved on. Caleb glanced around, but no one else was visible, and he and Katherine were presently out of sight of the tower. He detoured to-ward the steps to the shed.

Katherine glanced at his face, but then only smiled. They reached the steps, and she raised her hem and followed him up.

Wondering if one of the other couples had got there before them, he eased the door open and peeked in. Moonlight pouring through the panels in the roof lit the deserted space. He pushed the door wider, drew Katherine through, then nudged the door shut and set the latch in place.

He turned—and she slipped her arms about his waist and came up on her toes; as he instinctively bent his head, equally instinctively closed his hands about her waist, she offered her lips, and he covered them with his.

Days. They'd known each other for just days, yet sinking into her mouth, savoring her kiss, already seemed so familiar. Already so much a part of him, the natural appeasement of his desires and needs.

In seizing this mission as his own, he hadn't expected anything like this. He was only twenty-eight; he had years yet before he'd expected to settle down. Declan might have married at thirty-one, and judging by his journal, Robert, a year older, looked set to walk down the aisle very soon. But Royd was thirty-four and had yet to marry, so why should he?

Because she was here, in his arms.

Because she was kissing him, and he was kissing her, and for just these moments, nothing else mattered but her and him and what had grown between them.

And because one couldn't escape fate, and at some fundamental level, he knew she was his.

He'd known that from the first, and in his usual way, he'd elected not to fight but rather to travel with the tide.

And now she and that tide were tugging him on.

Into a sea of passion.

Katherine wanted—quite what, she couldn't have said, not

in words, but need of a kind she'd never felt before sank claws into her flesh and drove her on. She'd parted her lips and welcomed him in and gloried in her bold confidence—and in his as he claimed all she offered. Sensual hunger grew, his and hers, a complementary compulsion she now recognized.

Her arms looped over his shoulders, she backed and drew him with her, and he obliged. Step by step, she waltzed them across the floor, until her back hit the edge of the raised table and a stool, dislodged, scraped the floor alongside them.

Neither of them broke from the all-absorbing kiss, but one of his hands left her waist. She sensed him tugging the stool closer, then his hand returned, and he gripped her waist and hoisted her up. Her hands sliding to his throat, his jaw, she clutched and held him to the kiss and felt his lips curve against hers.

A second later, he flipped her skirt above her knees, parted her thighs so he could push between, and stepped closer.

Her breath caught in her chest. The sudden play of cooler air on her bared limbs sent awareness prickling over her skin. Sent her nerves, her senses, spiking. Compelled, she shifted her hands to his cheeks, framed his face—and held him steady as she kissed him with an ardor she hadn't known she possessed.

Or perhaps the flaring passion possessed her—it certainly seemed to drive her, to wield a power all its own. Regardless, he patently welcomed it; with a muted growl, trapped between their lips, he deepened the kiss and met her fire with his own. Yet he let her play, let her enjoy having the ascendency and direct the exchange for several heady heartbeats, but then his lips firmed, and he took control.

He leaned into her, tipping her until her back met the edge of the table.

Then his hands left her waist and rose to close about her breasts, and she stopped thinking, her mind, her wits, overwhelmed by feeling.

By the sensations he so knowingly stoked, that he drew forth, then sent rushing through her.

It might be wanton to so welcome his touch, yet the feel of his hands stroking and caressing and possessing her flesh, even muted by two layers of fabric, sent pleasure and delight coursing through her veins. And when his fingers firmed about her nipples, a delicious thrill spiked and shot straight to her core, igniting a wave of warmth low in her belly.

Caleb sank into the moment, into the pleasure of the exchange, a direct and straightforward foray into delight. Into the myriad little ways he and she could enjoy each other, could—for just those moments—take themselves from this world.

Away from the reality that neither could predict, neither could control, yet both prayed to counter.

To survive so that they could go forward.

He kneaded and caressed and rejoiced in the flaring heat of her response. He angled his head and ravaged her mouth, and her response—so fiery and demanding—nearly rocked him back on his heels. Before he'd even thought, his fingers had found the laces of her gown. A few quick tugs and he'd loosened the bodice enough to peel it down. By touch, he discovered that her fine chemise was held in place by a drawstring—one tug, a little pushing, and he slid his fingers, his hand, over her fine skin and cupped her breast.

They both stilled.

Stunned by the sensual jolt, by the sheer intensity of the tactile impact.

Their lips parted. From beneath their lashes, their eyes met. Just for an instant, they were both caught, flung adrift on a sea of physical feeling. Then her lids fell; a soft moan escaped her lips, and she pressed her breast into his palm.

He dove back into the kiss, and she met him. Her fingers tangled in his hair and then gripped, holding him tight, urging him on.

He needed no urging.

Katherine's senses were spinning—giddy and drunk on pleasure. She felt flushed, hot, her breasts swelling beneath his
hand—hands, now. *Oh, God.* She wasn't sure she could cope
with so much feeling—so much sensation sparking down every
nerve—yet the thud of her pulse drove her on.

His hands were so hot, burning against her skin, yet the fire
itself seemed to come from within. Like flames, that hot sensation licked over her flesh, spreading from her breasts over her
limbs and washing lower through her body.

She could so easily lose herself in this, with him. Some distant
part of her brain was mildly surprised that she felt no shame, not
even any awkwardness. This—this closeness, this sharing—simply felt new, with all the attraction of a novel activity. She felt
hesitant, but only because she didn't know what came next, what
was appropriate, and was having to rely on instinct to guide her.
Yet above all else, this closeness, this sharing, with him, felt right.

In this, with him, she was where she should be.

So she let go. Set her senses free to whirl and dance and savor.

Through the communion of their kiss, Caleb realized her direction and was only too happy to follow. To oblige. The feel
of her skin, so silken and warm beneath his callused palms, held
the promise of bliss, of glorious satisfaction.

He tightened his fingers about her nipples just enough to distract and focus her attention, then he drew his lips from hers and
sent them cruising. Over the delicate curve of her jaw and down
the slender column of her throat. He pressed an open-mouthed
kiss to the spot where her pulse beat so strongly, so hotly. Then
he trailed his lips down over the gentle swell of her breast. Down
to where his fingers rolled one tightly furled nipple.

With the tip of his tongue, he circled the tight bud, then gently
laved—and heard her breath catch, felt her fingers dig into his
skull as her nerves leapt.

He lipped her nipple, then drew it gently into his mouth—and her spine bowed, and her gasp filled the silence.

Inwardly smiling—gloating—he set himself to minister to her senses, to her needs and desires. She made those easy to read, conveyed by the pressure of her fingertips on his skull and by the breathy little moans she uttered.

His own needs, his own desires, welled and leapt, provoked by those evocative sounds. He was fully aroused, his erection a rigid rod restrained beneath his breeches. He shifted, restless, his baser self alive, awake, and intensely aware, but he told himself to forget the temptation her splayed thighs presented.

Easier thought than done, yet despite her ardent responses—despite her open encouragement—he knew acquaintance of mere days was not long enough to even think of ravishing her.

Much less there, in a place of no softness.

Manfully, he quashed all such thoughts, raised his head, found her lips, and reimmersed himself in the kiss. He returned his hands to her breasts, to their worship, and told himself again that, to this point, that was enough.

He hadn't expected her to disagree, yet as if she'd been privy to his inner argument, she made an incoherent sound; even trapped between their lips and muted by the kiss, it was clearly a sound of protest.

Then she squirmed closer, her thighs parting further, and she freed her hands from his hair and reached for his shirt.

Before he could react—before he realized her intent—she closed her fists in the fabric and hauled it up, then her hands dove under, and her greedy fingers and palms were on his skin—hungry and grasping, claiming and possessing...

Her touch burned with the silver flame of intense sexual desire. He felt seared, energized—shocked into a higher state of passion. Involuntarily, his hands firmed about her breasts, fingers tightening about her nipples—she just gasped through the kiss, and her sweeping, grasping, greedy hands urged him on.

Who was ravishing whom?

Then her hands drifted lower. *Oh, no, no, no.* Her palms molded themselves to his abdomen, her touch oddly innocent, tentative yet determined. Then with wanton deliberation, she slid those questing hands lower still.

He released her breasts and, without breaking the kiss, shifted back and caught her wandering hands. He found her wicked fingers and twined them—locked them—with his.

He drew her arms out to her sides, pressed their locked hands to the edge of the table—then stepped close again, angled his head over hers, and kissed her with all the searing passion she'd evoked in him. So much more than any other before her.

In that moment, he understood and fully accepted that Fate had brought him there—to her, to this.

To this moment of awakening.

To this second in which he finally comprehended what it was to desire, to want, to need, one specific woman.

To the recognition that his destiny lay inextricably entwined with hers.

And that there was *no limit* to what he would do, what he would give, to protect her. So that ultimately they could and would reach for and seize that destiny together.

He pulled back from the kiss.

His breath was coming in short, shallow pants.

Her lips were swollen, the delectable curves glistening, lush and ripe.

Her eyes, when she raised her lids and looked into his, were huge and passion drenched.

As he watched, her gaze turned quizzical.

He groaned, closed his eyes, and dropped his forehead to hers. "Kate."

"Caleb?"

He was in pain, and yet... It took serious effort, but he managed to find strength enough to straighten and say, "Not here. Not yet."

The words were gravelly, but at least they were clear.

Only then did she seem to recall where they were. She blinked and glanced around. "Oh."

Then she brought her gaze back to his face.

He met her eyes, his gaze steady. "Later." And just in case she doubted it, even after that incendiary kiss, he stated, "I want you. *After* we survive this, I want to and will ask you to be my wife. But not here, not yet."

Kate. Only he had ever called her that—only he had ever seen the woman she was inside. In her head, she used to think of herself as Kate; Kate was the woman she'd expected to be, that she'd thought she could be and should be, but everyone else had always called her Katherine. She'd never corrected them. And since her mother had died, she'd forced herself to be Katherine even in her mind. More formal; more proper and correct.

I want to and will ask you to be my wife.

She looked into his eyes and saw the unswerving commitment behind the words. Simple words—not a proposal but the promise of one. *After...*

He could have taken advantage of her with her enthusiastic blessing, but of course, he hadn't. Not him.

Not the man she—Kate—had already fallen in love with.

"Yes." Her eyes on his, she said that one word—the only word she could say in response.

He blinked, then his features eased, and the reckless smile she'd seen the first time she'd met him resurfaced.

"And you're right." She tugged, and he eased his hold on her fingers, and she drew them free.

He let his arms fall and stepped back, allowing her to slip from the stool and stand before him.

She wriggled her gown into place and swiftly tied the laces while he tucked his shirt back into his breeches. Then she smiled, stretched up, and brushed her lips across his. *"After."* Dropping back to her heels, she held his gaze. "We'll continue this after we win free."

Fifteen

Arsene returned to the compound with the replacements for the women's tools in just four days. Immediately thereafter, Cripps left with four other men to fetch more lamp oil and other supplies.

Kate—she'd reverted to thinking of herself by that name—wasn't surprised when Dubois carried the new tools to the cleaning shed himself. He laid them out along the raised table, then coldly looked at the women, calculatingly meeting each one's eyes. Finally, he returned his gaze to Kate's face. "You will all work from sunrise to sunset—as long as there is light. Only you and…" He glanced at Annie.

"Miss Mellows," Kate supplied.

Dubois refocused on her. "Only you two are excused for one hour each afternoon to attend to checking the children's work. Immediately that task is complete, you will return to your work here. There will be no ambling about while there is light enough for you to work." He glanced around the six women. "Are those instructions clear?"

None of the others spoke, although all of them nodded.

Kate waited until he returned his gaze to her, and nodded, too. "Quite clear."

She hadn't been there when Dubois had allowed his men to brutalize the young girl, but she'd seen the shadows in Harriet's eyes; neither she nor any of the others would willingly tempt Dubois, and they'd all heard of the letter he'd recently received from the mysterious backers.

Dubois held her gaze for a pregnant moment. Then, as if accepting her submission, he nodded. "Excellent." He turned for the door. "While there are diamonds to be cleaned, you will continue to work for as long as possible at the best possible pace."

The women waited until he'd left the shed, then waited for a full minute more. Even then, they held their tongues and waited until Gemma went to the open door, looked out, and confirmed Dubois had, indeed, returned to the barracks and that there were no guards lurking before they let down their guard.

Then they slumped onto their stools. They grimaced; some muttered. Grimly resigned, Kate reached for the new hammers and chisels, sorted them, and then shared them around the table.

Perched on her stool opposite, Harriet accepted the new tools and met Kate's gaze. "So what do we do now?"

Kate raised her brows. She reached into the basket sitting beside her, lifted out a large piece of ore, and started turning it between her fingers, searching out the planes between mineral concretion and diamond. After a moment, she said, her voice low, but strong enough to be heard by all the women, all of whom were listening and following her lead, "We obey Dubois's orders and work. We work at the same pace we always have, for the hours he stipulated. Meanwhile... I'll have a word to Frobisher and Lascelle about their idea." She glanced up and met Harriet's gaze.

Brightening, Harriet murmured, "The pieces of canvas?"

Kate nodded. "As long as Dubois and his men continue not to count the individual diamonds coming into the shed, I can't see how they can have any specific expectations over how many cleaned diamonds come out."

★ ★ ★

"Until Cripps gets back with more lamp oil," Caleb said, "the men are on short shifts, so Phillipe and I will see what we can do about creating pockets under your stools."

He and Kate—she was now Kate to him; that name fitted

the woman who was his better than the primly reserved Katherine—were sitting on one of the logs about the fire pit, surrounded by the other captives. They'd just finished their usual meager meal of meat of some kind, eaten with what passed for bread in these parts. Water, at least, was plentiful. He raised his tin mug and sipped.

"At least we can only work while there's sufficient sunlight."

He lowered his mug. "True. But you'll have to make a visible dent in that pile of rock outside the shed." Turning the mug between his hands, he thought, then said, "I suspect you'd better ensure that you and the ladies fill that strongbox at least a little faster than you were before—before you had a backlog to work through."

"Indeed, and the new tools will help us accomplish that." Kate caught his gaze. "But given the size of the backlog, we can keep our output at the higher levels Dubois will expect while also holding back a decent number of cleaned stones in case of later need."

Dixon, seated on Kate's other side with Harriet beyond him, had been listening. He leaned closer. "Harriet mentioned your notion of using canvas for the pockets. There are some old sails tucked away in the supply shed. If you tell me what you need, I can cut the pieces for you—easier to bring out the pieces than the whole sail."

Caleb called Phillipe over, and between them and the women they estimated the size of the canvas squares they would need.

Dixon nodded. "I'll make time tomorrow morning to cut them."

Caleb glanced at Kate. "Phillipe and I will drop by in the afternoon and set up the pockets. Ten minutes is all it will take."

She worried her lower lip with her teeth. "It might be best if you came while Annie and I are with the children." She met his gaze. "Less chance of one of the guards thinking something might be going on and coming to investigate."

"We'll keep watch anyway," Harriet said. "But I agree with Katherine—better you come when she and Annie aren't there."

Caleb discovered he agreed and nodded. Anything to minimize the chances of raising Dubois's suspicions, especially over anything involving Kate.

With that decided, they settled to discuss the current state and rate of the mining. Ultimately, that led to everyone wanting to know how much longer it would be before Dixon managed to get into the lower level and—they all fervently hoped—confirm that the rock face there was as densely packed with diamonds as in the upper level, so that they would face no insurmountable obstacle in keeping the mining going long enough to be rescued.

For them *all* to be rescued.

Ever since September the seventh had been flagged as the date, Kate had been counting the days. Today had been August the fifth, so they needed four weeks' grace—four weeks' more steady, straightforward mining.

According to Dixon, Caleb, and the others working on opening the lower level, they were hoping to sufficiently brace the crawl space they'd created to allow Dixon to check the quality of the vein of diamond-bearing ore sometime during the next day.

So by tomorrow evening, they would know.

Know if they would be safe—if they would be able to keep the mine going until the rescue force arrived—or if their lives still hung in the balance with an uphill battle before them.

Kate sent up a prayer that all would prove to be as they needed, and she was certain she wasn't the only one addressing the Almighty on their behalf.

Then it was time for the men to return to the mine. It was a part of Dixon's assumed role to chivvy them up and back to work. Although the others grumbled and cast him dark looks, that was all for show.

Kate rose to her feet as Caleb stood.

He looked down at her, hesitated, then reached out and tucked a stray strand of her hair behind her ear. "It might be better if you got what sleep you can. You'll be working under increased pressure from now on, and my group is going to push as hard as we can tonight to get the lower level shored up."

She frowned. "Won't you have to stop because of the lamp oil?" Dubois had had Dixon set up a rationing system to ensure the groups actually mining would have enough oil to keep production as high as possible through the shortage. Dubois had appointed Arsene to oversee the allocation of oil each day, so what Dubois regarded as non-essential works had limited hours of light.

He grimaced. "Yes, but we'll go for as long as we can."

Over recent nights, they'd enjoyed a quiet amble about the compound before retiring, but after their last interlude, perhaps he was right and they should play safe. She met his gaze and nodded. "All right." She touched his arm, then let her hand fall. "I'll see you in the morning."

With a nod, he turned and joined the other men, who under Dixon's urging were straggling back into the mine.

She watched until Caleb vanished inside, then returned to sit with Harriet and the other women. They chatted and watched over the children as, gathered in their smaller groups, they, too, talked about this and that. Just how much the younger ones truly understood, Kate didn't know, but the older ones...the expression in their eyes suggested that they understood the situation all too well.

Diccon came to sit at her feet and leaned against her legs. Kate smiled down at him even though he couldn't see, then gently stroked his fine pale hair.

After an hour of desultory activity, the children agreed to the women's suggestion that it was time for bed. There were rarely any arguments. The work the children did was strenuous and tiring, as well as largely boring; sleep was, to them, an escape from their waking hours—their dreams were doubtless better than their reality.

With the other women, Kate herded the children into their hut and into their respective hammocks. She busied herself wrapping the fine mosquito netting over and around each hammock; many of the children were already asleep, eyes closed and breathing softly, by the time she and the other women had them protected.

Then the women got themselves into their own hammocks. In the circumstances, they didn't divest themselves of their gowns but slept in them.

Gradually, the hut grew quiet, a quiet composed of the gentle murmur of thirty individuals breathing, punctuated by the occasional raucous call of some nocturnal animal hunting beyond the compound's walls.

Enveloped in the now-familiar dark, Kate lay in her hammock and stared up through the netting. She couldn't see the ceiling, but wasn't actually looking. Her mind had turned inward, following paths she hadn't trod for more than three years. Ever since her mother had fallen ill and she—Kate—had retreated from all contact with others to nurse her ailing parent. That had been when she'd finally and, at least in her mind, deliberately turned her back on marriage, but in truth, her view of that state had been equivocal at best from far earlier. Specifically, from the day her wastrel, always-laughing father had died and left her and her mother so deeply in debt.

So very alone, facing a largely hostile world.

But the one thing she'd never quite understood was the love—never dimming no matter what he did—that her mother had borne for that wastrel profligate. Even as young as Kate had been, she'd seen it—had felt the all but tangible force of it, that power people called love.

Her mother had loved her father, and despite all his flaws, he'd loved her truly, too. In that, he'd never been inconstant.

He'd just been him, and sadly incapable of dealing adequately with the practicalities of life.

And then he'd left them.

In her heart, she'd never forgiven him for that.

In her soul, she still blamed him for her mother's early death.

Men, she'd believed, were just variations on her father—lovable, but ultimately unreliable.

Nineteen days ago, she'd met Caleb.

And she now had some inkling of what had driven her mother's devotion to her father. Now she had a clearer vision of what it was to love a man.

And yet…from somewhere deep inside her, a little voice whispered, questioning how this could be. How could she have fallen so definitely in love in just days? Was it really love—the sort of love that wouldn't die no matter what the loved one did? And if it was, did she truly want it?

Did she have a choice?

Or was she, like her poor mother, doomed to being swept away—by a handsome face, a cheery smile, and circumstance?

How much of her attraction was due to their situation?

How much of his?

Unanswerable questions all, yet she knew she wasn't like her mother, and regardless of her distrust of most men, she knew—to her bones—that Caleb wasn't like her father.

She could trust Caleb. She could rely on him.

Was she up to trusting him forever? With her future, her life—her forever?

And what did it say of her and him that, after the past years of adhering to the name Katherine even in her own mind, it had taken Caleb two weeks to anchor her back in her true self, the self she referred to as Kate?

She stared upward into the darkness and found precious few answers there.

Especially to her most fundamental question: When it came

to Caleb, did she trust herself—or was she simply clinging to him and the safety he exuded because of the dreadful threat hanging over them?

All those questions, but especially the last, left her restless and unsettled. She wasn't going to fall asleep any time soon.

Accepting that, she rolled out of her hammock, fought her way out of the netting shroud, then silently wended around the children's hammocks to the partially closed door. They always left it slightly ajar so if any of the children awoke, they would see the sliver of light and not panic.

She slipped out of the hut into the cooler night air. She sank onto the single stool they left on the small, uncovered porch—more a landing at the top of the two steps. She leaned her shoulders against the hut's wall and let the quiet of the night wash through her.

Let her questions go, let them fade from her mind. She looked up at the stars, shining like the proverbial diamonds in the black velvet of the night sky, and let the constellations, so very far away, remind her of how infinite and ageless they were—and how finite and inconsequential she was in comparison.

Her mind had wandered to recalling the pattern of stars in the night sky over Aberdeen when the sound of men's voices reached her. She looked across the compound and saw the men who had been working the last shift leaving the mine. They made for their hut. With her eyes adjusted to the dark, she could see well enough to confirm that Caleb wasn't among them.

Nor was Dixon or Lascelle.

Even after the emerging men had tramped into their hut and the compound had fallen silent again, the glow of a lantern—distant, but still detectable—shone from the mouth of the mine.

She waited.

Gradually, the steady glow of the lantern started to fade.

Minutes later, she saw a group of men emerge, carrying the

last lantern, now almost out. Among those men walked Caleb, along with Dixon and Lascelle.

The men headed for their hut. Although she didn't move, did nothing to attract his attention, Caleb raised his head, looked across the compound, and saw her.

With a word, he parted from Dixon and Lascelle and came toward her. Intent invested his every stride.

She met him at the bottom of the steps.

His features set, he caught her hand and, without breaking his stride, towed her on—around the side of the women's hut and into the deeper shadows there.

Abruptly, he halted, spun her so her back met the wall, stepped into her, bent his head, and crushed his lips to hers.

His kiss was an explosion of heat and passion.

She parted her lips and drowned in the flames, in the raw, elemental tempest of desire he unleashed upon her.

And that she instantly, in the next heartbeat, gave back to him.

She caught his head, trapped his face between her palms, poured all he evoked in her back into the exchange—and hung on for dear life.

Like a spark set to the tinder of their passions, the kiss ignited a conflagration of need, of want, of desperate desire, and sent it raging through them.

On a groan, he straightened. His arms came around her, and he crushed her to him.

Need—raw need—reached her.

Without hesitation, she gave him all she had. She melded her lips with his, sent her tongue surging to tangle with his. She released his face, wound her arms around his neck, pressed herself to him, and together they rode the surging wave of unadulterated, well-nigh desperate wanting.

Hunger drove him and, beneath that, a yearning.

Both registered on her whirling wits, informed her giddy senses.

And she realized she was his anchor in this storm. Some cataclysm had flung him adrift, and he needed her to ground him.

She steadied. Stood steady within the maelstrom of their joint passions.

Gradually, the firestorm abated.

And eventually, the kiss became one of simple connection.

Of communication, although she still had no clue as to what had so affected him.

Finally, he raised his head, and their lips parted. His chest swelled as, eyes closed, he drew in a massive, steadying breath.

She gripped his upper arms and searched his face. "Caleb? What's happened?"

Eyes still closed, his long black lashes casting crescent shadows on his cheeks, he lowered his forehead to hers, then exhaled. "It's bad, Kate."

He drew in another breath and went on, "We got Dixon into the lower level. It's not yet properly shored up, and it's hellishly dangerous, but he was so determined to find out, he went in and...well, he says he can't be certain, but I think he just doesn't want to believe what he saw."

"It's not good." She made it a statement, which clearly it was.

He straightened and opened his eyes. "We don't yet know how bad it is, but from Dixon's reaction, it's nothing like what he expected—nothing like what we need." He paused. "We'll know for certain tomorrow. We have to do more shoring up, and then he'll be able to examine the entire rock face properly."

"So it's possible he missed something?"

"Possible, but not likely. When it comes to mining, Dixon knows what he's doing—he doesn't make that sort of mistake."

It was the first time she'd heard him sound even vaguely despondent. The realization that he was cast down hit her like a slap. She stared at him, tried to study his face, his eyes, shadowed though they were. "We will find a way through this—

you know we will." She hesitated, then added, "It's usually you who encourages and buoys everyone else."

And the entire company of captives would fall into a funk if he didn't do the same this time.

His lips twisted in a wry and distinctly self-deprecating smile. "Don't worry. By tomorrow, I'll have come around and will be my usual irrepressibly positive self again."

But he wasn't his usual indefatigably confident self now, and he'd come to her for comfort, for support.

She felt her heart squeeze. She released his arms and ran her hands down to grasp and grip his hands. "We *will* come about."

He sighed. "I know, sweetheart. I know." More quietly, he said, "But sometimes even I find myself asking Fate: What is it going to take?"

★ ★ ★

The bad news started to filter through the ranks of the captives in midafternoon.

During the usual brief midday break, Dixon, Caleb, Lascelle, Hillsythe, Fanshawe, and Hopkins, along with the carpenters and several of the men assisting with the work in the farther reaches of the second tunnel, had been notable by their absence. Anxious glances had been cast toward the mine, and by the time Kate, with Annie, went out to check through the children's daily discards, rumors abounded.

One of the girls, Heather, fixed her gaze on Kate's face. "Do you know if it's true, miss?"

Kate hesitated, but she couldn't not answer. "I'm not sure—I haven't heard. Until Captain Dixon tells us what he's found, none of us really know." She managed a smile. "Best not to worry until we know we have cause."

Isolated in the cleaning shed, until then, none of the women had heard the rumors. While she and Annie were with the children, Kate noticed Caleb and Lascelle going into the cleaning shed; despite the setback in the mine, apparently the men hadn't forgotten about tacking the canvas pockets beneath the women's stools.

Later, as she and Annie walked back to the shed, Annie murmured, "That was good advice you gave, about not worrying. Not that it's going to stop anyone doing it." She glanced toward the mine. "I just hope they tell us straight and don't think to keep it to themselves."

Kate could only agree.

When evening fell and they all gathered about the fire pit, the mood was subdued. And that was before Dixon made any report. Just one look at the men's faces—so many grim and strained— was enough to tell everyone that the situation had lurched toward the dire.

Finally, once the meal had been consumed and the plates ferried back to the kitchen and washed and stacked, and everyone was back around the fire pit, Caleb, not Dixon, who was seated alongside him, stirred—instantly attracting everyone's attention.

Once he was assured of that, Caleb said, "We finally completed shoring up the lower level of the second tunnel, and Captain Dixon and several of the rest of us have crawled down and inspected the rock face—essentially the continuation of the pipe of diamonds we're mining on the upper level."

He spoke calmly, factually, with no hint of dismay or desperation detectable in his tone. "As you all know, the deposit on the upper level is densely packed with diamonds. We'd hoped that deposit continued with the same density of stones on the lower level." He looked around the circle, scanning all the faces. "Sadly, that hope has not been borne out. For some geological reason, the diamonds in that pipe have been pushed into the section on the upper level. Overall, the number of diamonds in the second deposit is likely similar to what was in the first, but almost all the stones are in the rock face we've already exposed along the upper level, making them readily accessible."

He paused, allowing his words to sink in, then continued,

"The reality is that there are very few diamonds in the lower level of the second deposit."

Again, he paused. Seated tonight with the women and several logs from him, across the fire pit, Kate met his gaze.

For a moment, he returned her regard, then his gaze passed on. "The most important—indeed, crucial—aspect of this situation that we all must strive not to forget is that while *we* now know that this is the reality, Dubois and his men do not."

Kate heard the compelling steel in his voice as his tone changed from informative to commanding. When they spoke around the fire pit, they all kept their voices down; the guards weren't close, but strong voices might carry. So Caleb was speaking quietly, yet he still managed to fix the attention of every man, woman, and child about the circle.

"We have not reached a point of surrender—a time when there's no more hope. Not yet. We can still come about, and we will. But the first thing we all must remember is to say and do nothing that might bring on one of Dubois's inspections of the mine."

Caleb paused to let everyone absorb what he was saying, then went on, "He came into the second tunnel six days ago. If he follows what I've been told is his usual pattern, he won't come into the mine again for at least the next four days. We're going to use that time to plan our way forward. Meanwhile, the stockpile in the mine is growing, and we've taken steps to start another in the cleaning shed." He looked at the children. "Tomorrow, Mr. Hillsythe, Lieutenant Hopkins, and Miss Katherine will come and talk to you children about setting up another type of stockpile among your piles. We need you to be extra careful, but we need you to be a part of this, too. We'll each have our roles to play"—the quality of his voice changed, effortlessly capturing them all—"and if we all pull together, we'll still be here when the rescue force arrives."

He paused, then went on, quieter, somehow calmer, "That's

what our goal is, and we—each of us—need to never take our eyes from it." He looked around the circle, meeting everyone's eyes fleetingly but with intent, including every person. "We can do this, and we will. Remember that."

Kate felt emotion well up—pride, and something finer. She could feel a tide of dogged commitment rising in all those around the circle. He'd used his gift and turned that tide from despair, not to hope—not yet—but to resolution.

He'd given them what they needed.

He turned to speak with Dixon, who looked a trifle less grim. Gradually, the usual groups formed, talking quietly. Then the women rose, gathered the children, and shepherded them off to their hut and their hammocks.

Kate lingered by the pit. She circled to come up beside Caleb; he was speaking with Hillsythe. She rested her hand on his shoulder. Without glancing at her, he reached up and closed his hand over hers, holding it there.

Then Hillsythe nodded and turned to speak with Fanshawe, and Caleb lifted her hand, rose, swung around, and stepped over the log on which he'd been sitting.

She met his gaze. "From all of us, thank you."

His self-deprecating grin flashed. "No need. It's my role—it's what I do."

"No. It's what you are—who you are." And without him, they—Dubois's captives—would have fallen apart. If he hadn't come, if he hadn't been captured, where would they have been?

About him, men were getting to their feet and heading into the mine for the evening shift. He glanced at them, then looked back at her. "I have to go."

"I know." She held his gaze. "Come to me later. I'll wait up."

His trademark charming smile curved his lips. He raised her hand to his lips and kissed her knuckles. "All right. I will."

She tipped her head to the mine. "Go."

He released her and did.

Kate turned away. She didn't look back but walked slowly across the darkened compound toward the women's hut.

★ ★ ★

At midnight, Caleb left the mine with the other men who had worked the last shift—one group mining the diamond-bearing ore in a short section of the second tunnel as slowly as they could, while another gang had broken useless rock at the far end of the first tunnel.

He didn't head to the men's hut with the others but strode across the compound, his gaze on the slender figure seated on the porch of the women and children's hut.

She rose as he neared and, as she had the night before, met him at the base of the steps.

Tonight, however, she walked openly into his arms, and they shared a much more tender kiss.

Then she drew back, wound her arm in his, and, without a word, started them strolling counterclockwise around the compound, just as they so often had.

Bemused, he shook his head. How had she known that this was exactly what he needed? This simple reminder that she was there, waiting to embark on a future with him. The promise of gentleness in his life, of hope and succor—the sort of succor a man like him needed.

Tonight…the situation was so fraught, the tension so high, he couldn't focus on anything else and wouldn't trust himself to properly handle any other intense interaction.

But he'd needed this.

Her silent company, her unstated support, and the quiet, soothing cloak of her love.

Did she love him?

He rather thought she did. He certainly hoped she did, for he most definitely loved her.

But all that was for later, as they'd agreed. Now…

He sighed. Then softly said, "I have to go back."

She didn't look up at him but continued facing forward as they strolled. "Into the mine?"

"Yes. We need to plan."

They'd circled the barracks and drew level with the mine entrance. She glanced that way, saw no light shining, and frowned.

"We've doused all the lanterns. The others will be waiting not far inside."

She went to draw her arm from his, but he tightened his hold and kept her with him. "I'll walk you back to your hut."

He heard the wry amusement in her voice as she asked, "Is that you being gallant or not wanting the guards to notice you leaving me walking alone?"

He pondered for a moment, then asked, "Can't it be both?"

At that, she laughed.

The sound remained with him, echoing in his heart as, after seeing her into the women's hut, he walked back to the men's hut, then slipped into the shadows and followed them into the mine.

He came upon Jed Mathers and one of the other men just inside the mine entrance.

"We're keeping watch," Jed murmured. "Just in case any of the guards happen to wander in."

Caleb nodded. He clapped Jed on the shoulder and continued on, stepping carefully in the gloom.

He was used to the weight of command, but he'd never taken on such a heavy burden before. Shouldering responsibility for men was something he was accustomed to, but having women and children involved added several more layers, and weightier layers at that, to the load.

Hillsythe had insisted that he—Caleb—be the one to speak to the captives as a whole, and Dixon and the others as well as Phillipe, who knew him and his abilities better than most, had agreed.

But he knew that the trick to keeping spirits high, to carrying people with him, rested on ensuring that better times came.

People could bear a great deal of hardship and adversity as long as they could see at least a glimmer of sunshine on the road ahead. Now it was up to him to find that road and lead them toward their metaphorical sunshine.

He made his way to where the others were waiting, a few yards inside the second tunnel. They weren't in complete darkness, but the lantern they'd set on the rocky floor was turned down to a bare gleam; as they stood in a loose group around it, leaning in various poses against the tunnel's rough walls, the pale glow lit their faces from below, transforming their features into haggard masks and distorting expressions.

Hillsythe shifted, making way for Caleb to prop his shoulder against the wall beside him. As he did, Hillsythe murmured, "We took another quick look into the lower level before we turned the lantern down."

Dixon, beyond Hillsythe, raked a hand through his hair. "Given the way the stones are all but falling out of the wall along here"—he waved at the rock face on the opposite side of the tunnel—"then my best guess is that we've got a week. Maybe ten days, depending on how well we stretch things out."

"That takes us to mid-August at best." Hillsythe's tone was noncommittal; he was merely stating a fact.

Caleb glanced across the tunnel at Phillipe, who was leaning against the rock face directly opposite Caleb. Phillipe's expression gave nothing away, but when his gaze met Caleb's, Caleb could sense the tension underlying his friend's outer calmness. He and Phillipe had faced difficult—indeed, deadly—situations before. In the present case, Phillipe recognized the danger, but he knew they weren't at their last gasps yet.

Next to Phillipe, Fanshawe looked close to defeat, but not yet quite there—as if he was looking defeat in the eye and seeing no way around it. Beyond him, Hopkins appeared rather more resilient. Hopkins was younger and less willing to give up hope.

More, beneath his easygoing demeanor lay strength and determination—the sort that never yielded.

Caleb shifted his gaze to Dixon. He rapidly took stock of the engineer's drawn face and decided that Dixon was holding up better than he'd expected. Which was fortunate, as Dixon and his expertise had a critical role to play in Caleb's plan.

As for Hillsythe...he was Wolverstone's man, which told Caleb all he needed to know. He could rely on Hillsythe to do whatever needed to be done, effectively and efficiently.

"We need," Caleb stated, "to approach this step by step." Within this group, however it had happened, there was no longer any pretense that he wasn't the one in charge—that he wasn't the ultimate captain of their troops. "As I said earlier, at this moment, the preeminent danger for us lies in Dubois inspecting the lower level, or in any way learning of the dearth of diamonds there. He's seen this"—he waved at the rock face opposite—"and because of that, we've had to increase the output of stones enough to account for it. If he sees the lower level, he'll throw all the men into mining this stretch. Once he does that, nothing we do will be able to slow production enough—not without Dubois realizing, and we all know we can't afford to find out what twisted punishments he'll devise.

"*However*, if we block off the lower level *before* Dubois or any of his henchmen see it, then you, Dixon, can feed him the line that the rock face down there is every bit as good as it is up here." Caleb caught Dixon's gaze. "You thought it would be. All the unconscious signals Dubois would have picked up from you would have him expecting that. If the lower level of the tunnel collapses, but you tell him the deposit down there was just the same—or possibly even better—than the deposit up here, what's he going to believe?"

"More importantly," Hillsythe said, "what's he going to do?"

"He's going to have us mining this level as we have been—

assuming the collapse doesn't cave this in as well." Dixon's face suggested he was already calculating the possibilities.

"But," Hopkins said, "if he believes there are more diamonds in the lower level, he'll have a decent-sized gang working on opening that up again."

"And," Caleb put in, "given the tunnel there will have caved in once, we'll have reason to go extra carefully, which means extra slowly."

"Well," Dixon said, "obviously we won't ever go so far as to actually reopen the lower level, but yes—after a cave-in, it's easy to excuse moving very cautiously."

Phillipe stirred. "There's another consideration. Mercenaries tend to be superstitious. If there's a cave-in, you won't get many of them venturing into the mine, certainly not far, no matter what orders Dubois or his lieutenants give."

"And Dubois's own aversion to being in the mine will only increase," Hopkins pointed out, "so he, and Arsene and Cripps, too, will be even less likely to wander in, routine inspections be damned."

"Which will give us a free hand in managing what's done in the tunnels." Hillsythe nodded. "That's a valuable benefit in its own right."

Caleb stared into the gloom farther down the second tunnel, then he looked at Dixon. "So…how do we go about blocking off the lower level?"

Dixon heaved a heavy sigh, then he looked at Hillsythe, then at Caleb, then at the other three. "It can be done, but it's dangerous. I don't mean dangerous in the usual sense but *hellishly* dangerous and on multiple levels."

"Explain." Caleb hunkered down, resting his back against the tunnel wall.

The others did the same.

After several moments of cogitation, Dixon said, "We'll need to weaken the framing at the entrance to the lower level. The way we've constructed the bracing in the lower level, it's all… anchored, for want of a better term, by the framing around the opening, where we've stepped the level down." He paused, transparently mentally reviewing the structure he'd engineered, then he nodded to himself and refocused on Caleb. "If we take down the framing at the entrance, the rest will almost certainly collapse, too. That will necessitate a complete re-excavation of the lower level, and given it'll be after a collapse, it'll be touchy and tricky and very, very slow. If we bring it down in the next few days, we definitely won't have the lower level reopened this side of mid-September."

Caleb grinned. "That's what we need."

"Ah," Dixon said, "but that's the good news. The bad news is that, even though the lower level is an extension of the upper level—extending farther along under the hillside—the two tunnels abut. If we collapse the lower level by taking out the framework where the two levels meet, then we will inevitably take out some of the upper level as well." Dixon held Caleb's gaze. "The bad news is that I can't be sure how much of the upper level will go, too. A yard? Three? Or the whole damn lot?"

Hillsythe sucked in a breath through his teeth, then he looked at Caleb. "We can't risk losing the entire upper level. If we do, we risk the backers, if not Dubois himself, cutting their losses and calling an immediate end."

Caleb grimaced. For a long moment, he stared at the lantern. Then he raised his gaze to Dixon's face. "The only assessment we have to go on is yours." He paused, then asked, "Realistically, can we collapse the lower level enough to shut it off from view, preferably to collapse it entirely, without taking down more than, say, a third of the upper level?"

Dixon looked away. He stared at the rock face above the others' heads. Then he drew in a long breath, held it for several seconds, then exhaled. And nodded. "I think so." He glanced at Caleb. "And acting now, while the lower level is no bigger than a crawl space, would be best. The thing we have to consider is that that space is now empty. When the supports collapse, what's above—the hillside—will fall in to fill the gap. That's where subsequent destabilization will come from—if the shift in that mass makes the rest of the hillside unstable. It might not have much of an effect away from the immediate site, but depending on the composition of the hill, it might. That's where the wider risk lies, and there's no way for us to predict what might happen."

Silence fell while they all digested that.

Fanshawe shifted. "So what you're saying is that, if we do this—collapse the lower level—we'll be acting blind. That we won't know how much of the hillside is going to collapse until it does."

Grimly, Dixon nodded.

Caleb stirred. "As I see it, that's a risk we have to take." He looked around the circle. "One we have to face."

He paused, then reiterated, "We *have to* block off the lower level before Dubois or any of his men get a chance to see it. Everything"—he strengthened the conviction in his voice—"all and every possible chance we might have to survive and get out of this jungle—rests on that. If we don't take the risk, we have no hope."

He gave the others a moment to take in that stark reality before concluding, "As far as I can see, we have no choice."

Phillipe, Hillsythe, and Hopkins were already with him. Dixon and Fanshawe were reluctant, but they, too, saw no other option.

It was Dixon who asked, "Do we tell the others—the other men, the women, and the children, too?"

They discussed the point. It was immediately agreed that the rest of the men would need to be told; all worked in the mine and would be involved in one way or another with the operation.

All agreed that the children should be left in ignorance. Although many would be in and out of the upper level as well as helping in the continuing digging out of base ore surreptitiously going on at the end of the first tunnel, they'd grown used to Dixon and the others working on the timbers at the far end of the upper level and wouldn't see anything sufficiently out of the ordinary to pique their curiosity. But if they were informed, it was very likely that their anxiety would become apparent—possibly even to the extent that too many of them became fearful of entering the mine.

That, Dubois and his men would notice.

"The way we'll engineer it," Dixon said, "there'll be no more danger than there already is to anyone in the mine, not until we initiate the collapse." He went on to assure them that all danger would come after that point.

Caleb exchanged a wry glance with Phillipe; Dixon was throwing himself into the challenge of collapsing the lower level with significantly greater zeal than he'd invested in opening it up in the first place. It was hardly surprising that Dixon had such a sterling reputation in the corps.

They then moved on to the trickier question of whether to share their plans with the women.

Caleb was for; all the others were against.

Indeed, all the others were faintly aghast at the notion.

From their comments, Caleb realized that, all experience to the contrary, they saw the six women as weaker beings it was their duty to shield and protect. He could understand the protectiveness, but had trouble equating "willfully keeping them in ignorance" with protection. He knew beyond question how his mother, had she been there, would react to not being told—to not being trusted, as she would interpret it. As for his sister-in-law, Edwina—much less his soon-to-be sister-in-law, Aileen Hopkins—they would erupt. The thought made him wonder how well Will Hopkins knew his sister; as Will was adamant that the women not be told, apparently not that well.

At Caleb's suggestion, they called Jed in and asked what he thought.

Jed frowned and considered long and hard, but eventually, he stated that he would rather not have Annie worry.

Caleb inwardly sighed. "I still feel—strongly—that it would be wrong to keep this from the women." *Especially from Kate.*

Phillipe caught his gaze. "Do you really want Katherine worrying and fretting over whether the tunnel will suddenly give way and bury you—and everyone else—inside? Children and all?"

Caleb frowned and absentmindedly corrected him. "Kate."

Phillipe bent an exasperated look on him. "Exactly. Just *think*, man! She's going to be agitated—enough for Dubois to notice. We might think he's not watching, but he is. He knows damn well that we're plotting and planning. It's purely his arrogance—and his peculiar brand of malevolence—that makes him just watch and laugh at our helplessness, and believing we are ultimately helpless, he continues to let us amuse him. And remember, he caught the change in her—and whatever that was, it wouldn't have been overt—enough to think to follow her and capture us in the first place. And with this, she and the other women will be even more anxious, more than enough for him to notice. Then when the tunnel collapses, he'll know what to think."

"And we can't risk that." Fanshawe looked determined.

Hillsythe weighed in with, "At present, viewed from the perspective of getting the job done while fooling Dubois, one of the most attractive aspects of this plan is that it *is* so bloody dangerous. That it's such a crazy, desperate, reckless, and—given Dubois knows nothing about our impending rescue, as far as he will be able to see—stupidly senseless thing to do." Hillsythe spread his hands. "Why would we bring the hillside down on our heads? To him, such a notion will make no sense at all. He'll never think it was our deliberate doing—not unless something occurs to tip him off." Hillsythe caught Caleb's gaze. "We can't risk telling the women, because we can't risk alerting Dubois that something's afoot, even nonspecifically."

Phillipe leaned forward. "We can't risk him making the connection because he will retaliate." He paused for an instant, his gaze locked with Caleb's, then more quietly said, "And you know who he'll reach for first."

Not you. Kate.

Caleb heard the words Phillipe left unsaid more than loudly enough. He dropped his head back on his shoulders, stared upward for a second, then straightened his head and nodded. "All right. I agree. We'll tell only the men."

With that decided, they opted to get at least a few hours' sleep before they started on the work to put their plan—their bloody dangerous, crazy, desperate, reckless, and thoroughly sensible plan—into action.

Sixteen

First thing the next morning, Caleb, Phillipe, Hillsythe, Dixon, Fanshawe, and Hopkins separately broke the news of their latest plan to the men with whom they usually worked. Although the new plan was initially greeted with grave faces, nevertheless, as the day wore on, that they actually had a plan—one the leaders believed would work and were actively pursuing—sank in, and the atmosphere changed.

The men understood the danger, but they also fully comprehended not just the need to do something but the need to take this particular risk, and one by one, they, each in their own way, committed to the gambit.

Caleb, together with Dixon and the three carpenters, spent the entire day examining the timbers framing the opening to the lower level, then discussing and rejecting various ways to weaken them.

"The critical point," Caleb repeated, for the third time in different words, "is that we need to be able to set everything in place—have everything ready—without collapsing anything. We're not going to be able to have multiple attempts—it has to be exactly what we want on the first and only try."

Dixon threw him a frustrated look, but the engineer didn't disagree.

With his hands on his hips, Caleb watched and listened as Dixon and the carpenters examined, opined, and argued.

Having to make do with only one lantern didn't help.

Later, once the four had finally agreed on the most useful timbers to work on, and on a plan of attack, so to speak, Caleb reminded them, "The temporary bracing has to be set up in such a way that preferably one man, or at the most two, can initiate the collapse and still get out of the mine."

Dixon grimaced, but nodded. He surveyed the section of the framing they'd elected to weaken, then looked at the carpenters. "We've identified the timbers we need to work on. Given the lack of light, there's no sense starting on the work now." He glanced at Caleb and explained, "It's going to be exacting and will, as you said, have to be perfect the first time. We won't get any chance to make corrections, and one unwary slip—one cut too deep—and we could bring it down then and there."

His jaw set, Caleb nodded. He would have preferred to start active work today, but Dixon was correct. They couldn't afford to rush, and Dubois was unlikely to send anyone to examine the lower level just yet; they hadn't yet informed him it was possible to crawl in, and even if they had, while the space was so narrow, none of the mercenaries would be keen to go in, especially as Dubois himself wouldn't.

In those circumstances and with so much riding on the outcome, rushing would be foolish.

Instead, Caleb asked, "When do you think Cripps will be back with more oil?"

One of the carpenters who'd been a captive almost as long as Dixon replied, "If there's a rush, Cripps and his crew can make it to the settlement and back in three days. Because Arsene goes for the mining supplies, he and his group usually take five."

Dixon nodded. "Three days will mean tomorrow." He met Caleb's eyes. "I really don't want to even mark things up without better light, and the way Arsene is rationing the oil, using two or more lanterns at full light down here is going to leave too little for those mining."

"Let alone if one of Dubois's boys thinks to stick his head in and sees us here, bathed in light." Jed grimaced.

Caleb sighed and looked up at the beams, half of which were shadowed. "So our best bet is to hold off until Cripps gets back and we can work under full light." He was speaking more to himself than the others.

"What we can do, however," Dixon said, his voice gaining enthusiasm, "is to use the time—the rest of today and tomorrow until whenever Cripps gets here—to work out our strategy for holding off the collapse until initiation, and also how to delay the actual collapse *after* initiation to allow whoever triggers it to escape."

Caleb nodded. "Good idea. I take it we can do that outside, in the light?"

Dixon replied, "We can draw up plans and work on them."

He and the carpenters looked up at the beams, clearly fixing the structure in their minds.

Caleb was thinking of what might be achieved with a decent delay after the collapse was triggered. Several enticing thoughts were circling in his brain, along with several long-ago memories. "For the latter project—the delaying of the ultimate collapse—I think we should pick Lascelle's brain. And Hillsythe's, too, come to that. They might have experience that's relevant, not necessarily with collapsing mines but similar situations."

Dixon—who must have had at least an inkling of Hillsythe's background—nodded. "Excellent idea." He waved toward the exit. "Shall we?"

★ ★ ★

Caleb found himself cravenly grateful that Dubois's extended hours for the men, which the mercenary captain insisted on maintaining even in half shifts, meant he could take his turn in the mine late at night, and so avoid having to spend any significant time with Kate.

Even though he'd come to accept that the other men were correct, and that in this instance, sharing their plans with her and the other women wasn't the best path, he still felt...uncomfortable.

Nevertheless, when he walked out of the mine close to midnight and saw her waiting on the porch of the women's hut, his feet took him to her without further thought.

She met him with a kiss—sweet, full of promise—but then she drew back. Her hands gripped his forearms as she looked into his face. "I can't walk tonight—the children are so excited over being included in the plans and making a stockpile of their own that they're having trouble settling." She grimaced. "The other women are sleeping, but while the little ones are tossing and turning, my governessly instincts won't allow me to leave them."

His reassuring smile was entirely genuine. "Then let's sit for a little while." With an elegant flourish, he assisted her back to her stool, then sat on the open porch by her feet. He leaned back against her legs, then felt her hand lightly touch, then stroke over his unruly hair. "Tell me what was decided for the children."

In a clear, soft voice, she told him of the arrangements she, Hillsythe, and Hopkins had made with the children to create another stockpile of diamond-bearing ore concealed among the piles of discarded rock. "Even with the second tunnel yielding lots of diamonds, courtesy of those mining rock from the end of the first tunnel, there are still many more discards than diamond-bearing clumps. We gave the children a ratio of four to one. Four diamond-bearing rocks into the pile for the cleaning shed and then the next into their special pile. They can all count to four."

Even though he wasn't looking at her, he registered her satisfaction as she said, "And as Dubois relies on us women to check over the children's work, then that special pile will remain where it is—concealed between the true discards and, indeed, covered by them."

"Hmm." He leaned back, relishing the feel of her fingers absentmindedly combing through his hair. "And now that Dubois has caused such a large pile of diamond-bearing rocks to be created outside the cleaning shed door, then a few less being put onto that pile isn't going to be noticeable."

"With the stockpile in the mine, and now the stockpile by the discards, plus the cache of cleaned stones we've started in the cleaning shed…" She halted, then, in barely a whisper, asked, "Will it be enough, do you think?"

He reached up and caught her hand, stood, and turned to face her. He bent over her and looked her in the eye. "I said we'll manage, and we will." He managed a cocky grin. "Remember that. *Believe* in that."

She smiled.

He closed the distance between their lips and kissed her—long, assured, a kiss he ensured brimmed with confidence.

Then he raised his head, pressed her fingers and released them, and stepped back. He smiled. "Now go inside and sleep, and we'll see what tomorrow brings."

She chuckled and rose.

He saluted her, watched until she disappeared inside the women's hut, then turned and strode across the compound.

He didn't know why it should be so, yet every time he reassured her, he reassured himself.

★ ★ ★

What tomorrow brought was Cripps, a renewed supply of oil, a significant amount of dried meat, root vegetables, and flour, a massive amount of extra mining supplies, and a totally unexpected visitor.

"I can't believe it!" Along with Hopkins, Fanshawe stood glaring across the compound. "It's bloody Muldoon!"

Hopkins narrowed his eyes on the nattily dressed figure of the naval attaché. "Looks like my sister and Frobisher's brother were right. Muldoon *is* one of those involved."

"Interesting," Hillsythe laconically observed. "I wonder what's brought him here."

Dixon snorted. "What I'm looking at is all those extra supplies. It looks like they've cleaned out the fort's commissariat!"

"Either that," Caleb said, already thinking about what impact having even more supplies would have on their plans and on Dubois's expectations, "or Muldoon and his cronies have been stockpiling, too, and have decided it's time to clear out their warehouse."

His hands on his hips, he stood with the other leaders at the entrance to the mine and watched a long procession of native bearers march into the compound.

Phillipe, standing beside him, poked his arm. When Caleb glanced his way, Phillipe nodded past the side of the mercenaries' barracks. "Looks like your ladies are going to get us the relevant intelligence."

Caleb followed Phillipe's gaze and saw Harriet and Kate strolling along the side of the barracks. They passed the side window, saw the cavalcade, and halted by the front corner of the building. Folding their arms, they surveyed the bevy of men with apparently innocent curiosity.

They were close enough to hear what transpired in front of the barracks.

Dubois emerged and halted on the porch. He gave no sign of noticing the two women; his gaze had fixed on the naval attaché.

"What are you doing here?"

Kate studied the man to whom Dubois had addressed the not-entirely-welcoming question. European, possibly Irish if his dramatic coloring was any guide, the man had black hair and regular, somewhat sharp yet handsome features. Of average height, he was carrying a satchel slung over one shoulder and clutched a bulging traveling bag in his opposite hand. He was vaguely familiar.

"Do you know who he is?" Harriet whispered.

"No, but I think I've seen him around the settlement." Kate watched as the man climbed the porch steps.

He halted before Dubois. "We decided it was time I took the plunge and quit the settlement." The man turned and, from the vantage point of the porch, surveyed the compound. "This looks much more settled since last I saw it—quite the outpost of civilization."

"I'm glad you approve," Dubois returned. "Did something happen?"

"Yes and no." The man glanced at Dubois. "Nothing for you to worry about, however." He returned to surveying the scene. "It's just that with Decker back in port, matters were getting a trifle fraught. And after your news of the anticipated escalation in output, the three of us decided it was time I left and liaised with everyone from here."

Dubois's attention had shifted to the small mountain of boxes and timbers the native bearers were unloading in front of the supply hut. "What brought on this sudden generosity?"

The man smiled. "Winton has been stockpiling against the day when the mine went into full production. As we've reached that point, we decided the stuff would be safer here than in a tumbledown warehouse." The man turned to Dubois. "It's likely Winton will join us shortly. I assume you can adequately accommodate us?"

Dubois snorted. "I'm sure we can string up a hammock for you." He tipped his head back at the barracks. "In there, with my men." He looked across the compound at the men gathered about the mine's entrance. "I really wouldn't advise that you even contemplate sleeping anywhere else."

The newcomer grunted. "I see your point."

Dubois turned back to him. "What about our friend in the governor's office? Is he likely to turn up here, too?"

"At present, that's not part of our plan. He's more secure than Winton or I ever were, and of far more use to us where he is—neither Holbrook nor anyone else will ever suspect him."

Dubois humphed. "Best come inside, then."

Kate and Harriet drew back. They walked quickly across Dubois's window and returned to the cleaning shed.

★ ★ ★

Later that evening, they repeated all they'd heard to a fascinated and largely silent audience gathered around the fire pit; as Dubois and Muldoon had spoken relatively quietly, the men hadn't been able to hear the exchange.

When Kate reached the end of their report, Hillsythe grimly nodded. "So it's Muldoon, Winton—most likely the nephew, but we'll know when he gets here—and someone else in the governor's office." His eyes narrowed; his voice softened. "Who, I wonder?"

"No guesses?" Caleb asked.

Slowly, Hillsythe shook his head. "Holbrook has a staff of three. I was taken before I had a chance to get to know any of them. From all you've told us of your brothers' exploits, and from what we've just heard, it could be any one of the three." His features hardened. "And any one of the three might have learned the real reason I was sent to Freetown."

"Never mind that," Dixon said. "If we're to concentrate on surviving by stretching out the mining, with all those extra supplies over there, plus all the extra oil Cripps brought in, we're not going to be able to slow things down by running out of anything."

"True, but that's not going to matter. Not anymore." Caleb arched his brows. "In fact, all those supplies might end up being to our advantage."

Dixon, Fanshawe, and several other men stared at him. "How, for God's sake," Fanshawe asked, "do you imagine that might be?"

Fleetingly, Caleb grinned, but immediately sobered. He went to speak, then realized he couldn't explain what he'd meant to Dixon and the others without revealing their latest plan—the one the women and children didn't know about. But he had to say something. "It comes back to what I said earlier. Our first concern has to be to keep Dubois—and now Muldoon, too—

from learning of the true state of the rock face in the lower level. We need to ensure that doesn't happen."

As if that answered Fanshawe's question, Caleb looked at Kate, sitting alongside him, and at Harriet and the other women, a few places on around the circle. "It's possible Muldoon will call first at the cleaning shed to get a look at the raw diamonds. If he does, it would be helpful if you could keep him there for as long as possible—show him how you clean the stones and so on. Drag out his visit by showing him the children's work, too." He looked at the children. "And all of you will need to keep your eyes peeled in case Muldoon starts wandering about. Be alert. If he's around, make sure you're not adding anything to your stockpile—we need to keep that a secret."

The children all nodded.

When Caleb said nothing more, puzzled, Fanshawe opened his mouth—Caleb caught his eye just in time. Fanshawe registered Caleb's muted glare and desisted.

Caleb breathed again; keeping secrets had never been his forte. "I hope," he said, "that with only a narrow crawl space dug out so far, even if Muldoon comes into the mine, he won't push to go down to the lower level."

"If he does come into the mine"—Fanshawe's tone was all menace—"we'll—"

"Stand back and glare at him," Caleb cut in. "And by all means do—indeed, if we don't, Dubois might get suspicious." Caleb looked around at all the men. "But the one thing we won't do—*yet*—is harm a hair on the gentleman's head. Later, I'm sure that, between us, we'll ensure he meets with appropriate justice, but at the moment, taking revenge on Muldoon would not be in our best interests." He paused, then more quietly added, "Please remember that. No matter what provocation or temptation comes your way, don't lose sight of our goal."

Hillsythe came to his aid and asked the children a question, and the conversations about the circle moved on to other things.

Despite the very real tension among the adults, which Muldoon's appearance had only increased, they all did their best to put on a good face for the children.

As usual, Caleb rose to return to the mine with the other men. Now that there was ample oil to go around, Dubois had ordered all the lanterns filled and had directed that the mining of the upper level should proceed with as many men working the rock face as could fit along its length at all times.

Before retreating into the mine, Caleb crouched beside Kate. "I won't be around later—we're trying to work out what to do about the lower level, and Muldoon arriving has made that more urgent." At least that was nothing but the truth.

She nodded. "Yes, of course." She held his gaze for a moment, then raised her hand and touched her fingertips to his stubbled jaw. "I'll see you in the morning."

He caught her hand and pressed a hard kiss to her fingers, then he released her, rose, and headed into the mine.

On entering the upper level of the second tunnel, he skirted the men wielding pickaxes and shovels and made his way to the far end, where Hillsythe and Phillipe were consulting with Dixon. In the bright light of four lanterns trained on the framework at the entrance to the lower level, the three carpenters were arguing among themselves and marking chalk lines on various beams and supports.

Caleb halted beside Dixon.

The engineer swung to face him, a sheet of paper in his hand. "I think, between them, these two have come up with what we need."

The three proceeded to explain to Caleb how various weights, beams, and hinges could be constructed into what amounted to a trigger with a significant delay.

When they ran out of words, he looked at all three. "How long a delay are we talking about?"

Dixon looked at Hillsythe, who exchanged a glance with

Phillipe. Then Hillsythe looked at Caleb. "Best guess is fifteen minutes, but it could be half an hour."

Caleb grinned intently. "Perfect." He glanced at the carpenters. "Can we be ready to bring this down tomorrow during the midday break?"

All three carpenters looked at him and grunted.

"Let me see." Jed held out his hand for the trigger diagram. Dixon handed it over. Jed studied it; the other two carpenters looked over his shoulders.

Jed looked up, handed the diagram back to Dixon, then looked at Caleb. "Not by midday. But with luck, by evening, we should have it done."

Caleb grimaced, but nodded. "The evening break, then." He looked at Hillsythe, Phillipe, and Dixon and lowered his voice. "I daresay I don't have to point out that Muldoon showing his face here confirms that the backers, whoever they are, have a definite endpoint in mind—one that includes killing all of us."

Hillsythe snorted. "If we'd harbored any doubt of that before, seeing Muldoon openly showing his face put paid to it."

"We can't assume Muldoon suffers from the same affliction that keeps Dubois and the others from examining the lower level," Phillipe said.

"Exactly." Caleb looked at Dixon. "I haven't spoken with Fanshawe and Hopkins, but I imagine they'll see the situation as we do." He glanced at Hillsythe and Phillipe. "So are we all agreed that if these gentlemen"—he tipped his head at the three carpenters—"have the beams weakened and the trigger mechanism in place by dinnertime tomorrow, we pull the trigger?"

As grim-faced as he, the other three nodded.

"The sooner the better," Dixon said.

"Which," Caleb said, "means tomorrow evening."

All four remained nearby for the rest of the shift, assisting the carpenters as needed, until midnight came and they walked out of the mine, all praying that the struts they'd left bracing the partially weakened beams would hold long enough for them to complete the job the next day.

"The last thing we want," Caleb murmured to Hillsythe and Phillipe as he glanced one last time at the now-dark mouth of the mine, "is to wake up tomorrow to a partial collapse that's too limited to do what we need."

★ ★ ★

Their prayers were answered. They walked into the mine the following morning to find all exactly as they had left it.

Dixon studied the beams, then blew out a breath. "Thank God."

After leaving Dixon and the carpenters to continue with the delicate deconstruction, Caleb, aided by Phillipe and Hillsythe, spread word of what was planned to all the men before the children arrived to fill their baskets with the loose rocks chipped out of the rock face the previous night. Rather than mining more rock, the men stood back and let the children take their time clearing the tunnel floor. Only when most of the children had departed and one of the urchins posted on watch at the mine's mouth darted in and hissed, "Guards coming!" did the men hoist their tools and start mining again.

Even then, they worked as slowly as they could. Everyone understood the need to leave as many diamonds in the rock face as possible; they did everything they could to drag their heels in ways Dubois and his men wouldn't notice.

Throughout the day, Fanshawe and Hopkins took charge of overseeing the mining, making sure everything about how the men were working and what was coming out of the mine met Dubois's expectations and raised no suspicions. The pair directed the various gangs as well as overseeing the children who came in to collect the broken rock. While they kept the upper level thick with men supposedly mining, others went deeper into the first tunnel and continued to generate non-diamond-bearing rock to mix in with the richer returns from the second tunnel.

Several other men worked with the children to replenish the secret stockpile of diamond-bearing rocks in the alcove off the first tunnel.

Caleb, Hillsythe, and Phillipe spent their day assisting Dixon and the carpenters. As they were supposed to be working on opening up the lower level, no eyebrows were raised when Caleb, along with four of his men, accompanied Dixon to the supply hut to fetch more timber and the various nails and other bits and pieces required to build their trigger.

Possibly due to Muldoon being there, the guards—no doubt under Arsene's and Cripps's orders—increased their patrols into the mine. However, once inside, their inspections were just as cursory as ever. Even though they saw the group working at the entrance to the lower level, none of the guards evinced the slightest interest in what the men were doing.

"Not that there is anything much different to see between putting beams in and pulling them out," Jed huffed.

As it transpired, precisely because Dixon was the exemplary engineer he was, the structures about the entrance to the lower level proved so very strong and thoroughly braced that weakening the framing to the point that it would definitely give way proved to be no simple task. Especially as there was no way to test their best guess.

Although they were fairly certain they'd weakened the surrounding beams sufficiently so that once the anchoring frame at the entrance failed, the surrounding beams would fail, too, working out how to ensure the frame fell as completely as they needed it to had Dixon clutching his hair and the three carpenters muttering and shaking their heads.

Caleb, Hillsythe, and Phillipe exchanged glances, throttled their impatience, and bit their tongues against the impulse to urge the four to hurry, to remind them of the likelihood that Muldoon would all too soon come into the mine; regardless of the need for haste, with something this critical—this finicky and so finely balanced—they couldn't afford to make a mistake.

By midmorning, however, Dixon and the three carpenters believed they'd established how to make the critical failure happen. However, once the frame was weakened, how long it would be before it finally gave way was impossible to predict. So after Dixon and the carpenters had agreed on how to most effectively destroy their earlier work, rather than do the deed then and there, the group as a whole turned to building their trigger mechanism.

A complicated system of levers, pulleys, hinges, weights, and counterweights, with all of them working on it, it was almost ready by the time the midday break was called.

Caleb accepted his portion of bread and hard cheese, then went to sit beside Kate.

Kate looked up as Caleb stepped over the log and sat in the space between her and Gemma. As soon as he'd settled, she asked, "Have you and the others decided what to do about the lower level?"

On her other side, Harriet leaned forward to listen as Caleb replied, "We're working on it." He glanced at Gemma, then at Harriet, then looked at Kate. "Has Muldoon visited you yet?"

She nodded. "But first, he spent most of the morning with Dubois, getting a tour of the facilities."

Harriet made an unladylike sound. "The way Muldoon asked his questions, you would have thought this was some kind of sanatorium. Still, he seemed to approve of all the arrangements and amenities Dubois has put in place."

"Although he did float the idea that he and this Winton person should take over the medical hut as their accommodation." Kate smiled cynically. "I almost applauded Dubois's response—that if Muldoon wished to take responsibility for his own safety, Dubois saw no impediment to that, but that he—Dubois—could not afford to place guards about the medical hut while still maintaining the necessary perimeter patrols." She grinned as Dixon and Hillsythe, who had come up and overheard her comments, stepped over the logs and sat beside Harriet. "Muldoon decided that the barracks, although primitive, was adequate for the moment."

"It's the same as usual," Gemma put in. "They—Dubois and now this Muldoon—didn't care that we overheard."

Kate glanced at the faces around her; they all understood the implications of that.

"So what happened when Muldoon made it into the cleaning shed?" Caleb asked.

"He only came in a little before the break was called." Kate met Caleb's gaze. "But if the way his eyes lit up was any guide, he's absolutely fascinated with what we're doing—and with the diamonds themselves."

"Good." Across her and Harriet, Caleb exchanged a look—meaningful in some way Kate couldn't fathom—with Dixon and Hillsythe. Then Caleb turned his attention back to her. "Do you think you can keep him with you for the afternoon? In the cleaning shed and with the children?"

Kate exchanged her own glance with Gemma and Harriet. "We can try," she replied. "He's already asked for a demonstration of how we clean the stones."

"We can drag that out," Harriet said. "When we get back, we can hunt out some of the more difficult clumps to clean—that should keep him engrossed."

"I'll suggest he try to clean one himself." Kate glanced at Gemma. "One of the smaller stones with lots of aggregate clumped around it might challenge him and will take the most time."

Gemma nodded. "I saw a rock in the basket that will do perfectly for that. I'll pull it out and keep it aside when we get back."

"If we keep him in the cleaning shed for as long as we can, then take him out with us to go over the children's discards later than we usually do"—Kate looked at Caleb—"with luck, between us and the children, we should be able to keep him busy almost to dinnertime."

Hillsythe leaned forward. "If you could manage that, it will help enormously. If at all possible, we want to keep Muldoon out of the mine for the rest of the day."

"Can you word up one of the children ahead of time," Caleb asked, "so that when Muldoon is with you and the children, if he makes noises about coming to the mine, that child can run ahead and warn us?"

"Of course." Kate looked from one man to the other. "Is it really that important—keeping Muldoon out of the mine?"

Caleb's features hardened. "If we want to bury the truth about the lower level, then yes, it is."

They didn't have time for more. They'd finished their meals, and a stir on the barracks' porch heralded the re-emergence of Muldoon and Dubois. The women rose. With one last glance at Caleb, Kate went with the others, trooping back to the cleaning shed.

Caleb fell in with Phillipe and several of their men as they made their way back into the mine.

As they turned into the second tunnel, Caleb glanced at Phillipe. "We need to get this done today."

"You'll get no argument from me. Muldoon…makes my skin itch. Dubois is bad enough, and undoubtedly the greater nightmare, but it's occurred to me that Muldoon is one who could order any one of us put to death—and Dubois would obey."

Curtly, Caleb nodded. "Without a blink."

Their men went back to their assigned stations among the gangs supposedly mining. Caleb and Phillipe picked their way past the miners to the far end of the upper level and joined the small group on whose shoulders the future of the captives now rode.

Another hour and a half, and they had the trigger mechanism completed. Without attaching it to the beam it was designed to dislodge, they tested it—and breathed a little easier when the timing mechanism worked perfectly, giving them a delay of close to twenty minutes. They all exchanged grins, Hillsythe, Caleb, and Phillipe sharing in the sense of achievement.

Then their grins faded, and they got down to the truly tricky task of making the final cuts that, essentially, dismantled the frame holding up the entrance to the lower level.

This was the truly dangerous—truly scarifying—part of the procedure, with them literally standing beneath tons of rock and effectively removing the supports that held it up. For every beam they compromised, they had to brace the structure—initially with their own strength while others rapidly shifted temporary supports into place. They had to call on Quilley, Ducasse, and several of the taller, stronger men to help hold up the tunnel roof while Dixon and the carpenters quickly knocked in temporary chocks, struts, and bracing timbers.

Deep creaks and groans started emanating from the rock above their heads.

The sounds ignited a primitive impulse to flee, but they grimly stood their ground, put their faith in Dixon, and continued to work steadily.

They couldn't afford to panic now.

The men mining farther along the upper level started sending uneasy looks their way. But no one left; they held their positions and continued to mine the rock face, providing camouflage for the men working at the end of the tunnel.

When, late in the afternoon, a pair of guards looked in, Hopkins—deploying his own cheery, easygoing façade—intercepted them at the mouth of the second tunnel.

The men at the end continued to move, to appear to be working, but in reality, they did not shift any of the beams they were adjusting by even half an inch.

The guards joked with Hopkins.

Then a low, prolonged groan drifted through the mine.

The guards started. "What was that?" one of them demanded.

The men mining hadn't reacted. Hopkins looked nonplussed. Then he said, "Oh, you mean the noise?"

"Yes. That." Both guards' eyes gleamed white in the lanternlight.

Hopkins shrugged. "Just a noise. It happens now and then." Unhurriedly, he looked up at the roof of the tunnel, then grinned. "Perhaps it's the god of the hillside venting his displeasure."

At the end of the tunnel, Caleb caught Hillsythe's eyes; Hopkins had just turned near-disaster into an advantage.

Needless to say, after one shocked look down the tunnel, the guards couldn't get out of the mine fast enough.

Phillipe chuckled. "They'll rush to babble to their mates. With any luck, that will be the last interruption we'll get from them."

So it proved, which was just as well. It took their combined efforts to complete their preparations to Dixon's and the carpenters' satisfaction and then connect the trigger mechanism before the call for the evening meal echoed through the mine.

Dixon and the carpenters checked the installation one last time, then they all stepped back and studied the final structure.

Then Dixon turned and looked along the upper level, at the beams holding up the roof. "We have to do this, don't we?" The entrance would fall and would almost certainly bring down the adjoining section of the upper-level roof, but how much of the upper level would remain, not one of them could even hazard a guess.

"We don't have a choice. We have to take the risk." Caleb made the statements crisp and unequivocal. If they brought the whole hillside down, they would move from the frying pan into the fire, but with the flames threatening anyway, they had to place their faith in Dixon's expertise and roll the dice. Caleb nodded at the others. Hillsythe and Phillipe turned and walked out, falling in at the rear of the mining gang. The three carpenters took one last look at the framing, then followed.

Leaving Caleb and Dixon.

As the sounds of the others' footsteps faded, Dixon looked at Caleb, then waved to the timing mechanism's lever. "It's your plan.

Caleb met his gaze. "It's your tunnel."

Involuntarily, Dixon huffed out a laugh. "All right. You go on."

"No. I'll wait."

Dixon shook his head. He hesitated, then he wiped his hands on his dusty breeches, reached out, and tipped the lever.

They held their breaths.

The pendulum of the mechanism started to swing. Exactly as it was supposed to.

A little creak sounded, but nothing came crashing down.

Caleb wanted to say "Come on," but some primitive instinct had seized his vocal cords. Instead, he tapped Dixon on the shoulder and, when the engineer glanced his way, pointed up the tunnel.

They turned and, side by side, walked—unhurriedly—out of the mine.

Seventeen

Caleb walked out of the mine beside Dixon, and they joined the gathering around the fire pit. Many of the men briefly glanced their way as they accepted their plates and took their seats beside their respective ladies, but there was nothing in that to alert said ladies or anyone else to anything being afoot.

Seated between Kate and Harriet, after swallowing his first mouthful, Caleb thanked them for keeping Muldoon occupied for the whole afternoon, then asked for their impressions of the ex-naval attaché.

Perhaps unsurprisingly, both women were scathing. "He's unbelievably shallow," Kate said. "More so than most children."

"All he cared about were the diamonds." Harriet poked at the lumpy meat in her plate. "Nothing else even impinged on his awareness."

"I don't come from much." Annie spoke from beyond Kate. "So I can understand that, to him, the diamonds might mean a lot. But I'd never've thought greed could turn a body so blind. He didn't even notice how thin and worn-down some of the children are. Seemed he thought it was fine to have them slaving for him and his friends."

There were mutters of agreement from the rest of the women and even less laudatory comments from some of the children.

Caleb glanced around the circle and had to give the men credit for doing a reasonable job of appearing unconcerned and unaware, rather than alert and tense, waiting for something to happen.

During the debate over telling the women, one of the strongest arguments against had been that when the tunnel imploded, the women and children would be genuinely shocked—and Dubois and his men would notice and instantly discount any notion that any of the women or children had been involved in engineering the disaster.

Of course, their fondest hope was that the falling rock would shatter and bury the timing mechanism and hide all signs that anyone had engineered the collapse at all.

Regardless, the men clearly knew their role and were intent on keeping to the script. When the mine fell, they would ensure that no matter what happened, the women and children remained safe—pulling them away to the other side of the compound if necessary. No one knew how much of the hillside would cave in, so they'd formulated their plans on a worst-case basis.

Caleb glanced at Dixon just as the engineer pulled out his watch. As he was the one who timed their breaks, he was one of the few with both a timepiece and a reason to check it. By Caleb's estimation, Dixon had pulled the lever more than ten minutes ago.

A slight frown on his face, Dixon tucked his watch back into his pocket, then looked across the circle to respond to something Hillsythe had said.

Caleb finished the muddy stew, mopped up the thin gravy with the heel of bread he'd been given, then set his plate down on the ground before his feet. His expression relaxed, he looked around the circle. He was seated in the quadrant closest to the mine, with his back more or less to the entrance. The position gave him a clear view of the barracks' porch. Dubois was there, leaning against a post, his back to the fire pit as he conversed with Muldoon, who slouched at his ease in a chair that must have been carried out to accommodate him.

As Caleb watched, Muldoon waved his hand in response to

some comment, and light glinted on glass. No doubt the bugger was enjoying a postprandial brandy.

Caleb rarely entertained thoughts of summary justice; he usually left justice to those whose business it was. But for Muldoon, Winton, and whoever their coconspirator in the governor's office was, he would make an exception. He could very easily envisage a long, slow, and excruciatingly painful death for all three.

Bad enough what they'd done in enslaving the men and the women. But the children?

Children like Amy, a little girl who was currently circling the ring of bodies seated on the logs; her fair hair had caught Caleb's eye. He hadn't yet learned all the children's names, any more than he had all the men's, but he had noticed Amy. She was one of the smaller, nimbler children sent into the mine to clear the rubble from beneath the men's feet. Caleb guessed she was about seven years old, and she was a bright little thing. Despite the situation, she always wore a cheery smile and spoke in a light, piping voice that made the men smile.

Making people smile, especially when they were in godawful situations, ranked as a gift in Caleb's estimation.

He watched Amy stop beside each of the groups of children scattered about the circle. She would smile, talk, then apparently ask a question before, eventually, moving on.

Beside him, Kate rose.

When he glanced at her, she smiled reassuringly and laid a hand on his shoulder. "I'm just going to check on Amy."

Caleb returned her smile, caught her hand and gave it a light squeeze, then released her.

Hopkins asked him a question about Hopkins's sister. Tangentially, it was a question about Caleb's brother Robert and their family. Feeling he owed a certain duty to Robert and the Frobisher clan, Caleb seized on the distraction—it would keep him from turning around and looking at the mine.

Surely it would implode any second now.

After satisfying Hopkins at some length, Caleb sat back, aware of mounting impatience.

Then he noticed Kate hadn't returned to her place beside him.

He looked up and scanned the circle...

He couldn't see her anywhere.

A chill touched his spine.

He turned around—and saw Kate walking, slowly, toward the mine.

He couldn't race to her. He forced himself to rise slowly. As he straightened, he followed her gaze and saw the glow of a bobbing lantern fade into the darkness inside the mine.

He couldn't run. He couldn't rush. But he took very long strides as he closed the distance to Kate.

Ten paces from the mine, he reached out and seized her arm. Placing his body between her and any watchers, he hauled her to a halt and looked into her startled face. "Was that Amy who went into the mine?"

Her eyes wide, Kate must have heard the pounding terror in his voice. "Y-yes. She's looking for her hair ribbon—it's the last thing of her own she has, and she thinks she must have dropped it in the second tunnel."

He looked at the dark mouth of the mine.

He had no idea how many minutes remained before the timing mechanism reached the end of its cycle, jerked out the critical beam, and the tunnel came crashing down. "I need you to go back and sit down as if nothing at all troubling is happening." He met Kate's eyes. "Please—trust me." He put every ounce of command he possessed into his tone. "Go back. Sit down. And I'll get Amy."

Kate stared at him for a split second. Then she swallowed and nodded. "All right."

He released her. "Go. Please."

He didn't look back to see if she did but continued to stride—still unhurriedly—to the mine.

The instant the darkness engulfed him, he ran. Guided by the faint light ahead, he pelted down the main shaft and into the second tunnel.

Sure enough, Amy was there. She was at the far end—of course—shining the lantern beam onto a pile of rubble. As Caleb pounded toward her, she grinned, bent, reached into the rubble, and pulled out a piece of red ribbon.

Then she turned and, brandishing her find, beamed at Caleb. "It's all right. I found it!"

The timing mechanism lay still, the critical beam jutting at an angle with other timbers already slowly tumbling four yards behind her.

Caleb grabbed Amy up. The lantern went flying but didn't go out.

Holding her head against his chest, clutching her body to his own, he put his head down and tore back along the tunnel.

He felt as if he were moving underwater.

A shudder rippled through the air, then through the rock all around them.

A hideous, long-drawn groan of tortured rock followed.

Then, unexpectedly, came a high-pitched *ping*.

Then the air whooshed past them, and a roar filled his ears as the tunnel roof came crashing down behind them.

Stygian darkness fell.

Rocks tumbled and bounced; some hit the backs of his legs and shoulders, his hips and back. Unable to see, he'd slowed; he had no clear idea of how far he had to go to get them out of the second tunnel. He stumbled, but struggled back to his feet. Clutching a terrified Amy to him with one arm, he stretched out his other hand and tried to forge on.

The initial collapse had been the entrance to the lower level giving way.

Now the roof of the upper level started to fall.

Rocks rained down on them. Instinctively, he curled his head and shoulders about Amy.

A beam struck his back, and he felt himself falling.

Then something hit his head, and his senses shut down.

Blackness engulfed him.

★ ★ ★

Kate had reached the logs about the fire pit when a horrible moan came out of the mine. She swung about—in time to see dust start to billow out.

Then a deafening roar shook the compound, and a huge cloud of dust belched out of the mine.

Shock held her immobile. She and everyone else just stared.

Then reality crashed into her, and she screamed, "No! *Caleb!*" Picking up her skirts, she raced toward the mine. "Amy!"

The cloud of dust enveloped her, and she had to stop. She couldn't see. She could barely breathe.

She choked, coughed.

Then Lascelle was there.

He caught her arm in an unbreakable grip and drew her bodily back. "Is Caleb in there?" he demanded.

"Yes! *Yes!* He told me to come back and sit down while he went after Amy—" A coughing fit made her double up.

"Here." Lascelle pushed his neckerchief into her hand. "Try not to breathe so deeply."

Kate clapped the kerchief over her nose and mouth. Panic stricken and horrified, she couldn't calm her rapid, panting breaths. She went to press forward, but Lascelle wouldn't let her move.

"Wait!" he snapped.

The damned man was as fond of orders as Caleb. Her Caleb, who was somewhere in the mine.

Hillsythe materialized on her other side, a kerchief knotted like a mask over his nose and mouth. "Let's give it a moment and see if he comes out."

The dust cloud was still so thick they could barely make out the maw of the mine.

Then Dixon and the other men arrived, along with the women and most of the children. They all stood in a group ten yards from the mine entrance and waited as the dust cloud thinned.

As the rumbles from the hillside and the heavy thud of falling rocks and the clatter of loose timbers faded.

Everyone stared at the mine mouth, but it remained empty; no figures emerged, staggering through the murk.

Her jaw firming, Kate tugged against Lascelle's hold. "Let me go!"

"The whole hillside might be unstable." Dixon sounded as if the words were dragged from him—something he felt he had to say, rather than wanted to say.

Kate looked at him, then she wrenched her elbow free and rushed toward the mine.

Only to find Lascelle and Hillsythe flanking her.

"Go carefully," Lascelle warned. "We'll find him, but no sense getting all of us buried in the process."

Despite his words, Dixon must have been following close behind; as they neared the dark maw of the mine mouth and slowed, Kate heard him say, "Lanterns—Henry and you others, go and fetch as many as you can find. All the rest of the men, form up in single file. We're going to need to clear a path to get Frobisher and Amy out once we've found them. We're going to form a line to move the rubble—all the larger rocks and timbers—out of the mine. Fanshawe, Hopkins—take charge."

In an agony of impatience, Kate waited just inside the mine mouth, kept at bay by the dense darkness—then the first of the lighted lanterns was handed to Lascelle and Hillsythe. Expressions grim, they held the lanterns high, directing the beams into the settling murk.

Kate felt her heart constrict. She would have given anything to see Caleb walking out—even staggering out with Amy in his arms—but there was no sign of either of them. Yet other than the still-wafting dust and the heavy coating already deposited over every surface, the first section of the tunnel—the ten or so yards before the opening to the second tunnel—appeared undamaged.

"Caleb!" she called. "Amy?"

The only sounds to reach their straining ears were the murmurs of the rock and earth still settling.

Dixon joined them. He played the light from his lantern over the beams holding up the tunnel roof, then shifted his attention to scanning the tunnel walls, then the rough floor.

Kate felt Lascelle's restraining hand on her arm, but as she could sense the tension in him, and in Hillsythe and even Dixon—a straining against the impulse to rush forward and find their friend—she forced herself to draw in a slightly deeper breath and wait for Dixon's assessment.

Several rocks had bounced out of the second tunnel. Dixon's light remained on them for several seconds, then he pronounced, "This stretch looks solid. Nothing's even shifted. I'd say we're as safe as we've ever been in this section."

Immediately the words left his mouth, they—Kate, Lascelle, and Hillsythe—were moving forward. Others followed, but in an orderly way. Fear and trepidation over what they would find held them all silent.

Dixon quietly called, "Jed?"

"Aye?"

"Take some of the others and a couple of lanterns and assess the rest of the first tunnel. Check the joints where the side bracing meets the roof beams. If all's still tight, there'll be no reason to fear further collapse along there."

Jed called to several others.

After skirting several rocks, Kate and her company reached the opening of the second tunnel. Again, she had to wait, her heart in her mouth, while the men played the lantern beams over the scene.

There, the dust still hung heavy in the air.

And there was a lot more damage.

The debris reached to where they stood, rocks and rubble littering the previously reasonably clear floor. To their left, the diamond-studded rock face gleamed, fractured diamonds winking as they caught the light.

With every yard farther down the second tunnel, the density of rubble increased. About a quarter of the way down, shards of snapped timbers started appearing among the loose rocks. The men were directing their lantern beams along the roof, trying to gauge how far up the tunnel the failure reached; for at least half the upper level's length, the roof appeared to be sound.

The sullen mutterings of disturbed rock and earth were fading, to be replaced by an eerie silence.

Everyone behind them seemed to be holding their breaths.

Dixon pushed up alongside them. He stared at what the lanterns revealed. Then he barked out a seemingly incredulous laugh. "It looks like we've lost the last third of the upper level—the very best we could have hoped for. The roof's down to there, but it looks to have held—and held well—from that point on." He directed his own lantern at what was facing them—a cascade of jumbled rocks and a tangle of heavy structural beams flung like spillikins by the force of the implosion and now wedged diagonally across the tunnel. The blockage was much closer than where he'd placed the collapse. "All that has been pushed forward," he said. "It'll be loose, but if we move carefully and progressively, we should be able to safely dig it out again. Caleb and Amy…"

Dixon's voice trailed away.

But while the men had been looking at the tunnel's roof, Kate had been desperately searching the floor. Her eyes had finally adjusted to the dim light cast by the edge of the lanterns' beams and made hazy and diffused by the dust clogging the air.

It had taken her mind several seconds to realize what she was looking at, but finally...

A head and shoulders, thickly coated with dust, were just discernible in the shadows beneath and behind the first angled beam. And alongside lay a tangle of fine pale hair and a thin outflung arm.

As if Dixon's words released them from some invisible leash, Lascelle and Hillsythe started forward, but Kate gripped Lascelle's arm. *"There!"* She pointed. "Caleb!" Her heart twisted in her chest. Her voice gained strength. "He's there. With Amy."

She scrambled forward as fast as she could. She was lighter than the men—and possibly more desperate. She reached the tangle of beams first, ducked, and peered beneath the first beam.

Her eyes widened as she realized what had happened.

She held up a hand, palm outward. "Wait." She rapidly surveyed the cave-like space in which Caleb and Amy were lying. Three of the heavier beams—the one she was crouched beneath and two others—had wedged against the left side of the tunnel, the beams' ends roughly halfway up the rock face, with their other ends sunk into and held in place by the densely packed rubble crammed into the space between those ends and the opposite wall. A dozen or more smaller timbers, split and snapped, had fallen in a haphazard way on top of the larger beams, and a jumble of large rocks and smaller ones had fallen on top of them.

Kate turned to Lascelle. "Give me a lantern." She grabbed the one he held out, and her heart thudding wildly, she shone the lantern into the cave, centering the beam on the two bodies lying side by side. Caleb's arm was around Amy, her cheek pressed into his shoulder. Neither was moving, but Kate thought both their backs were still rising and falling. "Caleb?"

No response.

But Amy stirred, then whimpered.

Kate thrust the lantern at Lascelle and dropped to her knees; heedless of the jab of rocks through her skirts, she crawled and wriggled and squeezed her way under the thick beam, pushing rocks out until she was inside the cramped space.

There was only just enough space for her hard up against the wall near Amy's head.

Lascelle filled the gap where Kate had been. He shone the lantern in and softly swore.

Both Amy and Caleb had fallen on loose rocks—some small, some fist-sized or bigger. Other rocks had later fallen on top of them. What damage might have been done was impossible to guess.

Kate stretched across and stroked Caleb's dusty head. "I can't see any wounds."

"Check his pulse," Lascelle rasped.

Kate tried to reach the wrist of the arm tucked protectively around Amy, but in the cramped space, she couldn't tug it free. She tried for Caleb's neck and huffed in defeat. "I can't reach." Not without pressing her weight down on Amy.

She shifted her attention to the little girl. Brushing aside Amy's fine hair, Kate felt for a pulse at the base of Amy's slender throat and found it tripping, surprisingly strongly.

Then Amy whimpered and shifted her outflung arm, drawing it in.

"Hush, sweetheart." Kate leaned over the child. "We're going to get you out."

She picked up a rock that was pinning Amy's legs; she was about to toss it farther down the cave when Lascelle said sharply, "No!"

When she looked at him, he beckoned. "Hand the rocks out. You don't want to risk anything shifting." With a grim glance, he indicated the haphazard tangle that was holding a ton of rubble suspended over Caleb's back.

Kate looked, swallowed, and nodded. She and Amy were under the looming mass, too.

As quickly as she could, she freed Amy's torso, arms, and legs of rubble.

The little girl whimpered several times.

"Before we move her," Lascelle said, accepting the final rock, "see if you can rouse her and ask if she can move her fingers and toes."

Despite the near-overwhelming urgency to get to Caleb, Kate bent her head close to Amy's and spent the next minute coaxing the little girl into full awareness. When Amy's big blue eyes were finally staying open, Kate asked, "Tell me where it hurts, sweetheart."

Amy's lower lip trembled, but she clearly tried to assess… "Scrapes," she said. "I've scraped my knees."

Kate nodded. "All right. Now can you wiggle your toes?"

Amy looked at her as if she was strange. "Yes, but why?"

Relief swept Kate, and she managed a smile. "Never mind. How about your fingers?"

"They're all right." Amy drew in the arm that had earlier been outflung, braced herself on her elbow, and wriggled beneath the weight of Caleb's arm. "He's heavy." She glanced at Caleb, at the side of his face she could see. "He came to find me. He rescued me when the roof came down." Her little voice lowered to a hushed whisper. "Is he all right?"

"I hope so, sweetheart, but I need to get you out so I can get close enough to him to see where he's hurt." Kate glanced at Caleb. "It might just be his head."

"I 'member a piece of wood falling on him," Amy said, "and then we fell." She looked around, then pointed at a strut lying in the rubble beneath the large beam. "That one, I think it was." She'd used her other hand to point and now held up the bedraggled piece of dusty ribbon she was clutching to show Kate. "But I got my ribbon, see?"

Kate managed a smile. "Yes, darling. I see. Now you hold on

to that while we get you out so that Annie and Harriet can see to your scrapes, and the rest of us can get Captain Caleb out."

Lascelle, Hillsythe, and others had been busy clearing rocks and timbers out of the way and sending them back and ultimately out of the mine via lines of eager helpers. Luckily, Mary and Gemma had realized that there were lots of diamond-bearing rocks among the rubble, and the women and the older girls had set up a checkpoint at the entrance to the second tunnel to monitor the rocks taken out. Kate had been dimly aware of the whispered conference between Hillsythe and Dixon and had registered the arrangements to divert all diamond-bearing rocks to the stockpile still safely ensconced in the alcove in the depths of the first tunnel.

She'd also registered the implication of Dixon's comment regarding the stockpile—"I was worried that we might lose even that in the collapse, but the gods smiled on us, at least on that front"—but decided she couldn't think about that now.

Given she'd managed to wriggle her way into the cave, then once the rubble blocking the way was further reduced, Amy would get out easily enough. Kate worked with the little girl to get her up from her prone position to a crouch. She sympathized over Amy's badly skinned knees and scraped elbows and shins, then, once the men had cleared as much of the choking rubble as possible, she helped the little girl crawl out under the beam, into Lascelle's waiting hands.

He stood, lifting Amy, and turned. "Amy's free!"

A loud cheer went up. Distantly, Kate realized just how many of the captives had packed into the tunnels and were working to free the trapped pair.

But the instant Amy had left her hands, her attention had locked on Caleb.

Now the little girl was out of the way, Kate scooted around and half lay down, bending her head so she could look into his face. "Caleb?"

Was that a flicker of movement in his features? She couldn't be sure.

She eased her fingers under the curve of his jaw and down the strong column of his throat, reaching, hoping... It felt as if her whole world—her mind, her wits, her senses—came to a careening halt and just stopped. And waited...

Then beneath her fingertips, she felt the heat—and the heavy thudding beat.

For an instant, she closed her eyes, letting the solid repetitive thud of his heartbeat seep deep and reassure her, then she drew in a long, calming breath and opened her eyes.

The world crashed in again.

Looking up and out of the confining cave, she met Lascelle's eyes.

There was no expression on his handsome features, but he exuded a sense of suspended emotion.

She smiled. "He's very much alive."

Lascelle humphed, but he couldn't stop the smile that bloomed and wreathed his face. "He's always had the luck of the devil." He turned and called the news back—and a huge, even louder cheer rocked the tunnel.

"Not so loud," Dixon called.

Everyone hushed and waited, but there were no telltale creaks and groans. The hillside, it seemed, had done all the collapsing it was going to do, at least for the time being.

Kate looked back at Caleb. Crouched low over him—even with Amy gone, the beams above restricted her to that position—she twisted and looked back along his length. Rocks lay scattered over his back, hips, and legs. She couldn't see his feet and didn't think she had space enough to reach them; the cave angled downward to meet the floor, and another beam had hit the ground horizontally just beyond where his boots would be. She still couldn't see any wound, although there might be some beneath the rocks. At least there was no blood anywhere she could see.

She heard the men lifting rocks and rubble away, clearing the tunnel ahead of the cave.

Then Lascelle returned to look into the cramped space. "Even were he hale and hearty, getting him out of there wouldn't be easy. We're going to have to clear enough of the rock to get at least this first beam up and away before seeing if we can pull him out." His gaze rose to the weight of rubble suspended over her head. "That's going to take time."

When he returned his gaze to her face, she nodded. "I'll stay with him."

Lascelle regarded her, but to both her relief and his credit, he didn't argue. "Call if you want to get out."

With that, he rose and turned to the other men. Kate heard him confirm that she was remaining where she was. Rather than invite argument, he immediately started discussing with Hillsythe and Dixon how best to approach what she understood was a tricky task.

She left them to it.

Wriggling around, she managed to get into a half-sitting, half-lying position that allowed her to, very gently, send her fingers probing beneath Caleb's thick hair, dislodging the layer of dust coating it.

Within seconds, she found a lump the size of a goose egg above and behind his right ear.

She was carefully checking for any broken skin when he stirred. Her gaze locking on his face, what she could see of it, she froze.

He coughed, then grimaced—horrendously. "Head hurts," he grumbled, as if she should have known.

She drew her hand away and dipped her head closer to his. "Caleb?"

His lids fluttered, then rose. He blinked at her, then focused. "Amy?"

"She's all right. We've already got her out. Just skinned knees and scraped shins and elbows." She felt like she was babbling, but as she looked into the bright blue of his entirely lucid gaze, relief flooded her in such a massive wave she nearly slumped. "Thank God!" Gently, she touched his jaw. "Are *you* all right?"

He snorted. "Depends on your definition." He splayed his hands on the rock floor and tensed as if to push himself up.

"No." She pushed down on his shoulder. "You can't get up yet."

Lying as he was, his view of their position was severely restricted, but he looked at her, then tipped his head this way and that, trying to get some idea… "Ah. I see." He eased down to the floor again.

Lascelle must have heard their voices. He returned to crouch at the opening and look in.

Kate beamed. "He's awake."

Lascelle grunted. He had to tip his head to meet Caleb's gaze. "What's the damage?"

Caleb grimaced. He tested this muscle, then that, and eventually replied, "I can feel everything all too well, including the weight—whatever it is—on my feet. But everything appears to be functioning."

"Good. In that case, just lie there and let us lift this"—Lascelle nodded at the roof of their prison—"off."

"Can you send someone so I can hand out the rocks and rubble from in here—so he can move?" Kate asked.

Lascelle squinted down Caleb's back at the rocks and small pieces of timber scattered over him. "I'll get one of the older boys in here with a basket."

"Meanwhile," Caleb said, "send Dixon over. If I have to stay quietly trapped, at least let me know what result we achieved."

Lascelle grunted and rose.

Caleb watched him vanish. He glanced at Kate and thought of how, when he'd regained consciousness, it had felt so right to find her beside him. He shifted his right hand, found hers, and gripped it.

A minute later, Dixon crouched in front of the angled beam. Caleb was relieved to see the engineer smiling.

"It went better than expected, truth be told," Dixon said in reply to his query. "As far as I can see, the lower level's completely blocked off. In the upper level, we've lost about a third of the working rock face." Dixon glanced over his shoulder. "And we can stretch out the clearing up for all of tomorrow, at least."

In his mind, Caleb ran through what losing a third of the working rock face would mean. Delay enough or…?

Dixon shifted. "I need to get back to overseeing the removal of the rubble above you. Just rest. You've done your part. Now let us do ours."

He drew back and was replaced by Gerry, one of the older boys.

Kate started handing out the rocks that littered Caleb's back, weighing him down. She steadily worked her way down his body as Gerry eagerly took the rocks from her.

Eventually, Gerry said, "Let me go and empty this." He gripped the basket's handles. "I'll be back in a jiffy."

"On your way," Caleb said, "can you ask Hillsythe to look in?"

"'Course, Capt'n." Gerry grinned and saluted, then moved out of sight.

A short time later, Hillsythe crouched in the opening. "How are you feeling?"

"Bruised and a trifle battered, but I've been worse." Caleb studied Hillsythe's features. "Dubois? The guards?"

Hillsythe cracked a grin of his own. "Outside—and they're showing no signs whatever of wanting to come in, not even to see the state of things." He sobered. "But be prepared to meet

Dubois's questions when we get you out. He's seen Amy, so he knows why you came into the tunnel, but we're not yet sure what he's making of it all."

"Muldoon?" Caleb asked.

Disgust passed over Hillsythe's features. "All he's concerned about is what this means in terms of mining more diamonds. Dixon described the situation here"—with his gaze, Hillsythe indicated the pile beneath which Caleb lay—"and told Muldoon and Dubois that we won't know what's what until the tunnel is cleared, most likely later tomorrow."

"And the timing mechanism?"

Hillsythe's grin resurfaced. "Well and truly buried and almost certainly smashed to smithereens. Regardless, as it's us who'll be digging it out, I think we can be assured Dubois, Muldoon, and the guards will never see anything to stir their suspicions."

Kate had already realized that the men had engineered the collapse of the mine themselves—in secret—but had she needed confirmation, the comments regarding a timing mechanism provided it. But she held her tongue, and when Hillsythe drew back and let Gerry return to take more rocks from her, she resumed her task. She and Caleb still had to get free of the collapse the men had engineered. Time enough for upbraidings later.

As she worked, freeing Caleb's waist and hips and reaching as far as his knees—the farthest she could manage—she considered why they'd done it. That, she could understand—desperate times called for desperate measures, and they'd obviously set it up so that if it hadn't been for Amy going back into the mine, no one would have been hurt at all…

But why hadn't the men told the women?

Why hadn't Caleb told her?

With all the larger rocks removed, she smiled and waved Gerry away. "That's it for now. It must be late." She'd lost all track of time. "All you children should be in bed."

Gerry grinned. "Miss Harriet and Miss Annie are just round-ing us up." He looked at Caleb and sobered. "Me and all the others, Capt'n, we wanted to ask if you're really all right."

Caleb actually laughed. "Battered and bruised, but more or less intact. My thanks to you and all the others for your help, but you'd better head off before Miss Annie comes to tow you away."

Gerry saluted. "Aye, aye, Capt'n." Then he rose and dragged the basket away.

Caleb lowered his head and rested it on his left forearm. The position allowed him to tip his head far enough to look at her.

When his eyes met hers, she arched her brows. "Can you move your legs and feet?"

The space was still limiting, the beams angled over his back too close for him to turn onto his side and pull his legs up. He shifted, attempting various maneuvers, in the process dislodging the rubble about his calves and feet, but eventually, he grunted, gave up, and slumped flat as he had been. Meeting her eyes once more, he grimaced. "They'll have to lift all the beams off." He tried to look over his shoulder, but couldn't manage it. "How many are there?"

"At least three of the big ones, and there's several others in between. But I think they're going to lift this first one and then see if they can pull you out."

He grunted again. After a moment, he caught her eye. "You must be exhausted. You don't have to stay."

She held his gaze. "Yes, I do." In case he thought to argue, she added firmly, "More, I am."

His lips curved in his usual irrepressibly charming grin. He reached out and took her hand again, and she sat beside him and waited.

It took another half an hour before the men had cleared the debris sufficiently to safely lift the first beam away. Trapped by the remaining beams, Caleb still couldn't move—couldn't even raise up enough to crawl out—but after helping Kate out and to her feet, then urging her back, Fanshawe stepped in, gripped

Caleb's hands, heaved, and slowly dragged him out from beneath the remaining beams.

Finally! Caleb slid his hands from Fanshawe's, thanked the man, then pushed himself half upright into a sitting position. He drew in his aching legs and bent his knees, then swiveled to lean his back against the tunnel wall. Just that much movement made his head pound and his senses swim; he was grateful for Kate's steadying hand on his shoulder.

Dozens of men were crammed into the tunnel; they sent up a resounding cheer. In lieu of a grin, Caleb managed to hold up a hand and weakly wave in acknowledgment.

Dixon appeared, briefly gripped Caleb's shoulder, then addressed the men. "Now he's out, we'll leave the rest until tomorrow. No sense risking getting trapped in here if there are any further falls."

Everyone agreed. The men started to file out.

Phillipe crouched before Caleb and searched his eyes. "How are you feeling?"

Caleb wished he could grin as he had before, but now he was sitting, the blood was rushing through his limbs, making him acutely aware of each bruise and scrape. "I don't think I'm bleeding anywhere" was the best he could muster.

Phillipe held up several fingers. "How many?"

Caleb was fairly certain the answer was two and said so.

Phillipe grunted. "You're guessing. You have a concussion. No sleep yet for you."

"Actually," said Hillsythe, who had come to stand just behind Phillipe and had been studying Caleb, "I wouldn't attempt to appear too chipper. Dubois is waiting outside. Your pallor's quite convincing, but I wouldn't go out of your way to play down any weakness—not in this case."

"Ah." Caleb went to nod, but thought better of it. "I take your point." He reached behind him to push up off the wall.

Phillipe shifted to his side, seized Caleb's arm, and looped it over his shoulders. Hillsythe displaced Kate on Caleb's other side, and between them, the pair hoisted him to his feet.

When he swayed, they steadied him.

Caleb closed his eyes and sucked in a breath. "Damned head."

"Just as well it's still attached to your shoulders," Hillsythe drily remarked, "because we're still going to need it and you to get us through August and into September."

Caleb grunted, but as Hillsythe and Phillipe turned to half carry him out of the mine, he opened his eyes enough to find Kate's face.

She smiled, although the gesture didn't erase the worry in her eyes, then she spoke to Hillsythe and Phillipe. "Take him to the medical hut. I'll need to check his injuries, and we should bathe that lump and give him something for the pain."

Caleb decided he could live with that plan. "How's Amy? Is she truly all right?"

With their way lit by lanterns held aloft by other men, Kate walked beside the three of them and assured him Amy was better than he was and, more, had retrieved her ribbon. Apparently, that fact, combined with the usual resilience of youth, meant that Amy was already well on her way to being her usual sunny self.

Supported between Phillipe and Hillsythe, he staggered slowly out of the mine and into the open compound. As they paused to pivot toward the medical hut, he saw Dubois and Muldoon waiting ahead and to one side, backed by a semicircle of guards with muskets in their hands. Instinctively, Caleb tried to stand taller, only to have one ankle buckle beneath him.

Kate grabbed the hand of the arm slung across Hillsythe's shoulder, while both men grunted and heaved Caleb upright.

Beneath his breath, Hillsythe grumbled, "No need for histrionics."

Caleb murmured, "That wasn't an act."

Kate gritted her teeth. She wasn't at all sure what the truth was. Not that it mattered; his injuries needed tending, and he needed to stay awake. She released his hand. "Straight to the medical hut."

Dubois, of course, stepped across to block their way, his men ranging behind him.

Hillsythe and Phillipe drew up with Caleb swaying between them. He noted that Muldoon had remained where he'd been—on the sidelines and farther from the captives.

Dubois studied Caleb with cold detachment. "Captain Dixon informs me that the collapse of the tunnel was most likely due to a minor earth tremor that caused the newly constructed entrance to the lower level to shift and subsequently fail."

Caleb tried valiantly to raise his head high enough to nod, but couldn't quite do it. He managed, "I'm not an expert, but that seems about right. The ground did...tremble, and it was somewhere back there—around the entrance to the lower level—that collapsed first." He really didn't want to relive the moment—the sickening seconds before the roof had fallen in and he'd thought he'd finally pushed Fate too far—and if some of that reluctance crept into his tone, he couldn't bring himself to care.

Dubois said nothing for several seconds, but Caleb had a mother and three manipulative brothers; silence wasn't going to make him obligingly rush in to fill it.

Kate, however, wasn't so inured. "I was closest to the mine. I felt the ground shake, just a little, before the collapse." She offered the comment reluctantly, as if feeling forced to speak up.

Dubois glanced her way, then inclined his head. "As it happens, the guards in the tower felt the movement as well." He returned his gaze to Caleb. "Which leads me to conclude that the cause was, indeed, a natural one." Dubois's smile was as chilly as his tone as he continued, "Which is good news for you, Captain Frobisher. If part of the mine had collapsed inexplicably, even with you sending in a young girl to give you a reason to go in when no one else was there, I would have been sorely tempted to lay the blame at your feet."

At that, Caleb did raise his head enough to look Dubois in the eye. "Do you really think I would be fool enough to bring down the mine about my own ears, let alone with Amy in there with me?"

Dubois held his gaze steadily. "Do I think you would be reckless enough to arrange such a scenario, but misjudge the outcome and get caught in the collapse? Yes, Captain Frobisher, I do."

Caleb's frown was entirely genuine. "Well, I didn't." For once, his scheme had been determinedly nonreckless, and it certainly hadn't been any part of his plan to send Amy in as a decoy of sorts. He felt he had a right to be huffily indignant, but wasn't sure that wasn't his concussion talking. "It was an earth tremor."

"As Captain Dixon and my men bear that out, I accept that to be the case." With a coolly contemptuous nod, Dubois stepped back. His men followed suit, clearing their path to the medical hut. "I have been told," Dubois said, "that you are not so badly injured that you will not be able to continue to work as you have been."

It was Kate who snapped, "He has a concussion, but that appears to be all. He should be recovered enough in twenty-four hours."

"Excellent." With a cold smile, Dubois waved them on. "According to Captain Dixon, it will take that long to clear the debris. I'll expect to see you on your feet when Mr. Muldoon and I make an inspection of the mine tomorrow afternoon."

Caleb didn't bother attempting a reply.

Her head high, Kate swept past and on, leading the way to the medical hut, and he allowed Hillsythe and Phillipe to steer him in her wake. His mind buzzed with questions regarding the state of the mine and their plans for the upcoming inspection, but then he had to climb the steps into the medical hut.

Kate had gone ahead and stood holding the door.

He hauled in a breath and started up.

The change in elevation rocked his balance.

The buzzing in his head abruptly increased—and giddy dizziness rose and dragged him down into blessedly unfeeling darkness.

★ ★ ★

When he regained his senses, he was lying in the bed in the medical hut, under the mosquito netting. From somewhere nearby, a lamp shed golden light upon the scene.

He blinked.

Several seconds passed, then he realized he was naked.

He was also clean.

Someone had sponged the dust from all of him, from all his cuts and bruises, and everywhere in between…

Without moving his head, he shifted his gaze and saw Kate carrying a wide bowl to the chest against the wall.

He blinked again. Surely not?

He knew his brain wasn't working all that well. While her back was to him, he lifted the sheet and peered down.

Yes, he was naked.

And yes, he was clean.

Someone had washed all of him.

Eighteen

Caleb lowered the sheet and glanced at the door. Kate turned and saw. "What is it?"

He looked at her. "Is there someone else here?" *When did Phillipe and Hillsythe leave?*

She frowned. "I don't think so." Carrying a pot of salve in one hand, she walked to the door and looked into the corridor. "No. No one's about." She shut the door and latched it. Turning back to the bed, she said, "In case anyone else is brought in."

His wits, he discovered, weren't cooperating. "What time is it?" *How long had he been non compos mentis?*

"It must be nearly midnight." She advanced on the bed.

He watched her approach and reminded himself that he should be trying to keep a viable distance...shouldn't he? His wits were fuzzy about that, too. When she lifted the netting, ducked beneath and let it fall, then sat on the bed beside him, he cleared his throat. "How did I get here?" He waved. "In the bed?" *In this state?*

She'd been unscrewing the lid of the pot. She looked up and met his gaze. "Hillsythe and Lascelle carried you in, then Hillsythe had to go back. Lascelle helped me undress and bathe you." Her lashes lowered, but her lips quirked. "If that's what you want to know."

He wasn't at all sure what he felt about that—tantalized or horrified. But... "I can doctor my own cuts."

"Actually, you can't." She looked up, and he saw determination of a sort he hadn't previously encountered in her eyes.

Before he could decide what it foretold, she went on, "Most of your abrasions are on your back—you won't be able to see them much less reach them." She gestured with one hand. "Now turn over so I can rub some of this on. You know you can't risk infection in this place."

A second was all it took to convince him that he was really not up to arguing. He humphed, and clutching the sheet to keep it over his shoulders, he turned away from her onto his left side, then, gingerly, onto his stomach.

Of course, she promptly drew the sheet down, but only to his hips.

Then came the excruciatingly delicate touch of her fingertips as she dabbed the ointment around a scrape on one shoulder blade, but that was followed by the much firmer and definitely soothing pressure as she gently stroked, then rubbed the ointment in.

After she'd attended to several such scrapes, he found he was all but floating, relaxed and strangely content.

Then she stood, circled the bed, and came to sit on his other side, the better to reach the rest of the damage. She dabbed, then stroked. He felt her gaze on the side of his face, but didn't raise his heavy lids.

"You're supposed to stay awake," she said, her voice soft and low, "or at least, I'm supposed to make sure you don't sink into sleep for too long."

"Hmm."

"So why don't you tell me why you and the other men chose not to tell the women about your plan?"

Although he didn't raise his lids, he was immediately wide awake. And for a wonder, his brain seemed to realize that he needed all his wits about him. "I wanted to tell you—you and the other women—but the rest of the men made a convincing case."

"So Lascelle informed me. He also said the reasons the other men put forward were unarguable, and that if the same situation arose again, you would behave in the same way."

Caleb made a mental note to reward Phillipe appropriately for his help. First, Phillipe had acquiesced to Kate being involved in undressing and bathing Caleb, and then Phillipe had told her just enough to leave Caleb having to explain a point he was well aware women often didn't appreciate. "Phillipe's such a good friend."

"Indeed." The crispness in her tone suggested she understood enough to suspect Phillipe's motives. "But in the interests of keeping the peace among us all, why don't you explain what those 'unarguable' reasons were?"

Inwardly, he sighed. "They convinced me by pointing out that when the tunnel collapsed, the reactions of the women and children—your shock and surprise—would instantly eliminate all of you from Dubois's list of suspects. Moreover, we're all fairly certain that Dubois amuses himself by watching us plotting, so he knows that, generally, the women and children are included and involved in all our plans. So in this case, having you—the women and children—all reacting in obvious shock and surprise would also assist in keeping Dubois from thinking that we—the men—were responsible for engineering the collapse."

He paused, knowing the next part was actually the crux of the matter, at least for him and her. He raised his lids and shifted his head so he could meet her eyes. "We couldn't risk Dubois guessing the collapse was our doing, because if he did, he would retaliate." He held her gaze. "And the first person he would hold to blame would be me. So the first victim he would seize for his atrocities…would be you."

Kate found herself drowning in the vibrant blue of his eyes, in the steady, rock-solid, unwavering devotion that was so much a part of him, a cornerstone of his character, and in the knowledge that that devotion was now hers. This man would walk through fire for her. She knew that—could see it with her own eyes.

She would never have to doubt him, never need to question his commitment to what he patently had taken on as a new cause.

Her and him living a shared life.

He would never give up on that goal.

And after tonight, she knew that regardless of any quibbling of her rational mind, her soul had already decided that she should throw in her lot with his.

Tonight, she'd known what it was to care for another to the exclusion of self.

Tonight, she'd felt something inside her rise and break free, and fill her, drive her, to find him, rescue him, care for him.

Still holding his gaze, she tilted her head. "So you kept me in ignorance to protect me?"

He searched her eyes, then his lips and chin firmed. "Yes. And Phillipe spoke truly—if the circumstances were the same, I would do it again."

What Lascelle had actually said was that that was simply the way Caleb was, and she'd have to get used to it. She dropped her gaze from his, but knew he would see her lips curve. But she wasn't yet ready to explain why, after being exceedingly ir- ritated over being kept in ignorance earlier, having learned of his reasoning, she now found his actions...romantically endearing.

If this was a portent of their lives to come, then she was, in- deed, willing to get used to it.

She drew in a breath, then set about anointing another deep scrape on his side.

He shifted his head and studied her face. "Well?" he eventu- ally prompted.

She still hadn't found the right words. "Well...just as long as you had sound and solid—indeed, *unarguable* reasons...then I suppose that's all right."

She glanced at him and found him staring at her as if she was a puzzle for which he was missing several pieces. She smiled and looked away, continuing her careful ministrations. "And in this case at least, the ploy worked. When the mine collapsed, I screamed and tried to race in. Lascelle had to catch me and hold me back. There's no chance whatever that Dubois didn't believe my performance or those of the other women and children." She met his gaze briefly. "And you're also correct in that our shock and surprise is infinitely more convincing. You men just get more stony faced when something dreadful occurs—just more stoic. There's no telling what you're really feeling, much less why—you all so rarely show your emotions."

He nodded fractionally. "And never to an enemy. That's written in the rules of engagement."

She grinned, then patted his side. "There are several bad abrasions on the backs of your legs. I'm going to lift the sheet and tend them, and you'll just have to lie there and bear it."

His eyes flared wide, but when she rose and pulled the sheet up from his feet, he humphed and relaxed again, sinking his head into the pillow.

"How's your head?" She started with a long scrape down the back of one calf.

He frowned slightly as if taking stock. Eventually, he replied, "Not as bad as I thought it would be."

"Both Hillsythe and Lascelle said you need to stay horizontal until tomorrow—that the longer you do, the better you'll be when you eventually get to your feet."

He made a noncommittal sound that she interpreted as confirmation that his friends' prescription was an appropriate one.

Which only led her mind further along the path her emotions had been tugging her down for the past hour.

She let the thoughts, the impulses, brew as they would while she tended the rest of his injuries. When she finished, she stood back and surveyed all she could see of his back—the thin sheet now draped over his buttocks and little else. "Lascelle was right—he said you have the luck of the devil." His friend had also stated that the gods looked after such as he.

Caleb snorted. "He can talk. I've seen him come through pitched battles without even a scratch." He raised his head and tried to look over his shoulder and down his back. "I, at least, end with scratches."

"Scratches, scrapes, deep abrasions, and bad bruises—from being all but buried in a mine collapse." She shook her head at him, then ducked under the netting, walked to the dresser, and set down the ointment. "Incidentally, you have several deep bruises on the front of you, too. But I tended those earlier."

She'd rushed to salve the bruises before he'd woken; she'd been fairly certain he wouldn't have been as amenable about her tending those as he had been about the abrasions on his back. She smiled to herself, but didn't glance around; she could imagine his expression. For all his confident, pushy ways, there was a strong streak of the gentleman in him.

Rustling came from the bed. She turned to see him once more on his back, the sheet flipped modestly over him, and his gaze fixed on the netting above.

After a moment, he said, his tone utterly sober and serious, "It would have been a lot worse if those beams hadn't fallen as they did."

"Indeed." And that realization had been her turning point. Seeing and understanding that he'd come closer than a whisker to death—confronting what his death would now mean to her—had forced her to see, to acknowledge and admit, that there was only one path she could take. Only one path to the future that she wanted.

That she now craved.

She walked, slowly, back toward the bed.

His gaze lowered, and he watched her approach.

She paused beside the bed and reached for the laces of her drab, unflattering gown.

He blinked. His eyes widened. "Kate? What are you doing?"

Instead of answering, she wriggled her arms out of her loosened bodice, then pushed the fabric to her waist, then farther over her hips until of its own volition the garment fell to the floor. She rather thought that words would be superfluous, that her actions would speak clearly enough.

All she had on beneath the wretched gown was the fine lawn chemise she'd been wearing when kidnapped. Her walking dress hadn't lasted long in the conditions of the compound, and as Dubois had with all the women, he'd given her the dun-colored drab to wear.

She'd expected to feel self-conscious, but shedding the hated outer garment made her feel more herself.

And the stunned yet openly heated expression in Caleb's bright blue eyes made her feel...

As if she—Kate, the woman she truly was—was his ultimate prize.

She didn't hesitate but ducked beneath the netting and knelt on the bed.

She leaned over him, falling toward him, and he instinctively raised his hands to grasp her waist. His fingers nearly circled her, and she briefly closed her eyes; she didn't try to mute the delicious shiver that traveled over her skin, along her nerves. Felt through her thin chemise, the heat of his touch was all but scalding.

Then she felt him draw in a long breath—sensed the lift and swell of his chest. Before he could speak, she opened her eyes, looked into his, then she bent her head and fitted her lips to his.

This time, it was very definitely she who kissed him. She who pressed on; she who framed his face between her palms and dove into his mouth and claimed.

And he let her. He parted his lips and let her lead the way—let her direct, even dictate their play, even though he was hard on her heels, following every move she made and reciprocating gladly. With vigor, verve, and openhearted enthusiasm.

Just as she wished.

Just as she wanted.

Because she wanted him. Because she wanted the future he'd conjured. He'd committed to it already, in both words and deeds. She…she'd been sitting on a mental fence, too lacking in confidence in her own impulses—her own emotions—to take the plunge.

Tonight had put paid to that.

He and his plan and the collapse of the mine—let alone his selflessness in going after Amy—had slain every quibble, eliminated every uncertainty.

What was she waiting for?

Coming so close to losing him had set that question blazing in her mind.

There wasn't any sense in holding back. In not committing, in not openly acknowledging *this*.

This hunger, this desire. This burning wanting to claim him and have him claim her.

She released his face and traced one questing hand down the strong column of his throat to where the sheet was trapped across his upper chest. She gripped and wrestled the screening fabric down, then she spread her hands on his chest—and tactilely devoured, even as she pushed their kiss on into what, at least for her, was unchartered waters.

His hands rose to cup her breasts. Then those powerful hands closed and kneaded, shifting the fine lawn against her sensitive skin. Then his fingers found her nipples, teasingly circled, then tweaked until the buds furled so tightly she gasped.

She broke from the kiss, straightened her back, and raised her head high to drag in much-needed air. And realized that, at some point, she'd shifted to straddle his waist.

Good. The siren inside her purred in approval. Now she'd taken the plunge and made her decision, she felt remarkably at one with that rarely glimpsed side of her—the side only he had ever evoked.

Sitting half upright, she drew her hands reluctantly from the glorious width of his chest, cupped the steely muscles of his forearms, and traced them upward, feeling the flex of muscle and tendon as he continued to minister to her breasts. She skated over his wrists and finally closed her hands about the backs of his, and gave herself a moment to savor the sensation of his hands working as he pleasured her.

She found herself shifting to a rhythm that pressed her breasts into his palms—and gloried in the connection.

Her lashes had fallen; raising her lids, she looked down into his eyes. Watched him watching her, watched him drinking in her pleasure and delight.

She knew he wouldn't ask, much less move to do it; she had to do it herself.

She released his hands, reached down, found the hem of her chemise, then in one smooth movement, she drew it up and off over her head. After freeing her arms, she tossed the chemise away. She'd expected to feel his hands, temporarily removed, immediately return to her bared skin; she'd steeled herself for that intimate shock, but it didn't eventuate.

She looked at his face—and saw something close to reverence in his expression. Something akin to worship as his gaze traveled over her, from her bare shoulders to her breasts, swollen and flushed, their peaks rosy and so tightly ruched, down over her midriff to the indentation of her waist, then over the subtle curve of her taut stomach and the flaring of her hips, down to the triangle of dusky curls that screened her most private flesh.

His hands had fallen to her knees. Now they gently gripped, then he skated those large, hard hands up the smooth expanse of her thighs—to her hips. He gripped, long fingers splaying around and over to caress the curves of her bottom.

She closed her eyes and let her head tip back as heat and desire, love and passion, expanded and swirled higher and higher within her.

She could barely breathe for the force of the sensation.

Caleb stared at her. He'd never in his life seen any sight so fine. So entrancing.

So arousing.

He wasn't just hard; beneath the inadequate restriction of the sheet, he was as rigid as iron and aching.

But he still had time for this. For her.

To fully absorb whatever this was and to follow wherever she wanted to steer it.

He was hers, and he'd known that from the moment he'd first seen her—in the jungle, gathering fruit with Diccon.

And she'd been his from that moment as well, even if she hadn't known it.

He had to wonder if she knew—and accepted—that now. Was that what this meant?

If there was one thing he'd learned through all his many encounters with the opposite sex, it was that, despite his often quite firm convictions, he rarely understood what they were thinking.

She, and this, and even more what he was determined would be were too important to chance to his not-always-accurate understanding.

When she caught her breath and looked at him, although acutely aware of the heated compulsion already racing through his veins, he forced himself to meet her eyes and ask, "Where are you taking this—and more importantly, why?"

He wasn't surprised that she didn't need to think, that the answer came tripping from her tongue. They'd both just gone through a life-and-death experience—both survived that salutary shock. He knew what that did to one, how it focused the mind on the things that truly mattered. And how what was revealed could drive one.

So he wasn't surprised when, sirenlike, she licked her lips and somewhat breathlessly said, "Life is for living, but it's also short. We need to—and should—seize every moment and live it to the full."

His gaze locked with hers, he tilted his head. "That's my philosophy."

She nodded. "And I'm embracing it." Her hands fell to his chest; her fingers curled unconsciously, as if to hold him. But she didn't look away, didn't break their connection. "You told me what you want, what you intend to offer. You were clear, while I...I wasn't."

A hint of self-deprecation slid through her eyes. "I wasn't clear because I wasn't truly certain, not in my thoughts, although my emotions—my heart—knew better. So I didn't respond to your declaration then, but I am now."

Her eyes didn't leave his, but the hazel darkened, her gaze growing more intent as she said, "So this? This is me joining you. This is me joining my life to yours—irrevocably and forever. Because I want us—you, me, and both of us together—to have every last possible reason to fight for what we might have. To fight and survive, here and beyond. Because, like you, I firmly believe that the future we can both see will be worth it."

He wasn't about to argue. His heart swelled; he had to haul in a huge breath just to accommodate the expansion, or so it felt.

But she hadn't finished. She leaned closer; her head hanging over his, she looked into his eyes. "So I'm embracing your philosophy, and I'm embracing you. With all my heart. With all my soul and everything I have in me." She tilted her head. "Because I'm not frightened anymore. Because I've learned that there are far worse things to be frightened of than taking a risk on love. Now I know I have the fortitude to look death in the face—and still fight—I know I have the courage to embrace you, to embrace love. To seize yours and make it mine." She lowered her face until their lips—heated and hungry and yearning—were less than an inch apart. "And to give you mine with an open heart."

He didn't wait for more. He raised his head, set his lips to hers, and claimed.

She welcomed him and urged him on, her tongue dueling with his. She lowered her body to hover over his, swaying seductively, and the sensation of her breasts, heated lush silken flesh, brushing tantalizingly over his chest sent fire racing through his veins.

Heat rose like a furnace wherever they touched. He couldn't get enough of the feel of her smoothness caressing his rougher skin. His hands roved her back, greedily exploring the gentle dips, the satin planes, then with a will of their own, they swept over her hips, and he filled his palms with the ripe curves of her bottom.

He kneaded, and the flames leapt higher.

Then she undulated, pressing her hips to his, and the conflagration inside them roared.

Passion spilled through them, an incendiary elixir that ignited them both.

Her hands turned as greedy as his, searching, caressing, arousing. He found the softness between her thighs and delved, and she gasped and pressed down on his hand. He responded, sliding first one, then two fingers into her softness, probing, then stroking the sleek slick flesh, and she quickly found her rhythm. She rode each and every thrust, her body shifting and swaying over his in a shatteringly evocative dance. And through their kiss, through the tension gripping her body, through the pressure of her thighs gripping his hips, she wordlessly begged for more.

Demanded more. She reached between them and closed her small hand about his erection, squeezed, then stroked.

His reaction blanked his brain.

Before he could think again, she broke from the kiss, reared up, positioned the broad head of his erection at her entrance, and sank down.

Or tried to.

Despite the scalding slickness, she was untried, and he...

He shook his head. Then realized she couldn't see; her eyes were tightly closed, and she was biting her lower lip.

"Sweetheart, I appreciate the sentiment." His voice was so gravelly, so low, so starved for air he wasn't sure she would make out his words. But he gamely forged on, not entirely sure from which brain the words were coming, "But that's not going to work this time." He gripped her hips, half lifted her, and rolled.

Only then remembered his head wound, but to his intense relief, no adverse reaction assailed him.

Instinct surged, driven by the new position, by the sensation of her nubile body caressing his and the firm sliding grip of her thighs along his flanks; he settled her beneath him and rose above her, sinking his palms into the pillows on either side of her head. He braced his arms and looked down on the face of a madonna lost in lust.

Angelic, yet invested with so much passion that the sight locked the breath in his laboring chest.

Then she opened her eyes, and desire blazed in the hazel. With her gaze locked with his, she moved—deliberately—to draw him to her. Inviting him into her body, into her softness, into her warmth.

As she'd said, into her embrace.

For a fleeting second, he hung there and simply drank in the sight. Caught in wonder and trapped by hunger and the searing realization that they stood on the cusp of a forever he'd only recently glimpsed. He was breathing as hard, as desperately as she. The hot honey of her welcome, of her need, coated the engorged head of his erection, and he wanted nothing more than to simply sink home, yet it seemed he had to ask, "Are you truly sure?" He closed his eyes, gritted his teeth, and managed to grind out, "Please say yes."

"Yes. I want you—now."

That was all he needed to hear—exactly what he needed to

hear. With every rein he possessed gripped tightly in a mental fist, he kept his eyes closed and eased slowly—so slowly he thought he would go mad—into her tight channel.

Scalding velvet softness engulfed him. He pressed further—and felt the tearing rupture of her maidenhead, heard the quick intake of her pained breath.

He froze and held still, waiting, *waiting*...then he felt her ease beneath him, sensed the first faint stirrings of resurgent desire, and let the reins slide. Just a little.

Just enough to push home, then withdraw and ease into her slick heat once more.

Five strokes, and she was riding with him.

Ten, and she was driving him on, the cadence of her sobbing breaths a rapid tempo whipping him urgently on.

Kate gripped the bulging, flexing muscles of his arms, sank her fingertips in and clutched tight, desperately using the contact to anchor her as passion, and he, whirled her on. Into and through a landscape painted by passion and shaped by desire, one she'd never imagined could be, where every rasp of his hair-dusted limbs against her smooth skin sent a riot of sensations rampaging through her. But that was nothing to the until-then-unimaginable feeling of him filling her, stretching and impaling her. So large and steely, so hard—and so astonishingly and amazingly welcome.

Her body had yearned for this—for this closeness, this intimacy. Now she understood. Now she finally comprehended where passion and desire could lead—to another plane of connection, another level of fulfillment.

But as the heat and desperation built, as the flames that seemed to have enveloped them both flared ever higher, she knew she—and he—needed more. Something more. She caught her breath on an almost painful hitch, then surrendered to instinct, released his arms, and reached for him.

She wrapped her arms around as much of him as she could and pulled him down. To her.

He grunted and obliged. Without breaking the rhythm of their joining—something that now seemed vital and critical to them both—he came down on his elbows.

The change in sensation—the instant escalation—as his hard body rode directly over hers, the heavy muscles of his chest abrading her breasts, the hair at his groin more definitely riding over her mons, the altered angle as he thrust harder and deeper into her, sent her tension rocketing, ratcheting tighter and tighter.

Driven by a need she could never deny, she clamped her hands about his face and drew his lips to hers. Wantonly lured him back into an exchange even more fevered than before.

He plunged into her mouth and into her body. Again and again, to their own pounding beat.

She gasped through the kiss, clung, and poured all she was into urging him on.

Abruptly, a wave of intense sensation caught her up and swept her high.

High and still higher. Until she knew nothing beyond the coruscating delight of an intense pleasure that built and built.

Then sensation imploded in a starburst of brilliant, sharply exquisite feelings that streaked down every nerve, shot through every vein, then slowly sank, dissolving into her flesh.

Leaving her floating in a bliss-filled void.

One, two, three more deep thrusts and he joined her. She heard his low, guttural groan, felt the spill of his seed warm inside her.

Then he slumped, his weight pressing her into the bed.

And still she floated.

She reached up and stroked the hair at his nape, then gently touched his cheek.

Caleb felt that touch, that wordless blessing, to his bones.

It took effort, but he managed to lift his head enough to look into her face.

The madonna remained, although she now looked thoroughly ravished—and thoroughly sated.

Then her lashes rose, and he found himself looking into hazel eyes lit by a glow impossible to mistake. He let himself fall, let himself sink—let himself drown.

Then her lips, swollen and rosy, lightly curved. *"This,"* she murmured, "was everything I wanted. Everything I needed." Her tone was one of blissful wonder.

Her lids lowered. Her fingers stroked his cheek one last time. He only just caught her final whisper.

"I needed to, and wanted to, share the wonder, the joy, the bliss…to experience the sheer power of *this* with you."

He felt her slide into slumber, sated and replete.

Feeling the same lassitude creeping over him, he tried to do the gentlemanly thing and relieve her of his weight, but even though she slept, the instant he tried to move, she gripped him with her arms, with her legs—with her sheath.

He surrendered, slumped into her arms, and let sleep—and her—have him.

★ ★ ★

As it happened, through the night and into the morning, Kate had him several times.

They woke every few hours, but she took up the challenge and, on each occasion, succeeded in keeping him abed and largely horizontal.

She felt a ridiculous sense of achievement when, finally, they emerged from the medical hut in response to the call for the midday meal. Neither had got all that much sleep, but he was walking steadily, with his eyes alert and his wits about him.

As for herself, she felt like a new woman. As if overnight, through the heated hours, she'd matured—and perhaps she had.

She'd taken an irrevocable step. She'd put her faith in love and put her hand in his.

And from now until they died, she and he would face life together.

She didn't need to ask to know his mind.

Together they would fight, first to survive, and then to thrive—to claim the future they wanted and, even more now than before, were determined to make their own.

Nineteen

They faced their first hurdle later that afternoon. After Kate and Caleb joined the other captives about the fire pit, the short meal break had fled in a flurry of inquiries as to Caleb's recovery, interspersed with quips and a certain amount of ribbing. Quieter, teasing and approving comments from the women had had Kate battling blushes. Yet overall, she'd sensed a resurgence of hope, carried on a fresh—renewed—wave of camaraderie that now buoyed the company.

The men had stepped in and taken a desperate step, but their plan had worked, and everyone had great hopes that the result would stretch the mining into September.

After the break ended, Caleb changed into another shirt and called at the cleaning hut. He found the ladies gathered about their long table, pretending to work while they gossiped. Judging by the bright eyes that fixed on him and the light blush in Kate's cheeks, he was fairly sure as to the subject of said gossip; after asking after Muldoon and Dubois and being assured neither had put in an appearance there, he beat a hasty retreat.

He paused to speak with the children. What with all the rock being cleared from the mine, they were busy sorting, but he sensed a certain suppressed smugness. When he crouched beside them, raised his brows, and looked around encouragingly, one of the older girls whispered that they were hiding most of the rough diamonds in their stockpile and sending very few on to the pile still waiting to be cleaned outside the shed.

"Our pile's nearly as big as the one in the mine now," one of the boys proudly proclaimed.

"Excellent." Caleb grinned. "Keep it up, but make sure none of the guards see." He rose and saw Amy with a group of other children busily trudging back from the mine, lugging their baskets.

The little girl wore a cheery smile, and her red ribbon was tied firmly in her hair. On reaching the ore pile, she dropped her basket and hurried to him. She caught his hand in both of hers, squeezed, and stared solemnly into his face. "Are you really all right, Captain Caleb? Your head must still hurt."

Caleb assured her that he was almost back to normal. As she was transparently none the worse for her ordeal, he grinned, freed his hand and tweaked her ribbon, then, laughing at her delighted squeal, he headed for the mine.

He strode into the dimness and found the men loitering and lounging in groups. Their tools were beside them, but no one was even pretending to work.

"The guards are too frightened to come in," Quilley informed him. "Now the tunnel's completely cleared, the children are just darting about, making a good show while we wait for his highness to come make his inspection."

"His highness" was Dubois. Caleb had a vague memory of Dubois saying something about an inspection in the afternoon. With a nod, he walked on and turned into the second tunnel.

More men were propping up the walls there, relaxed and unconcerned; Caleb passed them with smiles and nods. Toward what was now the end of the tunnel, he saw Dixon, Hillsythe, Fanshawe, Hopkins, and Phillipe gathered in a group a short distance from the other men.

As he approached, Caleb scanned his fellow officers' faces. He'd expected some degree of satisfaction, even a touch of jubilation, yet judging by their expressions, matters had somehow taken a turn for the worse.

Deciding it behooved him not to leap to conclusions, he joined the group. "What's happened?"

The others glanced at each other, then they all looked at Dixon.

The engineer sighed. "We'd expected that clearing the upper level would take longer, but…" He gestured to the almost ridiculously neat stretch of tunnel.

"Once we got you out," Hillsythe said, "the rest of the rubble turned out not to be as densely packed as we might have wished. We still have to re-excavate and rebrace the last third, but that won't take more than a few days—and more pertinently, won't interfere with the ongoing mining along the rest of this level."

Looking down the tunnel, over and through the clutter of rubble clogging the section that was no longer roofed and braced to where the entrance to the lower level had been—and seeing a wall of densely packed large rocks—Caleb lightly shrugged. "At least the lower level is well and truly blocked. That was our primary objective. Anything else was to be a bonus."

Dixon snorted. "Sadly, our bonus has turned out to be a new and potentially worse problem." He waved at the remaining rock face the men were supposed to be mining. "Just look at it."

Caleb obliged, but he wasn't sure what to make of what he was seeing. The instant he'd walked into the tunnel, he'd known something had changed, but as the dimensions of even the tunnel floor had been altered—both by the collapse and by the consequent digging and clearing—he hadn't yet reached the point of deciding if the changes had any practical implications.

He surveyed the long rock face; for his money, there appeared to be many more fractured diamonds embedded in the rock… Was that bad? He shifted his gaze to Dixon. "You'll have to explain. I'm still not thinking all that clearly."

Dixon drew in a breath, then laid one palm against the jagged rock. "The collapse sheared a section off this rock face. Along with the rubble, we've cleared dozens upon dozens of di-

amond-bearing rocks. And yes, we've hidden most, but still…"
He paused, focusing on the rock face as if he could somehow
see into and through it. Then his features hardened. "I think—
I greatly fear—that we're all too soon going to run through the
pipe. The shearing thinned it, so effectively we've already removed more than half its depth. Soon—perhaps in as little as a
week—we won't have much of it left." Dixon met Caleb's eyes.
"I know we've kept back stones to tide us through for a short
time at least, but not only do I have reservations we'll be able
to string that out long enough, that tactic also relies on Dubois
believing that we're actually still mining."

Caleb realized he'd spoken the truth regarding his mind not
functioning all that well. Taking in Dixon's words was hard
enough; accepting the implications…he couldn't seem to get
his mind to believe.

He glanced at the others; at least he now understood their
downcast, almost disillusioned demeanors.

Before he could think of what to say—of what tack to take,
of whether there was any possible way forward—a warning re-
layed from the mine entrance had all the men moving. Hefting pickaxes and lifting shovels, they made a show of working.

"Damn." Hillsythe met Caleb's eyes. "We'd hoped that regardless of his statement last night, Dubois's aversion would keep
him out for another day or so." He glanced at the rock face. "At
least long enough for us to decide how to handle this."

A stir at the entrance to the second tunnel proved to be caused
by Dubois, Muldoon, and four heavily armed and sweating
guards.

"Out!" Dubois gestured to all those mining.

The officers glanced at each other, then fell in at the rear of
the column of men as they filed out.

But as they approached Dubois and Muldoon, Dubois waved
them back. "Not you." Strain was already apparent in the mercenary captain's face, but it appeared he was determined to con-

quer—or at least ignore—his fear of being in the mine, let alone a mine that had recently partially collapsed.

Along with the other officers—the captives' de facto leaders—Caleb stood back against the tunnel wall.

Once the men in the mining gangs had left, Muldoon walked into the tunnel, his footsteps echoing hollowly.

Dubois, they all noted, took up a stance barely inside the entrance. With his hands clasped behind his back, he stood and watched as Muldoon ventured down the tunnel.

This was the naval attaché's first foray into the mine. Eyes wide, his expression fascinated, he eagerly looked here, there, everywhere. Taking in the corridor-like tunnel and the beams lining its roof, he said to no one in particular, "I must say, I'd always envisioned mining tunnels as far more cramped."

Dubois looked at Dixon, and the engineer moved to Muldoon's side.

"It's because these are diamonds," Dixon said, "and they can shatter if struck wrongly. So it's imperative that the men mining have the space to swing their picks, not just with sufficient force but also with excellent aim."

"Ah." His gaze now on the rock face, Muldoon nodded. "I see." He halted halfway down the tunnel and peered at the rock face.

Caleb shifted so he could see the man's face; he caught the moment when Muldoon realized just what he was looking at.

"My God!" Muldoon's tone turned reverent. "Are these…" He stretched out a hand and all but caressed a winking stone. Then he swallowed and looked at Dixon, then at Dubois. "These are the diamonds?"

Dubois nodded.

Dixon stated, "These are diamonds in the rough, as it were."

Muldoon's mouth had gone slack. He stepped back and swept his gaze along the rock face—the two-thirds of the pipe presently exposed. "But…there's more than a king's ransom—hell, there's more than *ten* king's ransoms here!"

Dixon hurried to explain, "The collapse sheared along the rock face and exposed more of it. That's why there are so many diamonds visible."

"But…that's *excellent!*" Eyes ablaze with blatant avarice, Muldoon swung to face Dubois. "Fate has clearly smiled upon us. As I understand it, there's now no impediment to getting these stones out and off to Amsterdam, and our backers, with all speed." He paused, then rather challengingly asked, "Is there?"

For an instant, Dubois didn't react, then he stated, "I believe that is so. However, what about the lower level?"

Before Dixon could cut in with predictions and suggestions that would significantly reduce the number of men mining, Muldoon waved. "Forget the lower level. There's enough here, I tell you. And we only have so much time."

Muldoon's last sentence sent a chill down Caleb's spine and, he was quite sure, those of all the other men. Quickly, he said, as if reminding Dixon, but in reality for all to hear, "I thought you said we would need to shore up the far end properly or mining along the last third will risk another collapse."

Dixon picked up the lifeline without a blink. "Yes, that's right." He turned to Dubois.

Who coldly remarked, "With all the fresh supplies and timber we've already brought in, you should encounter no difficulties and no delays in making sure this tunnel—all of it—is properly shored up again." Dubois shifted his gaze to Muldoon. "So other than with that caveat, the mining can proceed apace."

"Excellent!" Muldoon had returned to eyeing the diamonds glinting like stars trapped in the darker rock. "I must say," he murmured, again reaching out to stroke a glimmering stone, "that seeing all this is a huge relief. As you know, our backers have been growing increasingly restive and ever more demanding. They've been making loud and still-louder noises about needing to see evidence and so be convinced that the risks they're taking will be as amply rewarded as we've promised they will be."

Muldoon smiled and stepped back, then looked at Dubois. "A steady stream of strongboxes filled with diamonds getting into Amsterdam will appease them and, more, will shut them up." Muldoon's expression shifted to reflect a cynical coldness worthy of Dubois himself. "There's nothing like a solid return to convince businessmen like our backers to leave their investments in place."

And when the tunnel's mined out?

Muldoon appeared oblivious to the impact the logical extension of his comments would have on the captives.

Dubois, however, saw matters more clearly. "And once all the diamonds from this level have been extracted, what then? Will these backers of yours want the lower level reopened?"

Muldoon frowned. He cast a glance down the tunnel at the rubble and rocks now blocking access to the lower level. "I really can't say. I suspect that will depend on how they—the backers— are placed at the time." Almost as an afterthought, he added, "But given their recent flightiness...."

Muldoon drew in a breath, then turned and paced back up the tunnel. He beamed at Dubois. "But regardless of that, at the moment, everything is very definitely looking up."

★ ★ ★

"Up is relative," Fanshawe grumbled. "Up for him and his damned backers, maybe, but very definitely down for us."

It was three hours later. The sun had set, and the captives had gathered about the fire pit for their evening meal. And if anything, in the matter of ensuring their survival, over the past hours, their prospects had got even bleaker.

Kate, Harriet, and the other women had reported that, after Muldoon's eye-opening experience in the mine, he had hotfooted his way to the cleaning shed and pored over the cleaned stones in the strongbox. And at the end of the women's day, he'd insisted on taking the box away with him into the barracks— doubtless to pore over each individual stone. "If he continues to do that," Harriet had pointed out, "we'll need to produce new stones every day at a believable pace. We won't be able to hold nearly as much back."

Worse, they'd overheard Muldoon telling Dubois to get in more strongboxes so they could send two or even three to the ships at a time.

"And we have another problem with Muldoon." Phillipe met Caleb's eyes. "He's not in the least nervous about going into the mine. Even after the collapse, he was oblivious to any danger. He's going to keep coming in and examining the rock face, which means we'll have to keep removing diamonds from it at a reasonable rate—and he's going to see when they run out."

"The truth," Fanshawe put in, "is that one of the critical factors that has allowed us to stretch things out this long is the guards' dislike of going deep into the mine. That, and Dubois's, Arsene's, and Cripps's aversion to going in at all, with them only venturing in when they're forced to it. If it hadn't been for that, we'd never have been able to pull off all the delaying tactics we have."

"But now," Phillipe said, "with Muldoon monitoring both the rock face and the stones going out in the strongbox, he'll notice if we try to slow things down."

The final blow fell when Dixon, Hillsythe, and Hopkins finally joined the circle. Earlier, the three had left Caleb, Phillipe, and Fanshawe to work with the carpenters over what timbers were needed to reshore up the last third of the tunnel and had gone to assess the stockpiles.

Caleb looked at Dixon's face and knew he wasn't going to like what they'd found. A glance around the circle showed that everyone else was also expecting bad news. How swiftly the upswing generated by their successful engineering of the collapse had dissipated. Their confidence, Caleb reflected, had become a very fragile thing.

He looked at the three latecomers, and accepting that no one else was going to, he baldly asked, "How long do we have?"

Across the pit, Hillsythe met his gaze. "We made as accurate an estimate as we could of the stones still in the rock face, plus those in our four stockpiles—in the mine, at the discards, outside the cleaning shed, and inside it. With Muldoon monitoring the ultimate output as he looks set to do...our best guess is somewhere between ten and fifteen days."

It was the tenth of August.

Caleb nodded. Ten days, or even fifteen, wasn't good enough—that wouldn't get them to September. He wanted to say something—the impulse to try to lift everyone's spirits rose inside him—but for once, he couldn't think of anything that might work.

Beside him, Kate shifted. Then he felt her hand come to rest on his thigh, and she lightly gripped. Simply a reminder that she was there, that whatever was to come, they would face it together...

And they would never give up.

He filled his lungs, then he raised his head and looked around the circle. "Obviously, that's not good news. Several negative things happened today that, acting together, have left us in what appears to be a hopeless situation." He swept the circle again, taking in the now-familiar faces. "However, I would like to remind you all that we are not dead yet."

Several snorts and brief smiles greeted that pronouncement, but he wasn't finished. "I know it's easier said than done, but we need to cling to hope. That's the one element we must never let slip through our fingers." He paused, then went on, "Around this circle sit quite a few who have sailed with me for more than a decade. They know that I, and they with me, have been in even worse straits than this. We've always come through—we've always survived. Because we never relinquished hope."

Something stirred inside him, and without pause he went on, "Often—even though some believe it to be a fantasy—yet often in the darkest hours, that's when Fate steps in and shines a light. Just like a lighthouse light, shining through the darkness to steer a ship to safe harbor. And like ships' lookouts, we have to remain alert, with our eyes wide open so we see the light. So that when Fate shines for us, we notice and take the right tack."

He looked around the faces and met all the eyes now trained on him. "We're not dead yet and we still have hope. And clinging to that hope is our *only* way forward."

★ ★ ★

On the evening of the eleventh of August, Lord Peter Ross-Courtney summoned the five gentlemen he'd recruited to his latest venture to a meeting in a private room at The Albion, a highly select gentlemen's club favored by the king's closest associates. As a Gentleman of the Royal Bedchamber and a close confidant of the king, Lord Peter definitely figured among that august tribe.

Somewhat to Lord Peter's surprise, the first of the five to arrive was Mr. Frederick Neill, a gentleman several branches down an aristocratic tree. Neill had bartered his birth and connections for significant wealth through not one but two advantageous marriages. Said wealth had also enabled him to acquire significant political influence, which was why Lord Peter had approached him; in Lord Peter's estimation, one could find wealth easily enough, but one could never hold too much political capital.

At fifty-five years old, three years younger than Lord Peter's fifty-eight, Neill was a stocky man not much given to social chit-chat. He accepted a glass of brandy, sank into one of the plush leather armchairs, sipped, then asked, "What news?"

Lord Peter merely smiled. "Let's wait until the others get here. There is news, but it'll be easier to relate it once."

Lord Hugh Deveny chose that moment to walk in.

Lord Peter greeted him. Another scion of an ancient house, well connected and supposedly wealthy, within certain circles, Lord Hugh was known to be a heavy gambler, and many suspected him to be deep in debt. Of course, that didn't mean he couldn't lay his hands on significant cash.

Lord Hugh was followed by the Marquis of Risdale, a nobleman who was widely regarded as having no real thought in his head beyond the next fad on which he could spend money. Risdale gave the word *profligate* new meaning. He, too, was a close acquaintance of the king, a connection that had only encouraged Risdale in his belief that whatever he wanted should be his.

Having Lord Hugh and Risdale present made Lord Peter feel more comfortable; although both men were several years younger, they were of a type Lord Peter understood well. A type he felt confident of controlling.

Not so the last two gentlemen to arrive. Mr. Frederick Clunes-Forsythe was, quite simply, a powerbroker. He was an extremely wealthy man of excellent birth and nonexistent morals. While Clunes-Forsythe had been an obvious candidate to tap on the shoulder for this venture, Lord Peter knew better than to imagine Clunes-Forsythe could ever be trusted. Not unless his own position, his own best interests, were at stake.

With respect to this venture, Lord Peter had taken steps to ensure that the last criterion would always be met.

The last man to join them was a bluff, outwardly hearty, rather choleric gentleman of significant stature—Sir Reginald Cummins, a close crony of Neill's. He was a man of similar ilk to Neill, with an aristocratic background and significant accumulated wealth, and despite his superficially genial façade, Cummins was every bit as shrewd as his friend.

Shrewd and ruthless; Lord Peter had decided that combination was a virtue.

Once everyone was settled in the armchairs and adequately

supplied with drinks, Lord Peter dismissed the self-effacing waiter with a wave. After the door had shut behind the man, Lord Peter surveyed his coconspirators. "Obviously, I have news. Some of it good. Some of it...potentially disquietening." He sipped, then went on, "First, to the good. We've received the latest report from our man in Amsterdam." Lord Peter reached into his breast pocket, withdrew a folded sheet, and handed it to Neill. "He's given us prices for the latest shipments, and the profit is totting up very nicely—as nicely as we could wish."

Neill had scanned the sheet. He humphed and handed it on to Cummins, then he looked at Lord Peter. "As we all know, return is a function of amount and time. The amount is good, but the time? I thought we'd agreed that they needed to speed things up."

"Indeed." Lord Peter inclined his head. "And we've dispatched several letters to that effect." He paused as Cummins handed the sheet to Clunes-Forsythe. "We also made it clear that, from the first, this venture was essentially running on borrowed time. That there was only a finite window during which our involvement could be guaranteed."

"It's been eight months since we invested." Clunes-Forsythe handed the sheet to Risdale, then looked Lord Peter in the eye. "We've been receiving dividends via Amsterdam for the last four months, but at a rate just enough to whet our appetites and with constant promises of an increase in production."

"And we've reminded our agents in the settlement that that increase needs to eventuate, and soon. However"—Lord Peter nodded at the sheet that Risdale was passing to Lord Hugh— "you will have seen Herr Grendel's postscript noting that the last three shipments have arrived closer together, suggesting an increase in production. But even more heartening is his comment that the quality of the stones has improved significantly. To the point where he, at least, seems rather excited at the prospect of more."

"So you're saying"—Lord Hugh handed the sheet back to Lord Peter—"that it *looks like* we're onto a good thing, with the supply of stones increasing and the quality as well. Consequently, now would not be the time to fold."

"Succinctly put." Lord Peter tucked the folded sheet back into his pocket.

"You said there was some disquietening news." Neill arched his brows. "What?"

Lord Peter frowned. "*Potentially* disquietening—what's worrying is that I can't be sure if it's anything to be concerned about at all. But in the interests of frank disclosure, at least between us—one of the captains we're using to ferry the stones from Freetown to Amsterdam reported that his ship was searched under orders from Macauley and Babington."

"They were looking for diamonds?" Risdale's eyes flew wide.

"No. I understand it was a general search for goods that might be destined for England. Macauley and Babington hold an exclusive license for England-bound trade out of West Africa, hence their interest."

"So it was a non-specific search?" Neill queried. "Something Macauley and Babington routinely do?"

Lord Peter tipped his head from side to side. "Apparently, they conduct such searches from time to time, but our captain reported that Babington himself was at the wharf, which isn't something that would normally occur. The captain himself wasn't sure how much weight to place on the event, but felt he should report it."

"They didn't find any of the diamonds, did they?" Cummins asked.

"No." Lord Peter's smile was smug. "Our agents have their wits about them—the ships don't pick up the diamonds until after they leave the harbor."

"So"—Neill turned his glass between his fingers—"this is one of those—as you correctly phrased it—*potentially* disquietening situations one occasionally encounters. It could mean nothing, or it could be a harbinger of more serious trouble."

Clunes-Forsythe nodded. "On the one hand, we've finally seen evidence that the profits we went into this venture hoping to realize have a real chance of materializing." He dipped his head to Neill. "Not just in amount but over a reasonable period of time. On the other hand, we have a *potentially* worrying report, one that might or might not have any actual connection to or impact on our venture." Clunes-Forsythe glanced around the circle of faces. "We're all looking for an El Dorado out of this venture, and we've caught our first glimpse that such a return might soon come our way. Against that, however, we have to weigh the risk of our involvement becoming known. Ever."

He looked at Neill. "We've discussed the return on our investment. That's one aspect we all have an interest in. Another is the risk—not to the investment so much as to ourselves." Again, Clunes-Forsythe looked around the circle, his gaze, as always, cold. "None of us need to be reminded that we each of us stand high enough that a fall will be…quite simply, the end."

Neill snorted. "Quite aside from enslaving Englishmen and the host of other laws we're breaking, both the Crown and His Majesty's government will take a very dim view of our illicit profits."

Risdale huffed. "That may be so, but one report from a nervous captain about something that might have nothing to do with our venture hardly seems sufficient reason to hike our skirts and run away from the best part of said profits."

"And," Lord Hugh put in, "if we do withdraw now, we're not going to recoup any of our investment beyond what we've already received."

"An excellent point." Lord Peter uncrossed his legs and sat straighter. "Gentlemen, I believe we've reached a point in this venture when in order to best protect our interests, both financial and personal, we need better and more reliable intelligence. Intelligence on the ground, as it were."

There were murmurs of agreement all around.

"So what do you suggest?" Cummins asked.

"I propose," Lord Peter said, "that I travel to Freetown and thence to the mine myself." He smiled. "I rather fancy a break from town, and I could assess the positions of our agents in the settlement—and I would point out that, from the first, we've accepted all they've told us about themselves and their various abilities. Although their performance overall has been satisfactory to this point, verifying their claims wouldn't go amiss. But it's the mine and its potential that I feel we really need eyes we can trust to reliably assess, especially in terms of how long we keep the venture going. Even more so should any threats emerge." Lord Peter's smile took on an edge. "After all, no one outside this room has the same degree of vested interest in this project that we do."

While his suggestion had, at first, met with some surprise, no one seemed inclined to argue.

Lord Peter was mentally congratulating himself with having so smoothly carried off his stratagem when Neill set down his glass and said, "If I might make a suggestion?"

All eyes turned Neill's way.

He looked around the circle. "Two pairs of eyes will be better than one." He brought his gaze ultimately to rest on Lord Peter. "So, my lord, if you're agreeable, I suggest we travel to Freetown—and thence to the mine—together."

Lord Peter thanked his maker that he'd been blessed with the ability to maintain a poker face. He did so now as his mind whirled, recalculating, reassessing.

The others were no help; Cummins and Clunes-Forsythe were all for Neill's inclusion—no doubt sensing that Neill would be more likely to react in ways better aligned with their needs. And Risdale and Lord Hugh had no reason to oppose Neill.

So Lord Peter smiled and dipped his head to Neill. "I would be delighted to have your company, sir." Lord Peter raised his glass and looked around the circle. "To Freetown. To our mine."

"To diamonds," Neill said, and drained his glass.

★ ★ ★

For the captives, the bad news continued to pile up—along with the rough diamonds that all but fell out of the rock face at the veriest tap.

"It's *shattered*." Dixon stepped back from examining the ore bed through the jeweler's loupe he'd borrowed from, of all people, Muldoon. In something close to despair, Dixon raked a hand through his hair, then waved at the rock. "It's as if the shearing pulverized the ore—as if it shook it almost to pieces. Instead of the rock holding in the diamonds, it's now the diamonds holding the rock in place."

In the face of such disaster, it was exceedingly difficult to hold on to hope. To even find any hope to cling to.

They were a subdued and quiet company as they gathered around the fire pit that evening. Someone had started counting the days. Caleb heard several whispers of "It's the twelfth."

He looked around the circle. When his gaze reached Kate, seated beside him, and she met his eyes, he saw the same certainty he felt—in life, in love—reflected back at him. That, he knew, was the sort of fundamental strength—the sort of elemental belief that reached beyond all logic—that everyone needed to fall back on.

He'd wracked his brains throughout the day, but had yet to find any new path forward.

He could only hope he would.

And there it was again—hope. He—they—had to keep hoping.

They were all quietly eating when footsteps suddenly thudded on the barracks' porch.

Most glanced across—and saw Muldoon striding swiftly their

way. Dubois, looking puzzled, was following more slowly, Arsene and Cripps trailing behind him.

But Muldoon…the man appeared elated. Excited, in alt—all but jumping out of his skin with joy.

His face alight, Muldoon strode straight to Kate. Halting beside her, he thrust out his hand. "Where did this stone come from?"

When she blinked at the raw diamond in Muldoon's palm, then, baffled, looked up at him, he made an obvious effort to rein in his excitement and clarified, "From the first tunnel or the second?"

Kate frowned and reached for the stone. For a second, Muldoon tensed, and she wondered if he would allow her to take it, but then he forced himself to stillness and let her lift it from his palm.

She turned the cleaned stone between her fingers. "Harriet—I think this is one of yours." They each had their own way of approaching the cleaning, and Harriet was left-handed, which made her work easy to spot.

Harriet glanced warily at Muldoon. When he curtly nodded, she took the stone Kate held out. Harriet examined it. "Yes. I did this one today."

"So from the first tunnel or the second?" Muldoon demanded.

"Well, if we cleaned that today," Kate told him, "it would almost certainly be from the second tunnel. Because of the earlier backlog, we've only just moved on to stones from there."

Muldoon's expression turned beatific. He filched the stone from Harriet's fingers.

Dubois approached.

Muldoon swung to face him and thrust out his hand. "Take a look at that."

Puzzled, Dubois took the stone and examined it. "A cleaned raw diamond."

"Not just any raw diamond. That, my friend, is a *blue* diamond." Muldoon all but snatched the rock back. He turned it in his fingers, then pointed. "See? Just there. You can see the color—the blue fire."

Dubois looked, then humphed. "So it's a bit blue. What difference does that make?"

"About ten times," Muldoon informed him. As if trying to contain his exuberance, he drew in a long, deep breath, then more evenly stated, "I spent all of my last home-leave in Amsterdam with the jewelers who are receiving our diamonds. They taught me about the various grades of stones. They had a few chips—just tiny things—of blue diamond. According to them, every diamond collector the world over will give their right arm for a decent-sized blue."

His expression almost fiendish with delight, Muldoon all but brandished the raw diamond in Dubois's face. "This, my mercenary friend, even when cut, will be more than a carat's worth of blue diamond. It, alone, is worth a small fortune." He swept an arm toward the mine. "And we have an entire rock face of the damned things!"

Kate cleared her throat, preparing to speak, but Dixon beat her to it.

"I've heard of blue diamonds. It's unlikely every diamond in the second pipe will be a blue."

Muldoon fixed Dixon with a commanding look. "But there will be more?"

Dixon nodded. "That would be my guess, but what percentage of the stones will be blue…the only way to know is to look and see."

Muldoon nodded. "My thoughts exactly. Just from what was in the strongbox today, I've already found two." He pointed at the women. "I'll come into the shed tomorrow and teach you what to look for." His gaze shifted to the children. "And then you can teach the brats. If they can pick the difference during sorting, we can keep aside the whites and concentrate on clean-ing the blues first.

"And as for you"—Muldoon swung to face Dubois and jabbed a finger at the mercenary's nose—"you can forget any notion of closing this mine any time soon. As long as there's even the slimmest chance of a blue diamond coming out, the mine stays open—and the men need to stop attacking that rock face with bloody picks! Chisels and small hammers—like what the women use. I want every diamond in that second tunnel *teased* out. Once they learn of this, just the thought of shattering a blue will be anathema to our backers—I can assure you of that. And trust me, I won't have to explain the value of blue diamonds to the likes of them."

Dubois had focused on Muldoon's finger.

For Caleb's money, the mercenary was giving serious thought to breaking Muldoon's digit.

But then Dubois drew in a breath and shifted his gaze to Mul-doon's face. A second passed, then Dubois shrugged. "It's all the same to us. You and your backers have paid our retainer, so as long as you keep the weekly payments coming in, we'll stay and keep the mine running."

"Excellent!" Muldoon slipped the rock into his pocket, then rubbed his hands with exuberant glee. He glanced around the circle of captives, his expression once more alight. "This find is going to make the history books."

With that, he turned and strode back to the barracks.

Dubois watched him go, then looked at his lieutenants.

"Blue diamonds," Arsene said. "I wonder if he's right about them being worth ten times the whites."

"Assuming he is…" Dubois's soft words filtered back to the silent captives, then he shrugged again and started following Muldoon. "I have to say this makes me inclined to view Mr. Muldoon's arrival in a more favorable light."

Arsene chuckled. He and Cripps followed Dubois.

The captives exchanged glances. Amazed, almost disbelieving—almost frightened to believe—they remained silent until the mercenaries had reached the barracks and were too distant to hear.

Then, after an audible *whoosh* as many released the breaths they'd been holding, everyone started talking at once.

Across the circle, Hillsythe caught Caleb's gaze and raised his voice to be heard over the din. "It's real, isn't it? We've just got our reprieve."

Grinning fit to burst, Caleb nodded and called back, "Courtesy of Muldoon."

"It just goes to show," Lascelle said, "that you can never tell from which direction unexpected help might come—or who Fate will decide to make her pawn."

Fanshawe snorted. "Just as well I didn't kill the bugger when he arrived."

Others laughed and slapped him on the back.

Kate watched as relief—giddy and overwhelming—took hold. Unable to keep still, some of the children started dancing, and then others—men and women—leapt to their feet and joined in.

So what if the guards saw? They didn't know rescue was coming.

Didn't know the true nature of the reprieve the captives had just been granted.

Then Caleb turned to her, and she looked into his face. She smiled, allowing every one of the myriad emotions welling inside her to show. She put a hand to his cheek. "You're allowed to say I told you so."

His grin widened into a glorious smile. "Oh, no. I would never do that." He looped his arm about her waist and hugged her tight, then he dipped his head and whispered in her ear, "Fate's a female—and one should never take females for granted."

Her peal of laughter was music to Caleb's ears. He smiled down at her—at his wife-to-be, at his future.

Then he rose and tugged her up with him, and they joined in the dancing.

Later, when they'd exhausted the exuberance engendered by so much giddy relief, he sat with his arms around Kate and looked around the circle of faces. All the captives, even the youngest children, were still there. The ease in their expressions testified to resurgent hope, to the lifting of immediate care, and the release of the tension that had held all of them in such a vicious and constantly tightening grip.

Also blatantly evident was a stronger sense of community—a strengthened belief that this community of theirs could and would survive.

Softly, Caleb spoke, his words falling into the gentle dark. "We're still captives. When the time comes, we'll still have to fight to survive—to overcome Dubois and his men and reclaim our freedom. But now we have hope. This is what it feels like."

He paused, then went on, "Fate just stepped in. I told you she would. No matter what hurdles might rise before us, if we look, if we believe, if we continue to cling to hope, we will find a way—a way to be here when the rescue force arrives."

He paused again and gave conviction full rein. "We will be here come September."

They didn't cheer—they didn't dare. That might have been too blatant.

But if uttered freely, the chorus of "Here, here!" would have been the equivalent of a roar.

★ ★ ★

The tide carried *The Prince* into the wharf at Southampton at eleven o'clock in the morning. Lieutenant Frederick Fitzpatrick, a close crony of Caleb's from their school days, understood the value of time. Although he'd crammed on every inch of sail, it was already the thirteenth of August. He wasn't amenable to wasting another minute in getting the documents Hornby had carried out of the jungle into Caleb's brothers' hands—but Fitz had to remain in Southampton to sign off on the voyage and ex-plain to Higginson why it wasn't Caleb fronting the office desk.

Which was why Hornby, in his best suit, was waiting by the railing, a satchel clutched in his arms.

The instant the side of the ship touched the wharf, a midship-man slid the rail aside. Despite his years, Hornby didn't wait for the gangplank to be rolled out. He leapt for the wharf, landed in an experienced sailor's crouch, then literally ran for the street and the coaching inn the company patronized.

"Godspeed!" Fitz yelled—and he wasn't the only one.

Without slowing his stride, Hornby snapped off a salute—and kept running.

★ ★ ★

At three o'clock that afternoon, Robert Frobisher, to his mind unfortunately, was relaxing at his ease in his brother Declan's library. Declan was seated behind the huge desk and pretend-ing to read a news sheet. Robert had given up; *The Times* lay discarded beside his chair. Neither he nor Declan was particu-larly good at waiting—interminably, it seemed—for news of an ongoing action, and as they'd both been involved in succes-sive stages of a mission that was presently being prosecuted by their youngest brother, Caleb, but hadn't heard so much as a peep from Freetown in weeks, neither Robert nor Declan was in any good mood.

Without looking up from his perusal of the printed page, Declan murmured, "What I wouldn't give for *something* to hap-pen."

The words had barely left his lips when a pounding on the front door brought both brothers to their feet.

Robert reached the library door first. He led the way into the front hall just as Humphrey, Declan's very correct butler, hur-ried to open the front door.

Belatedly recalling that this was not his house—that this was

London and who knew who might be calling—Robert slowed, but Declan, following at his heels, prodded him on.

When Humphrey swung the door wide, Robert and Declan were both close enough to recognize the sailor standing on the stoop.

"Hornby?" Declan pushed forward, shoving Robert before him.

Hornby's relief at seeing them was intense.

"Where's Caleb?" Robert asked.

"Captains." Hornby drew himself up and snapped off a salute. Then he hauled a heavy satchel from his shoulder. "Captain Caleb's keeping watch on the mining camp in the jungle. In case something happens to the poor souls trapped inside before you and the rest can reach them."

"He found the camp?" Declan asked as Robert took the satchel and opened it.

"Oh, aye." Hornby's gaze went past them, and he paused to bob bows, and Robert realized the pattering he'd heard from behind him had been Aileen Hopkins, his soon-to-be wife, and Declan's wife, Edwina, rushing to join them. As both ladies had been actively involved in their respective missions, and as both had met Caleb, they were as eager to hear any news as Declan and Robert.

"For goodness' sake, step back!" Edwina hauled on Declan's arm. "And let poor Hornby—it is Hornby, isn't it?—over the threshold."

Declan obliged, but his attention didn't shift from the documents Robert was extracting from the satchel. "What has he sent?"

"My damned journal, for a start." Robert brandished the slim volume, then handed it to Aileen. "And it appears he's had the sense to draw maps."

Declan looked at Hornby, now hovering just inside the open door. Regardless of the dictates of social custom, neither Declan nor Robert was about to tamely go and sit down, not before they'd discovered what Caleb had sent—and neither was Edwina or Aileen.

Reflecting that Hornby would understand, Declan left Robert scanning the documents he'd pulled forth and repeated his question.

"Easy as you please," Hornby said, "once we'd taken Kale's camp."

Robert looked up.

Declan stared.

"You took Kale's camp?" Robert finally asked. "What, exactly, do you mean by that?"

Hornby shrugged. "Nasty piece of work, Kale was, but Captain Caleb bested him."

When Robert and Declan appeared struck dumb, Aileen caught Hornby's eye and smiled encouragingly. "I note you're using the past tense with respect to Kale—I take it that means he's deceased?"

"Dead as a doornail, ma'am, begging your pardon."

"Oh, you can tell me things like that any time." Aileen beamed at Hornby. "Kale was the lowest form of scum, and I'm delighted to know Caleb removed him from this earth."

Edwina professed herself delighted, too. "How did you reach here, Hornby?"

Hornby duly related how he came to be delivering the satchel.

Declan and Robert barely glanced up, then again abandoned Hornby to their ladies in favor of wading through the information Caleb had sent.

Edwina smiled at Hornby and directed Humphrey to make the old sailor comfortable.

Hornby looked uncertain. "I daresay I should get back to *The Prince*, ma'am. Lieutenant Fitzpatrick will be waiting to hear that I handed the information over."

"We'll send a messenger." Edwina gripped Hornby's sleeve

and inexorably drew the old sailor deeper into the hall. "We can't let you return to *The Prince* until these two"—she waved at Declan and Robert—"and the others are certain they have no more questions for you. I take it you were with Caleb when he found the mine?" When Hornby confirmed that, Edwina beamed. "In that case, once we've digested Caleb's news, I'm sure we'll all have more questions for you."

With that, she consigned Hornby into Humphrey's care. "Don't worry about the door—I'll get it."

Robert and Declan were busy with various documents, and Aileen had commandeered the satchel and was examining a map. Edwina started for the door—only to see a carriage and four, the horses lathered, drawing up at the curb before their house. She halted. "Who on earth…?" She glanced at Declan. "Are we expecting anyone?"

Alerted by the sound of stamping hooves, Declan and Robert had looked up. At Edwina's words, the brothers walked to the doorway and halted on the threshold, shoulder to shoulder, effectively filling the space.

Edwina scowled and pushed to peer around her husband's arm, while on the other side of the doorway, Aileen stood on tiptoe to look over Robert's shoulder.

Aileen steadied herself with a hand on Robert's back. The carriage rocked on its springs, then the door opened, and a man stepped out. Aileen registered the tension that infused Robert's muscles, but her attention was riveted by the gentleman who, having gained the pavement, looked up—directly at Robert and Declan.

The man was tall—every bit as tall as Robert and Declan, and possibly an inch or so more. His hair was black as night and fell about his well-shaped head like ruffled silk. His features, while clearly hewn from the same mold as his brothers', were harder, more sharply chiseled, perhaps a touch more finely drawn. His jaw was uncompromisingly square, and there was an understated strength in the way he moved that was nothing short of mesmerizing.

He was dressed fashionably, but with a certain negligent ease, as if clothes were of little importance to him. His figure was long, lean, sleekly yet powerfully muscled, the thighs revealed by his buckskin breeches those of a man who rode frequently.

Aileen watched as, with a graceful elegance that was transparently innate, the gentleman turned back to the open carriage door.

"Royd," Robert unnecessarily informed her in an undertone.

Aileen reflected that everything she'd ever heard about the impact of the eldest of the Frobisher brothers was, quite evidently, true.

She was still staring at Royd when he straightened, stepped back, and handed a lady from the carriage.

If Royd's appearance had made Robert—and no doubt Declan, too—tense, then the sight of the lady shocked both brothers into rigidity.

Aileen had to admit the lady was stunning—an eminently fitting visual foil for Royd Frobisher. She was tall, too—her head reached to just below Royd's eyes—and she possessed the same ineffable grace. Her hair was pure midnight, a wealth of glossy curls frothing over her shoulders and down her back. She was dressed in a severely plain carriage dress, but her figure did wonders for the outfit. She was all sleek curves; given the way she raised her head, she reminded Aileen forcefully of a very fine Thoroughbred.

Royd turned to give orders to the driver.

The lady, retrieving her hand from Royd's, turned to speak with the postboy and pointed to a bandbox lashed to the roof.

Declan shifted. "Wolverstone said he'd written to Royd, telling him about Caleb and asking him to take on the final leg of the mission."

In a tone that testified to the depth of her mystification, Edwina whispered, "But who is she?"

Aileen leaned around Robert's shoulder to look at Declan. Only to see Declan's expression grow studiously impassive, then he shot a glance at Robert.

Hanging on Robert's arm, she looked at his face and saw that his expression had turned every bit as uninformative as Declan's.

Determined, Aileen pinched Robert's arm.

Focused on the lady, he didn't even flinch.

"Who is she?" Aileen repeated.

Sotto voce, Robert replied, "Trouble. Trouble with a capital T."

★ ★ ★ ★ ★

*If you enjoyed Caleb and Kate's adventure,
don't miss the thrilling conclusion of
Stephanie Laurens'*
The Adventurers Quartet,
*a set of sultry, sweeping adventure-romances
featuring four buccaneering brothers
and four adventurous ladies.*

Read on for a sneak peek from Volume Four,
LORD OF THE PRIVATEERS,
*as the eldest Frobisher brother
takes on the challenge of bringing
the dangerous mission to a triumphant end.*

Available from MIRA Books December 27, 2016.

Prologue

R oyd Frobisher stood behind the desk in his office over-
looking Aberdeen harbor and read the summons he'd just
received a second time.

Was it his imagination or was Wolverstone anxious?

Royd had received many such summonses over the years
Wolverstone had served as England's spymaster; the wording of
today's missive revealed an underlying uneasiness on the normally imperturbable ex-spymaster's part.

Either uneasiness or impatience, and the latter was not one of
Wolverstone's failings.

Although a decade Wolverstone's junior, Royd and the man
previously known as Dalziel had understood each other from
their first meeting, much as kindred spirits. After Dalziel re-
tired and succeeded to the title of the Duke of Wolverstone, he
and Royd had remained in touch. Royd suspected he was one
of Wolverstone's principal contacts in keeping abreast of those
intrigues most people in the realm knew nothing about.

Royd studied the brief lines suggesting that he sail his ship,
The Corsair, currently bobbing on the waters beyond his window, to Southampton, to be provisioned and to hold ready to
depart once news arrived from Freetown.

The implication was obvious. Wolverstone expected the news
from Freetown—when it arrived courtesy of Royd's youngest

brother, Caleb—to be such as to require an urgent response. Namely, for Royd to depart for West Africa as soon as possible and, once there, to take whatever steps proved necessary to preserve king and country.

A commitment to preserving king and country being one of the traits Royd and Wolverstone shared.

Another was the instinctive ability to evaluate situations accurately. If Wolverstone was anxious—

"I need to see him."

The voice, more than the words, had Royd raising his head.

"I'll inquire—"

"And I need to see him now. Stand aside, Miss Featherstone."

"But—"

"No buts. Excuse me."

Royd heard the approaching tap of high heels striking the wooden floor. Given the tempo and the force behind each tap, he could readily envision his middle-aged secretary standing by the reception desk wringing her hands.

Still, Gladys Featherstone was a local. She should know that Isobel Carmichael on a tear was a force of nature few could deflect.

Not even him.

He'd had the partition separating his inner sanctum from the outer office rebuilt so the glazed section ran from six feet above the floor—his eye level—to the ceiling; when seated at his desk, he preferred to be out of sight of all those who stopped by, thinking to waste the time of the operational head of the Frobisher Shipping Company. If callers couldn't see him, they had to ask Gladys to check if he was in.

But he'd been standing, and Isobel was only a few inches shorter than he. Just as the glazed section allowed him a view of the peacock feather in her hat jerkily dipping with every purposeful step she took, from the other side of the outer office, she would have been able to see the top of his head.

Idly, he wondered what had so fired her temper. Idly, because he was perfectly certain he was about to find out.

In typical fashion, she flung open the door, then paused dramatically on the threshold, her dark gaze pinning him where he stood.

Just that one glance, that instinctive locking of their gazes, the intensity of the contact, was enough to make his gut clench and his cock stir.

Perhaps unsurprising, given their past. But now…

Nearly six feet tall, lithe and supple, with a wealth of blue-black hair—if freed, the silken locks would tumble in an unruly riot of large curls about her face, shoulders, and down her back, but today the mass was severely restrained in a knot on the top of her head—she stared at him through eyes the color of bittersweet chocolate set under finely arched black brows. Her face was a pale oval, her complexion flawless. Her lips were blush pink, lush and full, but were presently set in an uncompromising line. Unlike most well-bred ladies, she did not glide; her movements were purposeful, if not forceful, with the regal demeanor of an Amazon queen.

He dipped his head fractionally. "Isobel." When she simply stared at him, he quirked a brow. "To what do I owe this pleasure?"

Isobel Carmichael stared at the man she'd told herself she could manage. She'd told herself she could handle being close to him again without the protective barrier of any professional façade between them, too—that the urgency of her mission would override her continuing reaction to him, the reaction she fought tooth and nail to keep hidden.

Instead, just the sight of him had seized her senses in an iron grip. Just the sound of his deep, rumbling voice—so deep it resonated with something inside her—had sent her wits careening.

As for seeing that dark brow of his quirk upward while his intense gaze remained locked with hers…she hadn't brought a fan.

Disillusionment stared her in the face, but she set her mental teeth and refused to recognize it. Failure wasn't an option, and she'd already stormed her way to his door and into his presence.

His still-overwhelming presence.

Hair nearly as black as her own fell in ruffled locks about his head. His face would make Lucifer weep, with a broad forehead, straight black brows, long cheeks below chiseled cheekbones, and an aggressively squared chin. The impact was only heightened by the neatly trimmed mustache and beard he'd recently taken to sporting. As for his body…even when stationary, the masculine power in his long-limbed frame was evident to anyone with eyes. Broad shoulders and long strong legs combined with an innate elegance that showed in the ease with which he wore his clothes, in the grace with which he moved. Well-set eyes that saw too much remained trained on her face, while she knew all too well how positively sinful his lips truly were.

She shoved her rioting senses deep, dragged in a breath, and succinctly stated, "I need you to take me to Freetown."

He blinked—which struck her as odd. He was rarely surprised—or, at least, not so surprised he showed it.

"Freetown?"

He'd stiffened, too—she was sure of it. "Yes." She frowned. "It's the capital of the West Africa Colony." She'd been sure he would know; indeed, she'd assumed he'd visited the place several times.

Stepping into the office, without shifting her gaze from his, she shut the door on his agitated secretary and the interested denizens of the outer office and walked forward.

He dropped the letter he'd been holding on to his blotter. "Why there?"

As if they were two dangerous animals both of whom knew better than to take their eyes from the other, he, too, kept his gaze locked with hers.

Halting, she faced him with the reassuring width of the desk between them. She could have sat in one of the straight-backed chairs angled to the desk, but if she needed to rail at him, she preferred to be upright; she railed better on her feet.

Of course, while she remained standing, he would stand, too, but with the desk separating them, he didn't have too much of a height advantage.

She still had to tip up her head to continue to meet his eyes—the color of storm-tossed seas and tempest-wracked Aberdeen skies.

And so piercingly intense. When they interacted professionally, he usually kept that intensity screened.

Yet this wasn't a professional visit; her entrance had been designed to make that plain, and Royd Frobisher was adept at reading her signs.

Her mouth had dried. Luckily, she had her speech prepared. "We received news yesterday that my cousin—second cousin or so—Katherine Fortescue has gone missing in Freetown. She was acting as governess to an English family, the Sherbrooks. It seems Katherine vanished while on an errand to the post office some months ago, and Mrs. Sherbrook finally saw her way to writing to inform the family."

Still holding his gaze, she lifted her chin a fraction higher. "As you might imagine, Iona is greatly perturbed." Iona Carmody was her maternal grandmother and the undisputed matriarch of the Carmody clan. "She wasn't happy when, after Katherine's mother died, we didn't hear in time to go down and convince Katherine to come to us. Instead, Katherine got some bee in her bonnet about making her own way and so took the post as governess. She'd gone by the time I reached Stonehaven."

Stonehaven was twelve miles south of Aberdeen; Royd would know of it. She plowed on, "So now, obviously, I need to go to Freetown, find Katherine, and bring her home."

Royd held Isobel's dark gaze. Although he saw nothing "obvious" about her suggestion, he knew enough of the workings of the matriarchal Carmodys to follow her unwritten script. She viewed her being too late to catch and draw her cousin into the safety of the clan as a failure on her part. And as Iona was now "perturbed," Isobel saw it as her duty to put matters right.

She and Iona were close. Very close. As close as only two women who were exceedingly alike could be. Many had commented that Isobel had fallen at the very base of Iona's tree.

He therefore understood why Isobel believed it was up to her to find Katherine and bring her home. That didn't mean Isobel had to go to Freetown.

Especially as there was an excellent chance that Katherine Fortescue was among the captives he was about to be dispatched to rescue.

"As it happens, I'll be heading for Freetown shortly." He didn't glance at Wolverstone's summons; one hint, and Isobel was perfectly capable of pouncing on the missive and reading it herself. "I promise I'll hunt down your Katherine and bring her safely home."

Isobel's gaze grew unfocused. She weighed the offer, then— determinedly and defiantly—shook her head.

"No." Her jaw set and she refocused on his face. "I have to go myself." She hesitated, then grudgingly confided, "Iona needs me to go."

Eight years had passed since they'd spoken about anything other than business. After the failure of their handfasting, she'd avoided him like the plague, until the dual pressures of him needing to work with the Carmichael Shipyards to implement the innovations he desperately wanted incorporated into the Frobisher fleet and the economic downturn following the end of the wars leaving her and her father needing Frobisher Shipping Company work to keep the shipyards afloat had forced them face to face again.

Face to face across a desk with engineering plans and design sheets littering the surface.

The predictable fact was that they worked exceptionally well together. They were natural complements in many ways.

He was an inventor—he sailed so much in such varying conditions, he was constantly noting ways in which vessels could be improved for both safety and speed.

She was a brilliant designer. She could take his raw ideas and give them structure.

He was an experienced engineer. He would take her designs and work out how to construct them.

Against all the odds, she managed the shipyards, and was all but revered by the workforce. The men had seen her grow from a slip of a girl-child running wild over the docks and the yards. They considered her one of their own; her success was their success, and they worked for her as they would for no other.

Using his engineering drawings, she would order the workflow and assemble the required components, he would call in whichever ship he wanted modified, and magic would happen.

Working in tandem, he and she were steadily improving the performance of the Frobisher fleet, and for any shipping company that meant long-term survival. In turn, her family's shipyards were fast gaining a reputation for unparalleled production at the cutting edge of shipbuilding.

Strained though their interactions remained, professionally speaking, they were a smoothly efficient and highly successful team.

Yet through all their meetings in offices or elsewhere over recent years, she'd kept him at a frigidly rigid distance. She'd never given him an opportunity to broach the subject of what the hell had happened eight years ago, when he'd returned from a mission to have her, his handfasted bride whom he had for long months fantasized over escorting up the aisle, bluntly tell him she didn't want to see him again, then shut her grandmother's door in his face.

Ever since, she'd given him not a single chance to reach her on a personal level—on the level on which they'd once engaged so very well. So intuitively, so freely, so openly. So very directly. He'd never been able to talk to anyone, male or female, in the same way he used to talk to her.

He missed that.

He missed her.

And he had to wonder if she missed him. Neither of them had married, after all. According to the gossips, she'd never given a soupçon of encouragement to any of the legion of suitors only too ready to offer for the hand of the heiress who would one day own the Carmichael Shipyards.

It had taken him mere seconds to review their past. Regardless of that past, she stood in his office prepared to do battle to be allowed to spend weeks aboard *The Corsair*.

Weeks on board the ship he captained, during which she wouldn't be able to avoid him.

Weeks during which he could press her to engage in direct communication, enough to resolve the situation that still existed between them sufficiently for them both to put it behind them and go on.

Or to put right whatever had gone wrong and try again.

In response to his silence, her eyes had steadily darkened; he could still follow her thoughts reasonably well. Of all the females of his acquaintance, she was the only one who would even contemplate enacting him a scene—let alone a histrionically dramatic one. One part of him actually hoped...

As if reading his mind, she narrowed her eyes. Her lips tightened. Then, quietly, she stated, "You owe me, Royd."

It was the first time in eight years that she'd said his name in that private tone that still reached to his soul. More, it was the first reference she'd made to their past since shutting Iona's door in his face.

And he still wasn't sure what she meant. For what did he owe her? He could think of several answers, none of which shed all that much light on the question that, where she was concerned, filled his mind—and had for the past eight years.

He wasn't at all sure of the wisdom of the impulse that gripped him, but it was so very strong, he surrendered and went with it. "*The Corsair* leaves on the morning tide on Wednesday. You'll need to be on the wharf before daybreak."

She searched his eyes, then crisply nodded. "Thank you. I'll be there."

With that, she swung on her heel, marched to the door, opened it, and swept out.

He watched her go, grateful that she hadn't closed the door, allowing him to savor the enticing side-to-side sway of her hips.

Hips he'd once held as a right as he'd buried himself in her softness...

Registering the discomfort his tellingly vivid memories had evoked, he grunted. He surreptitiously adjusted his breeches, then rounded the desk, crossed to the door, and looked out.

Gladys Featherstone stared at him as if expecting a reprimand.

He beckoned. "I've orders for you to send out."

He retreated to his desk and sank into the chair behind it. He waited until Gladys, apparently reassured, settled on one of the straight-backed chairs, her notepad resting on her knee, then he ruthlessly refocused his mind and started dictating the first of the many orders necessary to allow him to absent himself from Aberdeen long enough to sail to Freetown and back.

To complete the mission that Melville, First Lord of the Admiralty, had, via Wolverstone, requested him to undertake.

And to discover what possibilities remained with respect to him and Isobel Carmichael.

For alerts as new books are released,
plus information on upcoming books,
sign up for Stephanie's Private Email Newsletter,
either on her website,
or at: http://eepurl.com/gLgPj

Or if you're a member of Goodreads,
join the discussion of Stephanie's books
at the Fans of Stephanie Laurens group.

You can email Stephanie at
stephanie@stephanielaurens.com

Or find her on Facebook at
http://www.facebook.com/AuthorStephanieLaurens

You can find detailed information on all
Stephanie's published books, including covers,
descriptions, and excerpts, on her website at
http://www.stephanielaurens.com